Routine

Rock and Roll Gymnast Book Two

By

Margena Adams Holmes

Thanks to…

Ian Bristow for creating another beautiful cover.

Rebecca Camarena for editing.

Julie Stannard for again being my alpha reader.

All the bands I have watched and loved over the years that continue to inspire me.

Special thanks to my family—Reid, Vincent, Carter, and Aerin, Tony, Wolfe, and Mya for their love and support, as always.

Dedicated to all who aspire to be something. Follow your dreams!

Chapter One

"Sounds good, Kelly," Dean said through the studio intercom.

Her watch beeped softly, indicating one o'clock in the morning. As raw as her throat felt, and drained as she was, Kelly Brennen hoped that was the last take on her vocals. She listened to the playback in her headphones and finally got the thumbs-up from the producer and Dean Landry, Fate Struck's manager and their drummer Isaac's uncle. She smiled and picked up her now lukewarm cup of tea and took a sip.

Dean hadn't been joking when he said things would move fast once they signed the recording contract with Tyrian Records three weeks ago. A week after the signing, Tyrian Records booked them into a recording studio to record their first album. The guys in the band had already laid down their tracks. Kelly did her vocals next and then Ian and Jake would do their backing vocals. It had taken a week to get all the instrument tracks done, and another week for Kelly to do her vocals. Kelly found out that they aren't just sung, they are sung over and over again until the producer gets the sound he's looking for.

Kelly walked through the studio and went into the booth.

"I think they've finally got what they wanted," Dean said.

"Sorry to keep you so late," Johnnie, the producer, said, "but we were so close to getting it done, I didn't want to have you come back tomorrow."

"No worries," Kelly said, stifling a yawn. "I'm used to late nights now."

Used to the late nights as she was, Kelly still liked to get to bed at a decent time. Luckily, she didn't have to make the drive from Los Angeles back home to Lakewood. Dean had booked a room for her and Jayna, her best friend and personal assistant, at a hotel close by to stay in while Kelly recorded her vocals. At least tomorrow night she'd be in her own bed.

"The backing vocals won't take as long," Johnnie said. "We can probably knock those out in a day or two."

"I'll drive you back to the hotel," Dean said. He waved to the rest of the production team. "Good night, all."

Dean pulled up to the hotel a few minutes later and parked.

"Thanks for being such a trooper," Dean said as they walked down the hall to their rooms.

"You know me," Kelly said, a roughness in her voice. "I like to just get it done, whatever it takes."

"I'll be ready to take you home tomorrow after eleven."

"Fantastic," Kelly said. "See you then."

Kelly opened her door and stepped inside. Jayna was already asleep, having stayed there after having lunch with Kelly and Dean. Kelly tried to not wake her as she grabbed her pajamas and went into the bathroom to change. She brushed her teeth and then got into the bed across from Jayna.

"You're done, finally?" Jayna asked sleepily.

"Sorry, did I wake you?" Kelly asked.

"No, I just had a weird dream that woke me up. A huge donut was singing the Whitney Houston song 'How Will I Know?'"

Kelly giggled.

"Are you hungry? I think there's some donuts leftover from this morning."

Jayna shook her head.

"I don't think I want one if it's going to sing to me."

"Maybe we can have it sing back-up for the band if it's any good."

"Glazed donuts are always good."

The girls squealed with laughter.

"We're finally done with my vocals," Kelly said once she'd caught her breath. "I must've sung the same line ten times tonight. I'm so done." Kelly lay down and pulled up her blankets with a sigh. "Ian and Jake will do theirs this week."

"Good," Jayna said, turning over away from Kelly. "Good night."

"Good night," Kelly said. "Watch out for singing donuts."

Jayna snickered under her blankets.

Recording had seemed pretty glamorous before they started. In reality, it was tedious work, singing the same line or verse repeatedly. To Kelly, they all sounded the same, but to the producer, they sounded different, and he finally got the one he liked best.

Kelly finally got tired of looking at the ceiling and fell asleep.

***

Ian was almost asleep when his phone beeped, indicating a text message. He groaned and looked at his phone.

"Kelly's done w/vocals. Will need you and Jake tomorrow afternoon," the text read.

Ian tapped out his short reply.

"OK. B ready then."

Dean picked up Jake and Ian after lunch and drove them to the hotel where Kelly and Jayna had stayed to drop off their belongings before heading straight to the studio.

"Things still moving at light-speed, I see," Jake said as they got back into the car.

"Time is money," Dean said.

They were familiar with the studio by now, having spent a week in there before. While they did their vocal warm-ups, Dean left to buy them a six pack of beer. Jake and Ian each took one into the studio with them.

After working on two songs, they took a break for dinner. They ate while they listened to what they'd recorded so far.

"Sounds good, guys," Johnnie said. "I think we'll get this finished tomorrow."

They spent a few more hours after dinner working on the backing vocals, then Dean drove them back to the hotel where Ian and Jake shared a room.

"I thought Kelly's vocals turned out really well," Jake said.

"Was there ever any doubt?" Ian asked.

"No, not at all. Just that we pale in comparison."

Ian chuckled.

"Kelly can sing, that's for sure," he said. "I'm glad that we've only got one lead singer instead of two. Jayna can sing as well, but I think it would've made things difficult trying to have two female lead singers. I doubt there'd be any jealousy, but you never know. As it is, it worked out well."

"Yeah, we had enough jealousy with Jessica," Jake said.

"Don't remind me. Glad to be through with her. I wish I would've listened to everyone before things got serious, but of course, I thought it'd be different with me. Guess being in a band wasn't the best thing with her."

They went back to record at ten the next morning. Dean drove them to the studio where they ran through their parts a few times before doing the actual recording of the backing vocals. They spent twelve hours on the backing vocals, with an hour break for lunch, and Johnnie and Dean were happy with the results.

"Great job, guys," Johnnie said. "Come on into the control room."

Ian and Jake went into the room to hear the playback once more.

"It all sounds good," Johnnie said. "I'll get it all mixed and then we'll give it a final listen and decide the order of the songs on the album."

"About how long, do you think?" Dean asked.

"About six weeks, give or take a few days. I'll let you know if any issues come up, which I don't see happening. You all have been very cooperative."

"It's all new to us," Ian said.

"Yeah, give us a few years and we'll be coming in drunk or hungover," Jake said with a grin.

Johnnie laughed.

"You wouldn't believe how many musicians do come in like that and not ready to work," he said.

"Talk to you soon," Dean said, and he, Ian, and Jake left to drive back to the hotel.

"Check-out time is eleven, so be ready to leave by ten," Dean said.

"Will do," Ian said.

A few days later, the band and Jayna gathered at Dean's house for their usual weekly meeting with him, where he told the band that Isaac's father's company wanted them to play at their summer picnic again.

"Sure," Isaac said.

"It's fun playing there," Kelly said.

"Do we want to up the price at all?" Dean asked.

"No," Isaac said. "As much as I'd like to stick it to my dad, it doesn't come out of his pocket. We'll give them the same deal as always. And if it comes up, the same goes for the holiday parties."

"How weird will that be," Jake said, "if our CD is out by then?"

"It's possible it could be out by December," Dean said. "It's already the end of July. Six weeks is the middle of September. Get it into production—it could be out in October-November."

"Woo hoo!" Ian said.

"And then you know what that means?" Dean asked.

"Tour!" they all shouted.

"You all seem pretty eager to go out on the road again. It'll be a longer tour this time. Longer time away from your family and significant others."

"We'll live," Ian said.

It wasn't as much about getting away as it was to just play music and not think of Jessica, who'd still been trying to get back with him. She texted him constantly, which he ignored, then she'd call him. She'd already been to see him twice, where he told her in no uncertain terms that they weren't getting back together.

"Of course you can say that," Isaac said. "You're back on the prowl."

"Yep," Ian said.

"I've talked to Hayley, and she's very understanding about it."

"Hayley is a sweetheart," Jake said. "She's been talking to Missy about everything, keeping her head from wandering."

"Is Missy afraid she's going to lose you?" Paul asked.

"No, she's just afraid that I'll be tempted to do things on the road when she's not there."

"How do they feel about Kelly and Jayna being on the road with you?" Dean asked.

"Hayley's fine with it," Isaac said. "They've all known each other for years."

"Missy's got no issues with either of them," Jake said.

"Alexa is okay with them both," Paul said.

"Good, because nothing was going to change anyway," Dean said.

Later that night, Ian had to turn his phone off, Jessica was calling and texting so much. He worried about her mental state. It was almost like she was obsessed with him.

He woke up the next morning to a hundred text messages and twenty phone calls.

I'm going to have to deal with this, he thought. After breakfast, he called Jessica to arrange to meet her at the park in an hour.

"I'll be there," she said.

He'd bought himself an hour of peace and quiet, but it would be short-lived once he had that meeting with her. He deleted all the texts off his phone.

At the designated time, Ian drove to the park. He saw Jessica sitting on a picnic table under the trees. He got out of his car and took a deep breath as he walked over to her.

"Hey," Ian said.

"Hi!" Jessica greeted, a little too enthusiastically, Ian thought.

He sat down on the table, leaving space in between them so she wouldn't get the idea they were even remotely best friends.

"Jessica," Ian began. "You've got to stop calling me and texting me. It's getting annoying."

"But I want to talk to you," she said. "I still love you and I want to make it work."

"It's never going to work out, Jess. You're too jealous of other girls in general and Kelly in particular. There was never any reason for it, yet you still gave Kelly a hard time."

"You spent a lot of time with her at band practice and I'm not allowed to be there. It made me think something was going on."

"That rule was put in place by Isaac's father, who doesn't trust any of us. He almost blew a fuse when Kelly joined. Luckily his mother knew who she was and spoke on her behalf."

"Can't you make the same exception for me?"

Ian shook his head.

"You're not part of the band, and Isaac can't ask his father. We're thinking of moving someplace else to rehearse. But that doesn't matter because we're not getting back together. I've got a tour coming up later this year, and I'm going to be gone for months. What would you do then?"

"Couldn't I come with you?"

"For *months*? You'd have to quit school, quit gymnastics, and you'd be by yourself most of the time. No, no one is bringing their girlfriends on tour."

"I would keep all the groupies away," Jessica suggested. "When you start getting groupies."

"We already have them" Ian said. "When we were the opener for The Disciples of Man, they were backstage."

"But I know you didn't…"

"I did," Ian interrupted, knowing what she'd say.

Jessica sat silent for a moment, processing that information.

"I'm not real proud of the fact, but it was right after we broke up. I'm not telling you this to hurt you, but I've moved on. You'll find someone eventually who you'll love and not be jealous of."

Jessica finally found her voice.

"I thought that was you," she said quietly.

"I thought so, too, until we started the band and Kelly joined and you flipped out on me. I think we're just better apart."

"I promise I'll change," Jessica whined.

"You've made promises before, Jessica, and never kept them. I'm sorry, but we can't be together. It just doesn't work."

Jessica sniffled, then stood up.

"Ugh. I thought I'd try one more time. I love you so much, Ian, but I can't make you love me. Good luck with your record and tour."

"Thanks. Are you going to be okay?"

"Yeah, eventually. I'll see you later," Jessica said, and she walked to her car.

Ian watched her drive away. He hoped she'd gotten the message that there was no way they'd get back together.

***

Kelly got a group text from Dean.

"Need to go to the studio on Friday @ 2PM to decide the order of songs," the text read.

"OK," Kelly replied. The rest of the band replied in the affirmative.

Friday afternoon, Dean picked everyone up to drive them to the studio to meet with Johnnie again. Jim, the rep from Tyrian Records was also there.

"You want to start with a strong song," Johnnie said, "but not necessarily with what would be a single."

Isaac wrote down all the songs on index cards and spread them out on the table in the control room. They talked through which songs to put where in the order. It took them half an hour, but they finally had the order for the songs.

"I would agree with this," Jim said. "You've got a good mix of slower songs between the rockers. As far as singles, I was thinking 'The Lies That You Tell,' 'No Words,' since there is a video for it already and people know it, and 'Bad Vibes.'"

"What do you guys think?" Dean asked.

"What order would they be released in?" Isaac asked.

"I would think that order—'Lies,' 'No Words,' and 'Vibes.' You don't want to oversaturate with 'No Words,' so 'Lies' would be a good first single, *then* 'No Words,' coming back to a familiar song, and then 'Vibes,'" Dean suggested.

"You know your stuff," Jim said, smiling. "Exactly what I was thinking. We'll run it by everyone at Tyrian, of course. They have the final say on it."

Chapter Two

Dean met with Jim and the executives at Tyrian Records a week later about the album and singles, and they agreed with Dean and Jim on everything.

"Sounds great," Rob, the assistant executive of A&R, said. "Everything is moving along nicely. I'll get the booking agents to get the tour planned."

"We have two previous engagements in December, so hopefully we can work around those, maybe have the band play nearby for the month," Dean said.

"We can work it out. Give me the dates and I'll make sure they're blacked out and we schedule shows only in California for that time."

Dean texted him the dates.

"Great! I'll keep you updated," Rob said.

When the band met at his house, Dean told them what happened, and when the tour would start.

"Looks like November," Dean said. "They're going to work around the dates of the holiday parties. The single is coming out in three weeks, and the CD will follow two weeks after that. Which puts us at about October."

"Awesome!" Kelly said.

"Woo hoo!" Jake said.

"In the meantime, I'm going to try to get you some interviews, do some lives here and there, so you can grow your audience."

"What about doing interviews on college radio stations?" Isaac asked. "I know they've had a few of them at Fullerton."

"Not a bad idea," Dean said, making a note on his phone. "Be easier to get those right now until your album comes out, then we can get the bigger radio stations."

When Kelly got home, she had an idea and emailed her gymnastics coach at Cerritos College about it, and got back an answer in the affirmative. She texted Jayna to ask her if she'd come to her gymnastics class the next day to help her out.

"Of course!" Jayna replied.

Kelly picked up Jayna at two-thirty for class at three. Kelly had dropped all her classes except gymnastics, since she was so busy with the band, but she used the class to stay in shape for the shows.

"So, I guess just follow me around and record what I do and then I'll get Isaac to edit it down a bit before we post it to the band's social media pages," Kelly said.

"Awesome," Jayna said.

The students sat down and started to stretch, and Jayna recorded that, then they did some warm-ups, Jayna following Kelly around. The students broke into groups to work on different things. Kelly and a couple other girls who were a little more advanced worked on the uneven bars and floor routines. Dean didn't want her using the balance beam or the vault in case she injured herself.

Jayna followed Kelly for the entire hour and a half of class, recording everything she did, catching some good moments on the bars and floor.

After class, Kelly and Jayna sat in Kelly's car to watch the recording.

"This is going to be awesome once it's edited," Jayna said.

"I hope so," Kelly said. "Just trying to show stuff that we do when we're not playing, I think Ian and Jake are doing something, too."

Kelly called Isaac later that night to see if he could edit it for her.

"No problem," he said. "Send it to me and I'll watch it, then you and I can edit it."

"Cool, thanks," Kelly said.

She sent the recording to Isaac in an email, and he replied that he received it. He messaged her the next day to let her know he'd watched it and to come over anytime to edit it.

Kelly went to Isaac's house later that day. They spent a couple hours on the edits, and had it cut down to about forty-five minutes of footage, and broke that up into one-, three-, and five-minute pieces, the longer pieces going on You Tube, and the shorter ones on Instagram and Facebook. He added some fun comments to the footage and some sound effects to make it more interesting.

"It seems like a lot," Isaac said, "but people will watch it if they're interested, especially if we space it out over a couple of weeks. You never know what people will like, but you seem to have a good following, so I think it will entertain them."

"Especially when I fall off the bar," Kelly said.

"Yeah," Isaac said with a chuckle. "I've got Jake and Ian coming over tomorrow to edit what they've got. We'll have a lot of content on our social media platforms."

"Good! Just what we want."

Isaac uploaded and scheduled them to their different social pages, one every other day. They got quite a few Likes and more new fans.

Dean got interviews set up at college radio stations. Cerritos College, where Paul and Kelly went, Cal State Fullerton where Isaac went to school, and one at Cal State Long Beach where Ian and Jake took classes.

At each interview, the band were usually asked the same questions as the previous interview, but they always happily answered the questions. As the interviews went on beyond the colleges, they got better about answering the questions.

Dean contacted Kelly's brother David to see if he'd be interested in making the video for their single.

"I'd be an idiot not to be interested," he said. He had graduated from college with a bachelor's degree in film and was anxious to make more videos and films.

"I think Kelly would be more comfortable with you doing it, too," Dean said.

Dean, Jim from Tyrian Records, and David talked out the particulars, and put it in writing. David and his crew would get paid this time.

"I know we still owe you and your crew tickets to a headliner show," Dean said. "I haven't forgotten."

"Sounds like that could be pretty soon," David said.

A month later the band, Dean, and David and his crew were set up and ready to record the video. Fate Struck came early to get ready for the shoot. Jim had hired a make-up artist for Kelly and the guys. Kelly enjoyed being pampered, having someone else do her make-up for her. Jayna helped Kelly with whatever else she needed.

"This is such a big production," Kelly said as she sipped her energy drink.

"The record company really went all out, didn't they?" Jayna asked.

Kelly nodded.

"It's fun, but scary. This is *really* big time now."

Kelly had brought her own wardrobe to wear and change into for different parts of the video. The guys' wardrobe was less elaborate, mostly just shirt changes for them. Kelly had pants, blouses, and shoes to change between.

When everyone was ready, David called for the band to get into their places.

"I still can't get over how different you look as a rock star, Kel," David said as she walked out to her position.

"That's what I say every time I see her," Jayna said.

Kelly laughed.

"Gotta look the part, ya know," she said.

Kelly and the guys put in a long eight-hour day, not really expecting it to take so long to record. They had one long break for lunch and snacked in between takes. Kelly had changed her clothes twice for the video.

Jim came by to see how the shooting was coming along.

"I'll have this done in two to three weeks," David told him.

"Good," Jim said. "That's about the time the single should be out."

One week before their single would be released, Dean held another meeting at his house.

"The day's almost here!" he said. "I just wanted to touch base with everyone, to see how you're all doing since we haven't met up in a while."

"Doing well," Kelly said. "I'm only taking gymnastics at Cerritos now. I can't do all the work even for just one class with everything going on."

"Same," Jake and Ian chimed in.

"I'm only taking one class online," Paul said. "After this semester, though, I'm quitting for the time being."

"As much as I hated to do it," Isaac said. "I had to withdraw from my classes and give back the unused portion of the scholarship. My dad wasn't thrilled about it."

"I figured he wouldn't be," Dean said, "but you've learned quite a bit in business and did really well before I took over."

"Thanks," Isaac said.

"I've got a press release ready to go for the local newspapers, announcing the release of the single and the CD. Tyrian Records will take care of the press release for the major newspapers, et cetera."

Dean put together a listening and watch party for the band scheduled for when the record company released the single. He had arranged to have it played at a certain time on a radio station, and the video would debut at eight that night on You Tube.

Kelly and the guys had invited their families and friends to the party. Jayna had invited her parents and Marty. Food and beverages were on-hand, and Kelly indulged in her usual hard lemonade, the rest of the band had their Jack Daniels and Coke. Everyone had arrived before the time the radio station would play the song.

Kelly and Isaac had their phones out—Kelly to record and Isaac going live on their social media page, getting everyone's reaction to the song.

"And now, something new. An up-and-coming band from the Long Beach area, Fate Struck, has their very first single out, called 'The Lies That You Tell.' Enjoy this hard rock song here on 95.8 KRRQ," the DJ announced, and the song faded up.

Everyone cheered then no one said anything for the three and a half minutes the song played. Kelly looked around and saw that everyone looked to be enjoying the song. Even Isaac's father had what could pass as a smile on his face.

When the song ended, the DJ came on again to remind everyone of the band and song, then went on to play Collective Soul's latest single.

Everyone cheered and applauded, congratulating the band and Dean.

"The video will be on in five minutes," Dean shouted over the excited voices.

He pulled up You Tube on his Smart TV and went to Fate Struck's page, and everyone settled down again to wait for the video to start. Isaac made a couple of comments in the comment section, and got lots of replies, too many to answer. At exactly eight o'clock, the video came on. Kelly had a hard time watching, as she wasn't confident in how she looked on screen, even though

David and his crew thought she looked great. She mostly focused on recording the reactions from everyone on her phone.

Live comments popped up on the chat as they watched. Almost all were positive responses, with only a few mediocre comments. As they watched the comments, a familiar name popped up.

"Best new song of the year," Erik from The Disciples of Man posted.

"Oh my God," Kelly exclaimed, hand over her mouth.

"How awesome is that?" Dean said, grabbing Isaac's shoulder.

"They really like you guys," David said.

The video ended. The comments continued for a few more minutes, then just trickled in.

"That was great," Paul's mother said.

"You all should be very proud," Ian's father said.

"And a big round of applause for David and his crew," Dean shouted.

Everyone applauded loudly, and David waved his hand.

"It was fun to do," David said. "They are all really hard workers and did everything asked of them, never complaining. I think it made them more comfortable having someone they knew at the helm for this. All the applause goes to them."

Everyone cheered for the band again. Several friends and family went over to shake David's hand. As everyone still congratulated each other, phones started to go off everywhere in the room. Kelly looked at hers and saw the number of one of her other friends from high school gymnastics. She answered the phone and while talking, the phone beeped in her ear, indicating a text. She finished her call and looked at her text messages, which were up to five now. Kelly saw that even her mom had her cell phone out, talking and smiling.

So many people called Kelly. She felt like she was floating on air, enjoying the moment of knowing a song she sang on got airplay, feeling like a rock star. After talking with several of her friends, she put her phone on silent. She'd call everyone back later. It looked like others did the same as the amount of ringing diminished.

Isaac's parents left after talking to Dean and David. Both looked a little concerned.

"What did my dad say?" Isaac asked Dean.

"He liked the video and song but still thinks you're wasting your time."

"Did he not see all the positive fucking comments we got on the video?" Isaac asked. "Or hear what the DJ said?"

"I'm sorry," Dean said. "I'll let you know right now that he's never going to appreciate what you're doing. He thought it was just a phase, even though you're signed to a record deal. It was the same thing when I was in a band back in the nineties and when I managed a couple of bands in the early two thousands. He told me I'd never get rich doing that. I might not have gotten rich, but I had a hell of a lot of fun. I believe in you guys. Jim believes in you guys. That's all that matters."

"Unless you're trying to get the approval of your father," Isaac mumbled.

"Fuck his approval. The fans love you guys. I know your father loves you, Isaac, I don't doubt that. He just thinks rock music is beneath you, and him."

"Wonderful," Isaac said.

Isaac went to the kitchen and came back with another drink and sat down next to Hayley, who ran her hands through his hair and talked softly to him.

Kelly felt bad for Isaac. He was a good guy and tried so hard to be a good musician, and had managed to get a scholarship for music. She knew his father had wanted him to join an orchestra instead, or follow him into the corporate world, but that wasn't Isaac's passion.

Kelly's parents stepped over to her where she sat on the arm of the chair Greg sat in.

"We're going to go," Mom said.

"Already?" Kelly asked.

"Yes. Dad's still got work tomorrow," Mom said. "This was fabulous! I talked to your aunt in Redding who saw the video and she sends her love and congratulations to you."

"Tell her thanks," Kelly said.

She hugged her parents and thanked them for coming.

"We'll always support you, pumpkin," Dad said.

18

"Thank you. I'll see you when I get home."

Everyone had left and only the band members, their significant others, and Jayna and Marty remained. Dean brought out bottled water for everyone, which they all gratefully accepted.

"This is just the start," Dean said. "Wait until the album comes out."

Kelly yawned and looked at the clock. It had been nearly four hours since the video premiere. She looked at her phone and saw she had twenty-five texts.

"Good thing I put my phone on silent," she said, showing Greg the number of texts she had.

"Look at you, Miss Popular," Greg said. "Are you ready to go?"

"Yeah," she said.

Greg drove her home. Kelly still felt a little wobbly after drinking three hard lemonades, so Greg walked her up to her door.

"You gonna be okay?" he asked.

"Yeah," she said. "I'm going straight to bed."

Greg kissed her slowly, then made sure she got inside before leaving.

Kelly changed into her pajamas. Too tired and too tipsy to do anything else, she fell onto her bed. She managed to get under the blankets before falling asleep.

Kelly woke up at ten-thirty the next morning, feeling a little worse for wear. She hadn't awakened at all during the night, so had no opportunity to drink anymore water. She grabbed the bottle of water from her nightstand and drank a quarter of it down then fell back on her bed.

I know better than this, Kelly thought. *I should've drunk more water at the party.*

She lay in her bed for another half an hour before getting up to eat breakfast. Her stomach seemed okay for the most part. She'd eat some toast and take some ibuprofen with plenty of water to get rid of her headache.

"Are you feeling okay?" Mom asked when she came back in from gathering the laundry from the clothesline in the backyard.

"I'm not great," Kelly said as she spread butter on her toast. "I didn't drink enough water yesterday."

"Oh, yeah, that'll do it," Mom said. "What have you got going on today?"

"I've got a bajillion text messages to go through," Kelly said, "but after that, I don't know. Nothing planned with the band."

"A little calm before the storm?"

"Yes. Definitely need that right now."

Kelly took a bite of her toast as her mom went into the laundry room to fold clothes. When Kelly finished eating, she took a couple of ibuprofen tablets with water, then went back to her room to dress and start on answering the text messages. It took her an hour, thanking them for the support. She got one from Erik from The Disciples of Man.

"Nice job, girl! Good luck!" the text read.

Kelly tapped out her reply.

"Thx so much! U've been so supportive!"

She finished going through her text messages and turned her phone from silent back to vibrate.

***

Isaac taped up the box and set it aside, looking at the rest of his belongings in his room.

It should only take two more boxes, he thought.

Isaac and Jake were moving into their own apartment that day, and Isaac hadn't meant to leave the packing to the last minute, but with the single coming out and the party Dean had given them, he'd had no time. Luckily the next few days were off days, and he finally had time to get everything packed.

Isaac heard a knock on his door.

"Come in," he said, and his father stepped inside.

"Just checking to see if you needed any help," his dad said.

"No, I'm almost all packed up," Isaac said. "I'll have to make a few trips in my truck to get everything over there but shouldn't take too long. Jake will help load up my bed and dresser."

"Very good," his father said, and he left, pulling the door shut behind him.

Like I'd let you help me anyway.

20

Later that afternoon, Isaac loaded his truck with the first load and drove to the apartment complex where he and Jake were moving in. He drove around to his specific carport and saw Jake's car already there. He jogged up the stairs to the apartment and found the door open and Jake setting up his bedroom.

"Hey," Isaac said.

Jake turned away from his stereo.

"Oh, hi."

"Just wanted to let you know that I'm here," Isaac said.

"Cool. Let me know if you need help with anything."

"Will do!"

Isaac went back downstairs and grabbed a box from the back of his truck and took it upstairs to his bedroom. When he had unloaded his truck, he drove back to his parents' house to reload.

It took Isaac two trips to get all the boxes, then he and Jake loaded up his bed and dresser into his truck.

"I think that's the last of it," he told his parents.

"Come visit us sometimes," his mother said.

For all the issues with his father, Isaac did get along with his mother and would miss her being around. But he had to do this if he wanted any sanity in his life being in a band.

"I will," Isaac said. "And I'll let you know when we're playing and when we go on tour, which will be pretty soon."

"Take care, son," his father said, shaking his hand.

"See ya!"

He and Jake got into this truck and he pulled away.

"Glad to be out of there," Isaac said.

"I guess you don't get along with your parents?" Jake asked.

"Yeah, you've seen how my dad is," Isaac said. "My mom is okay, if a little judgey. My dad's a dick."

"I gathered that from seeing him backstage, and the parties we've had."

"It's time I got out on my own, anyway. I don't need his running commentary on everything I do with the band. I don't know how Uncle Dean dealt with that growing up."

"Dean seems to have a high tolerance for things," Jake said.

Isaac laughed.

"Good thing, since he's got to deal with all of us."

Later that night, Isaac and Jake invited the band, Jayna and Marty, and Dean over for a New Home party. They invited their neighbors and promised the ones who couldn't come they wouldn't be loud or late. They didn't want to make a bad first impression. Isaac had told their neighbors who they were and assured them they were not the rowdy type and promised them a free CD when it came out.

"I'm not above bribing people," Isaac had said to Jake after they'd talked to the neighbors.

Chapter Three

Kelly received a message from Dean, calling them all to a meeting on Saturday. She noticed Jayna was on the list, too, which meant he had news on the tour!

When the time came on Saturday, Kelly drove to Dean's house. She heard voices through the open door.

"Knock-knock," she said as she opened the screen door and walked inside.

"Hey, Kelly," Dean greeted, setting three bottles of beer on the table for the guys.

She sat down on the chair across from the couch where Ian, Jake, and Isaac already sat. Jayna sat in the other chair.

"Want anything to drink?" Dean asked.

"Just a soda, please," she said.

Dean went back to the kitchen and brought out a cola for Kelly.

"As soon as Paul gets here, I can let you know what's going on," Dean said.

"For a musician, he sure comes in late a lot," Ian joked.

Paul walked in a moment later.

"I heard that," he said, sitting on the floor next to the couch.

"Now that everyone's here," Dean said, handing Paul a bottle of beer, "I can let you all know that the tour has been finalized."

"Woo hoo!" they shouted.

"They've got us starting in Seattle and working our way down the coast for three shows. Then we've got Steven's company holiday party on December 3rd, then a couple shows around in the area, then Mr. Brennen's company holiday party on December 10th, then we just move on from there across the country."

"Are we flying or driving to Seattle?" Isaac asked.

"Flying, which reminds me, if you don't already have it, get started on your passports. We've got a couple of Canadian dates early next year, so you'll need those."

"Canada?!" Paul asked.

"Yes, just a couple of dates so far. We're going to see how well you do there and maybe add more dates later on at the end of the tour."

Kelly had a passport from when her parents took her and David to Cancun a few years ago for a vacation.

"Getting back to how we get there—we'll fly and then there should be a tour bus waiting for us that we'll use for the tour, plus a trailer to haul your gear in. Kind of like last time when you opened for The Disciples of Man."

"And we're headlining this tour?" Ian asked.

"For the most part, yes. There are a couple of dates where you'll be the support band, but that will be good exposure for you."

"Awesome," Ian said.

"Album comes out next week, and we'll see how sales go, but don't get discouraged if the sales are slow. It will pick up as the tour goes on."

Dean went over a few more items on his list.

"We need to update your rider," he said. "Do you want anything new added—sodas, alcohol, snacks, et cetera?"

"I think what we've got on there is still good," Isaac said.

"More bottled water," Jake said. "It seems like we get close to running out by the end of the night."

"Okay," Dean said, taking notes on his tablet. "I'm searching for rehearsal spaces, too. I know your dad isn't too keen on you rehearsing at his building anymore."

"Yeah," Isaac said. "We're all twenty-one now, but he still doesn't want us bringing beer into the place."

"Or girls," Ian said.

"Or guys," Kelly said.

"You may have to practice in my garage if I can't find a place we can afford."

He told them there were several local newspapers that wanted to do interviews with them.

"I'll get them set up ASAP," Dean said. "Maybe we can do them all in one day and get them over with."

Dean finished his list, and the band hung out for a little while to talk before heading home.

The following Tuesday, Kelly woke up early, knowing the band's CD had come out at midnight. She sat up quickly and grabbed her phone, going straight to the band's social media page. Kelly found quite a few friends and fans talking about it. She then went to the online store to see if there were any reviews of it, scrolling until she found the reviews. There were two already on there! Both were positive, saying how well the music sounded and how good the band was.

Her phone *dinged* with a message. She saw that Erik had texted her and the band.

"Congrats on the CD! Can't wait to listen to it!"

Ian had already replied. She tapped out her response.

"Thank you!"

Kelly got out of bed and went to the kitchen to eat breakfast. Her mom had made her favorite breakfast—pancakes and bacon.

"Good morning!" Mom said as Kelly walked into the room.

"Good morning!" Kelly said.

"Today's the day, isn't it?"

"Yes! And there's already two reviews of the CD online," Kelly told her.

"How wonderful! Dad says congratulations, too. He had to leave for work before you got up."

"It will be interesting to see what happens throughout the day. I may have to shut my phone off again."

Kelly finished eating and went to change her clothes. She got a text from Dean saying the record company wanted to do a photo shoot with them that day at two o'clock. She texted back, saying she'd be ready, then texted Jayna to make sure she could help her that day.

"Of course," Jayna replied.

Jayna came over half an hour later to help Kelly pick out her outfits for the photo shoot. They picked out her platform ankle boots and her Chucks, and a couple of blouses to change into that would go with her black flared pants. She would take her make-up bag and do her make-up once she knew what they wanted from her and the guys.

Dean came by in the van at one-fifteen to pick up Kelly and Jayna. He made stops to pick up the guys then drove to Monte Verde Park where some of the photos would be taken.

They met the photographer at the entrance of the park.

"Hello," the photographer, Brian, said.

"Hi," Dean said, shaking hands. He introduced Brian to the band and Jayna.

"I've walked around inside to find some great spots for the photos," Brian said. "I've made arrangements for you to use the lodge to change clothes and get ready."

"Awesome," Dean said. "Lead the way."

Brian took them into the lodge and showed them where they could get ready, which were the restrooms with a dressing room adjacent to it.

"Just dress how you normally would for the stage," Brian said. "We'll do some posed shots and then some casual shots."

Kelly and Jayna went to get ready while the guys went to their restroom to change.

Half an hour later, Kelly came out in her platform shoes and sparkly blue blouse with her black pants. She had on her usual stage make-up and Jayna had styled her hair into soft waves.

Brian led them back to the place where the tree branches had grown sideways then upwards. He had Kelly sit on the branch with two of the guys standing on either side of her. Kelly's phone *dinged*, indicating a message. She pulled her phone out to see who texted, then slipped it back into her back pocket.

"You can smile or not, just whatever you want to do," Brian told them.

Kelly had a hard time not smiling in photos, so she smiled. Ian and Jake smiled, Isaac and Paul did not.

"I want to take one not smiling," Brian said.

"That's always hard for me, especially today," she said, as her phone *dinged* again. She turned her phone to S*ilent* so she wasn't distracted by it for the photos.

Kelly tried her best to not smile, but ended up with half a grin.

"That'll have to do, I guess," Brian said.

Brian then took individual photos of the band. He had Kelly lean on the tree with her chin in her hand, then had her change her shoes to jump in front of the tree, doing a ring leap in the air, showing off a little of her gymnast prowess. He also had the guys lean against the tree in various poses.

Two hours later, Brian had everything he needed.

"Thanks so much for being so cooperative," he told them.

"It was fun," Kelly said.

"I don't know about fun," Isaac said with a laugh.

"Talk to you soon," Brian said to Dean, shaking his hand as he left.

"Now, let's go celebrate the release of your CD," Dean said.

They gathered up their belongings and got back into the van, and Dean drove them to El Torito for dinner and drinks. The hostess seated them quickly and when the server came, they placed their orders. Dean ordered margaritas for everyone.

"I can't wait to see the charts on Monday," Dean told them. "I think the CD will do well in New Releases."

"If Kelly's phone is any indication," Ian said, "it will."

"Yeah, sorry about that," Kelly said.

The server brought out their food. The guys and Jayna ordered another margarita, but Kelly and Dean stopped at one each. Dean's phone *dinged* and he pulled it out.

"Hey, it's a text from Jim," he said, "congratulating us on the CD release. He says it's moving at a slow but somewhat steady pace."

"It's moving, at least," Isaac said.

"Awesome!" Kelly said.

On Monday, the New Release sales came out. Their CD came in at number 19 on the list.

"Not bad at all," Dean said when they gathered at his house for an update. "Yes, it's not Top Ten, but you're in the Top 20. It's more than I expected, not for a lack of confidence, but you're still a fairly localized band. All the work you've done helped to get it in the Top 20, so congratulations."

"When's the tour starting?" Isaac asked.

"Two weeks from today," Dean said. "So make sure you've got everything taken care of to be gone for an extended time."

"I've got my brother and Jake has his sister coming to check on our apartment while we're gone," Isaac said.

"Good. You all have your passports in progress?"

"Yes," they said in unison.

"Good, and you guys are rehearsing tonight and the next couple of days?"

"Yes," Kelly said. "The rehearsal studio you rented is really great."

They finished up the meeting and went straight from there to the rehearsal studio.

"Since we don't have a lot of our own songs," Isaac said, opening a bottle of beer. "We're going to have to add a few cover songs, like the old days. Ideas?"

"Hit Me with Your Best Shot is always a good one," Kelly said.

"I knew you'd say that one," Ian said.

"It is our best cover," Isaac said.

"I'm not complaining. I like it."

"What else?" Isaac asked.

They tossed around song names until they had seven more songs to go with their ten originals.

"I hate that it's almost half the set list," Jake said.

"I think everyone will be happy. We'll eventually have all our own songs to play."

They worked on their originals first, then worked on some of the covers. They agreed to rehearse the next night to run through the entire set list and then work on individual songs as needed during the next week of rehearsals.

Five days before they were to leave on tour, Dean had their equipment packed up into a trailer and the band's two main roadies, Bailey and Scott, took it and the crew up the coast to Seattle.

Greg picked Kelly up in the morning the day before she'd leave for Fate Struck's tour so they could spend the day together. They went to Knott's Berry Farm and held hands as they walked around, and when they waited in line, Greg kissed Kelly gently, arms around each other. They went on a few rides, but it was mostly a day to be together and enjoy their time before she had to leave.

They went to the Chicken House there at Knott's for dinner. They waited in the short line and got seated quickly. They ordered their food and after the server left, Greg picked up Kelly's hand.

"I wish you didn't have to go," he said. "I hate being away from you."

"I hate to be apart from you, too," Kelly said. "Unfortunately, it's something we'll have to get used to. We got through it before."

"I know, I just don't like the idea of guys looking at you as someone to hook up with."

Kelly laughed.

"I'm sure they don't," she said.

"Bless you for being so naïve about it, but they do. I've heard comments from people. Guys want you, babe, and I'm afraid I'm going to lose you, especially when you're gone for so long. I don't want guys looking at you like that."

"So what should I do so guys don't look at me like that?"

"Leave the band."

She laughed, but noticed that Greg wasn't laughing or even smiling.

"You're serious?"

"Actually, yes."

That shocked Kelly. He knew that she loved to sing and loved entertaining people. Leave the band? How could he ask that?

"You know that's not going to happen," Kelly said.

"I also want you to stay away from Ian. You hang around with him so much and I think he's got a crush on you."

The server brought their food to the table. It gave Kelly a moment to let that sink in. Is Greg really jealous of Ian?

"Ian and I are just friends, and that's it. We're bandmates. You're sounding like Jessica, and I don't like it." She stabbed her salad with her fork and shoved it into her mouth. Tears formed, and she set her fork down and put her head in her hands.

Greg sighed deeply and reached for Kelly's hand.

"I'm sorry," he said, rubbing the back of her hand with his thumb. "I know this is important to you."

"Do you?" she asked, raising her head to look at him. "Because it sounds very demanding. You fell in love with me because of what I do. Now it sounds like you want me to make a choice."

"No, I don't want you to make a choice," he said quietly. "I know this is something you love doing. I'm sorry. I really am. I'm just not looking forward to you being gone for four months."

"I know, and I don't want to be away from you for that long. But it's something we'll have to learn to deal with."

Greg took both of her hands in his and leaned over to kiss Kelly.

"I don't want to fight on our last night together. Let's eat and go to my place," he said.

They finished their dinner and Greg drove them to his house that he shared with two other guys.

"It looks like the guys are out," Greg said with a smile. "I'm so sorry I made you upset."

He leaned down to kiss Kelly, gently at first, then more eager and they walked to his bedroom. He shut the door and continued to kiss Kelly as he backed her to his bed. When she felt the bed on her legs Kelly sat down and pushed herself up the bed and laid down, Greg following.

They kissed for a long time, his hands in her hair, her hands on his back. Greg moved his hand to her breast over her blouse, then slid his hand under her blouse and pulled the cup of her bra down and caressed it. They parted for a moment while Kelly took her blouse off and Greg took off his shirt. He slipped one strap off her shoulder, baring her breast. He licked it, then took it into his mouth. Kelly moaned softly, and he reached behind her and unhooked her bra and cast it aside. Her hands were in his hair as he teased her breasts with his tongue, then kissed her neck while playing with her.

Kelly wanted him inside her, and moved her hands to his waist and unbuttoned his jeans. As he took off his pants, Kelly unzipped hers and kicked them off. Kelly took his sex in her hand and caressed and stroked Greg to hardness, and he grabbed a condom from his side table drawer and rolled it on and quickly entered her. Kelly arched into him as he got fully inside her. He started to move and she moved with him, his arms around her, kissing her face and her neck. Her hands caressed his back and butt, pulling him inside her as far as he could go.

"Oh, God, Kelly," he breathed. "I love you so much."

"I love you," she whispered.

An hour later, they lay on the bed, spooned together.

"I'm going to miss this," Kelly said softly.

"Me, too," Greg said.

"Not just the sex, but being with you."

Greg raised his head to kiss her shoulder.

"I knew what you meant. It's going to be a long four months being without you."

"I'll be back in a couple weeks," Kelly reminded him.

"I know, but then you're gone again for four months. I want to be with you."

"That's the only reason I hope it goes by quickly, to be back with you."

They lay together for a few more minutes, then Kelly said she had to get home to finish getting everything ready.

Greg sighed, and he threw off the blankets so they could both get up and dressed. He drove her home when they were ready.

"I'll come by tomorrow to see you before you go," Greg said as he walked her to her front porch.

"Okay. Don't be late, because Dean won't wait for you."

He kissed her softly on her lips, and walked back to his car.

Kelly anxiously went down her list to make sure she had everything she needed.

"I know I'm forgetting something," she said frantically to her mom.

"Whatever it is I'm sure you can buy it somewhere," Mom said. "They have Walmarts almost everywhere."

"I know, I just wish I knew what it was."

"You're just excited and nervous, sweetie. What is it they say? 'Don't sweat the small stuff.'"

Kelly took a deep breath and blew it out slowly.

"You're right," she said. "It'll be fine. It'll be fine." She'd tell herself that the entire tour if need be.

"Jayna will help you, too. If you're missing something she'll know what it is."

"True. She's been so great. It's nice having my best friend with me for this."

Kelly woke up the next morning at six, well before her alarm would go off. She lay in bed and tried to get back to sleep but couldn't, her mind racing about the tour.

She got up to start her day. She changed her clothes and put on some make-up before packing her make-up bag into her luggage. She quickly made her bed, and by the time she finished, her mom had awakened. Kelly went to the kitchen to eat breakfast.

"Couldn't sleep?" Mom asked.

"Yeah," Kelly said. "I tried to go back to sleep, but I'm too excited about this tour."

"Let me make you some pancakes and bacon so you have a good breakfast for the start of your tour." Mom got the griddle and pulled out the box of pancake mix from the pantry.

"Thanks, Mom," Kelly said. "It'll be the last home-cooked meal I'll have for the next two weeks."

"You'll be back here for the holiday parties?"

"Yeah, we'll be here for a little over a week, then back out for about four months."

Mom finished making pancakes and put two on a plate for Kelly, along with four strips of bacon. Kelly poured orange juice into a glass and sat down and ate slowly, enjoying the taste of the food. She took a picture of her plate and posted it onto her social media page with the caption, "Last home-cooked meal before going on tour."

At eight o'clock, Kelly received a text from Dean, letting all of them know he'd be picking them up starting at nine-thirty. She replied that she'd be ready, and brought all her luggage out to the living room. She had two suitcases—one with her everyday clothes and one with her stage clothes. She wore her Chucks and packed her two pairs of platform shoes and a pair of flip-flops. Kelly had packed her make-up bag in her suitcase, along with her various styling products for her hair.

She could see she had everything, but still felt she was missing something, besides Greg not being there yet. By the time Dean came to pick her up, she remembered. She went to her room and grabbed the stuffed rabbit off her bed.

"Can't go without her," Kelly said.

"Is that what you've been worrying about?" Mom asked.

"I think so," Kelly said. "It's silly, but she needs to go with me, for luck."

Dean came up to help Kelly with her luggage. Her dad had delayed going to work that day to see her off.

"Call us when you can, pumpkin," Dad said.

"I will," Kelly said, hugging him tightly.

She moved to hug her mom.

"Have fun," Mom said, "and be safe."

"I've got eight guys watching out for me," Kelly said. "I'll be fine."

Kelly walked out to the van to see Jayna already sitting in there, and a driver in the driver's seat. Was Greg going to get there on time? Kelly turned to wave to her parents, and heard tires screeching behind her. Greg had almost missed her. He ran up to Kelly and hugged her.

"I'm sorry," Greg panted. "I over-slept. I'm going to miss you so much," he said.

"I'll be back in two weeks," Kelly said.

Greg kissed her slowly, then hugged her again.

"I love you," he said softly.

"I love you, too," Kelly said.

Greg helped her into the van and slid the door shut. Dean got into the passenger seat and the driver pulled away and Kelly watched Greg wave until they turned the corner.

They arrived at LAX three hours early for their flight that afternoon. Dean had wanted plenty of time to get things organized and checked in. The driver pulled up to the curb in front of their flight terminal and helped get everything out of the van.

Isaac and Kelly, ever the historians of the group, took photos with their phones of their luggage on the carts, the terminal, and themselves as they walked up to the counter while Dean checked them all in.

Once through security, they split up to walk around the shops to kill time until their flight. Kelly and Jayna went straight to the bookstore, where Kelly bought the latest release from her favorite author to read while they were on the long drives on the road.

"This is starting to feel real," Kelly said as she and Jayna got a coffee from Starbucks. "We're in an airport, waiting for a flight up the coast to start a tour."

"Never imagined that, huh?" Jayna asked.

"Nope. In high school, before I joined the band, I thought I'd join a college choir or something, and maybe coach gymnastics."

"And now you're headlining a national tour. Pretty awesome!"

"Yeah, it is!"

At three o'clock, Kelly and Jayna walked back to the gate. The guys joined them a few moments later.

"They just called to board," Dean said. He handed each of them their boarding pass as they walked to line up with the rest of the travelers. "We should arrive in Seattle in about three hours, so not a long flight."

They got to their seats and put their carry-ons in the overhead bins or under the seat in front of them. Kelly and Jayna were booked sitting together, Ian and Paul together, and Isaac and Jake together. Dean sat a couple rows back from them.

When the flight attendant came around for drink orders, Kelly requested ginger ale.

"I tend to get air sick at the least bit of turbulence," Kelly told Jayna, who ordered a rum and coke. The attendant brought their drinks to them a few minutes later. Jayna held out a five-dollar bill.

"Oh, your drinks are paid for already," the attendant said, gesturing toward Dean.

"Nice!" Jayna said, putting the money back into her purse.

Half an hour into the flight the attendants served dinner. Kelly had never flown first class before and was surprised at how good the food tasted.

"Check this out," Kelly said, as they finished dinner. "Greg and I went out to dinner yesterday, and he wanted me to quit the band."

"What the hell?" Jayna said, eyes wide.

"Yeah. He said he didn't like the way guys looked at me when I'm onstage. He even mentioned that Ian supposedly looks at me like that."

"Ian doesn't look at you like that at all. He's like our brother."

"Right? Anyway, it felt like a Jessica situation all over again, and I told him so."

"What did he say?"

"He apologized, but I'm not sure it was sincere. I'm not even looking at other guys, so I don't know why he thinks he's going to lose me while I'm on tour."

"Maybe being apart will help him realize how wrong he is. As much time as I spend with you and the fans, and guys coming to talk to me, Marty hasn't said one thing about it. I know I'm not up onstage, but I get hit on a lot at the merch table, though it may be to get to you."

"Marty trusts you, and he's known you since before we got popular."

"You sure have rotten luck with guys."

"Thanks for that," Kelly said, not unkindly.

"Sorry. I just mean it's their issue, not yours."

"No, you're good, and you're right. I feel like he doesn't trust me, and I've given him no reason to think that."

She put that whole issue out of her mind for now. She didn't want to start off the tour depressed.

The plane descended and five minutes later they were on the ground at Seattle-Tacoma International Airport and taxiing to the terminal. Once at the terminal the passengers gathered up their belongings. Kelly knew from an earlier discussion with Dean to wait until everyone else had gotten off before they got up and deplaned. As they walked to the luggage carousel, Kelly saw a man holding a sign saying *Fate Struck*.

"Dean, look!" she said, pointing.

Dean went over to the man and introduced himself.

"Welcome to Seattle!" the man said. "I'm Harry, and I'll be your driver to take you to your hotel. I have two carts over here to take your luggage to the cars," Harry said.

"Fantastic," Dean said.

They retrieved their luggage from the carousel and Harry had two other men there to help push the carts. Kelly and the others didn't have to carry anything.

"I could get used to this," Isaac said.

35

They followed Harry out to the street, where he opened the car door for them.

"We get a limo?" Kelly exclaimed.

"Tyrian Records must think very highly of you," Harry said with a smile.

While the men put their luggage into the van parked behind, the band, Jayna, and Dean got into the black limousine.

"People are looking at us," Ian said.

"Get used to it," Dean said. "Because it will only get worse as you get more popular."

Harry got into the driver's seat and started the engine.

"Make yourselves at home," he said. "There are drinks in the bar, and snacks in the console. It'll take about an hour to get to the hotel."

Dean opened the bar and saw bottles of Heineken beer and Mike's Hard Lemonade, shooters of various liquors, and cans of soda. Dean passed the beer to the guys and the Mike's to Kelly and Jayna. Dean abstained from the alcohol and took a can of Coke.

Kelly had her phone out, taking pictures of the inside of the limo and taking selfies with everyone. Isaac, also had his phone out, doing a Live on social media.

They arrived at the hotel. Harry came around and opened the door for them, Dean getting out first, then Jayna and Kelly, and finally the guys.

"We'll take care of your luggage while you check in," Harry said.

Dean went inside and the band and Jayna followed behind, looking at everything. They'd never stayed in such an upscale hotel. Kelly took pictures of the inside and then took a selfie with all of them inside the lobby. Harry and his men brought in the carts with their luggage on them and waited for Dean to finish checking in.

"We're on the third floor," Dean said, handing key cards to everyone. "Go on up and we'll follow with the luggage."

The band and Jayna went to the elevators and rode up to the third floor. They walked down the hall and found their rooms, a group of four at the end of the hall, two across from each other. Jayna and Kelly were booked together, Ian and Paul together, and

Isaac and Jake. Dean had his own room. The roadies had arrived the day before and had rooms down the hall.

Kelly slid the keycard into the slot. The light flashed and the door clicked open. She and Jayna went inside. Jayna opened the drapes and they had a great view of the city lights.

"Wow," Kelly said. "This is fantastic."

"Enjoy it while you can," Dean said, having come up with the luggage. "After tonight, with the exception of our shows in California, you'll be on a bus for the next four months."

They all went out to retrieve their luggage, and Harry and the guys wished them a successful tour, shook hands with Dean, and left.

"The bus will be here tomorrow at noon to pick us up and take us to the venue," Dean said. "We don't have to be there until four o'clock, but it will take time to get you guys settled in and everything."

Kelly and Jayna took their luggage into their room. While Jayna called her parents, Kelly called hers.

"Hey, Mom," Kelly said.

"Are you at the hotel?" Mom asked.

"Yeah, you should see this place! It looks expensive. We got picked up from the airport in a limo with a driver and everything!"

"The record company really went all out for you."

"They really did. It's kind of fun to be pampered like this."

"When is your first show?"

"Tomorrow night. The bus is picking us up and taking us to the venue. I'll try to call again before we go on, but can't make any promises."

"Just call us when you can," Mom said. "I know you're in good hands with Dean. He seems like he knows what he's doing."

"Yeah, Dean's been great. He really watches out for all of us."

Kelly spoke with her dad for a few minutes, then hung up so she could call Greg.

"Hey, babe," Greg said when he answered.

"Hi," Kelly said. "We made it to our hotel room. I'll send you pictures of this place. It's freaking amazing."

"I'll bet," Greg said. "That's the first time I've ever heard you say 'freaking' anything."

"It needed an adverb to describe the place."

The conversation went mostly the same as with her parents, letting him know when they were playing.

"Call me when you can tomorrow," Greg said.

"I will," Kelly told him. "I'll make more of an effort to call you than my parents. Not that I don't want to talk to them, but I miss you more than I miss them."

"Aw, thanks."

Someone knocked on the door, and Jayna answered. Dean had an armful of snacks for them.

"Ooh, Dean just brought us snacks," Kelly told Greg. "We ate dinner on the flight, but that was hours ago and I'm hungry."

"I thought you might be," Dean said. "I went to the convenience store around the corner."

"Thanks, Dean," Kelly said.

Dean and Jayna set the food on the dresser and Dean left. Kelly turned back to the conversation with Greg.

"I guess I better let you go nibble," he said.

"I love and miss you so much already."

"I love you, too," Greg said, making kissing sounds to her.

"I'll see you in a couple of weeks," Kelly said, and she disconnected.

Kelly went to see what Dean had brought them. Doritos, donuts, a couple of bananas and oranges, and some bottles of juice and water. Kelly picked up the bag of Doritos and tore open the bag, and picked up a bottled water. Jayna grabbed the bag of donuts and opened it.

"Oh, no," Kelly said. "Not donuts."

"I don't hear them singing," Jayna said, "so I think we're good."

The girls laughed together.

"It's been a little while since we've had a sleepover," Kelly said.

"Yeah, this is like old times, munching and laughing together. Staying together while you recorded was kind of fun, but we didn't get to talk much."

"I was too tired when I came in and you were usually asleep." Kelly took a sip of water. "I remember your dad playing tapes of old songs for us. I think that's when I learned to love music and appreciate different genres of music. I mean, Napoleon the Fourteenth? Who even listens to that nowadays?"

"You!" Jayna said with a smile. "I've heard your playlist."

Kelly giggled. Her playlist was heavy on seventies and eighties, and eclectic songs.

"I can't help it if I like the old stuff. Probably why I like 'Hit Me' so much."

"Hooray for oldies!"

Kelly held her hand out for a donut and Jayna tossed one to her. She held it up to her ear.

"Nope, definitely not singing," she said, and Jayna giggled as Kelly took a bite.

Chapter Four

Kelly awoke the next morning and, remembering what day it was, threw off her blankets and jumped out of bed. She went to her suitcase to get out something to wear for the day, pulling out a pair of jeans and a t-shirt with the band Sweet on the front. She pulled on her socks and purple Chucks, then brushed her hair.

Jayna stirred in the bed across from Kelly.

"Wake up, sleepyhead," Kelly said.

"You're very chipper today." Jayna rolled over and tossed her blankets aside and sat on the edge of her bed. "This is going to be so great today."

Kelly looked at the clock on the nightstand. 8:30.

"I know I'm up early, I'm just too excited to sleep any longer," she said.

Jayna got out of bed and rummaged through her suitcase for something to wear, then went in to take a quick shower while Kelly put on her make-up.

Kelly and Jayna were ready to go at nine-thirty. Dean texted to meet at the elevator in ten minutes to go down to breakfast in the hotel dining room.

Back in their room after breakfast, Kelly and Jayna got their suitcases repacked and everything organized for when Dean came to let them know the bus had arrived.

Dean brought up two carts for the luggage and helped them get it all downstairs. He stopped at the front desk to check them all out and then helped them take the luggage to the bus parked in the side parking lot.

"Wow, that's huge!" Kelly said.

"That's what she said," Jake said. Kelly smacked him on the arm.

"Is that what we've got to look forward to—silly innuendoes?"

"Of course!" Ian said with a wink.

The bus was bigger than the last bus they had; it looked more like an actual bus than a motorhome. Leaving their luggage outside, the band and Jayna went inside to check it all out. At the front of the bus behind the driver was the living room, with two couches on either side of the bus. Next was the kitchenette, which had a small microwave and stovetop, and a half-size refrigerator. A small booth with a dining table was between the couches and fridge. Above the counters were cabinets. Next were the bunks, six on either side of the hallway. They moved through the sleeping area to the lounge. A full-sized bed in the middle, small side tables on each side, and a TV mounted on the wall. It wasn't flashy but it looked comfortable.

"What do you guys think?" Dean asked. He stood at the front while they surveyed the bus.

"This is awesome!" Isaac said.

"Fabulous!" Kelly said.

The rest of the band and Jayna gave their approval as well. The driver stepped inside.

"Does everything meet your expectations?" he asked.

"Oh, yeah," Dean said. "I think they'll enjoy this a lot."

"Let me know what to put in storage and what comes on the bus," the driver said.

By the time they got everything situated, it was one o'clock. The driver got onboard and drove them the few miles to the venue, Dean pointing it out as they drove to the back loading area. It was a smaller venue, about the size of The Constellation Room in Santa Ana, and there were already about ten people waiting out front. Dean went inside to let them know they'd arrived, then came back out.

"Everything's all set," he told the band. "Bailey and Scott and the crew have everything already set up. You can take your stuff in and get settled now if you want, then you'll sound check at four."

They got their belongings together and followed Dean to the side door. A few fans had been watching the bus and shouted and waved to the band.

"Hi Kelly! Hi, Isaac!" they shouted.

"Break a leg tonight!" said another fan.

Fate Struck waved back to the fans as they went inside the door.

"We have fans here?" Paul asked.

"Apparently," Dean said with a laugh. "I'd venture to say they're here for you and not the opener."

"Woo hoo!" Ian said.

Dean took them to their dressing room. Bigger than their last dressing room, it had a men's and women's bathroom with a shower and toilet. The common area had a couple of couches and several chairs around the room. Kelly noticed a full-length mirror at each end, and a counter with mirrors running the length of one wall.

"This is fantastic," Kelly said, turning to Jayna. "We've got our own bathroom!"

"And a dressing area," Jayna said. "Plenty of room in there for both of us and our stuff."

Kelly and Jayna took their suitcases and set them on the bench near the women's bathroom and opened them up. Kelly took out her make-up bag and set it on the counter and made sure there was an outlet available for her curling iron. There was one about every four feet along the counter.

The guys, Kelly, and Jayna spent the rest of the time either on the bus or hanging out in the dressing room. The guys played video games on the bus while Kelly read for a while, then went inside to watch the crew finish the final touches.

At three o'clock the staff came in to set up a food table for them. They filled the table against the opposite wall with trays of various fruits and veggies, bottled water, Heineken and Mike's, and sandwich fixings.

The boys were already devouring the food by the time Kelly and Jayna had gotten their area set up.

"Hey, leave some for us," Kelly joked.

"Then don't lollygag," Ian said.

"Goofball," Kelly said.

She and Jayna picked up a plate and went down the table, picking up strawberries, carrots, grapes, and then made a sandwich. Kelly took a bottled water while Jayna took a hard lemonade.

The band finished just in time for sound check. Dean led them to the stage and helped get their in-ear monitors set up, making sure the batteries were good. When everyone was set, Kelly checked her microphone first. She said a couple of "check-one-two's" into the mic, then sang a song a cappella.

Ian and Jake stepped up to their mics for their checks, then the engineer moved on to the instruments, getting Isaac's drums first, then the guitars. Finally, with everything set, they ran through one of their songs to make sure everything sounded good and they were done.

Kelly showered before getting dressed for the show. She liked having a shower at the venue to use. She didn't like showering on the bus or in the hotel before sound check because she got sweaty during that time, and then had to just use a washcloth and the bathroom sink to try to feel refreshed.

After drying and dressing, Kelly came out to comb out her hair and apply her make-up. She let her hair air-dry.

An hour later, everyone was dressed and ready for the show. Jayna made sure Kelly had everything she needed before she headed out to the merchandise table.

"Let's do our pre-show drink before you go," Kelly said.

Ian got the cups and poured Fireball into each of them, Dean choosing to partake this one time.

"Here's to a fantastic tour," Dean said, holding up his cup.

"Cheers!" they all shouted, then touched cups before drinking. Dean pulled a face after downing his shot.

"You can drink this?" he asked, turning to Kelly.

"Yeah," she said. "It's not that bad."

"I prefer Jägermeister," Dean said.

"Yuck," Kelly grimaced. Dean laughed.

"I guess we all have our favorites." Dean tossed his cup into the trash while the boys had a second shot. Kelly declined and Jayna went out to the merchandise table.

"See you later!" Jayna said and with a wave walked out the door.

Kelly stretched her legs and back, then warmed up her voice, running through some scales with Ian and Jake. The opener started their set, and they went out to watch a little of their performance. Dean had suggested them to the record company and the band. The band liked them, and Dean persuaded the record company to book them for part of the tour.

The opener played for forty minutes, then the roadies made the changeover for Fate Struck. While they made the change, Kelly drank down her energy drink while the guys had one more shot of Fireball before they went out to play.

Isaac went out first, made sure his drums were set up how he liked, got the computer up and running, and then played the beat to one of their songs. Ian joined in with his bass as he walked onstage as the crowd cheered for the band. Paul and Jake walked out next, and finally Kelly came out to the loudest cheers. She set her water bottle on the floor next to her mic stand, then grabbed the mic.

"How's everyone doing tonight?" she asked with a smile.

The crowd cheered and waved their hands in the air.

"Let's rock and roll," she said, and they started their first song.

Even in her platform shoes, Kelly jumped and danced around onstage. She put her arm around Ian's shoulders as they sang the chorus to one of the songs, holding the mic in front of both of them. She stood next to Jake as he played one of his solos, moving to the music.

Between songs, Kelly thanked the fans for coming out.

"We love you guys so much," she said. "We really appreciate your support. Here's a throwback to the early days when we were doing covers in high school."

Jake started in on his guitar then the others came in, playing "Hit Me with Your Best Shot." The crowd clapped and sang along.

Fate Struck played for an hour and a half, playing their originals and some covers to extend the time. They had added a couple of new original songs to the set list to add length, but played all the songs on their CD, and the covers everyone loved.

"This is our last song for the night," Kelly said, brushing her hair back from her face. "Thanks so much for coming out. You've been great."

After they finished the song, they got together in the front to take a bow, then turned around for Dean to take their picture with the fans. Fate Struck waved as they went off stage, Isaac tossing out his drumsticks as he left.

Back in their dressing room, they all collapsed onto the couch and chairs, and Dean passed out water bottles to all of them. Kelly drank half of hers down.

"Awesome show, guys and girl," Dean said. "It looked like everyone was having fun and getting into the music."

"It was so fun!" Kelly said.

"Fucking awesome!" Isaac said.

They talked for a few minutes about the show, what needed to change, how the sound was, and a few other minor details, with Dean taking copious notes, before Dean extended an invitation to the opener, The Cat's Meow, to come hang out in Fate Struck's dressing room. They came in a few minutes later.

"You guys were great!" Kelly told the singer, Jensen.

"Thank you," Jensen said. "Thanks for inviting us over. That's totally cool."

"Well, when we were an opener," Kelly told him, "the headliner invited us to their dressing room to hang out for a bit and we always said if we had the chance, we'd do that, too. We gotta stick together and support each other."

"That's a fantastic outlook," Jensen said.

Kelly grabbed a hard lemonade, flipped off the top, and took a drink.

"Besides I think it'll be fun to hang out with you guys during the tour."

Isaac grabbed the plastic cups and poured in a shot of Jack into all of them and told everyone to take one. Kelly took one, even though she wasn't a big fan of Jack Daniels.

"To The Cat's Meow," Isaac said, holding his cup high. "Thanks for being here and I know I speak for everyone when I say that you guys were great and we look forward to you touring with us."

"Hear, hear!" Ian said.

They held their drinks up and then drank. Kelly only managed to drink half of her cup.

"It's just too hard for me," she said sheepishly.

"Girl, we need to get you used to alcohol," Jake said.

"Nah, I'm okay." Kelly smiled. She'd leave the hard drinking to the guys.

After about half an hour, the opener went back to their dressing room. Dean asked Isaac if they wanted any of the fans backstage.

"Are there people waiting?" he asked.

"There's a few people waiting, though management is about to make them leave."

45

"Sure, they can come back," Isaac said, looking at everyone for approval.

"As long as you-know-who isn't among them" Kelly said.

"Voldemort?" Dean asked, raising an eyebrow.

"Ha ha," Kelly said.

Dean winked. No one else said anything, so Dean went and let in a few of the fans, mostly women, but a few guys as well. Kelly suddenly felt self-conscious and nervous, especially after Mystery Guy admitted he'd sent the flowers to her after their last show in San Diego, and wished Jayna would come back to the dressing room. She'd never done well talking to guys, and now that she was in a band, it seemed like they only wanted to talk to her for one reason—sex. At least the guys in high school thought that. The women flocked round the guys, of course, as did a few of the guys who Kelly figured wanted to talk about their instruments. Several guys came over to Kelly, who shot Dean a wide-eyed look of panic. Dean came over right away.

"How's it going tonight?" Dean asked the fans.

"Going great!" one guy said.

"Fantastic show tonight," another said.

"I'm sure I don't have to introduce you, but I will anyway," Dean said, gesturing to Kelly. "This is Kelly Brennen, the singer for Fate Struck."

Kelly held out her hand to shake hands with the three guys and one girl there.

"So happy to meet you!" said the blond guy, who introduced himself as Denny.

The tall redhead was Joel, and the shorter blond guy was Nate. The girl introduced herself as Trina.

Dean hung around Kelly's group for a few minutes while Kelly got comfortable talking to them, then he meandered off to the side, but Kelly noticed he kept a watchful eye.

"I've been hoping your band would do a headlining show once the CD came out," Nate said.

"We've been following you for about two years," Joel said,

"Do you all know each other?" Kelly asked.

"Nate and I are friends," Joel said, "but we just met Trina and Denny tonight."

"Awesome. You know, I've made quite a few friends from the bands I've liked," Kelly said. "It's a fun way to make friends."

They talked about the show for a few minutes, then Nate, Joel, and Trina went over to the guys. Kelly saw that Ian, as usual, had his arm around a pretty brunette. Kelly asked Denny if he wanted to have a seat.

"These aren't the greatest shoes to stand in," she said, indicating her platforms.

They sat on the couch and a few minutes later one of the guys talking to Isaac came over to talk with her.

"You sounded fantastic," the new guy said.

"Thanks," Kelly said. She held out her hand. "I'm Kelly."

"I know!" the guy said. Kelly waited a moment. "Oh! I'm Chris."

"Nice to meet you, Chris."

"How long have you been singing?" Chris asked.

"Since I was fourteen," Kelly said. "I sang in my high school choir all four years."

"I'll bet all the guys hounded you."

Kelly shook her head.

"Nope. I was too nerdy, plus gymnastics didn't leave a lot of time for fun."

"Oh, yeah, I read you were a gymnast," Denny said. "I saw that flip you did on You Tube when you signed your contract."

"Everyone always asks me to do that," Kelly admitted. "Dean doesn't like me to do it very often because he's afraid I'll hurt myself."

"Who's Dean?" Chris asked.

"Our manager. That's him over there," Kelly said, pointing him out.

At that moment, Jayna walked into the room. Kelly watched her look around and, seeing Kelly, came over to her.

"How'd the merch go?" Kelly asked.

"We sold a lot," Jayna said. "Aren't you going to introduce me to your friends?"

"This is Denny and Chris," Kelly said. "This is Jayna, my best friend, personal assistant, and our merchandise manager."

"Ooh, that's sounds so much better than 'Merch Girl,'" Jayna said, giggling, and she shook hands with the guys.

47

Kelly felt much more comfortable with Jayna there. Kelly didn't really know how to talk to guys other than her band mates, and she figured Denny and Chris were looking to score with her. She wasn't looking for that; she was in love with Greg. Jayna had always been more confident talking with guys, and Kelly let her take the lead, though they all talked to one another.

***

"Would you like another drink?" Ian asked his busty companion, Junie.

"Sure," she said.

They stepped over to the table and Ian poured Junie and himself another drink.

"Has anyone told you how beautiful you are?" Ian asked softly when he came back, playing with her hair.

"Once or twice," Junie giggled.

Ian drank from his cup, then saw one of the guys who'd been talking to Jake move over to Kelly. He watched carefully for a few moments, all the while listening to Junie talk about how much she loved guitar players. He knew Kelly didn't have the experience of talking to guys and almost went over there to make sure the guys stayed in line when he saw Jayna come in and go over to her.

With the crisis averted, he turned his full attention back to Junie, who had started to run her hands through his hair.

"Hey, do you want to see our bus?" he asked.

"Sure!"

Arms around each other's waist, Ian and Junie walked to the door, stopping to talk to Dean.

"Keep everyone out of the bus for half an hour?" Ian asked quietly.

"That's it?" Dean joked.

"You're hilarious," Ian said.

"Will do," Dean said.

Ian and Junie walked out the side door to where the bus was parked. One of the roadies stood by the door to make sure no one without the proper badge went inside. He opened the door and Ian and Junie stepped in.

"Wow," Junie exclaimed softly. "This is fantastic."

"Home away from home," Ian said.

"You have everything here?"

"Yeah." He took her through the bus, showing her everything as they went. He ended up at the lounge at the back of the bus.

"That's just the lounge," Ian said.

"What's in there?"

"We play our video games in there, or if we're not feeling well it's got a bigger bed to sleep in."

"Ooh, can I see?"

"Sure," Ian said, and he opened the door and held it open for her. He shut the door and locked it, just in case.

"How cool is this?" Junie said.

The full-size bed took up almost the entire room, with just enough space on each side to walk between the bed and the wall.

"This is nice," Junie said, running her fingers along the comforter on the bed.

"We like it," Ian said. "It's comfortable and big enough for all of us to play in here if we wanted, though we usually just use the TVs in the dining area up front."

Junie stepped back to Ian, and put her arms around his neck.

"I'd love to try it out," she said, kissing him softly.

He didn't need any other invitation. Ian kissed her deeply, his hands in her hair. They sat on the bed and she pushed herself up to the head of the bed. Ian crawled up to her and she lay back as he kissed her again. He unbuttoned his shirt and peeled it off, then helped her with her blouse. They discarded the rest of their clothing and got in under the blankets.

Ian kissed Junie's face then moved down to her neck and chest, then back to her lips. He ran his hand down her arm gently, then brought it back up to her breast, gently caressing it, then squeezing it before taking the nipple into his mouth. She arched into him, making gentle moaning sounds, encouraging him to do more. He ran his hand down her body, feeling the swell of her hips, her smooth thigh, and back up between her legs. He pushed his fingers inside; she was ready for him. He stopped playing with her for a moment to reach into the nightstand and grab a condom.

He was hard, and rolled the condom on quickly with one hand. Ian shifted until he was on top of her and slowly entered her. They moved slowly together at first, sensing what the other wanted. Ian just wanted sex, but he had to go through the motions to meet Junie's needs, whatever they were. They turned out to be the same as his, however, because she grabbed his ass and pulled him even further inside her. Any pretense of anything other than sex went out the window as she grabbed her breast and licked the nipple.

"Oh my God," he breathed.

"You like that?" she asked.

"God, yeah," he said.

She did it again, and he ran his tongue around the same nipple, their tongues meeting, then he kissed her, his tongue stroking hers. She took both breasts in her hands and pulled the nipples erect. He took one in his mouth again, and massaged the other one as he came. Wave after wave moved through him until he had nothing more. He collapsed onto her for a moment, then rolled off onto the bed.

"That was incredible," Ian said finally.

"It was," Junie said, breathless.

They lay there for a few minutes until his phone *dinged*. He grabbed his phone and read the message.

"They're wrapping up inside," he said. "Unfortunately, that means it's time for you to go."

They got out of bed and dressed, Ian putting on his shirt but only buttoned the middle two buttons. He unlocked the door when Junie was dressed, and he walked her out.

"Thanks for coming to the show," he said, then whispered in her ear, "the after party was great."

Junie giggled.

"When will you be up this way again?" she asked.

"I don't know," he said honestly. "But I hope we'll see each other again."

"Count on it," she said, and she walked to the parking lot to her car and drove off while he went back inside to help pack up their belongings.

***

Dean walked around the room, telling everyone good night, his way of kicking everyone out that wasn't the band.

"It was so nice to meet you," Kelly said, standing up. "I loved talking to you both."

"Yeah, it was great," Jayna agreed.

The guys stood up, too. Kelly thought they looked a little disappointed, but were polite when they shook her hand again.

"I hope to see you again soon," Danny said.

"Watch for our tours," Kelly said. "I'm sure there will be plenty more."

"Definitely will."

He kissed Kelly on her cheek and left. Chris did the same, also kissing Jayna on the cheek as he left.

"Oh, my God," Kelly said, grabbing Jayna's hands. "I'm so glad you showed up when you did. I was so afraid they'd expect something from me, and I'm not about that."

"I saw Dean keeping an eye on you," Jayna said, "but thought I'd come over and help out."

"Thank you," Kelly said. "I'm not good at this stuff."

"You'll get used to it, eventually. You'll loosen up and feel confident about yourself."

Kelly went into the bathroom to wash off all the make-up she'd worn for the show and changed into her sweatpants and a t-shirt. She and Jayna gathered up all their belongings and Kelly packed her worn clothes into her suitcase. She'd organize it tomorrow when she woke up.

They all looked around to make sure they hadn't left anything behind, then followed Dean out the exit. A few fans hung around outside, waiting for them.

"Are you guys up for signing autographs?" Dean asked.

"Sure," Isaac said. "It's not a lot of people."

The others agreed. Jayna took Kelly's luggage onto the bus and Dean helped with the guys' luggage while they all signed for the fans.

"You look so different without your make-up on," one guy said.

"Yeah, I look like I'm about twelve without it," Kelly said.

"No, you look great," he said, touching her shoulder.

51

Dude, if you touch me anywhere else, you're getting an elbow, Kelly thought. *Why do they think they can just touch me?*

"Thanks," she said out loud.

The guy didn't do anything else, and Kelly stood next to the guy so he could take a selfie with her. They only spent about fifteen minutes signing and talking, since there were only twelve people there.

"Thanks for coming," Kelly called over her shoulder as she got onto the bus with a wave to the fans.

The rest of the band finished signing and stepped onto the bus. Artie started the engine and pulled away, taking them to their next venue.

"Glad that didn't last longer," Kelly said as they sat at the table.

"Why?" Isaac asked. "You always like meeting the fans."

"Not if they're going to paw at me."

"I saw that," Jake said. "One of the guys touched Kelly's arm like he was her best friend. If he'd done more, I would've stepped in."

"I appreciate that," Kelly said, "I was ready to hit him in the ribs, too. I guess it's something else I'll have to learn to deal with."

Over the course of a week, they played four shows. They drove to Spokane after Seattle, then Salem, Oregon, and Boise, Idaho, where they had a break before driving into Utah. Their next three shows were a little more spread out, but it got them back to California in time for the company holiday parties for Isaac's father and Kelly's father.

Chapter Five

Kelly was happy to be home even if it was for only a short time. She called Greg right away and he came over to see her.

"I've missed you so much!" Greg said, hugging Kelly, then kissing her quickly.

"I missed you, too," she said.

They spent the day together. They drove along PCH and stopped at the Huntington Beach pier to walk. Fate Struck wasn't so well-known yet that Kelly still had some privacy as she and Greg walked to the end. People fished over the rail and kids ran along with their parents trying to keep up behind them. Kelly and Greg leaned on the rail to look over the ocean and saw the outline of Catalina Island in the distance. The breeze blew Kelly's hair and Greg gently moved a strand from her face.

"You are so gorgeous with the wind in your hair," Greg said.

Kelly blushed and dipped her head. Greg took her chin in his hand and brought her face up.

"Why does that make you embarrassed?" Greg asked.

"I've just never been confident with my looks," Kelly said. "Even now, with you and guys wanting to talk to me after the shows…"

"What?" Greg interrupted. "What guys?"

"Dean let some fans backstage and a couple of guys came over to talk to me. I was scared to death until Jayna came in, although Dean kept an eye on me. We just talked, although I think they wanted more, but like I told Jayna, that's not me."

"I'm not sure I like that," Greg admitted.

"Dean won't let anything happen to me, nor will any of the guys in the band. I've told you before."

Kelly wasn't sure she liked Greg being so jealous. She'd seen it with Ian and Jessica and wasn't about to have the same thing with Greg.

"Don't you trust me?" she asked.

"Of course I do," Greg said. "It's the guys I don't trust. I'm not even sure I trust the guys in the band. I've seen how they look at you onstage."

"Are we seriously going to do this again? It's only an act, Greg. Once we're off stage they're my brothers. Ian told me that he's always watching what the fans do backstage around me. Isaac, too. And Jayna comes back from the merch table to sit with me. The guys kind of flock around her, too."

"Better her than you," Greg said.

"I don't want her and Marty to break up," Kelly said.

"Like I said, better them than us."

Kelly didn't want to fight with Greg on her first day back home after being gone for two weeks. She held back what she wanted to say and just looked out over the ocean. Greg put his arm around her shoulders.

"I'm sorry, babe," Greg said. "It's just hard on me with you being gone for so long."

"I'm going to be gone a lot longer on this next stretch of the tour," she reminded him.

"I know. I'm going to try to visit you on the road at some point."

"That'll be great," Kelly said, still ticked off at him, but she tried to remember that while she was occupied on the road, Greg wasn't except for being at work. His thoughts surely ran the gamut. She resolved to call him more often while she was gone. She'd only made a handful of calls to him on this first leg of the tour. Not avoiding him, just tired after the shows and being busy with all that went on.

They walked back up the pier and across the street to one of the restaurants for dinner.

After Greg dropped her off at home, Kelly had to do one of the more mundane things of being in a touring band, and got her laundry together and put in the washer, then went through her luggage to see if anything needed to be replaced or refilled. She'd need to buy more make-up, and she'd gotten a hole in one of her blouses she'd need to sew. She made a list and would do everything the next day.

***

Isaac was happy to be home, even for only a short while. He and Jake brought their luggage into the apartment and Isaac took his to his room to sort through everything, but before he did that, he wanted to see Hayley. He'd missed her so much. He called her and asked if he could pick her up.

"Of course!" Hayley said. "I've missed you."

Isaac grabbed his keys and went downstairs. His car was a little dusty from not being driven for so long, but at least it started. He'd need to invest in a car cover before they left again.

He pulled up in front of Hayley's house, and Hayley bounded out of her house and jumped into Isaac's arms.

"This is a nice welcome home," Isaac said, smiling.

He kissed her, then they both went into her house so she could pick up her purse before they went to dinner, then went back to his apartment afterwards and found that Jake had left.

"So, we're alone?" Hayley asked.

"Looks like it," Isaac said. Not that having Jake there would stop him, anyway.

They went to his bedroom and shut the door. Isaac took Hayley's face in his hands and gently kissed her. God, he loved her so much. Her sandy blonde hair fell in curls around her face, and that face! Light blue eyes with thick dark lashes that didn't need any help from make-up. Her skin was flawless. He had dreamed about her almost every night while he'd been gone. He may have had women hanging around him backstage, but he had eyes for only one woman—Hayley.

The twin bed was barely big enough for the two of them, but that didn't matter. They wouldn't be lying side by side, anyway.

After making love, they spooned together, Isaac's arm around Hayley's waist. He could smell the flowery scent of her hair, and nuzzled closer to her neck, placing soft little kisses on it.

They dozed off and on for an hour, when Hayley said she needed to go back home.

"Or I may end up staying here all night," she said.

"Is that necessarily a bad thing?" Isaac asked.

"No." She smiled. "But I don't think my parents would approve, even if I am twenty-one."

He knew too well that while her parents weren't like his, they liked to keep up appearances. He sighed.

"Okay, I'll take you home," he said.

They put their clothes back on and went out to the living room. Jake had returned.

"Hi, Jake," Hayley said.

"Hi, Hayley! How's things?"

"Great, now that you guys are back, even though it's just for a little while."

"I'll be back after I take her home," Isaac said.

Isaac drove her home and walked her up to her porch.

"I'll see you tomorrow," Isaac said.

"Okay," Hayley said.

He kissed her goodbye and waited until she went inside before going back to his car.

***

The next night, the band got together at Dean's house to rehearse for the holiday parties. They would play mostly covers, but add in their songs, too, for the sake of any fans there.

"I've hired a limo to take you to the hotel," Dean said. "Bailey and Scott will take the gear there and set up so all you'll have to do is show up early and do a short sound check."

"Easy gig, like the old days," Jake said.

"Though they didn't seem easy back then," Paul said.

"Old days, back then," Ian said. "Like it was sooo long ago." He laughed.

"Let's get a set list done so we can rehearse what we need to," Isaac said.

They all put in their choices for covers, then added in originals. They would play their usual length at the parties—play for an hour, take a short break, then play for another hour at the end.

When they got the songs picked out, they practiced. Kelly stepped up to the mic and they started to play, stopping to take a break at the end of the first set. Isaac, Jake, and Paul went to the backyard for their break while Kelly and Ian stayed inside.

"Thanks for always looking out for me backstage," Kelly said as she and Ian drank their hard lemonade. Dean didn't have any restrictions on what they could and couldn't do at rehearsal.

"You're welcome," Ian said. "I know it's overwhelming for you, and being the lead singer, all the guys want to meet you. Just know that I'll never leave the room if Dean or Jayna aren't there with you."

"I know that, and I appreciate that," Kelly said. "I don't want to cramp your style, though," she said with a laugh.

"There will always be girls, so I'm not worried about it," he said with a wry smile.

Kelly smiled sadly and turned away. Ian touched her chin and gently turned her face toward him.

"What's wrong?" he asked.

"Nothing, really," she said. "Greg and I had a misunderstanding the other day. I mentioned how guys want to talk with me after the shows, and he didn't like that."

"Talking doesn't mean anything," Ian said.

"He even mentioned how you and the guys look at me when I'm onstage. I told him that you guys are like my brothers, but he's still a little jealous."

"Oh, great."

"I didn't say anything else because I didn't want to fight with him. I'm going to have to figure this out or we're not going to last."

"He needs to be a little more understanding, too. You aren't looking for anything to happen, and he needs to understand that."

The other three came back in and they continued with their rehearsal.

"Sounds like a good selection," Dean said an hour later when they'd finished.

"It's pretty much what we've always done for the parties," Isaac said. "Just added a few originals."

"Also, while we're in town, the record company wants you to go to a party they're having a week from tonight," Dean said. "It's not a party *for* you, but they want you there. It's a good opportunity to mingle and get some photos of you out among your peers."

"Christ, we're far from their peers," Isaac said.

"Even so, you will be someday, and they say the other musicians want to get to know you."

"Awesome," Jake said.

On Saturday, Kelly got ready for the show at home. The limo would pick them all up starting at five-thirty to be at the hotel by six-thirty. They could eat and relax before they played two hours later.

At five-forty the limo pulled up to Kelly's house and Dean knocked on the door.

"I'll see you guys there," Kelly said to her parents as she grabbed her purse.

"Bye, honey," Mom said.

They stopped at Isaac's and Jake's apartment next, then picked up Ian, and lastly, Paul. The guys had dressed a little more formal in button-down shirts with their jeans. Kelly wore a red and white striped dress that hit just above her knees with short, puffed sleeves, and her platform Mary Janes.

They arrived at the hotel just before six-thirty. Dean got out from the front seat while the driver went around to hold the car door open for them all, assisting Kelly as she tried to get out while keeping her dress from riding up. They walked into the hotel and found the correct floor for the holiday party. Kelly recognized the event organizer, having spoken with him before.

"So glad you were able to work us into your schedule," the man, Shane, told them.

"We made sure it would work out," Kelly said. "We've all said that we'd make time for these for as long as you want us."

"Thank you, we appreciate it."

They did a quick sound check, then Shane led them to a small room where several trays of food were set up for them.

"This is fantastic," Isaac said.

"Let me know if you need anything else," Shane said. "Otherwise, I'll come check on you and let you know when you'll play."

"Sounds good," Dean said, and Shane pulled the door shut as he left.

The band was used to waiting around before they played, having to wait for changeovers and other things to be done. Kelly and the guys picked up a plate and placed a sandwich and some fruit from the trays. The guys grabbed a bottle of beer while Kelly took a bottled water, even though there were a couple bottles of hard lemonade. She didn't want those until afterwards.

Shane came back a few times to check on them and finally came in to tell them it was time. He led the band along the wall to the stage. Kelly saw that her dad would be introducing them.

"Our entertainment for tonight is the now Tyrian Records recording artists, Fate Struck," he said, and he smiled as they walked up to their instruments. He kissed Kelly's cheek as he held the mic out to her.

"Thanks, Dad," Kelly said. She turned to the audience. "Thank you for having us back to entertain you tonight. We hope you enjoy the music."

People danced to the songs for almost an hour before the band took a break. Shane took them back to their room where they could relax. Kelly asked for the restroom and Shane directed her down the hall. Kelly walked down the empty hall to the restroom. As she washed her hands afterwards, another woman came in and her eyes grew wide when she saw Kelly there.

"You're Mr. Brennen's daughter," the woman said when she got her composure back.

"Yeah. I'm Kelly," she said.

"Your band sounds great," the woman said.

"Thank you so much," Kelly said, smiling.

"All the times you've played for us, I didn't realize you wanted to be recording artists."

"It kind of evolved," Kelly said.

"Well, congratulations and good luck on your career."

"Thank you!"

Kelly went back to the band's room to wait for their next set.

At the end of the night several people came up to congratulate the band on their record signing and talk to them for a few minutes before Dean came to wrap things up. Kelly went out to say goodbye to her parents before they left, then returned to the group as they spoke with Dean.

"Home?" Dean asked.

"Denny's!" they exclaimed.

"Seriously? You want to go to Denny's?" Dean asked.

"It's tradition," Isaac said. "Even if we haven't been able to do that on the road."

Dean told the driver to take them to the nearest Denny's. The driver found one and drove straight there. There were only a few cars in the parking lot, which made getting out of a limo very conspicuous. Kelly didn't care. She was hungry.

When Kelly got home, she washed off her make-up, brushed her hair, and got changed for bed. She smiled as she got into bed, her own bed, not a small bunk on a bus.

Chapter Six

The band had a show at The Observatory in Santa Ana on Monday night. They had previously played The Constellation Room at the same venue, but were booked into the bigger venue for this headline show. Dean told them the show had sold out.

"Woo hoo!" Ian shouted.

"That's awesome!" Jake said.

Fate Struck arrived at the venue at four-thirty. Bailey and Scott and the other roadies had set up the gear earlier in the day. Dean had driven them to the venue in their van. Since there was no gear in with them, just their bags with their clothes and make-up, they weren't cramped together like they used to be. The band merchandise had also been taken to the venue; all Jayna had to do was organize it.

They stepped out of the van and several fans waiting in line shouted and waved to them. The guys and Kelly waved back as Jayna went on ahead inside. Isaac asked Dean if they had a few minutes to go say Hi to the fans. Dean looked at his watch.

"You have about ten minutes," he said.

"Cool," Isaac said, and they walked over to the fans, about twenty of them waiting in line. Dean kept a watchful distance from them. The fans cheered as the guys and Kelly got closer.

"How are ya?" Isaac said to the group.

"We're awesome!" said one of the girls in line.

The guys and Kelly took pictures and signed items some of the fans had with them, and talked to them until Dean came over and told them it was time.

"We'll see you all inside," Jake said as they walked toward the stage door.

"We should probably think about meet and greets," Dean said as they went inside. "Too late to do them for this tour, but the next tour we should do that."

"That would be fun to do," Isaac said.

The band dropped off their belongings in the dressing room before going to the stage for sound check. They got their in-ear monitors put in and hooked up, and when it was all set, they ran through a song, then went backstage to get ready.

Kelly showered, dressed, and then sat down to do her make-up. Jayna came backstage to see if Kelly needed anything.

"I'm okay for now," Kelly said, "but I'd love some company."

Jayna sat down next to Kelly while Kelly did her face.

"We talked to some fans waiting in line before we came inside," Kelly said.

"How'd that go?" Jayna asked.

"It was fun! They were all very nice. I think Ian saw one he'd like to hook up with."

"Doesn't he always?" Jayna giggled.

"There's no bus to go to, so I don't know where he thinks it'll happen."

Kelly had gotten used to Ian and his hook-ups. Kelly never knew him to be such a horn-dog, but maybe it was the thrill of being onstage and the fact that he wasn't tied down that made him want to explore that part of being semi-famous. It didn't even phase her anymore.

As it got closer to show time, Dean invited The Cat's Meow to the dressing room for the pre-show shot of Fireball before they went onstage.

"Break a leg!" the band told them as Jensen and the rest of his band left to hit the stage.

After the show, Fate Struck talked about the show for a few minutes. They really didn't have anything to deconstruct or want to change. Their sound engineer had everything down with how they liked things, so once the meeting was done, Dean allowed their families and friends in among the fans with backstage passes. Isaac's parents didn't attend this show, Kelly noticed, and Isaac didn't seem to be put out by it. Hayley was there, of course, as were the other's girlfriends and Greg and Marty.

"You sounded fantastic," Greg said. "As always."

"Thanks," Kelly said. "Do you want something to drink?"

"I'll have what you're having," he said. She went and got a hard lemonade from the table for him.

"Cheers!" he said. They clinked bottles and took a drink.

"You know, little sis," David said, coming over to join them. "You get better every time I see you guys."

"So, you're saying I sucked before?" Kelly joked.

"Yes, of course. It was like fingernails on a chalk board before."

"Thanks, Davy," she said, putting her arm around him and squeezing. "How did the crew like the show?"

Dean had finally been able to make good on the promise of getting them tickets to a headlining show for the work they did on the first video for the band.

"They thought it was fantastic, and were impressed with how professional you guys are."

"Tell them 'Thanks' for us."

"I will."

Mom and Dad came around to congratulate Kelly and tell her they were leaving.

"We'll see you in the morning," Mom said.

"Bye," Kelly said. David said his goodbyes too.

"Let's do lunch sometime, Kel," he said.

"Absolutely," Kelly said.

After the families left, there were just the fans and the significant others left. Isaac had eyes only for Hayley, though the girls there did vie for his attention. He spoke politely with them, and took pictures with them, but with Hayley there, nothing else happened. Isaac had been known to occasionally kiss the girls there and even make out with them, but it never led to anything else, and Kelly knew he was just trying to substitute them for Hayley.

Several guys came over to talk to Kelly, who felt a little more confident with Greg there and Jayna hanging out close by.

"You were awesome!" one of the guys said, shaking her hand.

"Thank you," Kelly said. "Is this your first show of ours?"

"No, we saw you guys a couple years ago at the Taste of Long Beach. I like your originals a lot."

"The CD is fucking outrageous," said one of the other guys.

They spoke together for fifteen minutes. Kelly wasn't sure if she should introduce Greg to the fans. He wasn't part of the band and she was afraid the fans would bolt after that, and while she wasn't looking for anything to happen, she did enjoy talking about music with them. They asked if they could get a picture with her and she said yes. Greg didn't look happy as he stepped out of the way while Jayna took the photo with their cell phones. After the picture, they tried to kiss Kelly on the cheek. Greg put his hand between Kelly and the guy.

"Nope. That's not gonna happen," Greg said.

"Greg…" Kelly started.

"No, I've been patient with them talking to you, touching you, but I draw the line at a kiss."

"Chill, dude," the tall guy said. "We're not hopping into bed."

"You're damn right you're not!"

"What's with this guy, Kelly?" another young man asked.

"He's my boyfriend," Kelly said quickly.

"You could've told them that earlier," Greg said.

Jayna and Dean both came over and escorted the fans away as Kelly took Greg into the dressing room.

"What the hell is wrong with you?" Kelly asked. "They weren't going to make out with me."

"I don't want anyone else kissing my girl," Greg said.

"It's a harmless kiss on the cheek, Greg. It's happened before."

"It has?" he asked.

"Yes. A platonic little kiss on my cheek. I wouldn't let anything else happen. I love you and want only you, not them. I've disappointed many guys on the road because I didn't ask them to sleep with me. You can ask Dean. He watches out for me because I'm the female lead singer and I'm not into having one-night stands with anyone."

"He can't be everywhere all the time," Greg said.

"So you think I can't think for myself and tell them 'no?'"

"You've been pretty sheltered, Kelly, and you've said that in high school boys were never interested in you. You may just get caught up in the moment."

"Oh my God! Are we really going to do this right now? This is ridiculous. It's like you've never trusted me."

"You're the lead singer for a band, Kelly, that's how I fell in love with you. Others will, too."

"But I'm not going to fall in love with them. It has to be mutual attraction and I'm not looking. You seem to think that I like the attention I get," Kelly said.

"Don't you?"

"No! I enjoy talking to the fans about the music, but I don't like the adoration, the almost worship that comes with it, and I definitely don't like the attention from all the guys."

Greg paced the floor.

"You really don't know me if you think I like all that stuff," Kelly continued softly. "You've been jealous from the get-go, and I've given you no reason to be. Ian went through this with Jessica. I'm not going to tolerate it with you."

"So, what are you saying?" Greg asked.

Kelly sighed. She loved him so much, but she couldn't be with someone who didn't trust her. He wasn't as overt with his jealousy as Jessica had been, but it felt the same. Why did he have to do this, too?

"I don't think we should be together anymore," Kelly said hoarsely.

Greg didn't say anything else. He stormed out of the dressing room and Kelly heard the door slam. She tried to fight the tears but couldn't. They fell quickly down her cheeks. Jayna came in a moment later.

"Kelly?"

Kelly turned and quickly walked over to her and cried on her shoulder. Jayna put her arms around her and held her as she sobbed.

"I'm so sorry, sweetie," Jayna said softly.

After several minutes, Kelly pulled back and wiped the tears on her cheeks, smearing her make-up, but she didn't care.

"Has everyone gone?" Kelly asked, meaning the fans.

"Yes, Dean kicked them out once he saw what was going on."

"I'm sorry," Kelly said.

"Don't be. It's not your fault. I'm glad you saw Greg's true colors before things went much farther."

Jayna got a wad of toilet tissue for Kelly to wipe her eyes and blow her nose.

"Thanks."

Once Kelly had gotten herself together somewhat, she and Jayna went back out to the common dressing room. The guys came up and hugged her one by one.

"I'm sorry, you guys," Kelly said. "I didn't mean to cause drama."

"Hey, it's okay," Isaac said. "You didn't. He brought it."

"I didn't want another situation like Ian had with Jessica. It seems he didn't trust me or you guys, and when he found out about getting kisses *on the cheek*, it was like I'd been to bed with every guy on the road."

Ian brought Kelly a shot of Fireball. She downed it quickly.

"Do you want another?" he asked.

"Yes, please."

Ian brought her another one. She drank it but stopped at that.

"Whenever you're ready, Kelly," Dean said. "I'll take everyone home."

Kelly went back into the bathroom and looked at her face, and she tied her hair back, turned on the water and washed her face. She dried and then touched up what hadn't come off and looked presentable to anyone who might be waiting by the van.

They went out and there were a few fans still waiting for them. Kelly plastered a smile on her face and signed for the fans with the guys and talked to them for a few minutes before the band got in and Dean took them home. Jayna put her arm around her and held her on the way home. Kelly lay her head on Jayna's shoulder and cried quietly. In light of things the band passed on the Denny's run after the show.

Kelly woke up late the next morning with a headache. She didn't know if it was from drinking or from crying most of the night. She'd finally fallen asleep at four. She got up and went into the kitchen to get something to eat.

"You look like heck," Mom said.

"Thanks," Kelly sniffed.

"What's wrong?"

"Greg and I broke up last night."

"Oh, sweetie, I'm sorry." Mom went over and hugged her daughter. After a moment she pulled back, holding Kelly's hands. "What happened?"

"He doesn't trust me. Some fans last night were talking with me about the music and when they left, they tried to give me a kiss on the cheek. Greg flipped out and it came down to the fact that he's never trusted me or the band. I wasn't going to go through what Ian went through, so I told him we should stop seeing each other."

"He has seemed a little possessive," Mom said. "He called us every day while you were on tour and asked us if we'd heard from you, because you hadn't called him."

"And one time I called him on the last tour, one of the guys made a comment and Greg got mad because they were sleeping four feet from me, and he knew that from being on the bus."

"That's too bad, I kind of liked him."

"I did, too. I guess this is something I'll have to get used to—guys being jealous because of what I do."

"Hopefully there will be someone out there for you who isn't."

Two days later, they had another show down in San Diego. Dean picked them up early and drove them. They would be staying overnight at a hotel before going home, Dean booking the usual roommates together.

"When we get to the venue," Dean said. "I'll make sure they know not to let Greg backstage. I know he's got a pass and I don't want him upsetting you again."

"Thanks," Kelly said. "I doubt he'll come, but you never know."

Dean got the band to their hotel at three that afternoon. They took a little time to rest before they had to head to the venue. As Kelly and Jayna walked to meet everyone at the elevators, Kelly got a text message. She pulled her phone out and saw that Greg had texted her.

"Don't read it now," Jayna said, putting her hand over the text. "You'll just get upset."

"I'm busy," Kelly replied without reading the text.

"Good girl," Ian said. "That bastard doesn't deserve you."

They got to the venue and went through the routine of sound check and running through a song before going back to the dressing room to eat and get ready.

Kelly showered and dressed, then sat on the couch and put her head in her hands. Despite what had happened, she missed Greg. They'd had fun together, and she lost her virginity to him. She thought they'd be together for a long time, maybe even forever, though they hadn't even come close to talking about marriage. The tears flowed again.

"Did you read Greg's message?" Jayna asked softly, sitting next to Kelly.

"No," Kelly said, sniffling. "I was just thinking about the good times we'd had. He'd been really supportive and caring, until the tour started. I'd seen bits of jealousy here and there, but I thought he was just joking. Apparently not."

"I'm glad you learned from my mistakes," Ian said, squatting in front of Kelly. He put his hand on her knee. "Don't think of getting back with him, no matter what he says. He won't change. They never do."

Kelly wiped her cheeks.

"Yeah, I know. It just hurts."

Ian sat on the other side of Kelly and both he and Jayna put their arms around her while she softly cried.

After a few moments, Kelly pulled herself together and wiped her eyes.

"Okay, enough of this," she said resolutely. "I gotta finish getting ready for this show."

"That's the spirit," Jayna said.

"And speaking of spirits," Kelly said. "I think I will have a hard lemonade right now."

Kelly got a bottle, opened it, and took a long drink. She went to her make-up bag and sat down and got to work on her face. Her eyes were slightly red from crying, so she put more concealer on to camouflage the redness.

When she'd finished, Jensen and his bandmates came in for the pre-show shot with the band, then it was time for Jayna to go work the merchandise table.

"I'll see you after the show," Jayna said, and she hugged Kelly before leaving.

Kelly finished her hard lemonade, then opened her energy drink and took a long drink from it.

"I can't believe you finished your lemonade before the set," Jake said.

"Are you okay?" Dean asked.

"Never been better," Kelly said.

"Well, I know that's bullshit, but okay," Dean said. "Be extra careful onstage, because the energy drink will just make you a wired drunk."

"I'm okay, I'm not drunk," Kelly said. "Just—relaxed."

"Awesome," Dean said. "Ian, keep an eye on her, will ya?"

"Of course," Ian said.

Kelly sat on the floor to stretch and then did her vocal warm-ups. She listened to the opener finish their last song and knew Fate Struck's set would start shortly. She went to use the restroom, and grabbed another bottle of Mike's to take onstage.

"Don't overdo it," Ian said. "Or Dean will have my ass."

Kelly smiled at him. She felt pleasantly relaxed, although she could feel the energy drink take effect. That's how she wanted to feel, relaxed with energy.

"I'm really okay," Kelly said, patting Ian's cheek. "Just because I've never finished one before a show doesn't mean I'm drunk."

When it was time for them to take the stage, Kelly had three drinks with her—her energy drink, her bottled water, and her Mike's. She set her drinks on the drum riser so they wouldn't get kicked over. Isaac started his drum beat and the band began to play.

In her more relaxed state onstage, she played up to and with the guys, putting her arm around them, or playfully tousling their hair. Kelly stood at the edge of the stage every so often and picked out faces in the crowd to sing to. She waved to the kids that were there at the front, and they jumped up and down, gleefully waving back.

When the band played "Jealousy Rules," even though Kelly didn't write it, the lyrics to the third verse had new meaning for her, and she teared up as she sang,

I gave myself completely to you
I thought you were the one

Making promises you just can't keep
I don't give a damn, we're done.

Her voice cracked with emotion on the last line. It broke her heart to not have Greg in her life, but she wasn't going to deal with his jealousy. When the song finished she wiped her eyes as she put the mic back on the stand and walked to the drum riser to take a drink of her water.

"Are you okay?" Isaac asked.

"Yeah, I'm good," Kelly said, taking another quick swipe of her eyes before going back to the mic.

At the end of their set, they got into position for their usual end of show photos that Dean took, then waved to the crowd as they went offstage, Isaac tossing a couple of his black drumsticks into the crowd as he left.

Kelly looked at her phone when she got backstage and saw that Greg had texted and called twenty times. *What the hell is he thinking? He knows I'm working.*

She opened the latest text. It said he'd be there tonight to see her show.

Glad I didn't see that until after, she thought.

"Hey, Dean?" Kelly called over her shoulder.

"Yes?" Dean said.

"Greg is here somewhere, so just be warned," she told him.

"Thanks for letting me know," Dean said, and he went out to check on the fans who waited to come backstage. He was gone for longer than she expected and she started to worry. Dean finally came in, leading in the pass holders and the opener.

"He was here, trying to get backstage," Dean said.

"Criminy," Kelly said. "What happened?"

"I had to call security to have him escorted out. He wouldn't leave unless he talked to you. I told him that wasn't happening."

"Thank you," Kelly said, relieved.

Kelly went and poured some Fireball into a cup and drank it down, then opened another bottle of Mike's.

As usual, the girls flocked to the guys, some of the male fans also wanted to talk to Ian, Paul, and Jake. A few of the male fans gathered around Kelly, who noted that Dean kept his usual watchful eye on the guys around her.

Tonight, she had no inhibitions while talking to the fans. Even after Jayna came back and joined her half an hour later, Kelly carried the conversation most of the time with the guys. A few girls came over to talk to Kelly, too.

"Your clothes are so cute," one girl said.

"Thanks," Kelly said. "Believe it or not, I get most of my stuff at Hot Topic."

"That's awesome," the tall redhead said. "I'm gonna have to start shopping there more often."

Kelly finished her hard lemonade and got a bottled water. She'd had enough alcohol for the night.

The fans asked if they could get some photos with Kelly.

"Of course," she said, and asked Jayna to take the photos with their phones. Jayna took a couple with each phone and the fans thanked her and Kelly.

"This is so cool!" the short blonde girl said. "You're not anything like I thought you'd be."

Kelly laughed.

"What did you think I'd be like?" Kelly asked.

"Well, kind of stuck on yourself," she said. "And more interested in the guys than us."

"You're all fans, and I appreciate you," Kelly said. "The guys do, too. If it wasn't for you we wouldn't even be here."

Dean walked around the room, thanking the guests for coming.

"Well, maybe we'll see you again," the redhead said.

"Sure," Kelly said. She shook hands with all of them and gave the guys she'd talked to a kiss on the cheek.

"They won't wash their face tonight," Jayna joked after the fans left.

They gathered up all their stuff and went out to the van. There were about fifteen fans waiting nearby. Tired as she was, Kelly hated to disappoint the fans. She and the guys put their luggage in the van and then went over to talk to the fans and sign some autographs for them. As they got into the van when they were done, Greg came out of nowhere, running up to the van.

"Kelly!" he shouted.

Kelly turned. Greg stood five feet away from her, and Dean, Ian, and Jake stepped between her and Greg.

"I just want to talk," Greg said.

"No," Kelly said flatly. "Leave me alone."

"You won't return my texts or calls."

"Yeah, because we're not together anymore. Not going through this again with you." With that, she got into the van and got into the back seat where Paul and Isaac sat. Ian and Jake got in after her and pulled the door shut. Dean got into the driver's seat and drove away, but not before Greg hit the van with his fist, which made Kelly jump. Isaac put his arm around her.

"You're okay," he said quietly.

"He's never been physical like that before," Kelly said, gaining some of her composure. "Looks like I may have avoided a lot of crap from him."

"Still want to go to Denny's, Kelly?" Dean asked.

"Yes," she said emphatically.

Dean took them to Denny's for food before driving back to the hotel.

In the hotel room, Kelly took a quick shower to wash all the sweat and make-up off. She dried and dressed quickly. She wanted to just go to bed and go to sleep.

A knock came on the door. Kelly wasn't about to open the door in case Greg had somehow found out where they were staying. Jayna looked through the peep hole and opened the door.

"It's Isaac," Jayna said, stepping aside to let him in.

"What's up?" Kelly asked.

"Weeeell," Isaac said. He looked hesitant to say something, then pulled a baggie out of his pocket and tossed it onto Kelly's bed in front of her.

"What's this?" she asked. She picked up the bag and held it up. "Oh, gummy bears."

"Not just any ol' gummy bears," he said.

"Oh, I know what it is," Jayna said with a grin.

"Someone wanna clue me in?"

"Ever so innocent Kelly," Isaac said. "I know you won't smoke anything, so I got these for you to help you calm down after what happened tonight."

"Edibles?" Kelly asked.

"Yes."

"Not interested," Kelly said, tossing them back onto the bed. Jayna grabbed them.

"We'll keep them, just in case," she said with a wink.

"I'm not eating them," Kelly said.

"If you do, only eat one. If you eat more than that, you will not feel good."

"I can vouch for that," Jayna said as she raised her hand. "I ate too much of a brownie once."

Kelly figured Jayna had tried them. Still, *she* wasn't going to. She wasn't into drugs.

"Well, they're there if you want them," Isaac said. "Goodnight."

Isaac left. Kelly was shocked Isaac would think she'd even want to try edibles. No, she'd fall asleep just fine without it.

Chapter Seven

Kelly rolled over and looked at the clock. It was nearly four in the morning. Her mind would not shut off from everything. She looked over at Jayna, who slept like a baby after eating one of the gummy bears. Kelly had always prided herself on how healthy she was. Years of being a gymnast had helped her stay in top shape. Yes, she drank alcohol on occasion, but that was different.

Still, the band had that record company party that night. She needed to get some kind of sleep.

It's just medication in a different form, right?

She grabbed the plastic bag off the nightstand. They looked like harmless little gummy bears. She took one out of the bag and smelled it. It had a strange yet fruity scent to it.

Kelly held it in her hand for a long time.

It's just medication. She shrugged. *What the hell.*

She popped the little gummy bear into her mouth. It tasted just like a regular gummy bear. She padded over to the bathroom to pee, then went back to bed and got comfortable.

When Kelly awoke the next morning, she thought she'd only been asleep for a couple of hours. The clock read eleven-thirty. She'd been asleep for nearly seven hours! She glanced over at Jayna's bed. Jayna sat on her bed, already dressed.

"Good morning, sleepyhead," Jayna said.

"I didn't plan on sleeping this late," Kelly said, throwing the blankets off and sitting up on the edge of her bed. She took a long drink from her water bottle, then went to the bathroom.

"How long have you been up?" Kelly asked from the bathroom.

"Since around nine," Jayna said.

"You should've woken me up," Kelly said as she walked back into the room.

"Well, I know you had a hard time falling asleep, so didn't want to wake you if you'd only just gotten to sleep."

"Those gummy bears definitely work," Kelly said.

"You ate one?"

"It was four o'clock in the morning and I still hadn't fallen asleep. It took me a long time to decide to take one. I was desperate."

"And the world didn't end, did it?"

Kelly looked down at her hands in her lap. She wasn't ashamed of what she'd done, but it felt weird talking about it.

"No," Kelly said.

"Well, let's get packed. Dean texted us around the time I got up. He arranged for a late check-out today, since you and some of the guys were still asleep."

"Awesome," Kelly said.

She texted Dean to let him know she was awake and getting ready to leave. She got a reply back right away.

"LMK when you're ready. All the boys are up finally, too. We'll drive through some place for breakfast."

"OK," Kelly replied.

She had gone to bed with her hair slightly wet, so it had some strange bends and curls. She got her straightener out and did her best to tame her hair. While the styling tool cooled off, she dressed and packed the rest of her belongings into her suitcase, throwing in the straightener last. She tied on her Chucks and then texted Dean that she and Jayna were ready.

"Meet us at the elevator," Dean replied to everyone.

Jayna and Kelly grabbed their keycards and took one more look around before heading out the door, pulling their suitcases behind them. The guys had just arrived at the elevator as well.

"Someone slept later than even Jake," Isaac said nudging Kelly's arm.

"Well, I'm gonna blame you for that," Kelly said with a smirk.

"Why me?" Isaac said, then he caught on. "Ooohhh…"

"Why 'ooohhh'," Ian asked.

"I bought her some gummy bears."

"Oooohh," Jake, Ian, and Paul said in unison.

"What did I miss?" Dean asked.

"Gummy bears," Isaac said. "You know—edibles."

"Seriously?" Dean asked, looking at Kelly.

"I managed to finally sleep," she shrugged.

The elevator doors opened. A gentleman stepped off, and the group stepped in and Dean hit the button for the lobby.

"Well, there's always a first time for everything," Dean remarked. "I'm sure it won't be the last time."

"Oh, I don't plan on making it a habit," Kelly said. "I just needed sleep."

No one said anything else about it. They arrived in the lobby and Dean gathered up all their keycards and went to the desk to check them out, then went out to bring the van to the front doors.

Kelly was quiet on the ride back home. She most definitely wasn't going to make a habit of eating edibles of any kind. It was a once in a great while kind of thing when she needed help to go to sleep.

She thought that her parents would somehow know what she'd done, so she kept to her room for most of the day when she got home. She only came out for dinner.

"You've been awfully quiet today," Mom said.

"Yeah, I'm sorry," Kelly said. "I'm just a little tired and got a little stressed last night. Greg showed up at the show."

"Oh, no," Dad said.

"Yeah, he said he just wanted to talk, but I'm done talking to him. I learned from Ian's lesson with Jessica. Not going to get back together with him."

"Good! Other than that, how did the show go?"

"It was fantastic!" Kelly said. "We had a great turnout."

After dinner, Kelly called Jayna and asked if she could come over to help her pick out something to wear for the party.

"Sure, I have a few minutes," Jayna said. "Marty is taking me to dinner, but I'll walk over and he can pick me up from there."

"Oh, I don't want to mess up your plans," Kelly said.

"It's okay. It won't take long to pick out something for you to wear."

Five minutes later, Kelly met Jayna at the door.

"Thank you! I really appreciate you helping me," Kelly said, letting Jayna in.

"You're welcome," Jayna said. "I'm happy to help."

They went through Kelly's closet, and Jayna pulled out a few things to consider. Kelly didn't want to wear a dress; she felt more comfortable in pants. Jayna put together a couple of outfits and Kelly picked the black flared pants with her sparkly red blouse and a black blazer over it.

"How are you doing your make-up?" Jayna asked.

"I figure something between no make-up and stage make-up," Kelly said. "Like I used to wear to school."

"Okay, that'll be good. How 'bout your hair?"

"Maybe curl some of it with my curling iron?"

"Perfect. I know you'll look great. You always do."

"I've just never been to a 'Hollywood' party before," Kelly said.

"You'll be fine."

Marty knocked on the door and the girls went out to meet him.

"Have fun at the party, Kel," Jayna said as she went down the porch steps with Marty.

"I'll text you when I get home."

Kelly went back to her room to get ready. She put on her clothes except for the blazer, then put on her make-up and styled her hair. She buckled on her platform shoes and grabbed her blazer and purse and went to the living room to wait for the limo to pick her up.

"You look great!" Mom said, pulling her phone out to take yet another photo of Kelly.

"Thanks," Kelly said.

The limo pulled up a few minutes later and Dean rang the doorbell.

"Bye, Mom!" Kelly called as she grabbed her purse and went out the door.

"Bye, honey," Mom said.

The driver opened the door for Kelly and she got into the back. Isaac and Jake sat in the back, dressed similar to Kelly—stage clothes with a jacket. Jake wore minimal eye make-up this time.

"Hey," Kelly said.

"How's it going?" Isaac asked.

"Good, though I'm nervous," she admitted.

"Same. This is new territory, being around celebrities," Isaac said.

"Which you all are now," Dean said from the front seat.

"I just don't feel like one," Kelly said. "I feel like I'm going to be like Miley Cyrus sings about in 'Party in the USA'. I just feel like…me."

They made stops to pick up Paul and Ian, then got on the freeway. As they travelled, they took advantage of the provided alcohol in the bar in the back. Isaac passed everyone a bottle of Heineken and a Mike's for Kelly, who gladly took it and drank it.

"You look great tonight, Kelly," Ian said.

"Thanks," Kelly said. "I had help from Jayna."

"She certainly knows how to put you together."

"I'm glad I have her, otherwise I'd probably look like a dork."

"I doubt you'd ever look like a dork," Ian said.

"Well, thanks! I appreciate that."

They arrived at the nightclub an hour later. The driver pulled up to the curb in front and the doorman opened the backdoor. Ian stepped out first, followed by Isaac, Kelly, Jake, and Paul. Dean got out of the front seat and led them inside.

"I think you'll be happy to know," Dean said, "that Erik from The Disciples of Man is supposed to be here."

"Really?" Kelly asked. At least she'd know one other person there besides her band. As they walked in, Jim from Tyrian Records saw them and came over to greet them.

"I'm so happy you came," Jim said, shaking hands with everyone, and giving Kelly a kiss on her cheek.

"They were a little hesitant about coming," Dean said, "but I told them that they'll know a few people here."

"The open bar is over there," Jim said, pointing across the room. "Hors d'oeuvres are along the wall in the back, and we'll bring around finger sandwiches later on. Give me a few minutes and I'll take you around and introduce you to a few people."

Jim walked off and Dean walked over to the bar, the band following at a distance so it didn't look like they were being led to the bar. Dean, who usually didn't drink while "on the clock," ordered a gin and tonic. Isaac and Paul each ordered a beer, Jake ordered a rum and coke, Ian a screwdriver, and Kelly her usual hard lemonade. She wanted something she could make last a long time.

Kelly looked around the room and saw many musicians and actors she'd only seen on TV or in concert. She felt so out of place at that moment and hoped to see a familiar face. She finally spotted Erik across the room and walked over to say Hi.

"Kelly!" Erik greeted, kissing her on the cheek and giving her a hug. "I'd hoped you'd be here."

"Yep, we're here," she said. *Boy, that sounded really lame.*

"I wanted to introduce you to my wife, Catalina."

"Oh, so nice to meet you!" Kelly said, shaking hands with her. "Erik has told me a lot about you."

"He's told me a lot about you, too," Catalina said pleasantly with a slight Spanish accent.

"How's the tour going?" Erik asked.

"So far, really good," she said. "We're at a kind of pause while we do these holiday parties for my father's company and Isaac's father's company."

"Oh, nice. You do those every year, right?"

"Yeah. We'll keep doing it as long as they'll keep having us."

Kelly, Erik, and Catalina talked until Jim came over.

"Do you mind if I steal Kelly for a few minutes?" Jim asked.

"No, not at all," Erik said. "We'll see you later."

"It was nice to meet you," Catalina said.

"Nice to meet you, too," Kelly said, and Jim slipped her arm through his and led her across the room to where a familiar-looking blonde woman stood, talking to a tall guy with long brown hair and several tattoos on his arms.

"Excuse me for interrupting, Nick," Jim said.

"No problem," Nick said.

"I wanted to introduce you to Kelly Brennen, the lead singer for Fate Struck. Kelly, this is Maggie Wilson, lead singer for MagNetic, and Nick Johnson, her guitar player."

MagNetic was a very popular hard rock band, having been around for about five years.

"Oh, wow," Maggie said. "So nice to meet you. I've heard your single. Your band kicks major ass."

Kelly was gobsmacked. *She's heard the band?*

"Nice to meet you," Kelly finally said, extending her hand.

Maggie took her hand, not really shaking hands, more like a friendly grip. Nick took her hand and shook once.

"Enchanted," Nick said.

"So, Jim is giving you the tour and introducing you to people?" Maggie asked.

"Yes," Kelly said. "We're kind of new to this."

"Eh, don't worry about it." Maggie waved her hand. "Most of the people here like meeting the new kids on the block, so to speak. It's like one big networking event."

"I'm going to get a refill," Nick said, indicating his empty glass.

"Okay, we'll be around here somewhere," Maggie said with a laugh.

As Nick ran off, Maggie sighed.

"Let's go find someplace to sit. My feet are killing me."

Oh my god! Maggie just asked me to come sit with her? Stay cool, stay cool.

They found a sofa to sit on. Maggie sat down with a groan, and took off one of her shoes.

"I probably shouldn't have worn these heels, but I'm really short if I don't."

"I know the feeling," Kelly said, looking at her own platform shoes.

"So, I hear you're on tour right now," Maggie said. "Tell me how you like it."

***

Ian watched as Jim took Kelly off to meet someone. When Ian saw who it was, he relaxed. He trusted Jim to keep her out of any questionable situations.

Jim came around and took each of them individually to meet someone. He'd taken Ian to meet Jensen, the bass player for Watson Road, a country-rock band from Arizona. They'd spoken for a while about their gear, then Jensen took off to talk with someone he hadn't seen in a long time, leaving Ian on his own for a moment. He finished his drink and went to get another one. There were a lot of celebrities at the party, but none Ian felt comfortable going up to. He did see Will, the bass player for The Disciples of Man, and went to talk with him.

"You guys got dragged into coming, too, I see," Will said.

"Yeah," Ian said. "Dean thought it would be good for us."

"It can be, and they can be fun, but they are also tedious. You gotta talk to the right people, yada yada yada. Jim's good about introducing new people around, though. Come over and talk to Stevie and me," Will said. "It'll make a good photo op."

Ian followed Will over to another couch where Stevie, the drummer for The Disciples of Man, sat with another musician.

"Hey, Ian!" Stevie said, standing up to shake his hand. "Glad to see you, but too bad it's here and not at a gig,"

"Yeah," Ian said. "We were hoping you'd be playing around here somewhere while we're on our holiday party break,"

"It'll match up sometime where we're playing and you're not," Will said.

"Hey, this is Liam, the drummer for Wreaking Havoc," Stevie said. "Liam, Ian Ketchner, the bassist for Fate Struck."

"Nice to meet you," Ian said, shaking Liam's hand.

"Likewise," Liam said. "How do you all know each other?"

"Fate Struck opened for us on the Western part of our tour last year," Will told him.

"Oh, yeah, okay, I know who you are now. You guys are really good. Your singer is hot!"

"She's great, isn't she?" Ian replied. He understood what Liam meant, but to Ian she was like a sister. Or at least he tried to keep it that way in his head. He sometimes failed when she looked like she did that night, thinking about kissing her red lips.

A photographer came by and took a picture of them as they spoke.

"Have you met any of the photographers here?" Will asked.

"No," Ian said.

"The one that just came by is okay, but see that one in the red jacket, with the messy gray hair?" Will pointed across the room.

Ian squinted to see the gentleman Will pointed out, finally seeing him at the bar.

"Yeah," Ian said.

"He works for one of the tabloids, and he'll write the shittiest stuff about everyone, making it sound like someone is dating someone or cheating on someone," Will said.

"Wonderful," Ian said. "Why is he here?"

"He gets credentials somehow." Liam shrugged.

Servers came around and offered finger sandwiches to the guests. Ian took one, as did Will, Stevie, and Liam. Will took a bite

"Not bad for catered," he said with a shrug.

Later in the evening, as Ian went up to the bar again, a woman with copper-colored hair came up next to him and ordered a drink as well.

"Hey, we drink the same drink," Ian said with a smile, then saw who the woman was— Lena Hendricks, an actress on the prime-time comedy series *All About Dad*. She played the eldest daughter on the show.

"Small world," Lena said, smiling warmly.

"That was a pretty lame line, wasn't it?" Ian asked, as the bartender gave them each their drink.

"I've heard worse," she said. "I'm Lena." She held out her hand.

"Ian," he said, taking her hand and shaking it. "Big fan of your show."

"Another pretty lame line," Lena joked.

"Oh, my God," Ian said, his face turning bright red. "Can we start over?"

Lena spun around quickly on her toes, then smiled at Ian. "Hi, I'm Lena."

"Ian," he said, trying not to laugh, but to no avail. "Nice to meet you."

"Likewise," Lena said, shaking Ian's hand again.

Ian and Lena spoke with each other for the rest of the night. She kept him laughing with her stories from her TV show until Ian got a text.

"Dean says we're leaving soon," Ian said.

"Who's Dean?" Lena asked.

"Dean is our wrangler, babysitter, and manager. We all came together and he doesn't want us to wear out our welcome."

"Here, let me give you my phone number," Lena said, holding her hand out for Ian's phone. He handed it to her and she input her name and number. She then handed her phone to Ian to do the same.

"I'd love for you to call me sometime," she said.

"Sure! We're getting back on the road here in another week, so I won't be able to see you much, but I can still call you."

"That would be great," Lena said. She leaned in to kiss Ian. Ian thought she wanted to kiss his cheek, but she kissed his lips, a slow, sexy kiss. "See you later."

She got up, placed her hand gently on his shoulder for a moment, then walked away. Ian watched her join a group of ladies on the couch. He wasn't really looking to date anyone, but damn, she was gorgeous, and she was funny. He'd definitely call her from the road; she'd certainly help him keep his mind off Kelly.

**

The evening turned into early morning, and Kelly got a text from Dean, letting her know they'd be leaving soon.

Kelly felt like she'd spoken with every guy at the party. A lot of them came up to introduce themselves, and many of those tried to pick her up. Even in her slightly inebriated state she had the presence of mind to politely decline, telling them she'd just gotten out of a relationship and she wasn't looking right now. Which was the truth. She'd only broken up with Greg three days prior.

Kelly went to say goodbye to Maggie.

"I'm so glad we met," Maggie said, shaking hands with Kelly.

"Same!"

"Here, let me give you my number so we can stay in touch."

Was this really happening? She was getting Maggie's number?

Kelly pulled out her phone and brought up her contact list and handed the phone to Maggie, who input her name and number. Kelly did the same for her.

"Awesome!" Kelly said.

As Kelly walked to the front door of the restaurant, she was stopped by several people, guys and girls, wishing her a good night. She felt a little unsteady on her heels, so Ian took her arm and put it through his. The photographer Will had warned him about took their picture as they left.

"Goddamn it," Ian said as they stepped into the limo.

"What?" Dean asked.

"Will warned me about that photographer that just took our picture," Ian said. "We'll be dating in tomorrow's edition."

"Most people know not to believe what that rag prints," Dean said.

"But you know who will believe it?" Kelly said. "Greg and Jessica."

"Even if they do, you both are not with them anymore. You can do whatever or see whomever you want."

With everyone in the limo, the driver pulled away and drove them home.

Someone shook Kelly's shoulder.

"Kelly?" Ian said.

Kelly opened her eyes and saw that the limo was sideways. She sat up and found that she'd used Ian's lap as a pillow while she'd slept.

"Oh, my gosh," Kelly said. "I'm so sorry."

"No worries," Ian said. "Remember we'll be dating later today." He laughed.

"I'll ask Jayna to monitor social media and quell any rumors," Dean said.

"Thank you," Kelly and Ian said.

"We're at your house," Dean said. "Do you need help up to the door?"

Kelly got out of the vehicle and stood there for a moment.

"No, I think I'm fine," she said. "See you all later."

Once inside her house, Kelly took off her shoes and went to her bedroom. She changed quickly and got into bed. She almost texted Greg, which is what she'd usually do after getting home from a band event, then remembered they weren't together anymore. Kelly quickly texted Jayna to let her know she was home, and to call her later. She plugged her phone into the charger and rolled over to sleep, but kept thinking about Greg and how much she missed him. Tears fell again. She wiped them away, and then turned over and put her pillow over her head as if to keep the thoughts from penetrating her head. She fell asleep soon after.

Chapter Eight

Kelly didn't get up the next morning until nearly noon. Her head throbbed and the bright sun-lit room didn't help. She lay in her bed with a pillow over her eyes, not wanting to get up. She couldn't stay there all day, however—the band had Isaac's father's holiday party that evening.

She made a promise to herself right then that she wasn't going to fall for all the trappings of the rock and roll lifestyle. It was so not her, but there she was, hungover after being at a Hollywood party. She rarely drank to that point, but had switched to rum and coke and hadn't drunk enough water in between drinks last night.

Staying in bed wasn't going to make her headache go away without intervention, so she got up and walked to the kitchen. Mom was there, making lunch for Dad and herself.

"Good morning, sleepyhead," Mom said softly. She set down the knife and gave Kelly a squeeze. "How was the party?"

"It was fun! I thought it was going to be boring because I wouldn't know anyone but the guys, but The Disciples of Man were there and then Jim introduced me to a few people. You know the band MagNetic?"

"Yes," Mom said.

"Jim introduced me to Maggie, and we exchanged phone numbers! She was super cool and laid-back. I met Erik's wife Catalina, who is also really nice and so beautiful.

"I want to warn you, though," Kelly continued, "there may be a story in one of the tabloids about Ian and me."

Mom stopped mid-spread of the sandwich.

"What do you mean?"

"Well, I was feeling a little unsteady, so Ian walked me out with my arm in his, and a photographer there took a picture of us. Erik said the guy is always stirring things up that aren't true, so, if you hear anything, it's totally untrue. He may not write anything, because we're not that popular yet, but you never know."

"Thanks for the heads-up," Mom said as she continued to make the sandwich. "But there are worse things that they could write, so I'm not worried about it. I like Ian, so even if it were true, it's not a bad thing."

"Except where Jessica and Greg are concerned."

"Oh," Mom said slowly. "That didn't occur to me. Hopefully it won't be too bad."

"Hopefully," Kelly echoed.

Kelly couldn't eat anything other than toast with butter on it, and some cran-grape juice. She went to the cabinet and got the bottle of Excedrin out. She shook out two tablets and drank them down with her juice.

"I'm going to shower and then pick out my clothes for tonight," Kelly said.

After her shower, Kelly felt better. She drank another glass of water to continue to rehydrate as she looked in her closet for an outfit to wear that night. Kelly went with a traditional holiday look and picked out her red blouse with her black pants.

Kelly's phone *dinged*, and she looked to see who the message was from.

"Hey, girl," Jayna wrote. *"Call me when you're up."*

Kelly called her right away.

"I'm up already," Kelly said.

"I didn't think you'd be up for a while," Jayna said.

"Yeah, we got in late, or early as the case may be, but I didn't want to sleep the day away."

"How was the party?"

Kelly told her everything she'd told her mom but also about the guys there trying to hit on her.

"I just don't understand why they want to talk to me," Kelly said. "I'm not that popular yet."

"You're the female lead singer for a band and you're beautiful. Of course guys want to talk to you, and…other stuff."

"Well, I shut them down. I'm not looking to get into another relationship so soon after breaking up with Greg."

"I got this weird message from Dean, saying he wants me to monitor social media? What's up with that?"

"Some photographer took a picture of Ian and me as we left last night. I was a little tipsy and Ian steadied me as we walked to the limo. Dean's afraid he might write something untrue."

"Oh, I get it now," Jayna said, "and he's afraid Jessica and Greg might over-react."

"Yep. Not real worried about Greg, but you know Jess. She'll flip out."

"I'll keep an eye on things, mostly on Instagram."

"Thanks, Jayna, you're the best."

"It's what I'm paid for, but I'm also your friend. I'll shut things down fast if I see anything."

Kelly needed to go to the store to buy her energy drinks. She'd definitely need one for the gig that night. She put on her sunglasses and drove to the grocery store, where she went down the drink aisle. Kelly got a couple of her usual energy drinks, but also saw some 5-hour energy shots. She grabbed a couple for the gig, too.

At the checkout, she piled the drinks onto the conveyor belt.

"You planning on having a heart attack later?" the checker asked.

"No." Kelly laughed. "I'll only be having one of these tonight."

"You drink it at night and you won't sleep."

"My band's got a show tonight, so I'll need it to keep going."

The checker rang up the items, and put them in a bag.

"Break a leg tonight," the checker said, handing her the bag.

"Thanks!"

Later that afternoon, Kelly dressed for the gig. Dean and the limo would pick her up around six to take them to the hotel where the party was being held. She drank the energy shot and hoped it did last five hours. She was dead tired.

At the hotel, the staff served dinner an hour before their set. The energy drink Kelly had drunk before she left home kicked in as she ate. The fork in her hand shook slightly as she ate, but once she had food in her, it counterbalanced the caffeine and the jitteriness subsided by the time she finished eating.

As they waited to go onstage, someone brought a bouquet of flowers in and handed them to Kelly.

"I wonder who they're from?" she asked as she pulled the card off to read it.

"We know it isn't from my dad," Isaac said.

"'You look beautiful tonight,'" she read aloud. "'From FP.' Who's FP and how does he know how I look tonight? That's a little unsettling."

"Mystery Guy?" Isaac asked.

Kelly's heart dropped.

"How does he even know where we are?" Ian asked. "We never tell the press where this is."

"Did he follow us here?" Kelly asked. She set the flowers on the table and played with the rings on her fingers. "Does that mean he knows where I live?"

"Let's not jump to conclusions," Dean said, "but just to be safe, I'll hire a security guard to watch your house at night."

"I'd feel a lot better with that," Kelly said.

"Here," Jake said, holding a shooter of Fireball in his hand. "You need this more than I do tonight."

"Thanks," she said. She unscrewed the top and drank it down.

The party coordinator came to let the band know it was time to go on, and led them out as the vice president announced them.

"Here is the Tyrian Records recording group, Fate Struck," she said.

They walked onstage and Kelly thanked her for the welcome, and the band started right in on a song. Once the shooter kicked in, Kelly relaxed a little, and concentrated on the songs instead of thinking about Mystery Guy.

The band played until midnight, taking a forty-five-minute break in the middle of the set. The energy shot Kelly had drunk lasted all the way through the night.

On the way home, Dean had the driver stop at Denny's for their usual after-gig meal and talked about the gig. Dean looked around as they stepped out of the limo, checking to see if anyone had followed them into the parking lot. He didn't see anyone.

"That 5-hour energy shot seemed to work," Ian said to Kelly.

"It did," Kelly said. "I was tired and slightly hungover, so I needed it. It felt really weird with the alcohol, though," Kelly said.

"You look like you're still ready to go," Dean said.

"She can always eat a gummy bear," Isaac said.

"We'll see," Kelly said with a smile.

After they ordered, Dean told Kelly some news.

"I called and got a security guard to watch your house tonight," he said. "I let your parents know, in case they see some strange car parked in front of their house."

"I'll sleep better tonight having him there."

When the driver pulled up to Kelly's house, Dean walked her up, and the security guard joined them to introduce himself to Kelly.

"Thanks so much," Kelly said, and she went into her house.

Kelly slept well that night, thanks to eating a gummy bear, and felt much better. It also helped that playing at the party wasn't as strenuous as a normal concert. She ate breakfast and got dressed, and then packed for the major part of the tour. She washed her clothes and got that packed when it was done.

Mom drove Kelly to Dean's house three days later, the security guard following in his car. Kelly saw Isaac and Hayley kissing and hugging, which made her miss Greg, or at least the kind and not jealous Greg. She didn't need the Greg that accused her of being with other guys while on the road. *Some trust he had in me*, she thought.

"Hey," Mom said, "are you going to get out, or should I take you back home?"

Kelly shook her head to clear it. She wasn't about to tell her mom about missing Greg.

"Bye, Mom," she said with a kiss to her mom's cheek. She got her luggage from the trunk of the car and took it into Dean's house. To avoid getting to the venue too early, the band wasn't scheduled to leave until eleven that night. Kelly, Jayna, and the guys played Risk until Artie pulled up in the tour bus at ten-thirty with their roadies Bailey and Scott already inside, pulling the trailer with their equipment in it.

The band took their luggage out to the bus for Artie to load into the storage compartments. They helped Dean and Artie take all the food and drinks onto the bus, organizing as they went. Kelly loaded the refrigerator with bottled water, beer, hard lemonade, and other perishables while Dean put away the boxes and bags of snacks into the cupboards.

They finished just before eleven o'clock and after securing his house, Dean was last on the bus. Artie started the engine and they drove off to Phoenix.

Too excited to sleep, Kelly, Jayna, and the guys played another board game at the table until one by one they went to bed. Kelly took the same bottom bunk as before, across from Jayna. She didn't bother changing into her pajamas and just slept in her shorts and t-shirt.

Kelly woke up to the bus parked at the venue. She got out of bed and got a bowl for her breakfast. Dean was up already getting everything taken care of, Scott and Bailey were getting the equipment set up, and Artie had gone to his hotel room for the day. Kelly sat down at the table across from Dean to eat. Isaac sat on the couch, playing games on his Switch.

"You're all checked in, just waiting for the stage to be set up," Dean said. "In the meantime you all can go explore the city or just hang out here."

"I'll see what Jayna wants to do when she wakes up," Kelly said. "And maybe Ian, too."

A couple hours later, after everyone had awakened, Kelly, Jayna, and Ian left to go walk around the area and check things out while Isaac, Jake, and Paul stayed on the bus and played games.

They got back to the bus a couple hours later.

"All right," Dean said. "Grab your luggage and we can go inside to the dressing room."

Dean led them inside to the fairly spacious dressing room. The size of the rooms didn't faze Kelly anymore, having gotten used to them on the tour.

The guys and Kelly staked out their place in the dressing room and spread out their belongings, Kelly and Jayna taking the left side of the room.

"Hey, did anything ever come up on social media regarding that picture?" Kelly asked.

"Nope," Jayna said. "I've been checking every day. Nothing."

"I think it was probably a long shot," Dean said. "You're not well-known enough to cause a scandal just yet."

"Thank God," Kelly said.

"But, something *did* come up with Ian," Jayna said.

"What?" Ian asked.

"A photo of you and Lena Hendricks talking at the bar, then you two kissing."

Ian smiled.

"I took her out yesterday," he said. "We had a nice talk there."

"Jessica doesn't think so," Jayna said, showing him her phone, open to Instagram, where Jessica had shared the photo she'd found online, with the caption, *"Who does she think she is?"*

"Jesus Christ, that girl's got issues," Jake said, looking at the photo on his phone.

Ian handed Jayna back her phone.

"I guess I'd better warn Lena about this," Ian said, and he stepped out into the hall to call her.

"Maybe she'll stop harassing me," Kelly said.

"Oh, no," Jayna said. "She mentioned you, too, asking how it feels for you to have Ian cheating on you."

"Oh, my God," Kelly said, rolling her eyes. "I have no words."

Ian came back a few minutes later.

"She said she doesn't care what Jessica says. She's used to it," he said.

"I think I will just ignore her," Kelly said. "She's just looking to get a rise out of me."

Fate Struck had a fantastic show as usual, and after the show, they invited the opener to the dressing room for the after-party. The alcohol flowed freely, at least for the guys. Kelly kept to just one bottle of hard lemonade. Several backstage guests, both male and female, came over to talk to Kelly. Kelly saw that Dean kept his usual watchful eye from a distance.

"You seem like a girl who everyone wants as their sister," the dark-haired young man said.

"Or wants to have as their sister's friend," said the blond guy next to him.

"I hope that's a compliment," Kelly said with a smile.

"Oh, it is," the first guy said. "I know that The Disciples of Man think of you all as their younger siblings."

"They've been really helpful, and they do kind of take care of us."

The fans each wanted a photo with Kelly. Jayna wasn't back from the merch table yet, so the fans just took a selfie with her, the fans barely touching Kelly around her waist, and Kelly flashing a peace sign.

"We heard about your break-up with your boyfriend," one of the girls in the group said. "We're sorry that happened."

"Thank you," Kelly said. "It was for the best, though I'm still heart-broken."

Jayna came backstage a few minutes later, having finished with the merchandise table.

"We sold a lot of stuff!" she told Kelly. "People really like the T-shirts and autographed photos the best."

"Awesome!" Kelly said. "Never in a million years did I think people would be interested in our little band!"

Jayna got herself a bottle of hard lemonade and came back to hang out with Kelly and the fans.

Half an hour later Kelly saw Dean go around to everyone to thank them for coming, their cue to leave. Kelly thanked the fans gathered around her for coming to the show.

"I hope you enjoyed the show," Kelly said.

"It was fantastic!" one of the guys said. "Can't wait for the next one."

After everyone had left, Kelly sat down heavily on the couch.

"I'm beat," she said.

"Gotta admire Ian's stamina, though," Paul said.

Kelly looked around. Ian wasn't in the room. She knew where he'd gone.

"I hope he changes the sheets," Isaac remarked.

The band slowly started getting their belongings together. Ian returned and gathered his stuff together. Once they had everything, they walked out to the bus. A few fans waited nearby for an autograph or photo with them. Kelly and the guys set their luggage down by the bus and while Artie put everything away, the band went over to talk to the fans, Dean standing off to the side.

They chatted with the fans and took pictures with them until Artie had finished storing the luggage and Dean whistled to them.

"Thanks for coming," Isaac said.

"We enjoyed talking to you," Kelly said.

***

Isaac lay on his bunk and tapped in Hayley's number on his phone. She answered on the second ring.

"Hey, baby," Isaac said.

"Hey, Isaac," Hayley said. "Are you done with your show?"

"Yeah," he said. "It went really well."

"Of course it did, with you being the drummer."

Isaac laughed.

"Well, most of it has to do with Kelly, but I guess I have something to contribute."

"You've only been gone a day and I already miss you so much," she said.

"I miss you, too," Isaac said. "And seeing Ian with the girls just makes me miss you so much more."

"You're not thinking about doing anything like that, are you?" Hayley asked.

"Absolutely not," Isaac said. "That's why I drink after the shows. Ha ha."

"I'm not giving you permission," Hayley said, "but if it ever happens, I don't want to know about it."

"I could never do that to you or us," Isaac said. "I'd feel too guilty."

He didn't mention making out with one or two girls while he'd been on the road. It didn't go beyond that, and he made sure the girls understood it wouldn't. He wasn't sure how he felt about Hayley saying that. Did she know? Or is that how she expected all rock stars to behave?

"Good," Hayley said.

94

They spoke for half an hour, until Isaac started to fall asleep while he talked.

"I'll call you tomorrow," Isaac said. "I love you and miss you so much."

"I love you, too," Hayley said. "I can't wait until you come back."

Isaac disconnected and plugged his phone into the charger and lay back on his bunk. Truth be told, he'd been tempted by the girls, but like he said, he couldn't do that to Hayley. But if she didn't know…

Chapter Nine

Fate Struck played nine shows over the next two weeks. It snowed when they arrived in Colorado Springs, but it didn't delay their departure later after the show. Now in Nebraska, it had recently snowed about five inches, but Artie managed to get them to the venue without mishap. Kelly, Jayna, and the guys put on their coats and gloves and went outside to have a snowball fight in the parking lot, Jayna taking lots of photos for social media.

"Whose idea was it to do this tour in the winter?" Isaac asked.

"Tyrian Records," Dean said. "But if your album had come out at a different time of year, you'd be sweating instead of playing in the snow."

"I much prefer the cold weather to the hot weather," Kelly said. "You can always add on layers, but you can only take off so much before it becomes indecent."

"I'm down for indecency," Jake said.

"You would be." Jayna laughed.

After the snowball fight, everyone came back onto the bus to rest before their sound check in a couple hours.

"You know," Kelly said, "every time I get back on the bus, the smell of dirty socks is just overwhelming."

"I don't smell it," Jake said, sniffing the air. "All I smell is your hair products."

"Do they have a scent?" Kelly asked.

"Oh, yes," Isaac said. "Flowers and citrus."

"I guess I'm just used to them."

"Wait until the end of the tour," Dean said. "You won't even notice the smells anymore."

Kelly laughed as she lay on her bed and called her mom.

"Hi, Mom," Kelly said.

"Hi, sweetheart," Mom said. "I was hoping you'd call soon. How are you?"

"I'm good. We just had a snowball fight in the parking lot of where we're playing tonight. How are you and Dad and David?"

"We're all doing well," Mom said. "Dad's at work right now, and David was over for dinner last night."

"I need to give him a call, too," Kelly said. She told her mom about every place they've played and how the crowds have been.

"It's been really awesome to meet some of the fans, too. The further we get from California, though, the smaller the venues, but that's okay, we're getting lots of airplay on the radio stations and people will know us better soon."

She spoke with her mom for half an hour before disconnecting. She hadn't gotten a text or call from Greg in over a week. *Good, maybe he's finally let it go*, she thought.

As the tour progressed, the band and Jayna fell into a routine—the band sleeping late and then getting ready for the show. Jayna setting up the merchandise table and doing whatever else the band needed. Dean checking and double checking the itinerary.

Along with that, they grew more tired with each day. As much as they liked playing the different venues and meeting their fans, they were exhausted. Each band member put on an energetic show, jumping, running, and moving with the music. Kelly had switched to extra strength 5-hour energy shots, and because she was wired after the show, she had started eating the gummy bears every night. She told herself it was just medication and once the tour was over, she wouldn't need them any longer.

They were getting ready to play their show in North Carolina. It was February 9th, Kelly's 22nd birthday, and they planned on having a party after the show.

"No singing to me onstage, though," Kelly said.

"You know the fans will want to do it," Ian said.

"It's just a birthday," Kelly said.

"We'll see," Ian said.

After sound check, the band and Jayna gave Kelly her gifts. She didn't know how they managed to keep them out of sight, but was pleased to receive them, especially since this was the first birthday she'd celebrated away from home. Cupcakes were delivered as she opened her gifts.

They played their usual set, but just before the band did their last song, Ian spoke for a moment.

"Since it's Kelly's 22nd birthday today," Ian said, "we'd like you to join us in singing happy birthday to her!" The fans cheered loudly for Kelly.

"Oh, my gosh, you guys," Kelly said, smiling. "I thought we talked about this?"

"What? I can't hear you," Ian said, shaking his head.

Jake started to play Happy Birthday on his guitar and the others joined in, getting the audience to sing with them. Kelly stood at the center of the stage while they sang, and the audience cheered when they finished singing.

"Thank you, everyone," Kelly said. She saw that Jayna had come into the room to sing, too, and waved to her, then stepped off the stage to ask Dean a question.

"Can I do a little flip for them?" she asked.

"In those shoes?" Dean asked, looking at her feet.

"No, I'll take them off first," she said.

"Are you in shape to do it?"

"Yeah, I've kept up with it a bit."

"Okay, something easy, though," Dean said firmly.

Kelly smiled.

"Thank you, Dean!"

Kelly ran back out to the stage and grabbed the mic.

"You guys gave me a treat, so I'll give you one," Kelly said.

Ian walked over to her.

"Are you doing a backflip?" he asked.

"A round-off and a back flip," Kelly said. "Same as I've done before."

"Dean's okay with it?" Jake asked.

"I asked him."

"Okay," Ian said, stepping back to his mic.

Kelly took off her shoes, and went to the left side of the stage. She got into position, and did the round-off and back flip. She left out the aerial since it had been some time since she'd done a skill like that.

The audience responded with the loudest cheers so far of the tour. She took a bow as the band clapped for her. She slipped her shoes back on and the band started their last song.

Backstage, the guys all gave Kelly a kiss on the cheek and a hug, then poured drinks for everyone, Dean included. The opener came over to celebrate Kelly's birthday with them.

"I just about had a fucking heart attack when you did that gymnastics thing," the singer said.

"I asked Dean first," Kelly said, "and I did the easier skill instead of doing an aerial."

"What you did was easy?" their guitar player asked.

"Kelly was an elite gymnast before stepping down to focus on choir in high school," Ian said.

"Elite? Like Simone Biles-type stuff?"

"Well, not as good as her, but yeah," Kelly said.

"They don't call her 'the rock and roll gymnast' for nothing," Jake said.

Dean let the backstage pass holders into the dressing room, and most of them went over to wish Kelly a happy birthday and a few gave her gifts for her birthday. She opened each one as they were given to her and thanked each fan for the gift. Kelly received artwork of the band, some books, and one fan gave her a jacket in her favorite color purple, with the band's name embroidered on the back.

"Thank you so much, everyone," Kelly said, "but you really shouldn't have. These gifts couldn't have been cheap."

"You're worth it," one fan said.

Kelly felt her face flush. The amount of affection they showed her overwhelmed her.

"Thanks so much," she said again as she quickly brushed the tears from her eyes.

Jayna came back into the dressing room, having finished taking care of the merchandise table.

"I was surprised when you did that flip," Jayna said.

"I think I surprised everyone," Kelly said. "I didn't dare do the aerial since I haven't done anything like that in a few months."

Kelly and the rest of the band happily took pictures with the fans, Jayna taking the picture with the fan's cell phone. Kelly felt a little less inhibited that night. She wasn't sure if it was the alcohol she'd been drinking, or that it was her birthday, or if she was just getting used to the fans being backstage and didn't have to worry about how it would look to others, especially Greg.

***

Against his better judgement, Isaac called his mom. He hadn't called her or his father in over a week. He hadn't talked with his father except for a couple of times, mostly talking to his mom and his younger brother. Tonight, after talking to his mom and brother, his dad got on the phone.

"Glad you finally called us," his father said.

Great, Isaac thought. *He's already pissed off at me.*

"Well, we've been a little busy, Dad," Isaac said.

"I'll bet you find time to call Hayley," his dad said.

"Yes, I do. She's my girlfriend, for Christ's sakes, I miss her."

"Watch the language, if you please," his dad said.

Isaac bit his tongue to stop saying what he wanted to say.

"Anyway, I just wanted to check in and let you know how I'm doing," Isaac said, getting ready to hang up.

"Thank you for the update," his father said. "Maybe try to call more often than once a week?"

"I'll try. No promises."

"Goodbye, Isaac."

"Bye," he said, and he disconnected.

"Was that your dad?" Ian asked.

"He gets on my last fucking nerve," Isaac said. He went over and poured himself another cup of Jack Daniels. "I'm so glad I don't have to go home to him anymore."

Isaac took a long drink from the cup, then went back to the fans. One woman stayed near him the entire time. He wasn't in the best of moods right then, but the girl seemed to recognize he was upset. How he wished Hayley were there at that moment.

"Aren't parents the worst sometimes?" the woman said.

"Mine certainly are," Isaac said. "Not my mom so much, but my dad—do you want a drink?"

"Sure," the woman, Jeannie, said.

Isaac went over and poured a drink and brought it back to her, having refilled his cup as well. They talked for a while, then Isaac put his arm around her and pulled her close to him on the couch. He played with her hair, then caressed her neck. He turned

100

her face to his and then gently kissed her on the lips, trying to get a sense of how much she wanted, and when she grabbed the front of his shirt, he deepened the kiss. This wasn't the first time he'd done this with a girl backstage; he did like the attention he got from them, playing every bit the rock star. He'd give the women a smile, and more often than not, he'd get a couple of them to fall for it. Then usually one of them would do more of the talking and the other girl would move on.

God, he missed Hayley so damn much. She always knew how to calm him down after talking with his dad, letting him vent for a minute then offering her thoughts on it. It always helped. After that, they would make love and all would be forgotten. Would having sex help him this time? In his inebriated state, he wanted to find out.

Isaac whispered to her, "Let's go to the bus."

Jeannie nodded, and Isaac took her hand and led her out to the bus. By the looks of things, Ian was already using the back lounge, so he and Jeannie would have to make do with the couch. He panicked for a moment, because he hadn't thought to bring condoms with him, but he remembered where Ian kept his and grabbed one, then grabbed a blanket off his bunk and they sat on the couch and kissed, then Isaac unbuttoned Jeannie's blouse. She pulled off Isaac's shirt and then they quickly undressed and he pulled the blanket over them while they had sex. Isaac didn't even care if anyone came in at the moment, he was oblivious to everything except what he and Jeannie were doing.

Half an hour later, they spooned together on the couch, catching their breath, Isaac holding Jeannie mostly so she didn't fall off the narrow couch. Reality set in as he lay there.

What the hell did I just do?

The door to the lounge opened and Ian and a girl came out.

"Hey," Ian said as he passed.

"Hey," Isaac replied. Neither of them said anything more as Ian and his girl left the bus. Isaac looked at his watch. It was about the time that Dean kicked everyone out from the dressing room.

"We'd better go back," Isaac said.

They dressed and Isaac walked Jeannie back to the backstage area. Dean had started making his rounds to everyone.

"I had a great time," Jeannie said.

"See ya." Isaac poured himself another drink as she left. Guilt overcame him and he drank his drink down and poured another. *God, I'm an idiot.*

The band got their belongings together. Isaac was too drunk to do much, so Jayna helped get his things together for him.

***

Once on the bus, they all collapsed on the nearest furniture, mostly on the couch and chairs in the dining area. Ian and Kelly sat side by side on the couch, with Jayna on the end. Jake and Paul ended up on the chairs, and Isaac managed to make it to his bunk.

Artie started the bus and pulled out of the parking lot, on the way to the band's next destination.

"I'm going to bed," Jayna said.

"Good night," Kelly told her. Jayna leaned over and kissed her cheek, then went to bed.

"I think we can finally make it to our bunks, too," Paul said, and he and Jake walked to their beds.

Kelly rested her head on Ian's shoulder. She probably shouldn't have drunk so much, but it's not like she did that every night. It was her birthday, and she just wanted to have a good time.

"I think I'm heading to bed, too," Dean said.

"See you in the morning," Kelly said as Dean walked down the hall to his bunk.

Ian wrapped his arm around her, but Kelly didn't think anything of it. They were good friends, and after Jayna, he was probably her best friend in the band. He kissed the top of her head as his hand caressed her shoulder, sending goosebumps down her arm. She looked up at him and they looked into each other's eyes for a long time, then without saying a word Ian bent down and kissed Kelly's lips. It was like being kissed for the first time again; Ian's kiss was gentle and soft. God, she missed Greg, but there was no way they could be together again. He was too jealous.

Ian deepened the kiss, and the kisses became longer and more eager, Ian's hands up in her hair, her hands on his back. He reached around her and unhooked her bra, then cupped her breast in his hand. Kelly's breaths came faster.

Her stomach fluttered as she kissed Ian. *Oh, my God, this feels so good!* she thought. She moved to unfasten Ian's pants, but stopped and pulled back.

"What's wrong?" he panted.

"We can't do this, Ian," Kelly said.

"Why not?" he asked, kissing her neck.

"We said we'd never do this. We're friends and bandmates. I don't want to mess that up."

Ian took his hands out from under her blouse and blew his breath out quickly.

"You're right," he said. "Of course, you're right. I took advantage of you, and I'm sorry."

"You're not the only one to blame here," Kelly said. "I let it happen. I think we both wanted it, but we shouldn't with each other, especially since we've been drinking."

"Well, it seems like it's always the guy that gets blamed."

"Not this time," Kelly said with a soft smile. "I guess I'm just missing Greg more than I realized, and getting drunk doesn't help. It lowers my inhibitions."

"Friends with benefits?"

"I'd have to think on that one. You have no trouble getting girls, Ian. Why would you want that?"

"Just for when you feel like you do tonight. I know girls are wired differently regarding sex, so I don't know if it'd be of help or not. You tell me."

"I'll let you know," Kelly said. She tousled his hair. "You're a good guy, Ian, and a good friend. Let's not lose that no matter what we decide, okay?"

"You got it," he said. He kissed her cheek.

"And with that, I'm going to bed, too," Kelly said, standing up. She swayed a little and Ian steadied her.

"You okay?" he asked.

"Yeah, I'm fine. I'm going to drink some water before I go to bed."

Kelly weaved down the hallway to her bunk, where she grabbed her pajamas and went to change in the bathroom. When she came out, Ian had gone to bed. She threw her clothes on the foot of her bunk, took a long drink of her water, then got into her bed and pulled the curtain shut.

She awoke the next morning feeling a little worse for wear. Even though she drank water before bed, she still had the mother of hangovers. Luckily the curtain on her bunk kept it fairly dark even in the daylight. She looked at her phone and saw it was already eleven. She didn't want to get up at all, but her bladder told her she must.

Kelly pulled the curtain open and slowly got out of her bunk. She used the bathroom, then went back to bed. The only person up so far was Dean, and he just nodded to her as she went back to bed. *I wonder if he knows what happened last night,* she thought. The bunks weren't that far away from the dining/living room area. *Well, it doesn't matter if he did, nothing really happened.*

Kelly fell asleep for another hour, then hunger made her wake up. The thought of food made her nauseous, however, but she needed something. She got up and made some toast and grabbed an orange juice from the fridge and sat at the table to eat.

"That was some birthday, huh?" Dean asked.

Did he know what happened, or almost happened?

"Yeah," Kelly said, pushing that thought out of her head. "I need to not drink so much. I don't like hangovers."

"Or remember to drink more water," Dean suggested.

"Yeah, that, too."

Kelly ate her toast and drank her juice and began to feel a little better. She probably didn't look that great, though. She hadn't washed the make-up off or brushed her hair before going to bed. She took her phone and looked at the selfie camera. She looked like a well-made-up panda, with her mascara smudged under her eyes and her eye shadow smeared off half her left eye. Her hair...

"Dean! Why didn't you tell me how bad I look?" Kelly exclaimed, tossing her phone onto the table.

"Because you look like you just got up, which you did," Dean said with a chuckle. "I don't expect any of you to be camera-ready first thing in the morning. Besides, you're not a vain person."

"There's vanity and then there's this monstrosity."

"You'll look and feel better after you shower."

"I'm going to do that right now."

Fifteen minutes later, out of the shower and dressed, she did feel better and looked like a normal person again. While she showered, Isaac, Jake, and Jayna had gotten up. It was one in the afternoon and they had crossed the state line into Minnesota. Artie had stopped to tune up the engine of the bus and eat lunch. Isaac, Jake, Jayna, and Kelly put on their coats and went outside to enjoy the fresh chilly air and sunshine. Isaac and Kelly ended up walking around the rest stop together.

"Are you okay?" Kelly asked. "You seem a little down."

"I'm struggling to come to terms about something," he said.

"About what?"

Isaac didn't say anything for a long time, and Kelly thought he'd rather not talk about it.

"Back a few weeks ago," Isaac said finally, "I talked to Hayley on the phone as I always do. I mentioned to her how Ian's always getting the girls, since he's the one who's single now."

"Go on," Kelly said.

"Hayley asked if I'd ever done that with the girls and I said 'No.' I don't count making out with the girls as necessarily cheating on her. Anyway, she told me that she's not giving me permission, but she didn't want to know if I ever did anything like that. Well, it happened last night. I brought a girl to the bus. The lounge was occupied by Ian, of course, so we just did it on the couch."

"And now you feel guilty," Kelly said.

"Yes! I just miss Hayley so much, and I drank a lot last night, too. I love Hayley, Kelly, why did I do that?"

"Why do you make out with the girls backstage?"

"I'm thinking of Hayley when I do that. I just imagine it's her. Maybe that's why I did that last night."

"You're not the only one feeling a little guilty today," Kelly offered.

"Why's that?"

"Ian and I almost gave the couch another workout."

He came to a dead stop.

"Are you kidding me?"

Kelly shook her head, staring off into the distance for a moment, then turned to Isaac again.

"Like you, I drank way too much, and I was missing Greg. It just happened, but we didn't do *it*," she said quickly. "I stopped us before it went that far."

"Are you two okay to work together?"

"Oh, yeah, totally. We talked it out. He offered to be a 'friend with benefits' but I don't know about that."

"As long as it doesn't break up the band, I don't care," Isaac said. "I'm just…surprised, is all."

"Yeah, I was, too, actually." She took Isaac's hand in hers. "Don't feel guilty. I know where your heart lies. It's none of my business what you guys all do. Fuck all the girls you want."

"Whoa!" Isaac said, stepping back slightly. "I've never heard you drop an F-bomb before. It's like hearing Sandra Bullock say it."

Kelly laughed.

"You guys are a bad influence on me," Kelly said.

"Well, now that we've both admitted our debauchery, let's get back to the bus. It looks like Artie's ready to go."

They hugged each other, and walked back to the bus. Ian and Paul had finally awakened.

"What was all the hugging for?" Ian asked when Kelly and Isaac got back on the bus.

"We were comparing notes," Kelly said.

"About what?"

Kelly gave him a pointed look.

"Oooooh," Ian said, looking wide-eyed at Isaac.

"It's cool," Isaac told him. "Everything's good."

Ian looked relieved.

"And we don't talk about it around Hayley," Isaac said.

"My lips are sealed," Ian said, pretending to turn the key on his lips.

Chapter Ten

The tour continued in Chicago; Lansing, Michigan; Pittsburg; up to Boston, back down to Philadelphia, and now in March they were in New York City. This was the one stop on the tour where they weren't the headliner, but were opening for their friends The Disciples of Man.

An interview was set at one of the hard rock radio stations in New York. Artie drove them to the station and as Dean went in to let them know they had arrived, the band got dressed in something other than sweats and t-shirts. Kelly put on just a touch of make-up and brushed her hair. She grabbed her sunglasses and was ready by the time Dean came back.

"Okay, we're all set," Dean told them. "I'll take you inside and introduce you to the deejays doing the interview. And Kelly, I know they'll probably ask you to do some kind of gymnastics thing. It's okay as long as it's like what you've been doing."

"Okie dokie," Kelly said.

Kelly, Jayna, and the guys followed Dean inside to the elevator, then down a long hallway to the control room where they were met by the director.

"This is Mike," Dean told them. "And this is Fate Struck—Kelly, Ian, Paul, Jake, and Isaac."

"Nice to meet all of you," Mike said, shaking hands with each of them.

"And this is Jayna, their assistant," Dean said.

Mike shook Jayna's hand, and then went over how the show would go. During a break, he introduced them to the deejays, Ed and Austin. He got them situated in the booth with headphones and mics for all of them. They were still settling in as the break ended and Ed and Austin gave a little background of the band and then played their single. When the music ended, Ed started the interview.

"So, first off, let's get an introduction of everyone," Ed said.

"I'm Kelly and I'm the singer," Kelly started.

"I'm Isaac and I play the drums."

"Ian, bass and backing vocals."

"I'm Jake and I play lead guitar and sing back-up."

"Paul, rhythm guitar."

"You guys have been on tour since November," Ed said.

"Yes, we have," Isaac said.

"And you are about halfway finished?"

"A little more than halfway," Isaac said. "At least for this leg of it."

"That's right, you're heading to Canada a few weeks after the US tour," Austin said.

"Yep, touring Canada for about a month, I think?" Ian said.

"Tonight is a little different because you're opening for The Disciples of Man, whom you've opened for before."

"Yeah, we're pretty excited about it," Kelly said. "They've really helped us along the way, so we're only too happy to open for them again."

The deejays talked a little more with the band, then played another song of theirs, which would most likely be their next single.

"Now, I've heard through the grapevine that you, Kelly, used to be an elite gymnast," Ed said.

"True," Kelly said.

"What made you switch to singing?"

"Jayna and I were in choir together in high school, and also gymnastics. Gymnastics was something I was good at, but my love is singing. I've always wanted to be a singer."

"Our record company calls her the 'Rock and Roll Gymnast,'" Isaac said.

"Do you do flips onstage?" Ed asked.

"Sometimes," Kelly said with a laugh. "Not very often. I'm usually not wearing shoes to do flips in."

"Hard to do a flip in platform shoes," Ian said.

"What shoes do you have on now?" Austin asked.

"Tennis shoes," she said, holding up her right foot.

"Can you show us one of your flips?" Ed asked.

Kelly looked around the small booth.

"Not in here," she said.

"How about the hallway?" Austin suggested.

Kelly looked out the window to the hallway. It was narrow but not too narrow and there was a length with no doors.

"Yeah, I can do it there," she said.

Ed and Austin took their mics and went out the door to the hallway along with Kelly, who left her headphones on the stool in the booth. People had come out of their offices or looked out their windows to watch Kelly do her flip. Jayna stood ready with her phone to take photos. Kelly got into position, and did a round-off into a backflip, landing with her hands in the air.

Everyone applauded as they went back into their offices and Kelly and the deejays went back into the studio.

"I have to say, that was pretty awesome," Ed said.

"Thanks," Kelly said. "I get asked to do that a lot. I have to keep it easy since I haven't practiced in a while."

"That was easy?" Austin asked.

"Pretty much," Kelly said.

"You seem so much bigger onstage," Ed said. "But here in the studio, you're tiny!"

Kelly laughed.

"That's why I was so good at gymnastics."

They talked a little more with the band, and at the end of the hour, Ed and Austin played another song off their CD.

"You guys were fantastic," Ed said.

"Thanks," Isaac said.

"I hope you'll stop by again on your next tour," Austin said.

"Sure!" Kelly said.

They shook hands with everyone and Fate Struck left the booth.

"Thank you for coming in," Mike said, shaking Dean's hand.

"Our pleasure," Dean told him.

They walked back out to the bus, and Artie drove them to their hotel, where a rental van waited to drive them to the show venue.

Fate Struck stayed at the same hotel as The Disciples of Man, and after the show, during which Erik called Kelly out to sing "Psychobabble" with him, they moved the party from backstage to the hotel. The Disciples had a suite, so the party took place there. The party grew in size at the hotel, with more guys and many more women than there were in the dressing rooms.

Stevie, The Disciples' drummer, sat on the couch with a beautiful brunette straddling his legs, not a care in the world. Adam had his arm around another woman's waist, sliding his hand down every so often to caress her butt. Even Jake, Ian, and Isaac had a woman with them. Kelly hadn't seen this side of the music business before. She wasn't so naïve to think this didn't happen, it was just weird that it was their friends. They hadn't done this when they toured with them, but also Kelly and the guys hadn't been at their after parties with them in their hotels. Paul, always faithful to Alexa, talked with Dean and Will off to the side.

Kelly knew that Paul had a hard time backstage with the fans. The women flocked around him like they did the other guys, but like the guys did with Kelly, they moved on once they figured out they weren't going to get laid. Paul had the brooding musician look onstage, never smiling, which women loved. But he only had eyes for Alexa, whom he'd dated since their junior year of high school.

A tall guy with long blond hair walked up to Kelly.

"You were fucking awesome tonight," he said, lightly touching her arm.

"Thanks!" Kelly said.

"I thought you were great with Erik on 'Psychobabble.' I was surprised when he called you out to sing with him."

"It took me a bit by surprise, too," Kelly said. "He hadn't mentioned it to me, but I was ready, just in case."

"He doesn't do that with just anyone," the guy said. "You two have a thing going on?"

"What? No! We're just friends. They've been really good to us."

"I think he's got a hard-on for you."

Okay, I didn't need to hear that.

"It's been nice talking to you, but I need to, uh, use the bathroom."

"I could join you," he said, rubbing her arm.

Ew.

"I think I can manage myself, thanks."

"See you later, I hope."

Oh my God.

She walked away quickly and went to the bathroom. She didn't need to use it, she just wanted to get away from the guy. Kelly sat on the closed toilet until she thought the guy had forgotten about her. When she came out she went to get another drink from the table.

Two more guys tried to talk her into having sex with them, one going so far as to unzip his pants and reach inside. Kelly bolted for the drink table again, her heart beating fast.

This is so not my scene. Is this what I have to look forward to when we get popular?

Kelly had stayed away from alcohol since her birthday, but with everything going on that night, she had started with a bottle of hard lemonade followed by several shots of Fireball, and a margarita.

The couch was free from people having sex, so she sat down at one end.

"You were fantastic tonight," Erik said as he sat down next to Kelly.

"Thank you!" Kelly said.

"And you look great," he added.

"Aw, thanks. Just a little bit of a change."

Erik played with the ends of her hair.

"I like the purple," he said. "It's one of my favorite colors."

"Mine too. Obviously," she giggled.

"It's just mind-blowing how confident you seem now, especially on 'Psychobabble.'"

"I really don't feel that confident, but thank you. I'm just doing my job to entertain people."

"It's really a turn-on," he said, and he leaned over and kissed her. It surprised her that he would do that, with him being married, and she didn't know what to do. She was a nobody. Why was he doing this? Erik kissed her neck, and whispered in her ear, "I'd love to show you how turned-on I am."

Did he just proposition me? Maybe that guy was right.

"I'm flattered," Kelly said, gently pushing on his chest as she came out of her shock. "But I couldn't do that to your wife. I'm sorry."

"You and your boyfriend broke up, though, right?"

"Yes, we did, but that still doesn't change the fact that you're married. I don't care what you do. We're friends, but I won't be the cause of breaking up a marriage."

Erik sat back.

"Well, women don't usually say 'No' to me," he said.

"You can have your pick of any woman here," she said, sweeping her arm around. "I'm just not it. I'm sorry."

"Okay, I respect your decision. Still friends?" He held out his hand.

Kelly took his hand and shook it.

"Still friends," she said, smiling.

Erik kissed her on the cheek then stood to mingle with the other guests.

Kelly pursed her lips and blew out a breath. She was starting to attract guys and she wasn't sure how to handle that. She got up and went over to Jayna, taking her arm and dragging her away from Adam, Jayna excusing herself as she left.

"What's up?' Jayna asked.

"Why do guys want *me*?" she asked.

"What do you mean?" Jayna asked.

"Well, first Greg, then Ian, some of the guys here, and now Erik."

"Erik? Like *singer* Erik?"

Kelly nodded.

"Well, you're gorgeous, confident…"

"Am I? Gorgeous and confident? Erik mentioned that, too."

"Hell yeah! You've really changed since the first days, in a good way. You own that stage now, girl. You look comfortable up there, and you can really belt out the songs now. Plus look at you! You look fantastic."

Kelly thought about that. She never saw herself like that, but maybe it was because she was just doing what she loved and the fans loved the band and the music. Guys did flock to her, but she thought it was because she was the lead singer. Was it because of how she looked, too? She'd never been confident about her looks. She didn't think she was ugly or anything, just average-looking, even after being made-up for gymnastic competitions or the stage.

"I just never see myself like that," Kelly finally said. "I'm just me."

"I know you don't invite the attention," Jayna said. "But it comes with the territory."

"I'm not sure how I feel about this."

Jayna put her hands on Kelly's shoulders.

"You do what is best for *you*," Jayna said. "You don't have to give in to the men who want to be with you."

"I know, and I haven't, because it's totally not me, but it's weird to me. The only reason I was popular in school was because of gymnastics and choir, but guys wouldn't give me the time of day then. Now, everyone knows who I am. It's weird," she said again.

Jayna hugged her friend, and Kelly nodded to her that she was okay to leave her and Jayna went back to her photography duties.

Kelly drank another shot of Fireball to calm down. Dean came over.

"Everything okay?" he asked. "You're putting that away quite a bit tonight."

"Why does everything have to be so fucking complicated?" she asked.

After recovering from the shock of her language, he said, "I don't know. Because life *is*, I guess?"

"You're no help," she said jokingly.

"I know. I'm sorry."

Kelly smiled, and went out to mingle a little, talking to some of the girls as well as the guys there. The girls talked to her politely but it was obvious they were there for the guys. Kelly felt a little out of place, and this was when she missed Greg the most. Kelly looked for Ian and spotted him across the room, talking to one of the many girls there. She pulled out her phone and texted him. She watched him pull out his phone from his front jeans pocket, read the text, and then look around for her. Kelly saw him excuse himself from the fans and came over right away.

"You need me?" he asked.

She bit her bottom lip.

"Yes," she finally said. She said nothing more, and he nodded his understanding. He took her hand and they left the party, going down the hall to his room, Ian hanging the Do Not Disturb sign on the door handle. They sat on Ian's bed for a long time before Ian broke the silence.

"Are you sure about this?"

She thought for a moment. He'd been talking to Lena fairly often during the tour.

"What's Lena going to say?"

"Lena and I aren't really together yet, so she's not a factor in this."

She kissed him passionately.

"That is my answer," she whispered.

He smiled, then returned the kiss just as passionately. They kissed for a long time before they took off their clothes and got under the blankets. Ian smoothed her hair from her face, and kissed her face softly. She ran her hand through his hair he'd let grow a little longer during the tour. He lay on top of her with his arms under her shoulders and his hands in her hair. Kelly looked into his blue eyes. *God, he looks good in make-up*, she thought. She could definitely fall for him, but that couldn't happen. She'd take this—Ian making her feel good when she was feeling down. He was very attentive to her and her needs. Ian reached into his nightstand and took out a condom and rolled it on just before he entered her.

They made love for half an hour, Ian making her feel like the only woman in the world. After they climaxed, they held each other for a few moments, spooning together, his hand on her stomach, softly caressing it.

"Are you okay?" Ian asked.

"Yes," Kelly said quietly.

He raised up on his elbow to look at her face.

"You're sure?"

"Yes," she said with certainty.

He lay back down and continued to gently stroke her stomach. Did she want to make this a thing with Ian, friends with benefits? It wasn't like her to do something like that, but she'd done a few things lately that was out of character. Getting drunk, eating edibles, and now this. Was it bad that she wanted to feel good?

"There's no strings attached," Kelly said aloud.

"I know," Ian said.

"And this isn't going to happen every night or even every week."

"Okay."

They lay there together for a long time, and Ian's breathing got longer and regular, and Kelly figured he'd fallen asleep.

She dozed off, too, because she woke up to Paul coming into the room. She glanced at the clock on the nightstand and saw that it was almost two in the morning.

"Is the party winding down?" Ian asked sleepily.

"Yeah," Paul said. "Sorry to disturb you two but I'm tired."

"No worries," Kelly said.

"Kelly?" Paul asked.

"Um, literally in the flesh."

"Okay, so not what I was expecting, but it's cool. I'm surprised it didn't happen sooner."

"We're not *together*," Ian said. "It's just…a thing."

"Hey, as long as it doesn't break up the band, I don't care."

"That's what Isaac said, too."

"Well, if he knows and is okay with it, I ain't got no issues with it," Paul said.

Paul went into the bathroom so Ian and Kelly could get dressed.

"It's safe now," Ian called to him.

Paul stepped back into the room.

"Have a good night," Paul said, as he sat on his bed to take off his shoes.

Ian and Kelly walked back to Erik's suite. The party had indeed thinned out, though there were still people hanging around. Dean saw them come in together. Kelly couldn't read his expression, but Dean didn't say anything to them. Ian and Kelly went their separate ways in the room.

At three in the morning, Kelly and Jayna both headed to their room. Kelly washed her face and changed before getting into bed.

"You are certainly full of surprises tonight," Jayna said.

"Why?"

"Well, Ian…" Jayna said.

"And I are still just friends. It was just something that I needed," Kelly told her.

"Okay," Jayna said, and she left it at that and turned out her light. Kelly got into bed and turned off her light. It didn't take her long to fall asleep.

On the bus the next day, Dean wanted to talk to all of them.

"First of all," he started, "that was a fabulous show last night, even if you were the opener."

"It was great!" Isaac said.

"Awesome!" Paul said.

"But I want to address the elephant in the room."

"What's that?" Jake asked.

"Us," Ian said, pointing to himself and Kelly.

"Why? Didn't you use a condom?" Jake asked.

"You know?" Kelly asked, eyes wide.

"Isaac told me."

"Okay, so no elephant, then," Ian said, looking at Dean.

"Well, there is if it starts to affect the band."

"There's nothing to worry about. We're still friends and nothing more," Kelly said.

"You say that now, but what if it turns into something else?" Dean asked.

"Not going to happen," Ian said. "I like my freedom."

"And so do I, right now," Kelly said. "And like I said earlier, I don't care who any of you sleep with. It's none of my business, and I'm not going to run and tattle on you."

"So, is everyone good on everything?" Dean asked.

"Yes," they all said.

"Great. Carry on, then."

Dean went to sit up front with Artie while the guys went to the lounge to play video games. Kelly and Jayna stayed at the table.

"How's Marty?" Kelly asked.

"He's good," Jayna said. "He was hoping to meet us in New York, but he couldn't get the time off from work. Got a big electronics project he's working on in the company. He's going to try for Texas. I miss him so much."

"It's too bad he couldn't come with you for part of the tour."

116

"Yeah, but that work thing."

"I'm glad you wanted to stay working for us on the tour. I know it's hard to be away from him."

"It is, but we talk every day while you guys do your sound check, and we video chat sometimes, too."

"And he knows that sometimes guys talk to you backstage?"

"Yes, but he trusts me, and I have no desire to do anything with the guys backstage."

"Yeah, trust is everything."

"I'm sorry, I didn't mean…"

"No, you're fine. It's Greg's problem, and if he'd been more trusting, there'd be no friends with benefits between me and Ian."

"I know. His loss."

"And I'm sorry I didn't talk to you about Ian before," Kelly said. "He asked me about it, and I wasn't sure what my answer was going to be."

"I know you're uncomfortable talking about stuff like that. But you know you can always come to me and talk to me about anything. Okay?"

"Okay. Thanks, Jayna."

They pulled into Baltimore late in the morning. Dean checked in with the manager and then showed Fate Struck to their dressing room where they snacked while they waited for the crew to get their equipment set up onstage so they could do their sound check.

Backstage after the show, the pass holders, mostly women, came backstage and flocked around all the guys. Several guys came over to talk to Kelly, but didn't stay long once they realized they weren't going to get anywhere with her, and moved to the guys to talk about their instruments. Kelly walked around the room, talking with all the guests as they spoke to the guys, feeling a little more a part of the crowd.

"It's funny how the women ignore me until one of you guys talk to me in the convo," Kelly said later when they were all on the bus.

"The guys don't ignore you," Paul said.

"Until they realize they're not getting anywhere with me. It's fine, though. I'm not looking for anything right now. Besides I'm not sure I'd want to date another fan. Didn't work out too well with Greg."

Chapter Eleven

The band played shows in Virginia, North Carolina, Florida, and Georgia before heading to Texas. They had two shows in the state—one in Houston and one in Dallas. In Dallas, Marty met up with the band and Jayna at the venue.

"I'm so glad you're here!" Jayna said, jumping into his arms and kissing him.

"I'm glad I was able to get time off," Marty said.

Kelly gave them a minute before going out to say Hi.

"Glad you could make it," she said.

"Me, too. I've missed her so much."

"She's missed you, too," Kelly told him.

Jayna took Marty with her to get him an all-access badge so she could set up the merchandise table while the band went to sound check.

After the show, Marty waited backstage for Jayna to finish with the merchandise sales.

"How long does it usually take for her to finish?" Marty asked.

"About an hour," Kelly said. "People usually finish their purchases about half an hour after the show, then she packs it up. You can go out there if you want. No reason you need to stay here."

"I think I'll do that," Marty said, smiling, and he left the room.

This time, some of the fans hung around Kelly and wanted to talk about the music and the band.

"I was so excited when I heard you guys were touring," said the tall blond guy.

"You've heard of us here in Texas before now?"

"We're big fans of The Disciples of Man and we caught one of their shows where you opened for them. We were surprised how good you were and hoped you'd do a tour when your CD came out."

"Thank you! Yeah, that was a fun tour with them. They're a great bunch of guys." *Even if the singer cheats on his wife,* she added in her head. But it was no different than what Isaac was

119

doing out on the road. She knew Erik loved his wife, she just didn't want to be part of that.

"They seem to have taken you under their wing," said the dark-haired girl standing next to him. "We've seen pictures of you all hanging out, and they've said on their website they consider your band their younger siblings."

"They've actually helped us a lot in our career so far."

Jayna and Marty came back to the dressing room and sat down in the corner, away from everyone, trying to be inconspicuous as they cuddled and kissed.

Dean made his rounds to kick everyone out. The fans around Kelly wanted some pictures so when Dean came by, Kelly asked him to take pictures of them for the fans. He took one photo then swapped out the phone for another fan's and took another. He did that two more times until everyone had gotten a picture.

"I'm sorry," Jayna said as she walked up. "I should have been doing that."

"It's okay," Dean said. "You were occupied."

"Well, I should have been doing my job."

"You're fine, Jayna," Kelly said. "How long has it been since you've seen Marty? Too long. "

"Thanks, you guys, but I'll be better next time."

Kelly put her arms around Jayna and hugged her.

"It's not a problem," she said, and kissed Jayna's cheek.

After everyone had left, the band cleaned up the room, getting all their belongings packed away again. Marty helped wherever he could, going around to do what was needed. They took their stuff to the bus and then signed a few autographs and took some photos with the fans waiting outside near the bus.

With everyone back on board, Artie pulled out of the parking lot and got back on the highway heading toward Albuquerque, New Mexico.

Before he went to bed, Isaac went and changed the sheets on the bed in the back lounge for Jayna and Marty.

"I think you two will be more comfortable there," he said.

"Thank you, Isaac," Jayna said. "You're a doll," and she and Marty went to the lounge and shut the door.

***

Isaac dropped the sheets off in the laundry basket outside the bathroom and then climbed into his bunk, using the lower bed for a foot hold, then the middle bed opposite of him, then launching himself into his bunk at the top. He plugged his phone into his charger and then shut his curtain.

He'd finally stopped feeling guilty about having sex with women after the shows. At first he couldn't call Hayley the next morning, the guilt overwhelmed him and he felt like she'd know what he'd done. He'd call her later in the day, after smoking a joint to calm down and ease the anxiety. Isaac didn't sleep with a woman every night after a show, but it became more than a once in a while thing. He loved living the rock star life on the road.

It would've been a harder decision if Hayley hadn't said she didn't want to know. It was like she knew it would happen. Isaac had never strayed once while at home with Hayley, but God, he missed her on the road. But he would always go back to her and not look twice at another woman.

Isaac lay there in the dark for a long time. He was tired but his mind wouldn't shut down and this was when he got the nagging anxiety. He opened his container of cannabis gummy bears and took two of them so he could sleep.

In the morning, Isaac awakened to the sound of the waste being emptied from the bus. He looked at his phone and saw it was noon. He got up and grabbed a blueberry muffin from the cupboard.

"We're almost to Albuquerque," Dean told him.

"Awesome," Isaac said. "We have a show tonight there?"

"Yes. We're about an hour away, so plenty of time. Sorry if the waste disposal woke you up. It needed to be done."

"No, it's okay. We don't want to have a shitty bus."

Dean laughed.

"No, we don't."

Isaac went back to his bunk and lay on his side propped up on his elbow to eat his muffin, then went back to sleep.

The bus had pulled into the parking lot of the venue and parked by the time Isaac woke again, and Artie had gone to his hotel room until after the show. He grabbed his phone and called Hayley.

"Hey, babe," Isaac said when she answered.

"Hi Isaac," Hayley said.

"Sorry I didn't call last night. I pretty much passed out in bed."

"It's okay. I think calling during the day is better, anyway."

"We just pulled into Albuquerque for our show tonight. Man, I'm beat, though."

"I bet it's so tiring."

"But once I hit the stage, I seem to find the energy. The crowds have been amazing."

"They seem really good from what I've seen on your band's social media."

"Dean and Jayna have been great with taking pictures of everything."

Isaac hoped none of the photos showed him with the female fans. He was pretty sure Jayna had been careful not to get those types of photos, but he hadn't looked in a week.

"Yeah, they've done an awesome job," Hayley said. "The tour is winding down in a couple weeks, right?"

"The US part, then we're going to Canada for a few weeks, then we should be home to stay for a long while."

"Good, I miss you so much."

"I miss you, too, babe," Isaac said.

They talked for a few more minutes, and in that time everyone had awakened and was moving around the bus.

"I better get going if I want to eat breakfast before we head out to the venue."

"Breakfast? It's lunch time."

"Not for me, it isn't." He laughed. "My schedule's going to be all messed up by the time we get home."

"I'll talk to you tomorrow, then?"

"Of course. I love you, Hayley."

"I love you, Isaac."

Isaac disconnected, and then opened his curtain and got out of his bunk to join the others in the dining area for breakfast.

***

"No hangovers to nurse today?" Dean asked once everyone was awake.

"Surprisingly not," Ian said. "Didn't drink much last night."

"Yeah. You were too busy with other things," Jake said, wiggling his eyebrows.

"Any port in a storm," Ian said with a wink.

"I'm going to go check in," Dean said, and he stepped off the bus.

"Is there anything to do around here?" Paul asked.

"I don't know," Kelly said, "but I'm too tired to go anywhere."

"Same," Jake said.

Ian pulled up the area on his phone.

"Nope, not really anything we'd be interested in," he said. "There's an area with a bunch of shops, but I'm not walking that far."

"I'm staying here," Kelly said.

Dean came back a few minutes later.

"All checked in, sound check is at four-thirty," he said.

"Cool," Isaac said. "Anyone want to play Mario Kart with me?"

"I will," Jake said.

"I'll come watch," Paul said.

The three of them went to the lounge to play.

"Thanks for making the bed," Isaac shouted from the back.

"You're welcome!" Jayna said.

"So, what do you guys usually do while waiting for sound check?" Marty asked.

"Pretty much what you see," Jayna said. "If we're not too tired and there's some cool things to do, we'll go out for an hour or so. We've been to a couple of museums, and botanical gardens and other places."

"Otherwise, we play video games or work on music," Kelly said. "Though I'm not much into video games. I like to read, though. I've finished a couple of books so far."

"Seems kind of boring," Marty said.

"It's not, really," Jayna said. "I'm not as tired as the rest of them, if you want to walk around a bit."

"Sure," Marty said.

Jayna changed her shoes to walking shoes, and she and Marty left.

"I feel like a fifth wheel," Dean said.

"Why?" Ian asked. "It's not like we're going to hop into bed every time we're alone," Ian said.

"Lovely way of putting it," Kelly said, slapping him on his arm.

"Ow!"

"I just didn't want to cramp your style or whatever it is you young 'uns say these days," Dean said.

"It's fine," Kelly said. "Want to watch a movie?" she asked Ian, changing the subject.

"Sure," Ian said.

Kelly turned on the TV and found a movie on Netflix.

After the show that night, Marty had to say goodbye to Jayna. They came backstage to the dressing room after packing up the merch and cuddled and kissed before the airport shuttle arrived to take him to the airport. He said goodbye to the band.

"We'll have your girl home in a couple of weeks," Dean said, shaking Marty's hand at the dressing room door.

"I'll be happy to have her home, even if it's only for a month," Marty said, acknowledging the Canadian tour.

"Safe travels! See you later!" everyone shouted as he left the room.

Kelly walked over and put her arms around Jayna, who brushed away the tears from her face.

"I miss him already," Jayna said.

"I know," Kelly said. "You'll be back home with him in just a short time."

"I didn't realize how much I missed him until he was here and then left again, and he's only been gone five minutes."

"I guess keeping busy will take your mind off of it."

Jayna returned the embrace and then went around and tidied things up to make it easier when it was time to go.

Kelly grabbed a bottle of hard lemonade and walked around and talked with the guests and the opening band. There was a good mix of male and female guests that night, with the girls hanging around the guys as usual, and some of the guys, too. A few of the guys talked with Kelly and they didn't even try to talk their way into her bed like usual.

"This is my third time seeing the band," the tall, dark-haired guy said.

"Really?" Kelly asked. "That's fantastic! Where have you seen us before?"

"When you opened for The Disciples of Man last year, and then when you did your mini tour, I saw you in Phoenix."

"Oh, wow. A true fan!"

"I like your music, and I like the fact that you don't sexualize yourself."

"Well, I thank you for being a fan. As you probably know, I'm a bit of a nerd, so I'm not into dressing like that. I'm here for the music, too!"

"We're going to see you in Phoenix again," the guy told her.

"Awesome! I'll look for you. Come backstage again if you can."

"Oh, definitely will!" he said.

Kelly spoke with more of the fans there. As they got closer to California, more of their true fans came out to see them. They had such a huge fan base in Albuquerque than anywhere else they'd been, with the exception of their home state.

A few fans wanted pictures with the entire band, so Dean got everyone together for a photo, exchanging phones so everyone got a photo if they wanted one. After that, Dean thanked everyone for coming, their cue to leave.

"See you in Phoenix," the guy said as he waved to Kelly.

"See ya!"

With the party over, the band and Jayna picked up their belongings and got everything packed away and onto the bus for their drive to Phoenix. They'd have an off day for rest tomorrow, even though the drive was fairly short, since their show wasn't until the following evening. The record company had also booked them into a hotel for the night.

"Yes! A pool!" Jake exclaimed as they walked into the lobby. The pool could be seen through the side windows of the lobby.

Dean checked them in, then led them up to their rooms, with the usual pairings together.

Once they were settled, Kelly and Jayna changed into their swimsuits, grabbed a towel and sunblock, and went downstairs to the pool. Isaac, Jake, and Ian were already there.

"Where's Paul?" Kelly asked.

"He'll be down in a while," Ian said. "He was talking to Alexa when I left."

"Everything okay there?" Kelly asked.

"I think so." Ian shrugged. "It didn't sound like they were fighting."

The girls slathered on the sunblock, got set up on a couple of lounge chairs, and then jumped into the pool.

"They have a poolside bar, too," Isaac said.

"I'm good for now," Kelly said.

Paul joined them a few minutes later and Kelly, Jayna and the guys played Marco Polo, then the guys wanted a margarita and swam over to the bar at the other end of the pool. They had shown their IDs earlier and received a wrist band. They got their margaritas and stayed by the side of the pool to drink them. Kelly and Jayna got out and lay on the lounge chairs to work on their tans.

That night the band and Jayna went to see the show at The Rebel Lounge, where Fate Struck would be playing the next night. The show wasn't sold out, so they got tickets easily at the box office. They got wristbands to buy drinks, then found a spot near the front of the stage to stand, Kelly and Jayna, being the shortest, standing in front of the guys.

At eight o'clock, the opening band came onstage and began their set. Kelly liked their music, and made a mental note to remember them when it came time to pick another opener for their tour.

The opener finished their set. Kelly remembered when they were an opener, and cheered loudly for the band as they ended their show and got their equipment off the stage. She and Jayna went to the restroom before the headliner came on.

"The opener was really good," Kelly said as she and Jayna washed their hands.

"I thought so, too," Jayna said.

"We might want to use them next time we tour."

They walked back to the main room, stopping at the bar to get another drink. They went back to their spot with the guys, who then went to the restroom, too. They came back just as the lights went down for the main band to play.

Kelly hadn't heard of the band, Midnight Ministers, and they played harder rock than Fate Struck played, but she enjoyed the music. She would look them up after they got back to their hotel.

Late in their set, the singer looked over at Kelly and the guys and Kelly watched his eyes get big and he smiled as he recognized them. The singer bent down to talk to them for a moment.

"Do you mind if I mention you guys?" he asked.

"No, not at all," Isaac said.

The singer went to the middle of the stage.

"It looks like we have some celebrities in our midst tonight," the singer said. "Fate Struck, who is playing here tomorrow night, came out to see us. Thanks for coming, you guys. That's awesome."

The fans cheered as Kelly and the guys waved, and the band started their last song.

After the show and the lights came up, Fate Struck were surrounded by a few fans wanting pictures and autographs. They signed and posed for a few of them, then someone from the venue came up to them.

"Hey, the guys would really love for you to be their guests backstage," the man said.

"You wanna go?" Isaac asked.

"Sure, why not?" Ian said.

"Yeah, let's go," Kelly said.

The man led them backstage to the dressing rooms.

"Hey, thanks again for coming to see us," the singer said. "I'm Draco."

"Draco?" Kelly said, shaking his hand. He had quite a few dragon tattoos on his arms and chest.

"I case you didn't notice, I love dragons," he said with a wink.

Kelly laughed.

"My real name is Don, but I go by Draco onstage."

The guys in the band looked close in age to Fate Struck, but were working to get to where Kelly and the guys were already at.

"Make sure you get a good demo recorded," Isaac said. "And good photos of the band. Play out as much as you can. It took us a long time to get here."

"Thanks for the advice," Don said.

The guys and Kelly and Jayna had a drink backstage with the band, took some photos with them, and talked a little more before they needed to get back to the hotel.

"It was nice meeting you," Kelly said, shaking hands with the band.

"Awesome job tonight," Jake told them.

"Come to our show tomorrow," Isaac said. "I'll get some comp tickets set up for you through our manager."

"Sounds great, thanks," Don said.

The guys, Kelly, and Jayna left and walked back to the hotel just a block away.

At breakfast the next morning, Dean asked how the show was the night before.

"It was really good," Isaac said.

"And more importantly, how was the venue?"

"It was good, too," Isaac said. "Kind of small, but the acoustics are good."

"The dressing room was fairly big," Jake said.

"You saw the dressing room?" Dean asked.

"The band invited us backstage after they saw us there," Isaac said.

"That was nice of them," Dean said.

"They also mentioned us playing there tonight, and I told them we'd comp them tickets for tonight," Isaac said.

"Okay, I'll get that set up for them," Dean said, making a note on his phone.

Kelly, Jayna, and the guys spent part of the day in the pool again, until it was time to head to the venue. Unfortunately, Paul forgot to reapply his sunblock and got a little sunburned.

"That's going to be fun tonight," he said as they were driven to the venue.

"I told you to put more on," Kelly said.

"I know, but I was too busy drinking," Paul said.

They went into the dressing room to grab some water before going out to the stage for sound check. Paul gingerly put his guitar strap over his shoulder, cringing at the pain.

After sound check, Kelly showered and dressed for the show, and drank her 5-hour energy shot. She'd had to switch from Rockstar to the energy shots since the energy drink didn't work for her anymore.

Fate Struck took the stage at their scheduled time. Paul grimaced as he put his guitar on again, and Kelly smirked. At least he didn't complain, because he knew he should have listened to her.

During one song while Jake played his solo at the front of the stage, as Kelly reached down for her bottle, a girl in front flashed Jake. Kelly caught part of it, and rolled her eyes. Jake, on the other hand, didn't miss a note, but both he and Ian smiled broadly.

"That was something I didn't need to see," she said to Ian as she went back to the mic to finish the song. Ian laughed at Kelly's reaction.

At the end of the night, Kelly thanked the fans for coming to see them.

"And thanks to Midnight Ministers for coming to see us tonight. We caught their show here last night and they were great, so next time they play, go check them out." Isaac counted off for the last song of the night. Kelly started to sing, and then noticed in the crowd, a couple of people back, stood the Mystery Guy that followed them around. Kelly glanced away quickly, though not quick enough, as the man smiled at her and winked. She looked over to Ian, who had seen her reaction and looked like he saw the man as well.

At the end of the song, the band quickly took their photos and Kelly nearly ran off the stage and was the first one into the dressing room, passing Dean in the hallway.

"What's got you so upset?" he asked, following her into the dressing room.

"That guy is here," she panted.

"He is?" Dean asked.

"Yeah," Ian said, walking into the room. "I saw him a few people back, near the flasher."

"There was a flasher?"

"Yeah, some girl sitting on a guy's shoulders."

"I wondered why you and Jake smiled so suddenly."

"Fantastic night," Isaac said sarcastically. "I'm bummed I missed the flasher."

"She wasn't that impressive," Kelly quipped.

"We'll be careful who we let backstage tonight," Dean said.

Kelly finished her Mike's and opened another.

"It was such a good night, too, the flasher notwithstanding," she said.

Dean carefully screened who came to the dressing room after the show, making sure they all had a pass, and the band also invited Midnight Minsters backstage. A lot of young women and a few young men came backstage and milled around, and the fans talked with both bands. Don joined Kelly for a drink.

"Here's to two of the best rock singers," Don said, holding up his bottle of Heineken. Kelly held up her bottle of Mike's and clinked with his.

"I'll drink to that," she said, and they both took a long drink.

The guy Kelly had spoken to in Albuquerque came backstage, and Kelly recognized him right away and walked over to him.

"You *did* come back!" she said.

"Of course, and brought a friend with me," the guy said. "He hadn't heard you before, but I think you've got a new fan."

"Fantastic!" Kelly said, shaking the friend's hand.

"Your vocals on 'No Words' were amazing," the friend said.

"Thanks so much! We worked a long time on that one to get it right."

"It shows," the guy said.

With the friend occupied later, the guy came over to Kelly again.

"I'm glad I got to come backstage again," he said. "It's all I thought about after the last show."

"How, how sweet," Kelly said, briefly touching the guy's arm.

"I was actually surprised that you invited me, knowing you'd just broken up with your boyfriend." The guy slid his arm around Kelly's waist.

Oh, crap. Did he think I invited him for some other reason?

"I think I may have given you the wrong impression," Kelly said, stepping away slightly. "I'm always happy to spend time talking to our fans and since you said you'd be here I thought we could talk more. I'm really not looking to hook-up with anyone right now."

"You sure? I could make you forget about him."

"I'm flattered, but I'm sorry. I really didn't mean to suggest that."

"Well, I guess I can say I almost made it with a rock star," he said, smiling sadly.

"You're a really cool guy, and if I *did* do that sort of thing, you'd be on the list," Kelly said.

The guy kissed Kelly on the cheek and stepped over to where his friend spoke with Paul. She sighed. She'd have to be better at what she said to fans.

When Jayna had finished at the merch table, she came back and started taking photos for their social media, getting photos of Fate Struck talking with Midnight Ministers, and she promised to tag them so they'd be on their social media as well.

Back at the hotel, Kelly, Jayna, Paul, Isaac, and Jake met in Dean's room. Ian passed on the meeting and took a girl to his room.

"Is there any way we can ban that guy?" Kelly asked.

"I don't even know who he is," Dean said. "Erik and Stevie told me that they don't even know his name, he just shows up at their gigs like he's doing with us. No name, no nothin'. Never gets a backstage pass, just comes to watch the band."

"He's creepy as hell, though," Kelly said.

"We'll try to ban him, but we don't even have a good photo of him, so it'll be hard."

"Just do whatever you can," Kelly said. "I'll just be happy to not see him ever again."

Chapter Twelve

The bus pulled into the parking lot of the venue in San Diego. This would be their last stop of the tour. Even though Kelly had thoroughly enjoyed playing concerts, she would be happy to be back home. The others expressed similar feelings.

"Well, tomorrow night, you'll be in your own beds," Dean said. "But you'll be in a hotel again tonight, because we're not driving home and coming in at four in the bloody morning."

"Thank God for that," Isaac said.

That evening, they played their hearts out for the crowd. Kelly really sensed the energy from the fans as they jumped and sang along with the songs and cheered for the band.

Kelly finished her bottle of hard lemonade and requested another. Dean brought one out to her and she set it on the drum riser behind her, alternating with water to stay hydrated.

After the last song, Kelly invited everyone up who had helped with the tour, calling Jayna up from the merch table. Dean joined them onstage, and the opener came out, too. Kelly put the mic back on the stand and they all linked arms and took a bow. Dean slipped out and took a few photos of the band with everyone, then the bands waved as they walked offstage.

There were a lot of people backstage, making it one big party. Dean had tried to make sure they all had a pass, but it seemed like everyone from the audience had come back there, it was so crowded. The press were backstage as well, taking photos and talking to both bands. Kelly tried to stick close to one of the guys, but that wasn't always feasible, as they had so many people surrounding them.

Kelly talked with a couple of fans about the show and some songs the band had worked on while on tour. People came and went as she spoke, and as she looked at the fans, she saw the Mystery Guy in the back.

"You!" she exclaimed, staring at him. The fans moved aside and the guy stepped closer to Kelly.

"What's this with you and Erik from The Disciples of Man?" he said, holding a paper out to her. Kelly grabbed the paper, which showed her and Erik on the couch after the show in New York, kissing. *Oh my God.*

"Where did you get this?" she demanded. *And how is there a picture?*

"It was in *Gossip Spot*," the guy said. Kelly knew of that site. It usually posted trash. "You were supposed to be mine, Kelly."

The guy tried to put his arms around Kelly, but she shoved him away. He came at her again, trying to kiss her this time.

"Dean!" Kelly shrieked, shoving the guy again, hard, making him fall. "Get the hell away from me!"

Dean and Ian pushed through the fans to get to the guy. As the guy stood up, Ian punched him in the mouth, knocking him to the floor again. Dean grabbed the guy with the help of one of the fans and security came in a moment later and hauled him out.

"Kelly! Don't let them take me! I'm your biggest fan!" he shouted as they took him down the hall.

Kelly, feeling brave moments before, couldn't stop shaking. Ian put his arms around her as tears fell down her cheeks. The fans gathered around them.

"He's gone now, Kel," Ian whispered to her.

She backed away for a moment, wiping at her eyes.

"Is your hand okay?" she asked, looking at his fingers. They had started to swell. "You need some ice on those."

"I'm okay," he said. The other guys had gathered around.

"How the fuck did he get backstage?" Isaac said.

"I knew I shouldn't have left it to the house security," Dean said. "I'm sorry, Kelly, it's my fault."

"It's not your fault," Kelly said, sniffling. "It's a damn circus back here. Security should have made sure he had a damn pass. My mom's going to freak out when she hears about this."

"Unfortunately, I can't do anything about what the press writes," Dean said.

"Why do all the weird things happen here in San Diego?" Kelly asked rhetorically. "That guy sending me flowers, Greg showing up, now this."

"That's the guy that's been stalking you?" a fan asked.

"Yeah, that's him," Kelly said.

"What a creeper," another said.

After that incident Dean cleared everyone out to head back to the hotel. Jayna helped Kelly gather up her stuff. Kelly was shaking so much she couldn't even roll up the cord to her curling iron.

"I got this," Jayna said. "Go sit down and take it easy."

Kelly objected at first, but when she dropped her shoes, she let Jayna do the work. Dean brought over a shot of Fireball. Kelly downed it quickly.

When they were ready to go, Dean led them out to the waiting van that would take them to their hotel. Some fans waited outside the venue, but Kelly didn't visit with them. The guys did for a few minutes, then they got into the van and Artie drove them to the hotel.

"Did they arrest that guy?" Kelly asked on the drive.

"I don't know," Dean said. "Are you nervous he might come to the hotel?"

"I don't know," Kelly said. "I'm just nervous, period."

"Do you want me to stay with you?" Ian asked softly. "If it's okay with Jayna."

"It's okay with me," Jayna said.

She really needed Ian that night, if anything, to just hold her tight.

"Okay," Kelly said.

"I'd feel better knowing you girls weren't vulnerable," Dean said, "since we know Ian packs a punch."

At the hotel, while the band and Jayna met in Dean's room, Kelly and Ian went to her room, dragging her bags with her.

Kelly took off her make-up, washed her face, and got ready for bed. Ian had taken his pants off.

"Luckily I didn't go commando tonight," he joked.

Kelly gave him half a smile.

"Just trying to make you laugh," he said.

She sat on her bed next to Ian.

"Not in a laughing mood," she said.

"I'm sorry."

"It's okay."

Ian put his arm around Kelly's shoulders and kissed the top of her head.

"Let's get you into bed so you can sleep," Ian said.

They stood and Kelly pulled back the blankets and got into bed. Ian covered her up and kissed her forehead.

"I'll sleep on the couch," he said.

"No," Kelly said.

"No?" Ian asked.

"I need you with me tonight."

"You're sure?"

She nodded. He climbed over her and got into bed next to her.

She lay her head on his chest, and he put his arm around her and held her close. Kelly felt safe in his arms. She slid her hand under his shirt and stroked his chest. Ian lifted her face to his and looked into her eyes, and in answer to her unspoken question, kissed her. She turned on her back and Ian lay beside her, kissing her face and neck. He took off her pajama top and caressed her breast while taking the other into his mouth, running his tongue around the pink center. Kelly arched into him and he moved his hand underneath her and pulled her close.

Eager to feel his skin on hers, she tugged at his shirt. He stopped what he was doing long enough to pull it off, then kissed her neck and chest. Those kisses made Kelly's skin tingle and her heart flutter. *God, that feels good.*

Ian moved his hand slowly down her body, barely touching her. His touch sent tingles through her, like a summer breeze on her skin, it was so light. His hand found its way between her legs, and his fingers inside her. He slid them in and out, and her breaths came short and quick. He grabbed his pants and found the condom in his pocket and rolled it on. He moved between her legs and slowly entered her.

Kelly kissed Ian as she put her hands on his back, feeling every muscle definition. Ian kept himself in shape even while on the road, working out when he could. She put her arms around him and he nuzzled her neck as they moved together.

Ian and Kelly climaxed and the waves diminished until they moved no more. Ian lay on top of Kelly, propped up on his forearms, kissing her face gently.

"That was fantastic," Kelly whispered.

"That was fucking intense," Ian said. He rolled off onto the bed and then pulled her to him, spooning together. He gently brushed her hair with his hand, kissing the back of her neck.

"I'm glad you're here tonight," Kelly said.

"This wasn't why I'm staying here, though," Ian said.

"I know. You were going to sleep on the couch. I wanted this. I *needed* this. You make me feel safe."

Just as Kelly started to doze off, her phone *dinged*. She reached over to the nightstand to see who texted her.

"What is it?" Ian asked.

Kelly giggled.

"It's Jayna," she said, "wanting to know if it's safe to come into the room."

Kelly tapped out her reply.

"Yes, it's safe."

Five minutes later, Jayna came in.

"Sorry, you guys," she said. "But I can't stay awake any longer."

"It's okay," Kelly said. "Sorry to make you wait."

Jayna went into the bathroom to change and wash her face.

"No worries," Jayna said when she came back. She got into her bed. "Good night."

"Good night," Kelly and Ian said in unison.

Kelly awoke the next morning, still in Ian's arms. She had a headache, and really needed to pee. She looked at the clock on the nightstand and saw it was almost nine.

She turned over and saw Ian sleeping soundly next to her. She tried to get out of bed without waking him, but as she pulled on her shirt, he stirred.

"Good morning," she whispered.

"Morning," he said.

She pulled on her pants and went to the bathroom, and came back a few moments later.

"How's your hand today?"

Ian looked at his hand and flexed it. It was bruised but nothing broken.

"It's good, just a bit sore. It's a good thing we're done with the tour, though. It would really hurt to play."

While Ian got dressed, Kelly pulled out a pair of sweatpants, a t-shirt, and a change of underwear and went back to the bathroom to change. She brushed her hair and her teeth, and came out again.

Ian used the bathroom next, and by the time he was ready to go, Jayna had awakened.

"Did we wake you?" Kelly asked.

"No," Jayna said. "I need to get up so we can get home."

"I'm gonna go get my stuff together," Ian said. He looked at Kelly. "Are you okay for now?"

"Yes, thank you," Kelly said. "I think it's okay for you to go."

"Just don't open the door unless it's one of us," he told her.

"Okay," she said.

He left and Kelly made a cup of tea with the kettle in the room, then continued getting her belongings together. She and Jayna were ready half an hour later, but before they could leave, Kelly's phone rang. She picked it up and saw her mom's number.

"Hi, Mom," Kelly answered.

"Are you okay?" Mom asked.

"Yeah, why?"

"There was an article online that said some guy got backstage and tried to attack you!"

"So you heard about that," Kelly said, looking at Jayna, who frowned.

"Yes! I just saw it and didn't care if I woke you up. I needed to know you're okay."

"Yeah, it was a little scary for a few minutes, but Dean and Ian took care of the guy. Ian's got a bruised hand, though."

"Why's that?"

"He decked the guy, then Dean threw the guy out, almost literally."

"You're really okay?"

"Yeah. Ian stayed in our room last night to make sure we were safe. The room has a couch."

"I wasn't going to say anything, but I'm glad you clarified," Mom said.

"We're in the middle of packing to come home, so I'll see you in a couple hours," Kelly said.

"Okay. I love you, sweetheart."

"Love you, too, Mom," Kelly said, and she ended the call.

"Nice way to word things," Jayna said.

"I didn't want my mom to be stressed more than she already is," Kelly said. "I'm an adult but I'm still their little 'pumpkin,'" she said.

Kelly and Jayna looked around to make sure they hadn't left anything behind. Kelly's and Jayna's phones *dinged*. Dean had texted them to meet him and the guys at the elevator. Kelly grabbed her bag and suitcase, got her keycard and she and Jayna left the room.

Back on the bus for the last time, everyone got the rest of their belongings together. Kelly's stuff had migrated all over the bus, along with the others' belongings.

"I kind of expected it," Dean said after Kelly apologized. "You're young adults and you need a lot of items to keep you busy and beautiful."

"It's hard to stay this beautiful," Jake said with a toss of his head. Kelly threw a make-up sponge at him, which he caught and pretended to powder his face

They finished getting their stuff together just as Artie exited the freeway to drive to Dean's house. Artie pulled up to the front of the house, and everyone got their luggage off first, then helped to unload all the snacks, game consoles, and everything else they'd accumulated in the four months they'd been on the road. Dean took the snacks into his house for meetings and rehearsals.

When the bus was emptied of all their stuff, Jayna told Kelly she could ride home with her and Marty.

"Thanks," Kelly said. It was a bittersweet end to the tour. She'd started the tour with a boyfriend and now they were no more.

Jayna called Marty and he'd be there to pick them up shortly. Ian called his mom to come pick him up. Isaac wasn't about to call his parents, and had Hayley come get him and Jake. Paul called his mom.

Marty was the first to arrive. Kelly and Jayna hugged the guys and Dean.

"It was certainly entertaining," Kelly said as she picked up her bag and luggage.

"We'll see you in a few days," Dean said.

"Bye," Kelly and Jayna said in unison.

Marty pulled up to Kelly's house and he and Jayna helped her take her bags to the porch.

"Text me later," Jayna said.

"Will do," Kelly said. "I love you, Jayna. Thanks for being such a good friend."

"Love you, too," Jayna said, hugging her friend.

"Thanks for the ride!"

"No problem," Marty said.

Kelly went inside, dragging her bags behind her.

"I'm so glad you're home!" Mom said, jumping up to help Kelly.

"Me, too," Kelly said, "even if it's only for a month."

"You can get rested at least," Mom said. "Did you eat enough? You look like you've lost weight."

"I might have," Kelly said. "I haven't weighed myself since I've been gone. We ate, but I burn a lot of energy onstage."

Kelly went and stood on the bathroom scale. She'd lost five pounds.

"I'll have to eat and gain that back before we go to Canada," she told her mom.

"Well, some home-cooked meals will fix that right away," Mom said. "I'm making lasagna tonight for dinner."

"Ooh, my favorite," Kelly said.

"I've had a lot of phone calls from your aunts and cousins," Mom said. "Wanting to know if you were okay after last night. I'm glad I called you this morning. They were all really worried. David was about to drive to San Diego and bring you back home."

"Gotta love David," Kelly said.

"He'll be here for dinner tonight, too."

Kelly took her luggage to her room and sorted through it to do laundry. Once she got the washer going, she went back and took stock of what she'd need when they went back on the road. She spread out everything on her bed. Her make-up looked okay, but she'd need to get more make-up remover before then. She put everything away and her bedroom looked back to normal.

At dinner, Kelly told her family about life on the road and all the places they visited.

"We visited a lot of museums," Kelly said. "Jayna, Ian, and I usually hung out together and did the artsy stuff while the others went to the bars or played video games."

"I'm gonna have to come with you," David said, "to keep an eye on you and keep creepers away."

"I've got four adopted brothers and an uncle with me," Kelly said, laughing. "They take care of me."

"They didn't last night," David said.

"He got back there because security was shit last night. Dean apologized, but it's not his fault. Ian decked the guy."

"Being around five guys didn't help your language any," Mom chided.

"Oops, sorry. Yeah, some of their bad habits rubbed off on me. That and sleeping until eleven, although when you get to bed at three in the morning, that's eight hours right there."

"How was life on the bus?" Dad asked.

"Cramped," Kelly said. "It's like a huge motorhome, but with bunks. The bunks have curtains so we get some shred of privacy. The novelty wore off pretty quick, though. I preferred using the showers in the dressing rooms to the one of the bus. More room and only Jayna and I used the women's side."

After dinner, Kelly texted Jayna.

"Did U get the 3rd degree when U got home?" Kelly asked.

Jayna replied a moment later.

"Yeah. My parents wanted 2 make sure there was privacy 4 us."

"I accidently slipped a swear word and my mom wasn't pleased," Kelly tapped out.

"Comes with the territory."

"That's what I said. LOL."

They texted a little more, then Kelly went to put her laundry away.

***

Isaac was happy to be home with Hayley. She helped Isaac and Jake bring in their luggage, and then she and Isaac drove to In

& Out for lunch. They drove back to his apartment to eat and found Jake had left, most likely to go see Missy.

After they ate, they sat on the couch and watched a movie, Isaac with his arm around Hayley, and she held his other hand on his lap. He had been away from her for so long, and had missed her so much. He felt a little guilty for being with other women, but he'd only wanted her.

Isaac kissed Hayley's neck. She turned to him and he kissed her lips. They kissed on the couch for a long time before Isaac stood up, took her hand, and led her to his bedroom.

Chapter Thirteen

Fate Struck had been home a few days when Dean texted them to meet at his house.

Kelly picked up Jayna and drove over that afternoon. She heard voices in the living room and knocked on the door then they walked in.

"Just waiting for Paul and Ian," Dean said.

"Technically they're not late yet," Isaac said.

Dean got the girls a bottle of Mike's while they waited for Ian and Paul. Ian walked in a few moments later, and Paul five minutes after him.

"Hey, not as late as usual," Isaac joked.

"I'm really trying to be better," Paul said.

After everyone had a bottle of something, Dean started the meeting.

"I have a few things that I didn't want to text about," Dean began. "First off—drum roll, please, Isaac."

Isaac drummed on the table with his hands.

"The CD has been certified gold!" Dean said.

"What?!"

"That's crazy!"

"Fucking awesome!"

"So, in a couple days, we'll drive up to the offices so they can present you with a gold record. Also, you've been invited to appear on *The Nightly Show with Anton*."

Oh my God! We're going to be on TV? Kelly thought. She'd never really thought about that. She thought it'd just be concerts and festivals. TV? She looked at Jayna, who gave her a broad smile and squeezed her hand.

"Hittin' the big time!" Jake said. "When?"

"Next week. We'll leave the day before and come back the day after the show. I'll send them your rider and see what they can do," Dean said.

"If they can't provide all of it, it's not a big deal," Isaac said. "It's not like we're going to be there for two weeks."

"We don't need *all* the alcohol backstage," Jake said. "Just beer and Mike's really."

Dean made notes on his tablet.

"Okay, I will get in touch with them and then let you know the firm details."

"Sounds good," Isaac said.

"And one more thing," Dean said. "We've added a few more US dates to the Canadian part of the tour. Just a couple places we missed, now that your record is certified gold, more venues are wanting you."

"Fantastic," Ian said.

"That's all the news I have for you. You can hang out here for a while if you want, play games, whatever, while I go make some phone calls."

Isaac got the Switch game console set up and they took turns playing games, even Kelly and Jayna, who knew nothing about the games.

"I'm more of a book person," Kelly said, as she died in the game for a second time, and handed the controller back to Paul.

The band stayed for just over an hour, then everyone left one by one. Kelly and Jayna left and went to the mall. Kelly wanted to see if there was anything new to buy for her stage clothes as they walked into Hot Topic.

As they browsed through the store, a couple of giggling girls came up to them.

"Are you Kelly from Fate Struck?" the taller girl asked.

That's something I didn't think about, Kelly thought.

"I am," Kelly said aloud, smiling.

"Oh my God! I didn't know you shopped here!" the girl's friend said.

"I buy a lot of my clothes here," Kelly said.

"Ooh, do you think we could get your autograph?"

"Sure!" Kelly said.

"Would you like a photo with her?" Jayna asked.

"Can we?"

"Sure!" Kelly said.

Jayna took a photo of the girls with their phones, then as Kelly signed their Hot Topic receipt, Jayna took photos of the interaction with the girls.

After the girls left, Kelly found a blouse she really liked.

"For *The Nightly Show*?" Jayna asked.

144

"Maybe," Kelly said.

"I think you should. It's great."

When Kelly checked out, the cashier also asked if she was from Fate Struck. When Kelly told him yes, he also asked for a photo, which Jayna happily took.

"I used to see you in here a lot," the cashier said. "Haven't seen you in a while."

"Yeah, we've been on tour for four months," Kelly told him. "We're about to go back out."

"Thanks for shopping with us," the cashier said.

"You're welcome," Kelly said, and she and Jayna left the store.

"You didn't mind taking the photo, did you?" Jayna asked. "I just thought it was nice."

"No, not at all! Unless they're being a bitch about it, I don't mind."

Kelly and Jayna walked up and down the mall, looking in other stores but not buying anything else. A few more fans recognized Kelly, then feeling slightly uncomfortable with the attention, she and Jayna left.

After dropping Jayna at home, Kelly went home and excitedly told her parents the news about the TV show they'd appear on.

"That's great, honey," Mom said.

"Things are moving quickly," Dad said, giving her a high-five.

"I got recognized in the mall, too," she said. "I'm going to have to do the whole 'baseball cap and sunglasses' like all the celebrities do."

"Well, you're one of those celebrities now," Mom reminded her.

"Hey, yeah." Dad got up from his chair quickly and stood by Kelly, holding his phone out to pretend to take a photo. "Can I get a picture with you?"

"Oh, Dad." She gave him a playful push. "Not now, I'm sooo busy," she said, smiling. "But seriously, I don't feel like a celebrity. I still just feel like me."

"That's good. It hasn't gone to your head," Dad said, as he put his phone away.

"Hey, Mom, will you take our picture? I don't have any photos of Dad and me, or you and me for that matter."

Mom stood and Kelly handed her the phone. Mom took a picture, then gave the phone to Dad, who took a photo of Kelly and her mom.

"Thanks. Love you guys."

***

Isaac's phone rang. He pulled it out of his pocket and saw it was his father.

What does he want now?

He hit *Accept.*

"Hey, Dad," Isaac answered.

"I just heard the news that the CD went gold, and you're going to be on *The Nightly Show with Anton.*"

Uncle Dean must have told him.

"Yeah, it's great. I think that's happening next week."

"I didn't realize how popular the band is, and the CD must be good if it's certified gold."

"Did you think it wasn't good? You've heard the songs."

"It's not that I thought it wasn't good," his father said. "I didn't think you were that well known."

"We have quite a following here, and with the single and CD releases, we have fans across the country now."

"Dean told me about the man who got backstage and harassed Kelly. Is she okay?"

"What's with all the concern all of a sudden? You never cared before, except how it made *you* look."

"I was upset when you quit school, because I didn't think you'd make enough to support yourself with music, and you'd be out of the scholarship, and then I'd have to foot the bill."

"Well, it's a good thing we're making money."

Was it really all about the money?

"That came out wrong," his father said. "You and I haven't been on the best of terms and I know it would've killed you to have me pay for it. I wanted you to do it on your own."

At least he acknowledged that, Isaac thought.

"I had hoped you'd follow in my footsteps into the business world. I was excited when you took business classes. I thought maybe you'd come around," his father continued.

"I took the classes so I'd know if we were getting ripped off as a group, as well as to learn how to manage the band, which I did for a while, and according to Uncle Dean, I did it well."

"He did tell me you had handled everything really well."

"To answer your question—Kelly is okay. Ian decked the guy and Dean tossed him out."

"Good," his dad said. "Well, good luck on *The Nightly Show*."

"Thanks," Isaac said. "Bye."

"Goodbye."

Isaac disconnected and tossed his phone onto the coffee table. Maybe he'd finally earned a little respect from his dad for what he's doing.

***

Dean led the band and Jayna through the airport to check in. Since they were only staying two nights, they all just brought a carry-on with their clothes and toiletries. The guys had their guitars in the checked baggage, but Isaac would use a rented drum set for the show. It wasn't feasible to drag his entire drum kit with him for just one show. Ian, Jake, and Paul would use rented amps. Kelly had brought her effects box with her, but would use the studio's mics.

They landed in New York five and a half hours later. They grabbed their luggage and made their way out of the airport to the waiting van that would take them to their hotel, which was only a half-block from the studio where *The Nightly Show with Anton* was recorded. At the hotel, Dean got them checked in and they went up to their rooms until it was dinner time, and walked across the street to a restaurant.

After dinner, Kelly and Jayna went back to their room while the guys explored the city. Kelly took a photo out the hotel room window and sent it to her parents.

"Look at this view!" she texted.

Kelly and Jayna went to bed early. Kelly wanted to be well-rested for the next day. They had to be at the studio at two for sound check, then they'd get ready for the recording of the show at five.

"Are you nervous?" Jayna asked.

"Not about the performance," Kelly said, "but for the interview after we play."

"I say let Isaac do the talking," Jayna said. "It's technically his band, but I'm sure you'll be asked some questions, too."

"I just don't want to sound like an idiot."

"You won't." Jayna laughed as she pulled up her blankets. "Just be yourself."

Kelly and Jayna joined Dean and the guys for breakfast in the dining room of the hotel. The hotel had an area partitioned off for them so they could eat away from other guests and prying eyes. After breakfast, they spent the morning in Isaac's and Jake's room playing video games. Kelly watched while the others played, cheering them on.

At 1:15, Dean had the band get their things together for the show. Kelly had hung her outfit in the closet in a garment bag to get out any wrinkles. She got her make-up kit and made sure she had everything she'd need, then took a quick shower before they met at the elevator to go downstairs to the waiting limo. Their instruments had been taken straight to the studio the night before.

Kelly had never been inside a television studio before. Right now, there was no audience, of course, and they were getting the sets ready for the taping. The music director greeted the band and Dean.

"This will probably be a little different sound check for you," the director said. He went over a few things with the band, and then had them put in their in-ear monitors to get that set up first, then they moved on to instruments and then voices. The band would be playing their single on the show. They ran through it a few times, which was nothing new to them, until everyone was satisfied. Kelly looked at her watch and was surprised it had been over an hour.

In the dressing room, Kelly dressed and put on her make-up, as did the guys, then someone from the make-up department came to touch up the make-up to prevent any shiny spots on their faces. A stylist took some mousse and scrunched Kelly's hair just a bit to add in waves and some curls. She wore it loose around her shoulders.

"Wow, Kelly," Jayna said as she watched. "You look fabulous."

Kelly and Jayna walked back to the dressing room and nibbled on some of the food there. Kelly left the alcohol alone, wanting to be at her best for the show. The boys drank a bottle of beer.

The group waited in the green room for their turn to go on. They could watch the show on the monitors in the room. Fate Struck would go on second to last.

Also appearing on the show that night was Dwayne Johnson. He came over and introduced himself.

"I'm sorry to say I've only heard a couple of your songs," Dwayne said, as he shook everyone's hand. "I've liked what I heard, though."

"That's awesome!" Isaac said. Kelly was too nervous to talk to him, and just smiled. He seemed even bigger in real life than on the movie screen.

"I've seen almost all your films," Jake said. "Loved 'The Rundown.'"

The door opened and the stage manager stepped in to take Dwayne out to the studio.

"Break a leg tonight!" he said, and with a wave, he left.

Kelly could hardly breathe. She'd just met Dwayne Johnson!

"Kelly," Dean said, bringing her back down to Earth. "They're probably going to ask about doing a flip or whatever, so do what you're comfortable doing."

"I figured they would. They always do." She laughed.

Isaac looked at the production schedule on the wall.

"We go on in half an hour," he said.

Kelly warmed up her voice and stretched her legs and back. She had worn her purple Chucks on the flight to New York, knowing that she'd need them just in case they did ask her to do a flip. Plus, she wouldn't have to bring another pair of shoes in her carry-on.

The stage manager came to the green room just as the show went to a commercial break.

"Let's get you out there," she said.

Fate Struck, Dean, and Jayna followed her out to the stage, where the music director helped them get in their places and put on their mics for the interview, Jayna and Dean standing off to the side of the stage behind the curtains. Kelly was excited but not nervous. It was just another gig to her—for the moment. She wasn't looking forward to the interview portion. She put that out of her head as the stage manager got the audience clapping as they came back from the commercial break.

"Our next guest is a band that is taking the country by storm," Anton began. "They're currently getting ready to head out on the Canadian part of their tour. Here to play their single 'The Lies That You Tell,' off their self-titled certified gold CD, let's welcome Fate Struck."

The audience applauded and the stage manager pointed at them. Isaac counted off the song and they began to play.

Kelly's voice was in perfect form and she used what she could of the stage, remembering what the director had said before she'd be out of range and camera view. The guys performed their parts well, Paul even gave a quick smile, something he hardly ever did onstage.

When they finished the song, the audience applauded and cheered loudly for them. They waved as they were directed to the couch by the stage manager. Isaac sat closest to him, then Kelly and the others.

Anton welcomed them to the show and then went into a few questions that Isaac confidently answered. After a few more questions directed at each of them, Anton had another question.

"You all were in high school together, right?" Anton asked.

Kelly took the question.

"Yeah," she said. "A couple of us have known each other since elementary school."

"So you just decided to form a band?"

"Well, I started the band with the guys," Isaac said. "But we needed a singer. I mean, Ian and Jake can sing, but we wanted a front person. We heard Kelly and Jayna sing in the school choir at their Spring Concert, and we asked them to join the band."

"But there's only one singer here," Anton joked. "You kick her out already?"

"No, no," Kelly said, laughing. "While she likes to sing, it wasn't what Jayna wanted to do. But she works for us, so she's with us anyway, and I have my best friend with me all the time."

"I also heard that in high school, Kelly, you were a gymnast."

"I was," Kelly said. "I still workout with a team at the community college, but I don't do competitions anymore."

"Would you do a flip for us?"

"Oh, I don't know," Kelly giggled. Of course she would, but she wanted to make it look like she wasn't sure.

"Oh, come on," Anton pleaded. "We've even got some mats set up for you."

Kelly looked over and they did indeed have several mats laid out on the floor. She hadn't noticed them before.

The audience chanted, "Kelly! Kelly!"

"Okay," she said. The guys and the audience clapped as she walked out to the mats. While the band had been home, Kelly had gotten her confidence back while practicing with the college team, and could do more than just a walkover.

She stood at the end of the mats, pointed her left foot, held her arms up, and then did a round-off, backflip, and aerial walkover, landing with her arms up again.

The audience cheered louder than before, and Kelly waved as she went back to her seat on the couch.

"Wow! That was awesome!" Anton said, clapping. "Was it hard to make the decision to do music instead of gymnastics?"

"Not really," Kelly said. "I stepped down from elite gymnastics while in high school to focus on singing, and I don't regret it."

"I don't think anyone does," he said. He held up the CD for the camera. "Fate Struck! Go get it now. Thank you so much for being on the show."

"Thank you!" they said.

The stage manager came up and unhooked their mics from their clothes and they shook hands with Anton again as they walked off the set to the audience applause. Dean and Jayna met them as they came off the stage.

"That was awesome!" Jayna said.

"Well done, guys and girl," Dean said.

"I didn't sound like a dork?" Kelly asked.

"No! You were great!" Dean said. "You all kept the conversation going. Sounded good and I think it was a success."

When they got back to the hotel, everyone called their family and friends to let them know the show would be broadcast that night at eleven thirty.

"Are you going to stay up to watch it?" Jayna asked.

"I don't know," Kelly said. "Not sure I want to hear myself talk."

"You sounded fine," Jayna assured her. "You sound like you always do."

After dinner, everyone went to their rooms until it was time for the show to start and then they gathered in Dean's room. Jayna had convinced Kelly to at least join everyone to watch.

Dean had bought snacks, and everyone passed around the bag of chips and grabbed cookies from the box as the show came on.

"Dwayne Johnson was super nice," Kelly said as they watched Dwayne talk to Anton.

After the second guest, the band would be next. Jayna got ready to go Live on Instagram during the show. The commercial break was over and Anton introduced the band, and they played their song. The song lasted three and a half minutes and Anton spoke with them for the fifteen minute interview, then Kelly did her gymnastic skills.

"That was the only time I wasn't nervous after we played," Kelly said.

"You looked awesome," Jayna said.

"You really did," Ian agreed.

The show went to commercial and everyone's phones started to beep.

"'Congratulations on the successful interview'," Dean read from his phone. "From Jim at Tyrian Records."

"'Lookin' good on those flips! Congratulations,'" Kelly read. "From Erik."

"Of course from Erik," Isaac said.

"'You all looked adorable on the show,'" Jake read. "From my mom."

Kelly scrolled through all the messages, which were up to twenty on her phone. She saw that Maggie from MagNetic had texted her.

"Maggie says 'Great job, everyone,'" Kelly said.

"You have Maggie's number?" Ian asked.

"Yes," Kelly said. "Why?"

"I just didn't realize you two were friends."

"She gave me her number at the party we went to. She's super cool. I called her before we left to ask her for tips on doing the show."

"The first of many TV spots, I hope," Dean said.

After an hour of talking about the show, Dean reminded them that they did have a flight to catch the next morning. Kelly and Jayna stood up.

"We'll get going, then," Kelly said.

Back in their room, Jayna read more of the posts from the band's social media accounts to Kelly. Kelly didn't want to see the negative ones, so Jayna looked them over before reading them aloud.

"So far there hasn't been one negative reaction," Jayna said.

"And how many of these posts are from family?" Kelly asked jokingly.

"Actually, hardly any of them. You guys did a great job on the show."

Kelly hoped that things stayed that way, hoping the bubble didn't burst.

Chapter Fourteen

The band arrived back in California the next afternoon, Dean dropping everyone off at home. Before anyone left the van, Dean reminded them about the gold record presentation.

"We'll be driving to the offices the day after tomorrow," Dean told them. "I'll send a text with the exact time we'll be going."

"Okie dokie," Kelly said as she stepped out of the van, pulling her bag behind her.

On the day of the presentation, Kelly was ready well before the time Dean had texted to them. She hadn't meant to get ready so early, but she was really excited about the presentation. People seeing their shows was one thing, but having a gold record showed how popular they had become.

The limo pulled up to Kelly's house and Dean stepped out and knocked on the door.

"Bye, Mom!" Kelly said as she went out the door.

"Bye, honey," Mom called after her.

After picking up the guys, the driver got on the freeway for the hour drive to Tyrian Record's building.

They arrived at the building and Jim greeted them on the fifth floor.

"Congratulations!" he said, shaking everyone's hand. "I've got some more great news for you! 'The Lies That You Tell' has also been certified gold."

"What?" Isaac asked. "That's fantastic!"

"We'll give you that one today, as well. Come on, let's get the champagne going!"

Jim handed everyone a glass and one of the assistants poured champagne into them.

The vice president of Tyrian Records stood to get everyone's attention.

"Thank you all for coming today," he started. "This is a happy day for all of us, but especially for Kelly, Isaac, Ian, Paul, and Jake of Fate Struck, and Dean Landry, their manager. It gives me great pleasure to present this certified gold record to Fate Struck."

154

Everyone applauded, and the VP asked, "Who gets this?"

"Isaac," Kelly, Ian, Jake, and Paul said in unison.

"It's his band," Ian said.

Isaac stepped up next to the VP and photos were taken of him being handed the framed disk and then holding the disk with the others around him.

"Also, we have a certified gold single for 'The Lies That You Tell,'" the VP continued, holding up the framed disk. "Who gets this one?"

"Kelly," the guys said.

"Why me?" Kelly asked.

"You wrote it," Isaac said.

"So did Ian," Kelly protested.

"You deserve it," Ian said, "for having to put up with Jess."

Kelly smiled, and stepped over next to the VP for the photo ops.

"Here's to Fate Struck," the VP said, holding up his glass.

Everyone held their glasses up and then drank.

"And here's to the many more gold records in your future," Jim said, also holding his glass high.

Everyone drank to that as well.

Kelly looked around at everyone there. She couldn't believe that all those people were there for the band, wanting to talk to them and take their picture. Her stomach was doing flip-flops with excitement, and it was hard to not giggle like a little kid at the attention they received that day. One of the photographers asked Kelly for a photo. She set her glass down, held up the disk and gave a peace sign with the biggest smile as the photographer took the photo.

The party died down an hour later and everyone started to leave. The band and Dean said their goodbyes to everyone and went downstairs to their waiting limo.

Kelly couldn't believe she was holding a gold record. Never in her wildest dreams could she have imagined this. She just liked to sing.

"Look at this!" she said when she walked into her house.

"You got to keep it?" Mom asked from her chair she'd been reading in.

"We got two today," Kelly said, handing the disk to her mom. "We got one for our album and one for our single. The guys said I get this one because I helped write it. We told Isaac he gets the album one."

"That is so amazing," Mom said, handing the disk to Kelly's dad.

"Well done, pumpkin," Dad said. "I can still call you that, can't I?"

"Of course you can," Kelly said with a smile.

Dad handed the disk back to Kelly.

"Can you take a picture of me with it?" Kelly asked.

"Sure," Dad said, switching off the TV.

Kelly handed him her phone and he took a couple of pictures for her.

"Thanks, Dad," Kelly said.

"My pleasure," Dad said.

Kelly went to her room and held it up in different places. She decided on the wall directly opposite of her door, so it was the first thing she saw when she entered.

"Perfect!" she said.

She found some hooks and put them up on the wall and then hung the disk up. Kelly heard a tap on her door, turned around and saw Jayna in the doorway.

"That is awesome!" Jayna said.

"Isn't it fantastic?" Kelly asked.

"You guys are totally on your way."

"Four years ago I never would've guessed that we'd have a gold record," Kelly said. "I was happy doing the corporate gigs, but we took it to the next level. I never expected this."

"You guys are a great band, and you have fantastic stage presence, plus you're not stuck on yourself in the least. People like that."

Kelly shrugged.

"I'm just me."

"And that's why they like you. You're approachable. Like those two girls in Hot Topic, they weren't afraid to come up to you."

"I hope I stay this way," Kelly said.

"I'm sure you will."

***

Isaac and Jake got dropped off at their building. Inside their condo, they decided on where to hang it.

"Before we hang it up," Isaac said. "I want to take it to show my parents."

"I thought you didn't like your dad," Jake said.

"I don't, but I want him to see something tangible for my efforts. He kind of made an effort the other day with trying to reconcile. I don't know if that will ever happen, but I want him to see this isn't just a hobby anymore."

Isaac took the disk to his car and drove to his parents' house.

"Anyone home?" Isaac called out as he stepped inside the house.

"In the family room," his mom called out.

Isaac went in and saw his parents watching TV.

"I thought you'd like to see the gold record we got," Isaac said, handing the disk to his mom.

"This is beautiful," his mom said. "It's heavy, too."

"I think most of that is the case," Isaac said.

His mom handed the disk to his dad, who studied it.

"Congratulations, Isaac," his dad finally said. "This is very nice."

"I wanted to show you before we hung it on our wall," Isaac said as his father handed the disk back to him.

"Your band is doing so well," his mom said.

"We really didn't expect this, but we'll take it," Isaac said.

"I guess it's really worked out with Kelly being the singer," his dad said.

"It's fantastic," Isaac said. "She's a great front person and singer. It's nice having a girl in the band. We draw the girls and she draws the guys."

"Doesn't anyone like you for the music?" his dad asked.

Of course he'd have a comment, Isaac thought, but he decided to keep the peace and not say anything sarcastic.

"Oh, yeah, they all do, but they get a bonus with the show."

157

Just before Isaac left his parents' house, he got a text from Dean.

"Hey, Dean says he wants to throw a party for us for our gold record status," Isaac told his parents. "He says he'll send out invites shortly."

"We'll look for it, then," his mom said.

Isaac picked up the disk.

"I'll see you later," he said as he went out the door.

Isaac drove to Hayley's house to show her the disk. Her parents were there and also wanted to see it.

"That is impressive," Hayley's father said.

"Isn't Isaac great?" Hayley asked, kissing Isaac's cheek.

Isaac told them all about the party and to look for an invitation soon.

"We look forward to it!" Hayley's mother said.

***

The party was held at the Marriott in Long Beach. Dean had invited several other bands, including The Disciples of Man and MagNetic. He told the musicians to bring their instruments if they wanted, and many of them did.

Kelly spoke with all the guests, and when she saw her parents come in, she ran over to them.

"I'm so glad you came!" she said, hugging them both.

"We wouldn't miss it," Dad said. "David should be in any minute, too."

As if on cue, David walked up to Kelly and their parents.

"Hey, big bro," Kelly said, hugging him as well.

"Hey, Kel," David said. "This is really cool, getting a gold record."

"Right? Never thought *that* would happen."

Kelly pointed them in the direction of the refreshments, and saw her former gymnastic teammates standing by the table and walked over to them.

"I'm so happy to see you!" Kelly squealed, throwing her arms around a couple of girls.

"Goin' big time," Emily said, smiling.

"I know! Couldn't believe it when Dean told us."

"Ian's looking good with Lena Hendricks on his arm," Tinley said. Kelly turned and saw Ian and Lena talking with Dean. Kelly felt a twinge of jealousy, but only for a moment. She and Ian weren't together, and she was genuinely happy for him to have found someone that wasn't a complete psycho.

"Yeah, he does," Kelly said.

"And Erik looked good on your lips," Emily said.

"God, I hate *G-Spot*," Kelly said. "I don't know how they got the photo."

"So it didn't happen?" Elena asked.

Ugh, Kelly thought. *Do I lie or tell the truth?* She decided the truth was better.

"It happened, but it was without consent. We'd been talking, then he started to flirt and then he kissed me."

"Is he a good kisser?" Tinley asked.

Kelly blushed.

"That kiss was like two seconds long. Not long enough to gather info about it. I pushed him away."

The ladies groaned, but Emily smiled at Kelly. Kelly knew that Emily thought she'd done the right thing.

The parents and siblings had gathered off to the side of the room while the friends all mingled together. Kelly couldn't believe that all these people were there for *them*.

When it looked like everyone had arrived, Dean got on the microphone.

"I'm so glad you all were able to come tonight," he acknowledged. "I wanted to give Fate Struck this party to show how proud I am of them. They've worked really hard to get to this point, never complaining, not even when they'd been on the road for four months.

"They're very smart about things and always want to learn what they can about the business, and they just go with the flow when things go wrong." Dean grabbed his bottle of beer and held it up. "Here's to Fate Struck! It seems fate has struck and you're where you're meant to be. Here's to another five hundred thousand sales!"

Everyone held up their drink and toasted the band.

"Oh! I wanted to mention one other person. Jayna has been such a tremendous help to us with everything we do. She works the merchandise table, helps clean up the dressing rooms, and watches out for all of the band, but especially for Kelly. It not easy living with a bunch of guys for months on end in a cramped glorified motorhome, so it's been nice for Kelly to have a friend there with her to keep her company. So, here's to Jayna!"

Everyone held their glasses up again. Kelly hugged Jayna, who blushed and stood wide-eyed by Dean's speech.

"I'm happy to do it," Jayna said to Kelly.

"I know, but you really are a big help, especially to me."

"In a few minutes we'll have some entertainment by some of the guests here tonight," Dean was saying. "I hope you'll stick around for that. Thanks, everyone."

Loud cheers went up from the guests and the music was turned back on low.

Half an hour later, Dean got Fate Struck up onstage to play. After they played three songs, Kelly asked the other musicians to come up and play with them. When everyone was set up, they settled on "Interstate Love Song" by Stone Temple Pilots. Kelly, Erik, and Maggie took turns singing the lead, and the other musicians played together on their parts, improvising if they didn't know the part.

The musicians played a few more songs together and got the crowd dancing. Kelly saw her parents dancing and David danced with Jake's sister, who was a couple years older than Jake.

After the jam, Kelly stepped down from the stage and got a hard lemonade and went to sit along the wall where it was a little quieter. Erik came and sat down next to her.

"You guys should be very proud of yourselves," he said.

"I never even thought about gold records," Kelly said. "I just wanted to make music."

"And make music you did! That was fun jamming up there with you guys."

"Yeah, it was! We need to do it more often."

"Do you want to go outside and get some air?"

"Sure."

They went out onto the balcony and looked out over the city and the ocean. The hotel was only a block from the beach.

"I'm glad Dean invited us to come, because I hardly ever get a chance to relax and see scenes like this," Erik said. "I miss it."

"Are you from here?" Kelly asked.

"I grew up in Anaheim, close enough to go to the beach, but didn't go very often once I was in a band."

"That's unfortunate. I'd die without the beach, I think."

The sea breeze blew Kelly's hair from her face. Erik stroked her hair, then moved to her back.

"You really are beautiful," Erik said quietly.

"I don't think I am, but thank you. I always see myself as a nerd."

"Well, nerds can be beautiful, too."

He caressed her neck, then bent down to kiss her. She knew she should pull away, but God, it felt good. *This gorgeous guy could have anyone he wants, and he wants to be with me?* His kisses were light at first, then more passionate, his tongue stroking hers. Her mind raced as she tried to reconcile what she felt at that moment.

They kissed for a few minutes, then Kelly backed away.

"We talked about this, Erik," Kelly said breathlessly. "You're married. I can't do this."

"Catalina knows I have other women on the road. Besides, you seemed to enjoy it."

"But I've *met* her, and I like her. It just feels wrong. We can't do this. I want to stay friends, but this can't keep happening."

"Okay." Erik rans his hands through his dark hair. "I'm sorry. You are just so gorgeous I can't keep my hands off you."

"Try," she said with a smile. "I know you can do it."

"I'm gonna go get another beer. You want anything?"

"No, I'm good still," she said, holding up her half-full bottle.

Erik gently touched her shoulder, then went back inside. Kelly leaned on the balcony wall and looked out at the moonlight glittering on the waves. *Why does being in a rock band have to be so complicated?*

"There you are."

Ian came up next to Kelly and leaned on the wall, facing her.

161

"Yep, here I am," Kelly said. She didn't turn to look at him.

"What's wrong?" Ian asked.

"Oh, just Erik again. He keeps wanting me to sleep with him, and I keep telling him 'No.'"

"He does?"

"I guess I haven't told anyone but Jayna," Kelly said. "Yeah, after the show in New York, when we were in Erik's hotel room for the party, he wanted to 'show me how turned-on he was' by my confidence onstage, and he kissed me."

"Seriously?"

Kelly nodded.

"He promised to be friends, but then tonight, he kissed me again and wanted more. I told him we can't keep doing this. I like his wife, I won't do that to her. Although I think Isaac thinks there's something going on. During the CD party I got that text from Erik and Isaac said 'Of course from Erik' like we've got something going on. My friends saw the photo in *G-Spot* and thought the same thing. It's very one-sided, though. Yeah, he's gorgeous, but I just can't."

"It doesn't have anything to do with me, does it?" Ian asked.

"No, not at all. I know where I stand with you and I'm very okay with it." *At least I think I am.*

"Okay, just wanted to make sure." He stopped to think for a moment. "Do you want me to say anything to Erik?"

"No, I think we're good. I want to stay friends with him and all the guys in the band, so I don't think anyone needs to say anything to him."

"Okay," Ian said. He chuckled. "So much for you being the 'little sister he never had.'" He put his arm around her and she lay her head on his shoulder.

"Where's Lena?"

"She had to leave because she has an early call at the studio tomorrow morning."

They stayed on the balcony until Dean came to tell them that some of the guests were leaving.

"Okay, we'll be right in," Ian said. Dean went back inside.

Ian kissed the top of Kelly's head. She raised her head to look at him, and he slowly kissed her lips. Again, he made her tingle inside with his kiss. She liked this part of being FWBs, though she wasn't sure if this really was part of that.

Once back inside, Kelly saw that her parents and David were ready to leave.

"I'm so glad you guys came," Kelly said, hugging her parents. "You, too, Davy."

"This was fun," Mom said. "We'll see you in the morning. I'm sure you're going to be here a while."

"Yeah, most likely," Kelly said.

"Can we do lunch tomorrow?" David asked. "It'll probably be the last time I see you before you head to Canada."

"Yeah, definitely! I'll call you when I get up."

"Awesome," David said as he hugged his sister.

"Bye, you guys!" Kelly said, and she watched them make their way to the door.

Kelly met David at Stonefire Grill the next day at just after noon. They placed their order and a server brought it to them a few minutes later.

"I love their Caesar salad," Kelly said, stabbing the lettuce with her fork.

"This place is fantastic," David said.

"I'm going to miss you while I'm gone," Kelly said.

"I know it's not cool to call your big brother, but maybe call me sometimes?"

"I will. I need to be better about that."

"So, what's up with you?"

"What do you mean?"

"I don't want to sound like a prude, but you've got a few guys on the line."

Kelly was still confused.

"I'm not following."

"First you were making out with Erik from The Disciples of Man, then you were making out with Ian."

Kelly set her fork down.

"You saw all that?" she asked.

"I'm always watching out for my little sis. What's going on? It's not like you to play like that."

"Erik has a thing for me," Kelly said. "He's come on to me once before, but I turned him down. Last night was the same thing. He's married and I like his wife. I'm not going to be part of breaking up a marriage, even if he says she knows. I know I let last night go on for too long, but I told him I want to stay friends. If he keeps doing that, we can't be friends."

David looked slightly relieved.

"Okay, that explains that. What about Ian?"

"It's a little more complicated," Kelly said. "He was there one night when I was feeling sad about breaking up with Greg. It wasn't planned but it happened. We're not together, but we're FWBs."

"Friends With Benefits? That's not like you, either."

"It's only happened twice. He makes me feel better when I'm sad or lonely. The other guys know and we've got parameters set."

"Sorry, I don't mean to get up into your personal business," David said.

"And not really the convo I want to have with my brother, but I guess better you than Mom and Dad."

"I just want to make sure you're okay and taking care of yourself. Touring can take its toll."

Kelly smiled.

"Yeah, I'm okay. I was afraid of gaining weight with all the snacks I ate, but I've actually lost weight. I think I get enough sleep, even though I sleep until eleven or twelve, but we don't go to sleep until like three or four in the morning because of the after parties."

They talked about other things besides the band and tour as they finished their lunch. Kelly didn't mind her brother checking on her, but didn't want to have to explain everything she did on the tour. Her personal life was hers and she had told him far more than she intended.

In the parking lot after lunch, David hugged his sister.

"It was nice to catch up with you," he said. "I'll miss you while you're gone."

"I'm glad we got to talk," she said. "I'll miss you, too."

Two days later at Dean's house, his entire living room was filled with luggage and young people for their flight to Canada.

"Do you guys really need all this stuff?" Dean asked.

"Yes," they said in unison.

"Gotta look good onstage," Jake said.

"I know your make-up bag rivals Kelly's," Paul said.

"It takes a lot to look gorgeous," Jake said, tossing his hair. Kelly and Jayna giggled.

"Oh, my God," Kelly said. "And I worry about me becoming a diva."

A driver picked them up in a van to drive them to the airport. They loaded everything into the van, and Kelly was surprised the tires didn't go flat.

At the airport, they found their gate and waited until their flight was announced to board. Dean, Jayna, and the band boarded last. There wasn't much carry-on space left, so Kelly and Jayna shoved their bags under the seat in from of them.

"Whoa! Head-rush," they both said as they sat up and laughed.

Kelly didn't particularly like flying, and was happy to have Jayna sitting next to her. Jayna held Kelly's hand as they took off, then the flight attendant brought drinks around.

"First time going to Canada," Kelly said.

"I'm sure there's going to be a lot of firsts for you and the band," Jayna said. "But soon it'll all be routine for you."

"Yeah, I guess after a while, it will become old."

"You still get so excited, though, for these tours."

"It's where I have the most fun, besides hanging out with you," Kelly said, squeezing Jayna's hand.

"Good save there," Jayna said, smiling.

They arrived in Vancouver several hours later. They went through Customs and then headed to the baggage claim. Dean left and came back with the driver for their van.

"We'll be in a hotel for tonight," Dean told them as they followed the driver out to the van. "The bus will come tomorrow to pick us up from there."

"Last night in a normal bed," Paul said.

"The bunks aren't too bad, though," Kelly said.

"That's Kelly, always seeing the bright side of everything," Jake said.

They arrived at the hotel. Dean checked them in, then with the help of staff, got the luggage loaded onto a couple of carts and took them to their rooms on the eighth floor.

Kelly got up early the next morning. Too excited about the Canadian tour, she couldn't sleep much. She got up and did some stretches until Jayna woke up, then they both got dressed and waited for Dean to text them.

"The bus has arrived," Dean's text read.

Kelly texted back that they were ready. They went out into the hallway and loaded their stuff onto the carts Dean had brought up.

Dean checked them out and they got on the bus while Artie loaded their luggage into the storage bins outside of the bus.

"Home sweet home," Isaac said when he saw the bus.

"At least it's a little shorter time this time," Paul said. "Only what? Two months this time?"

"Give or take," Dean said. "And luckily a little warmer now that it's almost summer."

They all claimed their previous bunks and then sat in the lounge area and played a board game as they got on the road to the venue, which was four hours away in Kelowna.

At the venue, Dean went to check them in, then came back and they went to the dressing rooms, handing them their All Access badges. The band got everything set up before heading onstage for sound check.

The only thing Kelly could think about after getting her levels set was food, since they hadn't had a chance to eat breakfast before they left, just snacks that Dean had bought. She hoped Hospitality set up while they sound checked, and wondered if her growling stomach would be louder than her vocals, she was so hungry.

Kelly could smell the food as she walked into the room.

"I'm starving," she said. She grabbed a plate and piled on the food, and got a bottle of water. The others grabbed food before Kelly ate it all.

Before the show, Kelly pulled out her 5-hour energy shot and was about to drink it.

"I have something better than that," Isaac said.

"What's that?" Kelly asked.

"Nick gave me these pills to try," Isaac said. "I tried them at the party the other night."

"What are they?"

"Ritalin."

"Oh. I'm good with this, thanks." Kelly unscrewed the cap and drank the shot.

"If you ever change your mind, just let me know."

"I won't."

Kelly and the guys finished preparing for the show, and asked the opener to come in for the pre-show shot of Fireball.

***

As Isaac got ready for the show, he thought about his offer to Kelly. He really didn't think she'd want them, but thought he'd ask anyway. She was too strait-laced for that, though she'd been getting looser lately. He never thought she'd have sex without a commitment, but she did. Her language had gotten saltier, too. He liked the change, but she could've stayed the same and he'd have been okay with it. She was a great singer either way, but he was sort of glad she was coming out of her shell.

He'd seen the exchange between Kelly and Erik the other night at the party. He knew she'd blow him off, though he worried that it would strain the bands' relationship with each other. But Stevie, their drummer, still texted him, so all seemed good.

Isaac and the other guys popped their pills as the opener went onstage. The medication would be in full affect by the time they took the stage.

"I'm surprised you wanted to try this," Isaac said as Ian popped the pill into his mouth.

"Just because I don't smoke pot doesn't mean I'm not open to other things," Ian said with a wry grin.

"The wonders never cease," Dean said. "I'm not surprised, though. Been there, done that."

"*You* did drugs?" Isaac asked, shocked by that revelation.

"Back in my band days," Dean said. "Never developed a problem, though."

Isaac started to limber up, using one of the chairs to drum on. The others did the same, stretching and loosening up their fingers.

The opener finished their set and after they had moved their equipment offstage, Fate Struck went out to play their set.

***

Kelly didn't really see much of a difference with the guys after they took the Ritalin, except maybe they moved around more, but then she never really watched the guys much unless she interacted with them. Her energy drinks worked just fine for her to give her the needed energy for their shows, but she didn't have an issue with the guys taking anything. That was on them.

Chapter Fifteen

The Canadian tour became a monotonous routine for them--gig, after party, drive to the next location. They each adhered to their own—Kelly drank her energy shot before the show, then drank her hard lemonade after the show, and a gummy bear for sleep. The guys popping Ritalin before and drinking afterwards.

After a show in Winnipeg, Kelly grabbed a cup and poured in a shot of Fireball, drank it down quickly, and poured another.

"That mistake wasn't that bad, Kel," Isaac said. "We recovered."

Kelly had started one of their songs with the second verse instead of the first. She had motioned for the band to continue playing and came in with the correct verse.

"It was horrible," Kelly said. "I don't make mistakes like that."

"You're human, Kelly," Ian said. "It happens. How many times have I fucked up the bass line?"

"Only once that I know of," she said.

Ian laughed.

"Oh, it's been more than once, babe," he said.

"And I've started songs too slow a few times," Isaac said.

"We all mess up," Paul said. "It's not a big deal. Didn't you hear the crowd singing along, cheering you on?"

"I did," Kelly said, opening a bottle of Mike's.

"They're there for you just as we are," Isaac said. "It's not a big deal."

Kelly took a long drink from the bottle.

"It felt like a big deal," she said. "I hate to mess up."

"It's okay to not be so damn perfect, you know," Jake said. "We're not kicking you out over something that trivial."

Isaac hugged Kelly.

"It's okay, really," he whispered into her ear. He kissed her forehead.

"Thanks," Kelly said, wiping the tears from her face.

"Can I let the pass holders in now?" Dean asked. "I can wait if you need more time."

"No, it's fine," Kelly said.

Soon the room filled up with people—guys, girls, and press. It was the usual circus, and Kelly did her best to talk with everyone that came up to her, but she was still upset about the goof. She finished her bottle and opened another. After an hour, Kelly told Dean she was going to the bus.

"I just want to be alone right now," she said.

"Okay," Dean said. "Artie's out there so you should be fine."

Kelly walked out to the bus. Artie was indeed outside keeping watch on things. She stepped inside and went to the back to the lounge and shut the door. Kelly lay back on the bed and stared at the ceiling. As she lay there, she realized that it wasn't such a big deal. She'd acted like a prima donna, and that wasn't her. Still, the mistake bugged the hell out of her.

Half an hour later, she heard a knock on the door.

"Kelly?" Ian said. "Dean wanted me to check on you."

"You can come in," she said. "The door's unlocked."

Ian opened the door and stepped inside, closing the door behind him.

"Are you okay?" he asked.

"Yeah, I'm okay," she said. "I'm actually more embarrassed now than upset. I didn't mean to act like a diva."

"It's fine," Ian said. He sat down on the bed next to her. "We understand. I know you're a perfectionist, so things like that disappoint you."

Ian pulled out his phone.

"I'm going to let Dean know you're okay," he said, and he tapped out a message on his phone, then set the phone on the side table. He put his arm around Kelly's shoulders. Kelly leaned into him. He always made her feel better no matter what he did.

They heard footsteps coming down the hall to the lounge, and then someone knocked.

"Go away," Ian said, laughing.

"Sorry," Isaac said.

Ian turned back to Kelly and she tilted her head up to kiss his lips.

"You are so sexy with your make-up on," she whispered to him.

Ian shrugged playfully.

"I bet you say that to all the guys," he said.

They kissed for a long time, Ian's kisses making Kelly feel better. After a short while they took off their clothes and got into the bed.

Half an hour later, Kelly lay on her stomach propped up on her arms. Ian lay on his side, leaning on his left elbow, slowly stroking Kelly's back with his fingers.

"My brother knows," Kelly said. She paused for a moment. "About us."

"What did he say?" Ian asked.

"He said it wasn't like me, but I pretty much told him not to worry about it. I'm an adult."

"Yes, you are," Ian said, lightly smacking her butt. He looked at the time. "We'd better get back. Dean'll want to be loading up soon."

They got out of bed and dressed, remade the bed, and Ian stuck his head out the door.

"Is the coast clear?" Kelly asked.

"Yeah, they're just talking now," Ian said, indicating Isaac and his girl.

Kelly and Ian walked down the hall, passing Isaac and the woman he was with on the couch as they left the bus.

The fans and others that had been in the dressing room had thinned out. Kelly went over to Jake and joined the conversation. The fans seemed happy to see her and talk with her, assuring her that her mistake wasn't a big deal.

"I've seen other bands mess up lyrics before" said one of the guys. "It happens."

"Thanks," Kelly said. "I was upset, but I feel better now."

"I bet you do," Jake whispered in her ear.

Kelly smiled, but said nothing.

As the band walked to the bus, a few fans waited along the fence, and the fans called out to them. The friends put their luggage down next to the bus for Artie to load while they went over to talk with the fans and take a few photos with them. The girls all wanted selfies with the guys, mostly Jake and Ian, and the male fans wanted selfies with Kelly. She obliged, taking turns with

171

them, being polite, but made sure she did nothing to provoke them to try to get an invitation into her bed.

Dean whistled to them, calling them to the bus when Artie had finished loading their luggage. The guys and Kelly waved as they walked back to the bus.

As Artie pulled away from the venue, Kelly apologized to the guys.

"I'm sorry for acting like a diva," she said. "It really wasn't that big of a deal, but it just made me mad that I'd messed up."

"You wouldn't be a singer if you didn't have a diva moment every now and then," Isaac said. "It's really okay."

"If that's you being a diva, we have nothing to worry about," Paul said. "When you start asking for ten dozen flowers to decorate the dressing room, then we might have a problem."

Kelly laughed.

"It will never come to that," she said.

"You need to just laugh it off," Ian said. "That's all you can do."

The guys were still wired from their Ritalin, so were nowhere near ready to go to sleep. Kelly and Jayna stayed up with them for a while, drinking with them but finally they both needed to go to bed.

"It all just hit me how tired I am," Kelly said.

"You've been putting that away pretty good tonight," Jake said, indicating her empty bottle of hard lemonade.

"My tolerance has built up a bit," Kelly said.

"Good night," Isaac said. "See you tomorrow."

Kelly didn't get up the next day until early afternoon. Her head throbbed, and she could kick herself for not drinking enough water. She slowly rolled out of her bunk and went to use the bathroom, then went to the dining area. Dean was up, as usual, going over things for the next show.

"I'm surprised to see you up already," Dean said.

"I had to pee," Kelly said, "and I've got a headache the size of Texas, so I need to take care of that."

Kelly took a bottle of orange juice out of the fridge and got a slice of bread to put in the toaster. When that was ready, she buttered it and ate before taking two Excedrin with water, then drank her juice.

"Just kill me now," she said, laying her head on the back of the chair.

"Drink some water and go back to bed," Dean said. "No show today, so you've got plenty of time to recover."

"Thank God," she said. She took her water bottle and went back to her bunk.

She must have slept more because it was nearly four when she got up. Jayna, Jake, and Paul sat in the dining area finishing breakfast. She got out of her bunk and walked over to them.

"Hey, she lives!" Jake said.

"Barely," Kelly said, sliding into the bench seat next to Jayna. "I do feel better, though, than I did at one o'clock."

"When did you guys go to bed?" Jayna asked.

"It was almost five," Paul said.

"No wonder they're still asleep," Kelly said.

"Crash and burn," Dean said. "Ritalin will do that."

That didn't sound like fun to Kelly, who again resolved to not take that stuff. Her energy shots worked well enough for her and didn't make her suddenly crash once it wore off.

The band headed back to the U.S for several festivals and concerts that had been hastily booked after their album went gold. They were headed to Milwaukee for a summer festival with several other bands. MagNetic and The Disciples of Man were booked there as well, though on different stages.

Fate Struck had had a few days off in order to recuperate from the late nights, and felt rested when they got to the festival. Dean got them checked in before going backstage, which was an enclosed tent. They used their tour bus to get ready, then waited in the tent, eating and drinking. They would go on at four o'clock that afternoon.

Kelly decided to forgo drinking before the show since it was pretty warm that day. She'd stick with her energy shot and bottles of water. The guys, however, drank a couple of beers before the show, and did the usual preshow routine of popping Ritalin. She did some thinking as she sat there. What if no one showed up for them? There were still relatively unknown.

"Watch no one be there when we go on," she said aloud.

"What the hell are you talking about?" Jake asked.

"We're not a big name yet," Kelly continued. "What if no one shows up for us?"

"That's ridiculous," Isaac said. "Even if they're not here for us, they're gonna hear us and remember us."

"I love your positivity," Dean said. "Kelly, don't worry. There will be people out there to hear you."

Half an hour before they were set to go onstage, Kelly slathered sunblock on her arms and face. She didn't bother with make-up other than lipstick. She planned to keep her sunglasses on since the sun would be directly in their faces while they performed. She wore black jeans, a red tank top, and her ankle boots for the show, and left her hair loose. Jake, Isaac, and Ian applied minimal eye make-up for if they decided to not wear sunglasses.

"Okay, five minutes to show time," the stage manager told them.

Kelly used the restroom once more and stretched her legs and back. As she did so, she heard how loud the crowd was and butterflies started up in her stomach. Dean came up next to her.

"Are you okay?" he asked.

"I've never really had stage fright before," she said, "but oh my God the crowd sounds massive."

Dean disappeared for a moment, coming back with the bottle of Fireball and poured her a shot and held it out to her.

"I know you didn't want to drink, but this will be okay and help you to calm down."

Kelly took the shot and drank it down, then held it out for another one. Dean poured and she downed it, and handed the glass back to Dean.

"Okay?"

"Yes," Kelly said, and she headed out onstage at the appointed time. She grabbed the mic off the stand as Isaac and Ian started the rhythm for their first song.

"Hello, Milwaukee!" Kelly said. "Thank you so much for having us today. We're Fate Struck and we're here to rock!" On cue, Jake and Paul started to play.

Kelly was happy she'd kept her sunglasses on. Even with them on she couldn't see much of the audience for the sun being in her eyes, but she could hear them as they cheered and applauded. Ian had taken his sunglasses off and mostly looked down at the crowd or at his bass. The sun went behind the awning of the other stage as Fate Struck hit their last few songs.

"Thank you again, Milwaukee, for having us today," Kelly said. "Let me introduce the band to you. On lead guitar we have Jake DeHerrera!"

Jake waved at the crowd.

"On bass—Ian Ketchner!"

Ian bowed elaborately.

"Paul Slaney on rhythm guitar."

Paul gave a mock salute.

"On drums we have Isaac Landry."

Isaac did a drumroll.

"And I'm your singer, Kelly Brennen. I hope you had as much fun as we did today. Thank you again for having us!"

With that, they launched into their last song.

At the end of the song, Kelly and the guys came to the front of the stage and clasped hands and bowed, then turned for Dean to take their picture with the crowd behind them, then they walked off the stage while Scott and Bailey tore down their equipment.

Back in the tent, the guys drank beer, but Kelly just drank more water. She wasn't fond of the hangovers she'd been getting lately by drinking with the guys and Jayna until the early morning hours after the shows.

While Bailey and Scott loaded the trailer with their gear, Kelly, Jayna, and the guys walked around to listen to some of the other bands. They got to the stage where MagNetic was playing. They managed to find their way to the side of the stage with their All Access pass and watched the show from there.

After Maggie's set, the friends walked around to the other stages and saw some good bands, some familiar and some not so familiar. Isaac jotted down the newer bands' names for potential openers for them. They never made it to The Disciples of Man's stage, which didn't bother Kelly much. She'd had to turn Erik down twice and she didn't want things to affect Fate Struck so she'd steer clear of him for a while.

Night had fallen by the time the friends got back to the bus. Artie was still sleeping at his hotel, so Dean went and got them all dinner from the concession stand, bringing hot dogs, pizza, burgers, and chips.

"Are you guys going out again after you eat?" Dean asked.

"Yeah, I'd like to go see the headliners," Isaac said.

"Same," Kelly said.

The others replied in the affirmative.

"Picking up pointers?" Dean joked.

"Possibly," Kelly said. "Always seeing what I can do better."

After dinner, Isaac, Jake, and Paul went outside to smoke a joint before heading out with the girls and Ian to see the other headliners. They found the stage where the Foo Fighters were playing, and were let in to the front of the barrier where the VIPs stood. They watched for an hour, then wanted to see Evanescence on another stage, and walked over to that stage. Kelly loved to watch Amy Lee sing. She kept it feminine and didn't scream the lyrics. Kelly tried to be like her onstage. She just needed Amy's confidence.

The band and Jayna got back to the bus at midnight, having seen a few more acts, but never staying for the entire show, since there were so many they had wanted to see. Artie was back from his hotel and was ready to go.

Fate Struck hit a few more cities on their tour over the next two weeks, then by the next weekend, they arrived in Tucson for another festival. It was the last stop on their tour, then they'd head home and start writing some new material for their next album.

They got into Tucson at nine in the morning and it was already blistering hot. While it was still cool in the bus, the air conditioning had trouble keeping up.

"Not looking forward to playing in this heat," Isaac said.

"No shirts?" Ian asked.

"Definitely," Paul said.

"Oh, that'll be a wonderful look for me," Kelly joked.

"It would definitely bring in a crowd," Jake said.

Dean let the promoters know they had arrived and got everyone's badges, then he had Artie pull up as close to their stage as he could. They were set to go on after lunch at one-thirty. There were already four other buses there. Kelly recognized Maggie's bus, which was quite a bit bigger than theirs, and went over to say Hi.

Kelly spoke with the driver standing outside of the bus, who then went inside to talk to Maggie. Maggie came out a moment later.

"Girl!" Maggie exclaimed, hugging Kelly. "We gotta stop meeting like this."

Maggie stepped aside to let Kelly in.

"It's going to be a hot one today," Maggie said. "Not looking forward to it."

"Me, either," Kelly said. "Definitely going to drink plenty of water during the show."

"If I remember correctly, you drink hard lemonade, right?"

"Yep!"

Maggie got a bottle from the fridge, flipped off the top, and handed it to Kelly.

"Cheers!" Maggie said, holding her bottle of beer out. Kelly *clinked!* her bottle and drank.

Kelly and Maggie talked for a couple of hours. Kelly hadn't realized how much they have in common. Both were in choir in high school, and both had been into sports. Maggie had been on the softball team.

Kelly's phone *dinged.* She pulled it out and saw Dean had texted her to let her know lunch had arrived.

"I'll see you later," Kelly said. "We'll be watching from the audience when you go on."

"We're gonna catch your show, too," Maggie said.

Kelly took her half-full bottle with her when she left to go to her bus.

"Oh, yum!" Kelly said when she saw what was for lunch.

Dean had gotten tacos from one of the vendors there and they looked delicious.

"Hopping off the wagon today?" Dean asked, indicating her bottle.

Kelly shrugged.

"Can't say 'No' to a drink with Maggie," she said.

They dug into the tacos and rice, then Kelly showered before getting ready for the show. She pulled out a pair of gray shorts that hit mid-thigh. She looked at her white legs.

"Gonna need to get some sun here," she said.

"The life of a rock star," Jayna said.

Kelly pulled out a red sleeveless blouse that had sequins sewn on the shoulders and down the front of the blouse.

"People should be able to see you in that," Isaac said.

"Yeah, if I don't blind them with my white legs," Kelly said.

Kelly rubbed sunblock on her arms, face, and legs, then put on minimal eye make-up, planning to wear her sunglasses again.

They followed Dean to the backstage area. The previous band had just finished and Bailey and Scott got Fate Struck's equipment moved into place and got the band wired up. When everything was set, Isaac went to his drum kit and checked to make sure all was set properly, then began to play a beat to one of their songs. Ian walked out, playing his part in the song, followed by Paul and Jake. Kelly ran out last, grabbed the mic and stand, and started their first song.

Between songs, Kelly took a long drink of her water bottle, then a sip from her hard lemonade. The sun was blistering hot, even with industrial fans blowing on the stage. After their fourth song, Kelly ended the song near the drum riser, and stumbled a bit, putting her hand out to catch herself on the riser, which she saw two of. Ian stepped over to her.

"I feel really dizzy," she told him, and he motioned for Dean to come out. He ran out and grabbed her hand to steady her.

"Are you okay?" he asked earnestly.

"I don't know," Kelly said.

"Not what I wanted to hear," he said. He told Jake to play a song Ian could sing. The fans at the front shouted encouragement as Dean led Kelly offstage.

Dean took Kelly to a chair and had her sit down. Sweat poured off her face and she wiped her forehead with the back of her hand. Jayna stood next to Dean, concern etched on her face. Kelly handed Jayna her sunglasses to hold.

"I shouldn't have let you drink that alcohol," he said. He asked Jayna to bring him a bottle of water and had Kelly drink it, then she yanked out her in-ear monitors, leaned over and poured water over her head.

The guys had started their second song without her when she said she felt better. She put her monitors back in her ears, and waited until the guys finished the song before walking back onstage soaking wet, with another water bottle in hand, as the fans cheered. Dean confiscated her bottle of hard lemonade.

"Are you okay?" Jake asked.

They met at Isaac's drums for a moment, a look of concern on all their faces.

"Yeah, I'm okay," she said. "It's just too hot today."

"We'll cut the set short," Isaac said.

"No!" Kelly shook her head. "Absolutely not. I'm good to go."

They took their places again and Kelly stepped up to her mic.

"Sorry about that," Kelly said to the fans. "Let's get back to it."

They started a song and Kelly took the mic off the stand, moving around the stage, though somewhat slower than before. Whenever she became light-headed again, she put the mic back on the stand and held onto it to keep from falling over and took a long drink of her water, then poured some on her neck and chest, much to the delight of the men in the audience. Her blouse clung to her body, showing her curves without taking anything off.

They finished their hour set and took their usual photos before heading offstage amidst the cheers from the fans. Jayna met Kelly on the side of the stage.

"Don't fucking do that again," she said. "I was scared shitless, woman!"

"You and me, both," Kelly said.

Jayna put her arm around Kelly and helped her offstage and down the steps on the side leading to backstage. They all went inside the tent meant to function as backstage and sat down and drank more water. She took out her in-ear monitors, took off the power pack and poured water over her head again.

"Are you okay?" Bailey asked when they finished tearing down the equipment.

"Yeah, I'm better," she said. "Thanks for asking."

"Let's get you back on the bus to cool off," Dean said.

Kelly walked back to the bus on her own, but Dean and Jayna stayed on either side of her, just in case. Once back on the bus, she fell onto the couch and didn't move. Jayna went to get a wet washcloth to put on Kelly's forehead.

"Thanks," Kelly said

The guys came in a few moments later.

"Are you really okay?" Isaac asked.

"Yes," Kelly said. "I just shouldn't have been drinking in this heat."

"Little Miss Five-foot Nothing Rock and Roll Gymnast," Jake said. "Gotta take it easy on days like this."

"Hey, I'm five-foot-three," Kelly corrected. "I need all the height I can get."

"Well, that is the last show for this tour," Dean said. They all cheered.

"As much as I like playing out," Isaac said, "I miss home."

Kelly's cell phone rang. She looked at the caller ID.

"It's my mom," she said, and she hit *Accept*. "Hi, Mom," Kelly greeted cheerfully.

"Are you okay?" her mom asked. "I got a call from your cousin James who's at the festival and he said you left the stage?"

Kelly told her mom what happened and assured her she was now fine.

"Okay, but I'll be glad to see you at home tomorrow," Mom said.

"Me, too," Kelly said. "See you then." With that, she hung up.

Chapter Sixteen

The sun was setting as the bus arrived at Dean's house, turning the few clouds in the sky orange and pink. Kelly saw her mom's car parked in front of the neighbor's house. Everyone got off the bus and Artie opened the storage bins and pulled out all the luggage. The band, Jayna, and Dean got together for a group hug, then hugged each other before going their separate ways.

Kelly dragged her luggage to her mom's car. Her mom got out and helped her put the bags in the trunk before taking Kelly home.

"You look a little worse for wear," Mom said.

"I'm tired," Kelly said. "It was fun but these last couple of weeks have been exhausting. Whoever thought an outside festival in Tucson during summer was a great idea is an idiot."

"Well, hopefully there won't be many of those," Mom said.

"I know it's good exposure for us—no pun intended—but not my idea of a good time."

Mom pulled into the driveway, and helped Kelly take her luggage into the house. She took it to her bedroom and left it there. She'd unpack tomorrow.

"Are you hungry, sweetie?" Mom asked. "There's leftovers from dinner. Sloppy Joes if you want some."

"Yes, please!" Kelly said. "A home-cooked meal, even leftover, sounds fantastic."

Mom helped Kelly heat up the food, then left Kelly to eat on her own. She poured herself a glass of milk, sat at the table, and ate. She'd missed her mom's cooking while on the road. They'd eaten well at the shows, with the food provided by the venues, but they'd also eaten a lot of junk foods. Nothing could replace a home-cooked meal.

Kelly put the dishes in the dishwasher when she finished eating, then went to take a shower. The shower on the bus was small and cramped, and Kelly always felt the need to finish quickly since there were six others who used it, too. Now that she was home, she could enjoy the water running over her body, and wash and condition her hair without fear of someone banging on the door.

After she dried and dressed, she went to the living room and sat on the chair opposite her parents.

"Glad to see you home, pumpkin," Dad said.

"It's nice to be back," Kelly said. "Hopefully I can get back into a normal routine again."

"And not pass out from heat exhaustion," Dad said.

"Yeah, that, too," Kelly said. "I wish I'd been able to see James at the festival, but I didn't even know he was there until you called."

The band had only been back for a few days when Dean texted them for a meeting at his house.

"I know you're all happy to be home," Dean said, "but Tyrian Records has just scheduled a European tour starting in a month."

"Europe?" Isaac asked.

"We're doing that well?" Kelly asked.

"Jim says record sales there are great and there's been interest in a tour. They've been booking for the last month."

"That's amazing!" Jake said.

"And your album and single just went gold in the UK and Germany. They said to be prepared for an Asian tour soon after," Dean said.

"We're gonna be on tour all year," Ian said. "But I guess it's what we gotta do."

"I promise after this, we'll get you home for a good few months."

The thought of going to Europe excited Kelly, though she'd have to leave home again. But this was a great opportunity for them.

"Your next single is also about to be released," Dean told them.

"Woo hoo!" they cheered.

"So, enjoy your time at home. We'll be back on the road soon."

When Kelly got home, she told her parents about the European tour.

"We're going to be back on the road," she said. "And after Europe, possibly Asia."

"It sounds like your record is doing really well," Dad said.

"Yeah, and our next single is about to be released, too."

"Lots of things happening," Mom said. "But it seems awfully fast."

"We have to do it while we and our CD are hot," Kelly said. "If we wait too long, sales will fall."

A few days later, Kelly and Jayna went to the beach for some girl time.

"How's Marty?" Kelly asked.

"He's fantastic," Jayna said. "Though he's not happy about me leaving again."

"Are you thinking about quitting?" Kelly asked. She didn't know what she'd do without her friend there.

"No, not at all," Jayna said.

Kelly relaxed.

"So happy to hear that!"

"Marty isn't happy, but he knows that I like this job and that you count on me for things. He'll try to visit when he can."

"Yeah, he can visit any time."

Jayna squeezed Kelly's hand.

"I knew you'd understand," Jayna said, showing Kelly her left hand. Kelly grabbed her hand and squealed.

"He asked you to marry him?" Kelly asked.

"He did!" Jayna said. "Obviously I said 'Yes'."

"Oh my God, Jayna!" Kelly got up and hugged her friend tight. "I'm so happy for you!"

"Thank you," Jayna said. "I wasn't sure how it would affect my job, but Marty is 100% behind me staying."

"I'm so thankful." Kelly sat in her chair again.

"And now," Jayna said. "Will you be my maid of honor?"

Kelly was honored to be asked, but she had to be practical.

"Are you sure you want *me*? I might be a distraction."

"Of course I want you! You're my best friend and we've been through so much together. There was never any doubt you'd be my maid of honor."

"I will absolutely do it," Kelly said. "Thank you for asking me."

"We want to do this before we set off to Europe, so it will probably happen in about three weeks."

"Holy shit, that's fast," Kelly said.

"I've got someone working on everything for me, since I can't do it all. Marty has help, too. I'll let you know when we need to take measurements for the dress."

"I'll be available, no matter what."

"We mostly have the same schedule, so it should be easy."

Kelly and Jayna talked about the wedding and all she's got planned for it. Kelly was happy that they could still be friends and talk on the beach without being noticed. They didn't have people following them around yet.

Over the next few days, Kelly helped Jayna with her wedding plans, and got measured for her dress. Jayna asked to have a meeting with Dean and the guys. Kelly went to the meeting, too, and tried to not smile too much so as to not give away anything.

"What's this meeting about?" Isaac asked when they'd all arrived.

"Well," Jayna said, turning to them all. "I just wanted you all to know that," she held out her hand with the ring on it. "Marty and I are getting married!"

"That's fantastic!" Dean said.

"Awesome! Congrats!" Ian said.

They all stood up and hugged her.

Dean turned to Kelly.

"You knew, didn't you?" he asked with a smile.

"She told me a couple days ago," Kelly said.

"Kelly's my maid of honor," Jayna said.

"When's the big day?" Paul asked.

"June 30th," she said.

"That soon?" Dean asked.

"We wanted it before I left for Europe," Jayna said. "Otherwise it'd be months, and I couldn't plan anything while on tour."

"Do we get to play?" Isaac asked.

"Do you want to?" Jayna asked. "I didn't know if you'd want to since it would take you away from your girlfriends for a bit."

"It'd be fun," Ian said.

"Sure, why not?" Jake said.

"You okay with doing that, Kel?" Jayna asked.

"Sure, it shouldn't be a problem," Kelly said. "I think we still remember the old covers we used to do."

"You guys, that's fantastic," Jayna said. "But only for a little while. I don't want your dates mad at me."

Jayna's wedding day was fast approaching. Kelly did what she could to help out, and asked Jayna if she wanted a bridal shower or a bachelorette party.

"Bridal shower," Jayna said. "I'm not sure I could contain myself at a bachelorette party."

Kelly got the shower together quickly, having it two days before the wedding at her home. She invited the guys' moms and girlfriends, and other friends from school. It was held in the late morning, and Kelly had mimosas, punch, and finger sandwiches for refreshments, and cake for dessert.

After playing several games, Jayna opened her gifts. She received a lot of nice things for her wedding and wedding night. Missy gave her a red lace teddy, and the other girlfriends gave her matching accessories to go with it.

"These should be fun!" Jayna said with a laugh.

Kelly gave Jayna a gold bracelet with a Best Friend charm on it.

"Oh, Kel, this is gorgeous," Jayna said.

After the shower, Kelly helped Jayna and her mom take all her gifts home.

"Thank you so much for today," Jayna said as Kelly walked to her car.

"You're very welcome, my dear," Kelly said. "Happy to help."

"I'll see you on Saturday," Jayna said.

Kelly went over to Jayna's house to help her get ready on her wedding day.

"A little role reversal today," Kelly said. "Usually you're helping me get ready."

Kelly got dressed first, then watched as Jayna did her make-up, and Kelly helped her with her hair. Jayna's mom also helped, and when Jayna was done, Kelly stood awe-struck.

"You are absolutely gorgeous," Kelly said.

Jayna turned to look in the mirror. Her dark blonde hair was pulled back at the sides, but left loose around her shoulders. Her make-up was flawless. Her white dress reached to the floor with a short train in the back, with lace and pearls covering the skirt. Short cap sleeves and a lace veil completed the dress.

"Just stunning," Jayna's mom said.

They finished and put away everything and waited for the limo to pick them up.

"We'll see you at the church, Jaynie," her mom said.

"Bye, mom," Jayna said.

An hour later, the limo arrived at the church. Kelly would walk in first, followed by Jayna. Jayna's dad met her at the limo to help the girls out of the back, and to walk Jayna down the aisle.

The music started and Kelly walked down the aisle. Her dress was a dark pink tea length dress with matching pumps. Her hair was left loose and curled around her shoulder. She walked slowly down the aisle, smiling as she did so. Some of the guests murmured as they recognized Kelly, but she tried to ignore it and looked straight ahead until she saw her family. Her dad winked at her and she smiled broadly at him. Once she reached her place, she glanced at Marty, who smiled nervously, and the music began for Jayna's walk. Everyone stood as Jayna entered the church and her father walked her down the aisle to Marty.

The ceremony was over quickly and everyone followed the wedding couple to the reception, held at The Centre at Sycamore Plaza in Lakewood. Kelly remembered playing some of their first gigs there. It looked quite different this time, with tables set up and flowers everywhere. A long table in front of the stage had been decorated with small flower arrangements. The wedding party would sit at that table.

After the meal, Jayna and Marty went over to the wedding cake while the wedding party and guests gathered around.

"This is going to be fun," Marty said.

"Oh, you think so?" Jayna asked, her hand on her hip.

"Oh, I know so."

"We'll see about that."

Jayna's mom brought over the cake knife for Jayna and Marty to cut the cake. With the photographer ready, Marty placed his hand over Jayna's as they cut the cake together. They each took a piece and held it up to the other for a bite, but before Marty could bite into his, Jayna smashed it into his face.

"Oh, I see how it is," Marty said, and did the same to Jayna. Jayna squealed, and they both laughed as they posed for the photographer, cake covering their mouth, chin, and cheek. The guests cheered and applauded.

"You shouldn't have said anything," Jayna said, wiping the cake off her face.

"I knew you'd do it anyway. It's tradition."

"I love you." She kissed Marty, then licked the cake from his chin.

An hour later, Kelly and the guys got up to play, the guys in their suits and ties and Kelly in her maid of honor dress. Not a very rock and roll look, but they played some upbeat covers for everyone to dance to, plus a few of their songs, which everyone loved.

After Fate Struck played, the DJ took over, and the friends said their goodbyes to the happy couple. Marty and Jayna left the party for their honeymoon in the Bahamas.

The week that Jayna and Marty were gone just flew by as Kelly and the guys worked on songs, new and old, getting them perfect for the tour. The tour would start just a few days after Jayna and Marty got back.

Kelly had an idea and asked the guys and Dean how they liked it.

"It's okay with me," Dean said. "The only thing is it will cut into a few of your escapades."

"We can work around that," Isaac said.

"Okay, sure! Let her know it's okay with us," Dean said.

Kelly went to Jayna's house to help her move things into hers and Marty's apartment.

"I had an idea," Kelly said. "I know that Marty has a few more weeks off from work. Why don't you have him come along on tour with us for that time?"

"Are you sure it's okay?" Jayna asked.

"I asked Dean and the guys and they're okay with it."

"Really? Thank you!" Jayna said, hugging her friend tight.

"What's so exciting?" Marty asked, entering the room.

"We can be together on the tour!" Jayna said.

"Really?" Marty asked.

"Absolutely. You guys can have the back lounge."

"What about Isaac and Ian?" Jayna asked.

"They'll have to figure it out. They have before."

"That means you, too."

"It's okay, really."

"What does that mean?" Marty asked.

"Can I tell him?"

"You might as well, he'll find out soon enough." Kelly said.

"Kelly and Ian are kind of friends with benefits."

"Ooooh," Marty said, nodding his understanding.

"So, anyway, are you game?" Kelly asked.

"Yes! This is fantastic!" Marty said. "Thank you so much."

Chapter Seventeen

Isaac picked Hayley up from her house and took her to dinner. It was their last night before the band had to fly to England for the start of their European tour. He drove to downtown Long Beach near the beach, to L'Opera Restaurant. He'd reserved the most secluded table they had for them.

After dinner, they walked around the area, then Isaac drove them back to his apartment. Jake was out for the night with Missy, so they had the place to themselves.

They went straight to his bedroom, where he started to kiss her, gently at first, then with more passion, almost a hunger. He'd miss her so much while he was gone. Hayley unbuttoned Isaac's shirt. He pulled her blouse off then tore off his shirt. They took off their pants and sat on his bed. He ran his hand over her neck and shoulders, slipping off her bra strap. She took her arm out and he pulled the cup down. He caressed her breast then reached around and unhooked her bra. They lay down on the bed and Isaac took her nipple in his mouth, running his tongue gently over it.

He wanted to feel every part of her, and he slipped off her panties and took off his shorts. He ran his hand down her body slowly, feeling every curve. Hayley softly touched his shoulder, moving to his chest and down his body. Her hand found its way between his legs and stroked him to hardness. They kissed a little longer, then Isaac rolled on a condom before shifting between her legs to enter her. He wanted to savor this moment, kissing her face and neck, before they started to move together.

They rolled over until Hayley was on top. He cupped her breasts as she moved her hips to fully envelop him. She leaned down to kiss his lips, her tongue stroking his.

"Oh my God," he breathed when their lips parted. "I love you so much, Hayley."

"I love you, too," she whispered.

They changed positions a few more times before they climaxed, Isaac feeling wave after wave of orgasm until he could move no more.

They lay in bed for a long time, lying next to each other, kissing and cuddling.

"Stay with me tonight," he whispered in her ear.

She didn't hesitate.

"Okay."

They fell asleep in each other's arms.

In the morning, Isaac opened his eyes and saw Hayley's beautiful face. She was still asleep. He didn't want to move, but nature called. He slowly moved his arm out from under her head, then slipped out of bed to use the bathroom. When he came back, she was stirring.

"Hey, sleepyhead," he said gently. She opened her eyes.

"Good morning," she said, smiling. She stretched and he put his arm under her back and pulled her close.

"Good morning," he said, kissing her.

Hayley got her phone out of her purse and saw her mom had texted her. She opened the text and read it to Isaac.

"I'm assuming you're with Isaac for the night," she read. *"Next time can you let us know you won't be home?"*

"Well, I guess that takes care of that," she said, putting her phone back into her purse.

"Unfortunately there won't be a next time for a few months," Isaac said, frowning.

They got up and showered together, then dressed and Isaac took her back home.

"I'm going to miss you so much," he said.

"Me, too," Hayley said.

He kissed her passionately, hands in her hair, her hands on his back.

"Hey, you wanna get a room?" Hayley's fourteen-year-old sister Jenna said through the screen door. She made smooching noises.

"Hey, Squirt," Isaac said, laughing.

"Go away," Hayley said.

"Mooooom," Jenna said, running to the kitchen.

"I love you," Hayley said.

"I love you, too," Isaac said.

He backed down the steps, both of them holding hands and reaching as far as they could until their hands fell to their sides. Isaac walked quickly to his car and drove back home.

The day came for them to fly to England. The butterflies in Kelly's stomach fluttered as she prepared to board the airplane. She had never been on an airplane for more than a few hours. This would take up to ten hours to fly. Kelly brought some Benadryl with her to help her sleep while they flew across the Atlantic. Dean, Scott, and Bailey had their gear shipped overseas and it would be there when they arrived.

"I would suggest you all try and get some sleep on the flight," Dean said. "We'll land in England at around eight their time tomorrow morning."

Jayna nudged Kelly awake when they touched down at Heathrow Airport the next morning.

"Are we there?" Kelly asked.

"Yep," Jayna said. "We're taxiing to the terminal."

Kelly took several deep breaths and took a drink from her water bottle to wake up. She still felt a little groggy when they got to the terminal. She dug into her purse and pulled out a 5-hour energy shot and drank it down.

By the time they all picked up their luggage at the carousel, the energy drink had kicked in. Dean led them through the airport to the waiting limos. The record company had sent two to handle all the luggage they'd have with them. Marty stood still, looking at the limos.

"Never been in a limo before?" Jayna asked.

"Only the one at our wedding," Marty said.

"I'll ride with Marty, Jayna, and Kelly," Ian said.

"Okay, we'll see you at the hotel," Dean said.

People stopped and stared as they got into the limos. They were used to it by now, though it still made Kelly just a little self-conscious.

When they were all situated, the limos pulled away from the curb. It took half an hour for them to reach their hotel in London. Kelly took lots of photos on their drive to post on their social media pages. She figured that Isaac was doing a live from inside the limo. She pulled up their Facebook page and sure enough, Isaac was live.

"This is so cool," Kelly said. "I never thought I'd ever go to Europe."

"I'm sure you never thought you'd be a rock star, either," Jayna said. "But I'm with ya. Thanks for this opportunity."

"Of course! Gosh, we've been through so much together, I'm just glad you wanted to stay on with us," Kelly said. "I don't know what I'd do without you."

They pulled up to their hotel a few minutes later. Isaac was still live, and he caught Kelly and Ian getting out of the limo. Kelly waved at the camera and made a kissy face.

Isaac signed off as the driver got the luggage out of the trunk of the limo. They were greeted by the assistant manager of the hotel.

"Welcome to London!" he said, shaking their hands. "I hope you'll find your stay comfortable."

"I'm sure we will," Dean said.

Several porters came out to take in their luggage. Once it was all loaded, the manager led them inside to the desk, where he personally got them their keycards and led them up the elevator to their rooms on the eighth floor.

They were all in one suite, with three bedrooms, a kitchenette, and a bathroom with a full shower.

"Wow, this is awesome!" Ian said, looking around.

Kelly went to the window and pulled the drapes open.

"Look at this view!" she exclaimed.

"You'd think you've never been in a hotel before," Dean joked.

"Not one this nice," Isaac said, clamoring to see the view out the window, too.

"Thank you so much," Dean told the manager, and he gave the porters a tip with the bills he'd exchanged before they left the States.

The manager and porters left, and the friends walked around to look at everything in the suite. Kelly found coffee and tea in the kitchenette with several mugs in the cupboard and lots of sugar and cream. The window overlooked the London Eye, the world's largest cantilevered Ferris wheel, and the River Thames.

The guys found terrycloth bathrobes in every bedroom, which also included two double beds.

"This is amazing!" Jake said.

"So, how do you plan to divvy up the rooms?" Dean asked.

"How we usually do it," Isaac said.

"Except there's three rooms and eight people," Dean said.

Jayna and Marty spoke together for a moment.

"Kelly can share with us," Jayna said.

"Jake and I can room together," Isaac said.

"Whoever I room with," Dean said, "someone will have to share a bed."

They all talked it out again, and came up with a solution.

"I can share a bed with Kelly," Ian said. "I don't think any of us want to share a bed with anyone of the same gender."

"Are you all good with that?" Dean asked the group in general, but looked at Kelly.

"Yeah, we're good," Kelly said.

"Okay, that's settled. We're here for two nights, then we'll be on the bus while we tour through the UK. When we're ready to go to France and Germany we'll take the Eurotunnel, and we'll be on the bus until we're done with Europe."

They took their suitcases to their rooms while Dean went to find a store to stock up on snacks and drinks.

"I'm sure this wasn't how you envisioned married life starting out," Kelly said to Marty.

"Hey, I'm just happy to be here with my wife for as long as I can," Marty said, hugging Jayna tight.

After they got their belongings settled into their respective rooms, they came out to the common area again and Jake grabbed the TV remote to find something to watch. He found a movie channel and selected a James Bond movie—*View to a Kill.*

"We're in England," Jake said, "we should watch something English."

Dean arrived back at the hotel an hour later with snacks and drinks, including beer for the guys and Mike's for Kelly and Jayna.

"They didn't have lemonade," Dean said. "They have hard sparkling water here. I got black cherry for you since I didn't know which you'd prefer."

"That should be fine," Kelly said. "Thanks."

The itinerary for the day was a couple of radio spots and a TV show. They had time to eat and relax before they had to go. The guys and Jayna and Marty went to their rooms to try to sleep. Kelly couldn't sleep, and neither could Dean. They were wide awake after having drunk their energy drinks.

"Those things really work," Dean said.

"That's why I drink 'em," Kelly said.

She used this downtime to call her parents. It was now ten in the morning in England which, after doing some calculating, made it two in the morning in California. Her parents had told her to call no matter what time so they'd know she arrived all right.

"Hi, Mom," Kelly said when her mom answered.

"Oh hi, sweetheart," Mom said groggily. "You got there okay, then?"

"Yes," Kelly said. "We're in our hotel now. Everyone is sleeping a little before we start our day. I slept on the flight and drank an energy drink when we landed, so I'm wide awake now."

"Well, I'm glad you're there safely," Mom said. "Call us when you can, though I know you're going to be pretty busy."

"I'll call you whenever I can. I love you guys."

"We love you, too, Kelly."

"Good night, Mom."

"Good night."

That taken care of, Kelly decided to get a head start on getting ready. She went quietly into her room and got a change of clothes and went in to take a shower. Since no one else waited for the shower, she could take her time, washing her hair and just enjoying the refreshing water.

After she dried and dressed, she came out to put her make-up on.

"Enjoying the solitude before the storm?" Dean asked.

"Yes," Kelly said. "It was nice to not have to take a speed shower."

Kelly sat on the floor, set up her mirror on the table to put on her make-up. She went with something in between normal day make-up and stage make-up, and by the time she was ready to style her hair, Jayna came out.

"You're ready early!" she said.

"I wanted to be able to take my time in the shower," Kelly said. "But now that you're up, want to help me pick out something to wear?"

"You don't want to go in what you've got on?" Jayna joked.

Kelly had on gray sweatpants and a Beatles T-shirt.

"Not really the style I'm known for," Kelly said.

"Sure, let's take a look," Jayna said.

Kelly followed Jayna into their bedroom and Kelly pulled out a few things. Jayna took the blouses and matched them up with pants, then swapped them around again, finally narrowing it down to two outfits that were casual but still fashionable.

"Well, I'm always partial to purple," Kelly said. She picked the purple short-sleeved blouse with the black jeans, and her platform ankle boots.

"I thought you'd pick that one," Jayna said, picking up the other outfit and putting it carefully into the closet.

Kelly dressed, leaving her shoes last for when they left. She then went back out to finish her make-up, and saw the guys had awakened.

"The car will be here in about half an hour," Dean told them all. "It'll take us to both radio stations, then bring us back here so you can get your stuff for the TV show."

"Awesome," Isaac said. "Is this TV show live or mimed?"

"Live, I believe," Dean said. "Scott and Bailey are handling getting your equipment to the station. We'll be there in time for sound check and to get ready."

The guys went to change their clothes while Jayna helped Kelly with her hair. Although it was radio, there would most likely by photos taken while in the studio. Jayna left Kelly's long hair loose and scrunched in some waves with some mousse.

They were all ready to go by the time Dean got a text from the driver, letting him know he was at the front of the hotel. Kelly grabbed her purse and they all headed to the elevator and out to the car. With Jayna and Marty, it was a tight fit, but not too uncomfortable for everyone.

They arrived at the radio station twenty minutes later. Dean got out and went inside as everyone got out of the car, Jayna taking photos while they waited for Dean to come back.

"Follow me," Dean said, and he led them inside to the elevator. They got off on the fifth floor, where Dean led them down the hallway and checked in with the show director.

"Happy to meet all of you," the director said. "I'm sure you've done this before. We'll go in and get you setup for the interview with the DJ, which should last about half an hour."

"Sounds good," Isaac said.

The director took them into an office and then into the studio where the DJ was doing his show. He waved to them as they came in.

"We've got a treat for you today," the DJ was saying. "Fate Struck has just walked in, and we'll have that interview in just a few minutes."

Kelly and the guys got settled onto the stools in the studio and the assistant helped them with their headphones and got the microphones set up. Jayna, Marty, and Dean went into another room where they could watch the interview take place, and Jayna could get a few photos from where she sat.

The DJ went to a commercial, and said hello to all of them and told them how the interview would go.

"We'll do some fun questions besides the typical band stuff," the DJ said. "I'm sure you're tired of all the same questions."

"At least we always know what to say," Jake said.

The DJ came back from the commercial and started the interview.

During the last ten minutes of the show, the DJ asked them the fun questions.

"Who's the bad boy of the four of you gentlemen?"

"Ian," Isaac, Jake, and Paul said in unison.

"Thanks, guys," Ian said.

"Well, who was it that was voted most likely to get the first groupie?" Isaac asked.

"Fair enough," Ian said with a laugh. "But to be honest, I was the only single guy."

"Who's the most innocent?"

"Kelly," the boys said.

Kelly giggled.

"When she joined the band, she had no clue what she was getting herself into," Jake said.

"And I haven't quit yet," Kelly said.

"Who's got the biggest brain?"

"Isaac," Paul said.

"He had a full scholarship to college when we graduated high school," Ian said.

"And wasn't he managing you for a while?" the DJ asked.

"Yes, he was," Kelly said. "And he did a very good job of it."

"Who sleeps the latest?"

"Jake," Paul said.

"What do you guys like to do when you're on the road?"

"Us guys usually play video games," Isaac said.

"What do you do, Kelly?"

"I read a lot," Kelly said. "Or I try to write down ideas for songs. I tried playing their video games, but I'm not very good."

"Favorite snack?"

"Doritos!" they all shouted.

The DJ ended the show by thanking the band for stopping by and reminding the listeners that Fate Struck would be playing the next night.

The "On Air" light went off, and the DJ thanked them all again for coming to the studio.

The next interview went pretty much like the first, and the band answered them as if they were being asked the questions for the first time. They'd learned to just go with it and answer the question rather than get annoyed. Dean had told them to get used to it and they had.

The driver took them back to their hotel and waited for them to get what they needed for the TV show. Kelly had her outfit in a garment bag, including her make-up. She'd wear the same shoes she already had on. The guys had their clothes in duffle bags. The driver opened the trunk and put everything in there for them, and drove them to the TV station.

After taking their belongings to the dressing room, they then went straight out to do their sound check and rehearsal of their song. Back in the dressing room, the studio staff brought in dinner for them consisting of gourmet sandwiches and fruit plates.

Alcohol was provided, though Kelly decided water instead of alcohol would be better for her that day. The guys drank the beer.

Kelly touched up her make-up, then changed into her stage clothes. Jayna then took the curling iron and curled Kelly's hair just a bit more.

"I'm going to have to touch up the purple ends soon," Kelly said, looking at her hair that had faded to a dark lilac color.

"I'll look into getting that done," Jayna said, making a note on her phone.

The stage manager came back and told them it was time for them to go out to the stage. Fate Struck followed her to the stage, where she and her assistant helped them with their in-ear monitors. Dean, Jayna, and Marty stood just offstage as the assistant got the audience clapping as they came back from commercial.

"Our next musical guests are from the United States," the host said. "Here to play their single 'The Lies That You Tell' is Fate Struck!"

The audience applauded and the stage manager cued them to play. Isaac counted off and they started the music. Kelly came in and sang the song perfectly. When they finished, the audience applauded louder than before. The host came over to talk to them as they stood on the stage.

The interview was a quick five minutes. They went back to the dressing room to change and then they left to go back to the hotel. They were able to see the London Eye lit up now that it was dark as they headed back to their hotel.

"Wow, that's pretty cool," Paul said as they passed by the Ferris wheel.

"Any of you going up in it?" Dean asked.

"I will, if there's time," Kelly said.

"Nope," Jake said. "Scared of heights."

"Wimp," Ian said as they went inside the suite.

"It's going to feel so nice to get into bed," Kelly said after she'd removed her make-up and changed for bed.

"Yes, it is," Ian said with a grin.

"Look, you," Kelly said. "No funny business tonight."

"Damn it," Ian said, snapping his fingers.

"Am I going to have to get an Amish bundling board for you two?" Dean asked.

"No," Ian said. "I'll behave."

Kelly and Jayna went to bed before the guys did. Marty stayed up to hang out with the guys to get to know them better, then he and Ian came to bed. Kelly stirred and looked at the clock and saw that it was only one in the morning.

"Did we wake you?" Ian asked.

"No, nature did," Kelly said as she got up to use the bathroom.

Everyone awakened by ten o'clock the next day. Dean ordered breakfast, then gave them the run-down for the day.

"The limo will be here at one o'clock to take you to the photo shoot for Pop Star Magazine," he said. "That will last for a couple hours, then we'll be taken to the venue for sound check and then dinner after. The show starts tonight at eight o'clock. You guys take the stage at nine."

"Sounds like an easy day," Isaac said.

"The calm before the storm," Paul said.

"Tonight will be the last night in a hotel for a while," Dean said. "So enjoy it while you can."

They got everything together that they'd need for that night, since they wouldn't be coming back to the hotel until after the show. Jayna helped Kelly get some outfits together for the photo shoot and the show that night.

"You do quite a bit for the band," Marty said.

"She is a big help to all of us," Dean said.

Kelly thought that Marty looked proud of his wife. He'd never seen her do anything pertaining to the band except running the merch table until now, and saw that she was good at what she did.

The limo arrived at one o'clock. They gathered up their bags to take down to the car. The driver drove them to Windsor Castle, where the photo shoot would take place. A small tent had been set up for them to change in. Jayna helped Kelly with her hair and make-up, then helped the guys with their make-up. The photographer took photos of Kelly and the guys at the castle entrance. An outfit change and lunch, then they went to another part of the castle grounds for more photos.

At the venue later that afternoon, they did their sound check, with Jayna taking some photos during that time. After dinner they had a chance to meet the opener, a local band called Another Day. Fate Struck invited them to their dressing room for the usual pre-show shot of Fireball.

The stage manager came back to tell Another Day it was show time.

"Break a leg!" Fate Struck told them.

While Another Day was on, the guys went through their current ritual of popping pills and drinking alcohol before the show. Kelly drank her energy shot.

Another Day finished their set and Bailey and Scott made the changeover. As soon as Isaac walked out to his drum set the fans cheered. Paul, Ian, and Jake went out next, and they started the first song as Kelly went out and took her place at center stage. She took the mic off the stand and began to sing as she waved to the fans.

The fans cheered and sang along with the band the entire show. Kelly was overwhelmed by how many people had shown up for the show and she loved hearing the fans sing along to every song. She smiled as she sang, and patted her heart at the smiles and gestures from the fans.

"You all are absolutely amazing!" Kelly said in between songs. "I'm sure I speak for the entire band when I say you all are awesome and we are so, so happy to hear you singing along with us."

"Yes, thanks so much," Jake said.

The fans cheered even louder, and the band continued on to their next song.

At the end of the set, the band came to the front for their usual photo. Fans tossed flowers and stuffed animals onto the stage for them. Kelly and the guys picked up several items and waved to the fans, then turned so Dean could take their photo. Kelly and the guys waved as they walked offstage.

"Did you hear them singing along with us?" Kelly asked Dean in the dressing room.

"I did," Dean said. "You guys are a lot bigger here than you think you are."

"I didn't think this part of the tour was going to be real great," Isaac said. "But I think we're going to do pretty well."

Kelly grabbed a bottled water and drank as she put some veggies on a plate to nibble on.

After they'd had a chance to relax and talk about the show, Dean let the backstage pass holders in. All the girls flocked to the guys, and the men made a bee-line to Kelly, who was still eating from her plate.

"Sorry to be rude," Kelly said. "I was just really hungry after the show."

"Not rude at all," said a blond young man, who looked to be in his early twenties.

"Rock stars gotta eat, too," said another slightly older young man.

Kelly spoke with the guys for a while on her own, then Jayna and Marty came back into the room, Jayna making her way over to Kelly. Marty stood off to the side, taking everything in.

"We heard you just got married," one of the fans said to Jayna.

"I did!" she said, showing off her ring. "That's him over there." She pointed to Marty, who had gotten a beer from the table.

"Lucky man," said another.

The fans wanted photos taken with Kelly. Jayna became the photographer, switching out phones with all of them to get everyone's photo taken with Kelly. Some of the fans moved on to talk with the guys while some stayed to talk with Kelly and Jayna. Marty came over and sat next to Jayna.

"Are you in UK for long?" one fan asked.

"I think we're here for a couple weeks," Kelly said. "Then we're heading over to Germany and hitting other countries for the next couple of months."

"Sounds like a great time," another fan said.

"I'm hoping to be able to do more touristy stuff during this part of the tour than we did in the US. I've never been to Europe before," Kelly said.

Bailey came into the dressing room with his arms full of stuffed animals and flowers. He put them on the coffee table and the band went through and picked out what they wanted, asking

Dean to have the rest donated to a children's hospital there in London.

Dean made his usual rounds a couple hours later, thanking the fans for coming. Ian and Isaac were nowhere to be seen, and Kelly figured they'd hooked up with fans somewhere in the building, since they had no bus. Sure enough, Isaac came in a few minutes later with a cute redhead. Ian made his appearance after that, a short blonde in tow.

"Aren't you mad?" Jayna whispered.

"Why would I be?" Kelly asked. "He's not my boyfriend. I don't care what or whom he does." That was the truth. It's not like she had feelings for him other than friendship. Or so she told herself.

"Just wanted to make sure," Jayna said.

Once the fans had gone, Kelly and Jayna started to clean up all Kelly's belongings while the guys got their things together. Marty helped where he could, and they finished getting it all packed up. The car arrived and while Dean and the driver loaded everything into the trunk, Kelly and the guys went and signed some autographs for the fans.

Back at the hotel, Kelly took off her make-up and took a quick shower before heading to bed, the guys staying up for some time until the Ritalin wore off, or they took something to make them fall asleep.

Chapter Eighteen

The bus waited for the band in the back of the hotel where there was ample parking for it. Fate Struck, Dean, Jayna, and Marty got out to the bus at noon. The guys in the band were slightly hungover, but managed to get their belongings together with minimal help from Kelly, Jayna, and Marty. When everything was ready, the driver pulled out from the parking lot, on their way to another venue a few hours away.

That night after the show, Kelly felt a little sad since her best friend wasn't in the bunk across from her, instead Jayna was in the lounge with her husband. Jayna had stayed up for a while to talk with Kelly, but eventually went to bed in the back. Kelly knew it was only temporary, until Marty flew back home, but it would be a long two weeks without their late night talks.

The band played six shows in eight days, three in England, one in Wales, and two in Scotland. They had a short break of a couple days to take in a few of the sights before taking the Eurotunnel to France to continue the rest of the tour.

They played one show in France before heading to Spain for another show. Both were in a small venue, and were sold out. They played one more show back in France before heading to Belgium and The Netherlands for more shows.

Marty had to leave at the end of the week. Dean had hired a car and driver to take Marty to the airport. Jayna and Marty said their goodbyes just outside of the bus. Kelly could see Marty wipe the tears from Jayna's face, then he kissed her and got into the car. Jayna waved until the car was out of sight, and came back onto the bus.

"I'm so sorry you had to say goodbye to him," Kelly said.

"I knew the day was coming, but it didn't make it any easier," Jayna said, wiping her eyes.

Kelly embraced her friend.

"You'll have to Facetime him a lot," Kelly said. She stepped back. "And he's only a phone call away."

"I know," Jayna said. "I just didn't think things out when we got married so quickly."

"Yeah, it's hard to think of that in the here and now."

The tour continued, the band now driving into Italy for a couple of shows. They arrived at the venue in Milan early in the day, which gave the band time to look around and enjoy the area. Kelly, Ian, and Jayna walked around together, with both Kelly and Jayna buying several items to take back with them. They got back to the venue at three-thirty that afternoon, which gave them time to relax before sound check an hour later.

There was only one bathroom in the dressing room, which meant only one shower. Kelly said she'd use the one on the bus so the guys could take turns with that one. She and Jayna went to the bus where Kelly showered and dressed before heading back to the dressing room to put on her make-up.

Kelly drank her energy shot just as the opening band went onstage. She could feel it kick in half an hour later, but Kelly didn't feel like she had the same energy as she usually did for the show. She always had a rush of adrenaline once she hit the stage, but even that faded after the first few songs. She slowed down a bit toward the end of the hour and a half set.

Back in the dressing room, Kelly flopped onto the couch, resting her head on the back.

"Great show, as usual," Dean said. "How are you doing, Kel?"

"I'm dead tired," she said.

"You're not coming down with something, are you?" Dean asked.

"I don't think so," Kelly said.

"Pregnant?" Isaac asked.

"God, no!" Kelly raised her head. "No chance in hell. I started taking the Pill when I was with Greg, and Ian and I are very careful."

"We've been going at a pretty good clip," Dean said. "I'm sure resting will help."

"I thought I had been resting," Kelly said. "But maybe going out around the city today wasn't such a great idea, but I may never get the chance again."

As the driver drove the bus out that night, Kelly was already in bed, foregoing the usual band hang-out after the show.

If it was just tiredness, she wanted to get back to 100% before the next show in two days.

By the time they got to Munich, Germany, Kelly felt a little better, having rested and pretty much done nothing on the drive, only getting out the few times they stopped to get some fresh air. They didn't have a show that night, and instead of having to spend the night on the bus, Dean booked a hotel room for all of them so they'd have a decent bed to sleep in instead of the bunks, which weren't too uncomfortable but not a lot of room to move around.

"I'm hoping this will help your exhaustion," Dean told Kelly.

"Thanks, Dean," Kelly said. "I'm sure this will help."

Kelly and Jayna again shared a room, with no one else in it with them. Ian would stay in a room with Paul, Isaac and Jake in another room, and Dean and the driver shared. The roadies and sound tech were down the hall from them.

Kelly and Jayna didn't do anything, not even going down to the pool with the guys, instead Kelly read and Jayna got some work done on her phone.

Jayna set her phone down on the table.

"We should get your hair touched up while we're here," she said. "That just came up on my phone."

"They have a salon in the hotel," Kelly said. "Let's book an appointment and we can do that."

Jayna called them up and they could fit Kelly in in half an hour.

"I think you being a celebrity had something to do with the quick appointment," Jayna said.

"However it works out, I'm ready," Kelly said, examining her faded purple ends of her hair.

They walked down to the salon and the stylist offered Kelly and Jayna a glass of wine, which they accepted. She washed and towel dried Kelly's hair, trimmed the ends of her hair that had gotten straggly over the past four months, and then touched up the color. First the stylist lightened the ends more, then after washing and drying again, colored the ends dark purple, and touched up the pink and purple streaks.

The appointment took two hours, but when Kelly was finished, she looked gorgeous.

"You're gonna knock 'em dead tomorrow night," Jayna said.

Kelly paid the bill, adding a generous tip to it, and she and Jayna went back upstairs to their rooms. They ran into Jake and Ian, who were headed back to the pool after eating lunch.

"Wow!" Jake said. "Stunning!"

"I love that color on you," Ian said.

"So do I," Jayna said.

That was the only thing Kelly did that day, wanting to rest as much as possible. She loved being pampered at the salon, not having to do anything but sit there.

Kelly woke up early the next morning, ready to start the day. She felt well-rested, but still planned to take things easy that day, to save up her energy for the show that night. While Jayna slept, Kelly picked out her outfit for that night's show and then dressed for the day, pulling on her sweat pants and a t-shirt. She pulled her hair back into a ponytail, and slipped on her flip-flops. She checked her phone and saw that Dean had texted them, giving them the itinerary for the day, which was nothing more than meal times and sound check time. She looked at her watch and saw she had an hour before breakfast, so got a protein bar from her bag and ate that to hold off the hunger until they went to eat.

Jayna stirred in the bed across from Kelly and woke up.

"Good morning," Kelly said.

"Good morning." Jayna rubbed her eyes. "You're up early."

"Yeah," Kelly said. "I hope it doesn't bite me in the butt later on."

Jayna checked her phone and mentioned Dean's text.

"We're going to get spoiled, eating here twice in one day," Jayna said, tossing her phone onto her bed.

Jayna got dressed and was ready to go downstairs for breakfast. She and Kelly went to the elevator and met up with Isaac and Jake.

"Have Ian and Paul gone already?" Kelly asked.

"I don't know," Isaac said. "I haven't seen them."

The elevator doors opened and they stepped inside. Jake hit the button for the lobby.

"Hopefully we don't have to wait for them to order," Kelly said. "I'm starving."

"How are you feeling?" Jake asked.

"Much better! But not going to do anything crazy today before the show. Might take a nap later."

When they got to the hotel restaurant, they saw that they were the last ones there, Ian and Paul sitting at the table already.

"I guess we're the late ones," Isaac said. "Surprised to see you here already, Paul."

"Hey, where food is concerned, I'm there," Paul said.

They were seated in a corner of the restaurant, away from the rest of the guests there. A server came over to take everyone's order and then he and another server brought their food fifteen minutes later.

"Are any of you going out today?" Dean asked.

"We are," Isaac said, indicating himself, Jake, and Paul.

"I'm staying in," Kelly said.

"So am I," Jayna said.

"I'll hang out with the guys," Ian said.

"Okay, just make sure you're back by sound check," Dean said.

After breakfast the guys went out to explore the area while Dean, Kelly, and Jayna went back to their rooms. Kelly and Jayna didn't do much of anything. Jayna was still sad about Marty leaving, and Kelly didn't have much energy.

At sound check, Kelly had some energy back, having rested all day, doing nothing but reading or writing. Even during sound check, however, Kelly toned down the exertion, just walking around instead of the usual jumping and running.

Kelly made sure she ate lots of protein and carbs at dinner, hoping it would give her the strength to get through the show that night. She also didn't drink any alcohol before the show, only the shot of Fireball that they shared with the opener, sticking with water and tea, then drinking her energy shot as the opener went onstage.

As the roadies made the changeover onstage, Kelly did her stretches and voice warm-ups, then grabbed her water bottle and followed the stage manager out to the stage. They each went out in their usual order, Kelly walking out last as the others played the intro to their first song.

During the first few songs, Kelly felt like her energy level had returned, but as the set went on, Kelly's energy vanished and she found it hard to even walk across the stage. She managed, though, but even the guys noticed it.

"Are you sure you're okay?" Isaac asked as they sat in the dressing room later. "The last half-hour you looked like you hadn't slept in a week."

"I think I'm fine," Kelly said.

"We should have you checked out by a doctor," Dean said.

"It couldn't hurt," Ian said.

"I'm just tired, is all," Kelly protested.

"But you've rested and you still lack energy," Dean said.

"Fine," Kelly relented.

The next day Dean told Kelly that he got her an appointment with a doctor just around the corner for that morning.

"Will we still make our next gig?" Kelly asked.

"We should," Dean said. "We'll have to not make as many stops, and I can give Artie a break and drive part of the way so he can rest."

Dean and Kelly walked to the doctor's office. Luckily the staff spoke English, since neither of them spoke German at all.

The doctor came in and examined Kelly, checking her heart, pulse, blood pressure, and oxygen level. He drew some blood to have it checked, putting a rush on it so they would know that day. The doctor would call Kelly and let her know what they found, if anything, and prescribe any medications that she might need that she could get filled along the way.

"Thank you," Kelly said, and they left to go back to the hotel. They needed to get everything back on the bus to drive to their next destination.

That afternoon, Kelly got a call back from the doctor while she was sleeping. She listened to the message, then told Dean and the others.

"The doctor said my iron is low," she said, "but it's really not low enough to make me feel so drained. He suggested an iron supplement, however, which we can get anywhere they sell vitamins. He also said it could be from lack of exercise. Real exercise, not running on stage for ninety minutes a night, and suggested I do some walking every day. I miss my gymnastic workouts, but there's no place to do that on the road."

"Great! I'm glad it wasn't anything bad," Dean said, looking relieved. "We can get the iron supplement the next time we stop for gas."

"He also said to stay away from the energy drinks for a while. I've gotten used to them so they don't work anymore. He said to eat bananas and drink green tea."

"We'll get right on that," Dean said, making a note on his phone.

At the next gas stop, Dean and Kelly went inside the store and bought what she needed, stocking up on bananas and other fruits, and getting the iron supplement. Kelly took one right away, eager to feel better. It wouldn't take affect right away, but the sooner she started, the better.

She still had the problem of not having energy for the show, however. The iron supplements wouldn't take affect for a few days, and the energy drinks didn't work at all. Kelly tried the bananas and green tea at the next show in Frankfort, but it didn't work as much as she expected. She walked several times, at each stop they made, but it didn't help.

As they drove to the next city of Berlin, Kelly did some serious thinking. The guys all used Ritalin before the shows, but did she want to go that route? She hated the feeling of being tired and run-down, but she also didn't want to get into drugs, legal or not. The edibles were a little different, at least in her mind. She needed to talk to Jayna. She got up and asked Jayna to come to the lounge with her.

"Ooh, girl-on-girl action?" Jake asked.

"In your dreams, dude," Kelly said over her shoulder, and she shut the door behind them.

"What's up?" Jayna asked.

Kelly sat down on the bed and Jayna followed.

"I need your opinion," Kelly said. "I'm tired. Exhausted, even, when I get on the stage. It's going to take time before anything works that the doctor prescribed."

"Okay…" Jayna said.

"The guys take Ritalin before the shows. You know how anti-drug I am, but there doesn't seem to be a quick solution and I can't get through a show without wanting to just sit down for the show."

"I'm not going to judge you if you're thinking of going that route," Jayna said. "I know you. Heck, you wouldn't even eat the gummy bears without thinking and re-thinking about it. I know you wouldn't consider taking anything unless it was a necessity. Adrenaline only goes so far. You can always try it and if it doesn't work out for you, there's always the doctor's way of doing it."

Kelly considered what Jayna said. She knew Jayna wouldn't judge her, but just needed a sounding board to work this out.

"Thank you, Jayna," Kelly said, hugging her friend.

"You're welcome," Jayna said. "It's what I'm here for."

Kelly opened the door and she and Jayna walked out.

"That was quick," Paul said.

"God, you guys," Kelly said, laughing. "Get your minds out of the gutter."

"Too late for that," Jake said.

Kelly did a lot of thinking as they got ready for the show the next day, and after sound check, Kelly stopped Isaac to talk to him, alone.

"What's up?" Isaac asked.

"I, um…" Kelly hesitated. She still wasn't sure if this is what she wanted to do, but she *needed* to do something. Without looking at him, she said, "I really hate this, but I need to try what you guys use before the show."

"Are you sure about this, Kelly?" Isaac asked.

"No," Kelly said, turning to Isaac. "But I need to do something while waiting for what the doctor suggested to kick in. I'm desperate."

"Truth be told, I wanted to suggest it to you again, but I know how you feel about drugs, and I decided to just wait and see if you came to me."

"And here I am," Kelly said softly. Her stomach was doing flip-flops. She felt defeated, and she'd never felt like this, not even after losing a gymnastics meet.

"Is this what you and Jayna talked about yesterday?"

Kelly nodded.

"I just needed to hear someone else's opinion about this. I wanted to make sure she wouldn't judge me."

"None of us do, Kelly," Isaac said, putting his hands gently on her shoulders. "You held out as long as you could, and none of us look at this as not being strong. You're tired, Kel, and we've got a lot of tour in front of us, and you always give 110% during the show. We'll support you whatever you want to do or however you want to handle this."

"Thanks," Kelly said, forcing a smile.

"Come here," Isaac said, and he pulled her into a hug. "Just think of it as a needed medication. You take Benadryl for sleeping, right? Or the gummy bears? This is just something else you need."

Kelly stepped back, and nodded that she was okay. They walked back to the dressing room together.

As she got dressed for the show, Kelly put the idea of taking a drug out of her mind and focused on her make-up and getting dressed. After the opener came in to share the preshow shot of Fireball and went out to perform, Isaac came over to Kelly and handed her one tablet, which she drank down with water.

"I've told the others, just in case anything happens, which it shouldn't," Isaac said. "It's perfectly safe to take."

"Thanks," Kelly said.

By the time Fate Struck went onstage, Kelly was jumping around, ready to perform. As the guys began the first song, she ran out onstage, grabbed the mic off the stand and greeted the crowd, then started to sing

Kelly had remarkable energy during the show, back to her old self again. She'd even forgotten what gave her the energy while onstage, only remembering once the show was over.

"I could've gone another hour out there!" Kelly said, grabbing a hard cider from the table.

"Best show we've had in a long time," Ian said. "Not that you've performed badly, Kelly, you just looked like you were having fun again."

"It was fun again," she said. "It's always been fun, but lately it just felt like a chore more than anything."

Dean let in the pass holders, and as usual, the girls went to the guys, and the guys surrounded Kelly. Despite the language barrier, Kelly enjoyed talking with the fans. There were a couple who spoke English, and they helped to translate what the others said. They all wanted a photo with Kelly; by that time Jayna had come back from the merch table and helped take the photos. They got the band together for a group photo with everyone's phones, Dean and Jayna taking the photos.

Back on the bus, no one was remotely tired, so they played a spirited game of Cranium. They split into three teams of two—Kelly and Jayna, Ian and Paul, Isaac and Jake—and played for a couple of hours, mixing up the teams after each win.

By four in the morning, Kelly was ready for bed. Jayna had called it quits earlier, and the guys were still going. Once she was in her bunk, she made a quick call to her parents, who were surprised that she was still awake.

"I guess the adrenaline is still running through me," Kelly said. "I hadn't been feeling well, really tired, so Dean took me to a doctor. I'm fine," she quickly said before her mother said anything. "But I'm taking an iron supplement and eating better, so I feel better, and I'm getting regular exercise, not relying on the performance for my workout."

"Well, I'm glad you're feeling better," Mom said. "I worry about you."

"I know." Kelly smiled. "But rest assured that Dean does watch out for all of us."

There was no way she was going to tell her mom what she'd actually done to get more energy, and she was sure that everything the doctor suggested would start working soon. She just needed some help until then.

Later, as they got near the next city, Isaac told Dean they'd need more Ritalin soon.

"I'll get someone on that when we get to the venue," Dean said.

Kelly wasn't sure how Dean got stuff like that, but as long as it didn't get anyone in the band in trouble, it wasn't her concern. She figured some of the crew knew how to get things like that.

Dean had some news for them once they were in the dressing room preparing for sound check.

"Tyrian Records wants to record one of the shows for a DVD," he said.

212

"What?" Kelly asked. "That's amazing!"

"When and where?" Isaac asked.

"When we go back to England in a couple of weeks," Dean said. "And because they liked the video so much, they want your brother David to do it."

"Really?" Kelly exclaimed. "That's awesome."

"They also like the recordings you guys are posting on social media. That's what gave them the idea to record a show. They've already contacted David and he's dropping everything to do this."

Kelly did some quick calculating and figured it was seven o'clock in the morning in California, a little too early to call. She'd call David later.

During sound check, as always, Kelly and the guys took it fairly easy, not expending any energy. They'd save that for the show.

When they were done, Kelly, Jayna, and Ian walked around Copenhagen, and Kelly called David.

"Hey, I hear you're going to record our show," she said.

"Hey, sis!" David said. "Yeah, isn't that amazing? I get a free trip to England and get paid to do it."

"I'm so excited to see you," she said.

"I'll be there in a couple weeks with a crew. Anything you want me to bring?"

"I'll let you know," Kelly said.

"So what are you up to right now?"

"We just finished sound check and Jayna, Ian, and I are just walking around Copenhagen. It's so beautiful here, but chilly for this California girl."

David laughed.

"Not beaches and sunshine?"

"Sunshine, yes, beaches, no. But there's a river nearby."

They talked a little more before David had to get ready for work.

"I'll see you in a few weeks," Kelly said.

"See you then," David said.

Kelly disconnected and put her phone back into her purse.

"What do you want to do first?" Jayna asked.

"Let's go see the Little Mermaid statue!" Kelly said. "I've always wanted to see that in person."

Ian looked it up on his phone, and found that they were only two blocks from the statue. He led the way and a few minutes later they were at the harbor where the statue stood. There were quite a few people surrounding the statue, so they patiently waited their turn to get close to the statue.

"So beautiful," Kelly said as she stepped next to it. Jayna took a picture of Kelly standing next to it.

"Never thought I'd ever get to see this." Kelly touched the rock the statue sat on, then stepped away to let others get a photo.

"Being in a band has really opened up our world," Ian said.

"It certainly has," Kelly said.

Chapter Nineteen

Two weeks later, the band was back in England for another couple of shows, one of which would be recorded for a DVD. Tyrian Records sent a van to pick David and his crew up at the airport and they would stay at the same hotel as Fate Struck. Kelly waited downstairs in the lobby and when she saw David arrive she ran out and jumped up to give him a hug, wrapping her arms around his neck.

"I'm so happy you're here!" she said.

"Hey, little sis," David said. "Let a man breathe."

"Sorry," she said, stepping back with a smile on her face. "It's just been so long!"

The porters got the luggage onto the carts and Dean met them in the lobby with their hotel key cards.

"Thanks for doing this," Dean said, shaking David's hand.

"I'm happy to do it," David said, "and happy that the record execs want me to do it."

They followed the porters to the elevators, getting out on the same floor the band was staying on, just a few rooms down.

When the band arrived at the venue the next afternoon, David and his crew had already been there for four hours, getting everything set up. The record company had rented all the equipment David and his crew would need, so David only had to bring his mixing board and a few monitors.

"Sound check is going to be a little longer than usual," Dean told the band. "We need to run through for your benefit and then another run-through for the film crew. David and I have already spoken to your opener and they're cool with it."

"No problem." Isaac looked over the table of food. "Can we eat first?"

"Of course," Dean said.

Kelly, Jayna, and the guys filled their plates with food, grabbed a bottled water, and sat down at the round dining table to eat. There was twice as much food as usual so David and his crew could eat as well. David came in a few minutes later with his crew.

"I was told there was food here?" he said.

"Over there," Kelly said, pointing to the back of the room.

"Fabulous," he said. He and his crew of six went over and filled their plates. "Can we sit with you guys, or are you too hoity-toity to be seen with the hired hands?"

"I don't know," Kelly said. She turned to Jake. "Do you think we can associate with them this once?"

"I think it'll be okay just this once," Jake said.

"You guys as really swell," David said, and he and his crew sat at the table or on the couch to eat.

"This is really good!" David said between bites. "Do you guys eat like this all the time?"

"When we have a show, yeah," Kelly said. "On the road, though, it's fast food."

"Or Hot Pockets," Ian said.

"But I've been thinking about having them add six dozen pink carnations to the room every time we play," Kelly said. "To pretty up the place where we have to hang out."

Isaac and Paul nearly choked on their food trying not to laugh.

"I'm sorry, what?" David asked, putting his fork down. "You going diva on us?"

Kelly and Jayna burst out laughing.

"No!" Kelly said.

"We made a joke one time about Kelly being a diva and wanting flowers put into the dressing rooms like Beyoncé," Paul said.

"I fu--, um, messed up the words one night and threw a little hissy-fit," Kelly said.

"Thank God." David picked up his fork again. "I was hoping this wasn't going to your head."

"Far from it," Ian said. "Kelly is really easy to work with."

When they finished eating, Kelly and the guys went to get wired for sound check while Jayna took photos of everything going on, since this was going to be a little different.

"I'll post these on all the socials," Jayna said. "Give the fans a little teaser of what's coming."

Once the band had the levels set, they ran through one of the songs, with David and his crew recording it, checking out different camera angles. When they finished with the sound check, David had them run through a couple of songs so he could continue to work out the angles and get his levels set, asking them to do what they would usually do onstage. Kelly grabbed her mic and moved around the stage as usual, and the guys did their thing. David got the entire stage covered with four cameras—two stationary cameras on each side, and two hand-held ones at the front.

"Thanks, you guys," David said. "I think we've got what we need."

"Awesome," Kelly said, putting the mic back on the stand.

The band went back to the dressing room to relax before they got ready for the show. David and his crew followed them to take some footage of them getting ready, and Jayna, as always, played the band photographer for this, taking some photos of them as well.

Kelly nibbled on the food a little more before she got ready for the show. She went in to shower and dress, then came out to put on her make-up and style her hair, Jayna helping her as needed. David had a camera and recorded his sister as she got ready. After she put on her lipstick, she turned to David and his camera and puckered up, then stuck out her tongue.

"Nice, sis," David said.

"Well, I can't decide if I should treat you as my brother or as a videographer, so I did both," Kelly said, winking at him.

With David watching her, she didn't know how she'd be able to take her pill before the show. Kelly watched as the guys took their pills, camera crew recording it all, and turned to Jayna, staring wide-eyed at her. Jayna picked up on Kelly's unspoken question, and grabbed the bag Isaac had given Kelly from the make-up bag, shoved it into her pocket, and walked into the bathroom. Kelly went in a few moments later.

"Thank you for figuring out my panicked look," Kelly said as Jayna handed her the bag. Kelly took one of the small tablets out, popped it into her mouth and took a long drink from her water bottle.

"That's what I'm here for," Jayna said.

They walked back out to the dressing room together.

Dean went to the opening band's dressing room to invite them over, making sure it was okay with their manager for them to be recorded with the band. He agreed.

The opener came over for the pre-show shot of Fireball, Isaac doing the pouring honors, asking the crew if they wanted one as well.

"Sure," David said. "One shot won't hurt."

After the toast, the opener hung out for a few more minutes, then went back to their dressing room for their own ritual before heading to the stage, and Jayna went out to work the merch table. Kelly heard the fans cheer and the opening band started their set.

Kelly took a hard seltzer water from the table and took a long drink while the guys drank their beer.

"No beer for you?" David asked.

"Beer tastes nasty," Kelly said, shuddering. David laughed.

"It does take some getting used to," he said.

"I'll never get used to it," Kelly told him.

When the opener announced their last song, she stretched her legs and back, then did her voice warm-ups, David recording all of it and asking her questions on camera.

"You do this before every show?" he asked as she sat on the floor to stretch her legs.

"I do," Kelly said, treating it like a regular interview. "Being a gymnast in high school has made me keenly aware of how I can pull a muscle by doing simple things if I don't stretch first."

"You do a lot of dancing and moving around in general onstage."

"Yeah. We want to give the fans a show, not just a concert."

"Is that why you sometimes do flips at the end of the show?"

"If I get asked I'll do it." Kelly stood up to stretch her back. "But the show isn't about me, it's about all of us. I don't want to take anything away from the band."

"And you don't," Isaac said, stepping over to join them, putting his arm around Kelly's shoulders. "It's kind of cool that you do that sometimes. I just don't want you to get hurt doing it, otherwise I'd incorporate it into the show. But that's also extra

218

work you'd have to do and we're already exhausted by the end of the night as it is."

David turned off the camera.

"Mom told me about that," he said. "Are you feeling better now?"

"Yeah," Kelly said. "I saw a doctor in Germany and he suggested supplements and I feel better. Not 100%, but a lot better." It wasn't really a lie. She was taking the supplements the doctor suggested. She was just also enhancing it with other things—for now, until the supplements kicked in.

The opener joked and laughed down the hallway as they headed back to their dressing room. David kissed Kelly on the cheek.

"I gotta go. Break a leg!" he told her as he headed out the door to go run the production.

"Thanks!"

Just before the band went onstage, Dean asked Kelly if she was going to do her flips for the cameras.

"If you think it's okay," she said.

"Are you in good enough shape to do it?"

"I haven't practiced lately, but I think I can do a round-off and backflip."

"Okay, but don't let the Ritalin 'talk' you into doing anything else."

"I won't. I promise."

With that, the band ran out onstage to start their set. They all knew where the cameras were and during certain segments of the show, they would walk up to the edge of the stage to the camera and play their part of the song. Ian and Jake stood back to back as they playfully pushed against each other as they played, and Kelly stood on the drum riser a few times to make sure Isaac was featured during some of his incredible drum parts.

Kelly bent down to take a drink of her hard cider and then followed that with a long drink of water.

"We're going to slow things down for a minute," Kelly said, putting the mic back on the stand. "Sing along if you know it."

The band started their power ballad and everyone took out their phones and turned on their lights and waved their arms back and forth during the song, which they did sing along to. When the song ended, they went right into another fast-paced song.

By the end of the show, Kelly and the rest of the band had worked up a sweat. They went offstage, waiting just a few moments before returning for their encore of two more songs. When they finished, they stood at the front of the stage for their bow and photos, then Kelly took off her platforms and the audience screamed, knowing what was about to happen.

The guys stood on the side of the stage and watched as Kelly did her round-off into a backflip. The applause was deafening as she picked up her shoes and waved as she ran offstage.

Backstage, the band relaxed, drinking water and more beer and hard cider.

"Best fucking show in a long time," Jake said.

"It was really fun," Kelly said. "Though I probably should've worn my Chucks instead, then I wouldn't have had to take off my shoes."

"But did you hear the crowd's reaction when they saw you take off your shoes?" Ian asked. "They knew what was coming. I thought that part was fantastic."

"They knew they were getting a bonus at that point," Dean said. "Well done, all!"

David came in with one of his crew and a couple of cameras to get some after show shots while Dean let the backstage pass holders in.

***

No making out with the fans tonight, Isaac thought, since Hayley would probably see the video. As the fans were let in backstage, most of the female fans and some of the male fans swarmed around him and the other guys, with a few scrambling to meet Kelly. The usual press people came in as well, interviewing the guys and Kelly, and also talking with Dean and David about the video that would be made from the concert footage.

Isaac talked with the fans, making sure to not to encourage the girls, though he did kiss them on the cheek after taking photos with them. He watched as Ian, on the other hand, having nothing to worry about, put his arm around several girls, and disappeared with one of them.

He hoped Dean would be involved in what shots to select and what to leave out. While they popped their pills out in the open in the dressing room, he wasn't about to have *that* conversation with his father.

A couple hours later, Dean started his rounds to thank everyone for coming, his subtle way of kicking everyone out. Isaac got his belongings together and when everyone was ready, they went out to the waiting van to take them back to the hotel. David would meet them there while his crew tore down the equipment at the venue.

"This is such a glamorous side of the band," Isaac said as they got out of the van and loaded a cart with their bags to take upstairs.

"Someone will find it interesting, I'm sure," David said, following the band with his hand-held camera.

They were all tired and a little drunk, but no one got too crazy as they congregated in Dean's room for pizza. They may be tired but they were all wide awake and would be for another couple of hours. David recorded them playing cards until one by one they headed to their own rooms.

"Good night, big brother," Kelly said, giving David a hug.

"See you in the morning," he said.

***

Ian pulled his phone out from his pocket to see who could be texting him this late, or early, as the case may be.

Any chance of getting together tonight? read the text from Kelly.

He smiled. It didn't happen very often, but when it did, Ian knew Kelly's adrenaline was running high.

Sure. Be at my room in five minutes, he replied.

"Meeting that hot redhead you passed on earlier?" Paul asked.

"Wouldn't you like to know." Ian got up and bid everyone good night.

"You've got an hour, then all bets are off."

221

He went into his room and cleaned up a few things off his bed, mostly clothes, and moved the snacks to the table. A knock on the door came, and Ian looked through the peephole to make sure it was Kelly and opened the door.

"Hey," Ian said, closing the door quickly.

"No one with a camera saw me," Kelly said.

"You're living dangerously, suggesting this with your brother and his camera crew here." He took her wrists in his hands and lifted her arms, pinning her to the door as he kissed her lips.

"He won't put this in even if he does get it on camera," Kelly said breathlessly.

Ian let go of her wrists and she grabbed the front of his shirt and pulled him to the bed. Once she hit the bed, she lay down and Ian lay on top of her, kissing her neck. Since they didn't have much time, they quickly took off their clothes and got under the covers.

Afterwards, they lay breathless in a tangle of sheets and blankets.

"You are amazing," Ian said softly. "I think your confidence has carried over to other areas."

Kelly chuckled.

"Why is that funny?" Ian asked.

"Because I was a virgin when I met Greg," Kelly said. "And we didn't do it very often."

"You're a quick study," Ian said.

Ian heard the keycard being inserted into the door and the door opened.

"Jesus, has it been an hour already?" Ian asked.

"Time flies when you're having fun, I guess," Paul said. "I'll step out while you guys make yourselves presentable."

"Thanks," Kelly said.

"Oh! So, *not* the hot redhead from earlier," Paul quipped.

"No, it's the hot lead singer for that new band. Maybe you've heard of them? Fate Struck?" Ian joked.

"I might've heard of them. I hear their rhythm guitar player is fantastic."

"In your dreams, dude," Ian said.

Paul smiled as he walked out the door.

Ian and Kelly dressed quickly, then Kelly left. Paul returned a few moments later.

"I made sure David wasn't in the hallway," Paul said. "Or any cameras for that matter."

"She said her brother knows about us," Ian said. "But thanks. We don't need any pictures of us showing up anywhere."

***

David's crew left the next afternoon, taking the drives and tapes with them to screen the footage while David stayed a few more days to visit with his sister and see more of England.

"I know I've said this before," David said at lunch, "but you're amazing onstage, Kelly."

Kelly blushed and lowered her head.

"Thanks," she said.

"It's true, you know," Jake said. "You've really gotten good onstage. I don't mean singing, because you've always been great, but using the stage, singing to the fans, playing around with us onstage. You're entertaining."

"I've been watching a lot of concert videos, especially for Evanescence, watching Amy Lee."

"Well, it's working," David said.

David and Kelly walked around London after lunch, taking in the sights and spending some quality time together, something they hadn't done in a long time.

"It's funny," David said. "I had to come to England to hang out with my little sister."

"I'm sorry I'm always so busy at home," Kelly said.

"Busy is good, though. It means the band is busy."

"I still should make time for family."

"We know where you live if we want to see you more," David joked.

"I know. I just feel bad that I don't see you all very often, even Mom and Dad. I see them when I eat dinner and that's it. I'm off with Jayna or the band."

"Well, I know this is an important time, being a new popular band. You have to do a lot of promos and such."

"Yeah. It will probably slow down a bit once this tour is done."

Kelly and David returned to the hotel in time for Kelly to grab her bags to go to the venue. They were playing in the same place as the previous night. Dean gave David an All Access pass so he could be free to roam around backstage and, since he offered, help where needed.

Back at the hotel after the show, Kelly said her goodbyes to David, who would be leaving early in the morning while Kelly still slept.

"I'm glad we got to hang out for a while," Kelly said.

"Me, too," David said.

"I'll be home in a week or so. I'm anxious to see the video footage."

"So am I. It should be great."

She hugged her brother, who kissed the top of her head.

"Safe travels," Kelly said.

"Break a leg on the rest of the tour," David said.

"Thanks!"

The tour ended in Belgium a week and a half later. Kelly couldn't wait to get home. It had been fun but tiring, even with the added help from the pills and supplements. Once she was fully rested at home, she'd be much better.

As they stood in line to board their plane, Kelly and Jayna received a text. Kelly didn't recognize the number, but saw it was from California, so she opened it.

This is Miss Suzy from high school. We're having a gymnastics exhibition and inviting all the alumni from school to participate. I've sent a letter with all the information, but wanted to let you know since I know you're on tour right now. Let me know if you'd like to participate.

"Did you get..." Kelly started.

"Yep," Jayna said putting her phone back in her purse.

"Should be interesting," Kelly said.

"What should be interesting?" Dean asked.

"Our high school is having a gymnastics exhibition and they want Jayna and me to participate," Kelly told him. "I guess there's more info in a letter at home."

"Well, let me know," Dean said as they lined up to board the plane home.

Kelly had wanted to do more gymnastics, and looked forward to this opportunity to see her former teammates again, Jessica notwithstanding, and to do a little more than just the occasional backflip onstage.

Chapter Twenty

Kelly was happy to be home. She loved touring Europe, but it was long and exhausting. Now that she was home, she hoped to be able to rest enough before training started for the exhibition, which would be in two months.

Two days after Kelly got home, the fatigue returned since she'd stopped taking the Ritalin. Not only that, she was irritable. She snapped at her mom over something small. Her mom took it in stride, but let her know it wouldn't be tolerated.

"I know you're tired, Kelly Margret," Mom said. "But you're not on tour now. Time to adjust to the real world."

Kelly was horrified at how she'd spoken to her mother.

"I'm so, so sorry, Mom," Kelly said, feeling rather small at the moment. "It won't happen again."

"I know it won't," Mom said, squeezing Kelly's hand.

Luckily Tyrian Records hadn't booked the tour of Asia yet, so they would book dates after the gymnastics exhibition, which would give Kelly a little time to recover before they toured. They thought that the exhibition would be a good promotional tool for the band, but they had to get permission from Miss Suzy and the organizers, who agreed that it would be a great promo for the gymnastics team as well.

"I don't like the idea of using me to promote the exhibit when all the other girls are just as good as or better than me," Kelly said as the band had a meeting at Dean's house after they'd been home a week.

"Unfortunately, you're the big name draw," Dean said, "and they want lots of people to show up."

"I think they'd get a lot of people just by using Jessica's name."

Jessica, Ian's old girlfriend, was a gymnast at UCLA, and as a senior there, she got lots of attention online. Some of her videos had gone viral.

"Maybe use both?" Dean asked.

"If you can get them to do that, that'd be awesome," Kelly said.

"As much as you dislike her, you still want her to be featured?" Ian asked.

"It's the right thing to do," Kelly shrugged.

"You're too damn nice," Dean said.

"I'm working on it," Kelly said with a grin.

Four days later, Kelly and Jayna drove up to their old high school to practice for the exhibition. Kelly had told Jim from the record company that she'd be more comfortable having David do the recording of the event, and they agreed.

"I may as well be on their payroll," David said when they met in the parking lot of the school. "Thanks to you, though, I'm getting a lot of work and getting noticed in the music industry."

"Yeah, you did the music video for Fluffy Brain, didn't you?" Jayna asked.

"I did," David said. "They were a little harder to work with than you guys, though. But it turned out well."

Kelly picked up her gym bag.

"Okay, I guess we'd better get inside and do this," she said.

David turned on the camera and his sound guy got the mic ready, and they followed Kelly and Jayna into the gym. As they walked in, a lot of the gymnasts stopped what they were doing, and the spectators whispered and pointed to them. Kelly and Jayna saw some of their old teammates from high school and ran over to them and they hugged each other and screamed with delight.

"I'm so glad to see you guys!" said Emily. "I wasn't sure you'd be able to come."

"I wouldn't miss this for anything," Kelly said, smiling. She saw Jessica standing by the water cooler, getting a drink, looking daggers at Kelly. Kelly turned away as Miss Suzy, their old coach, walked quickly over to them.

"I'm so happy you two came!" she exclaimed, hugging them both tightly. "I was afraid either you or the record company wouldn't want to do it."

"I'm glad it worked out," Kelly said. "This is my brother David," she said, pointing to her brother. He shook hands while holding the camera, then turned the camera off for a moment.

"I'll make sure to get everyone as much as I can," David said.

"Oh, good. They've all signed the waivers you sent us, so it should all be good to go."

David was not the only media present. The local newspaper and the news station were there, too, most likely because of Kelly. She hoped that they wouldn't just focus on her, but figured they would. She wouldn't encourage it, however, and stayed away from them.

At eleven o'clock, Miss Suzy whistled to get everyone's attention.

"Thank you, everyone, for joining in and being willing to participate in this," Miss Suzy said. "We're hoping that this will stir up enough donations for the organization. You're all equally important to this exhibition, so just do your best. It's not a competition, so if you're not perfect, it's no big deal."

Kelly silently thanked Miss Suzy for that. She wasn't even close to perfect at the moment

Miss Suzy looked around at all participants and smiled. "Okay, let's get to training."

They spread out on the mats and started to stretch. Kelly had been doing this before every performance so she was still fairly flexible. Jayna, on the other hand, hadn't done quite as much as Kelly and was a little stiff.

"It'll get better, Kelly said.

"I should have joined you whenever you stretched before shows," Jayna said.

"Well, you can do that with me next time," Kelly suggested.

After they stretched, they ran a few laps around the gym. Kelly and Jayna stayed together, and Kelly saw Jessica way ahead of everyone. She wondered if she was trying to show everyone she was the best and draw the attention away from Kelly. Kelly didn't care if she did. It wasn't about her or Jessica. She decided she'd steer clear of Jessica as much as she could.

That didn't last long, as Jessica made a point to come over to Kelly and Jayna as they stood in line to work on their floor skills.

"So, you decided to grace us peasants with your presence here," Jessica said.

"Hello to you, too, Jessica," Kelly said. "Yeah, you know, I like to go out amongst the people to see how you commoners live."

Jayna choked as she turned her laugh into a cough.

"Well, just stay out of my way, Brennen," Jessica said. "As it is, I'm the gymnastics queen with several viral videos on You Tube."

"Hey, me, too!" Kelly said. "But for different reasons. You don't have to worry, I've seen your videos and you're good. I'm not here to steal your thunder, I'm just here to help out Miss Suzy. I've told my brother to make sure he gets lots of shots of you and everyone else."

Jessica scoffed, then took her turn on the floor mat. Most of the spectators shouted and applauded as Jessica finished her pass, which was impressive. She stuck her landing with a smile. Or was that a smirk at Kelly?

"Well, I can't beat that," Kelly remarked to Jayna as she stepped up to the position as the audience applauded. Kelly waved then started her pass. She ran and did a round-off, back flip, and an aerial, before landing with a slight wobble. The audience applauded and cheered anyway.

Damn it! she thought. *I've gotten sloppy.*

As she walked off to make room for Jayna, Miss Suzy caught up to her.

"Don't worry about it," she said, knowing what Kelly was thinking, having coached her for four years in high school. "The landings will come along."

"Thanks," Kelly said.

Kelly watched as Jayna did her tumbling pass, doing a round-off, backflip and a tuck. She hopped on her landing as well.

"We've got work to do," Kelly laughed.

After spending an hour on floor, Kelly, Jayna, and a couple other girls moved to the uneven bars. Kelly tried to remember her old routine. She got about halfway through, but when she missed the bar during a transition from low to high and fell, she stepped aside to let one of the other girls have a turn.

"Yeah, I've got work to do," Kelly said again. She turned and saw David recording nearby. "Did you get that?"

"Of course," David said.

"Thanks, bro."

Kelly and Jayna spent another half an hour working on the bar routine, then Miss Suzy called everyone over for a lunch break.

After lunch, the girls met with Miss Suzy to let her know what events they'd be performing on. Jessica, of course, would do all four—floor, uneven bars, vault, and beam. When Miss Suzy got to Kelly, Kelly knew there's no way she could vault, and the beam seemed too dangerous with her lack of conditioning. She picked floor and bars. Jayna picked floor, bars, and vault. Jayna had been particularly good at vaulting in high school.

"Oh, not doing balance beam?" Jessica asked in her fake high-pitched voice.

"Nope. Can't, manager's orders," Kelly said.

"Darn, I was hoping to see you fall on your face."

Ugh, that girl. Kelly took a moment to rein in her emotions.

"So sorry to disappoint you," Kelly said in the same sickly-sweet voice Jessica had used. Jessica flounced away.

Kelly and Jayna worked on their skills on floor, Kelly trying to get more height with her flips, and Jayna working on her handstands.

Practice ended at three-thirty, and Kelly was beat. Miss Suzy asked all the girls to gather around her, where she told them all how proud she was of the work they'd done that day.

"It may seem like a daunting task right now," she said, "but it will all come back to you and you'll do great! I'll have an additional practice every Wednesday at six o'clock if you'd like to get some extra work in. Great workout, ladies. See you next Saturday."

The girls applauded and stood up to get their belongings.

"See ya around, Brennen," Jessica said as she flounced past her and Jayna.

"Bye." *Bitch*, she added in her head.

One of the reporters for the newspaper stopped Jessica and spoke with her for a few minutes, then she met up with a blond haired guy in the stands, and kissed him quickly. With their arms around each other, they walked out of the gym.

"I guess that's supposed to make me jealous?" Kelly said under her breath.

"Probably had to pay him to go out with her," Jayna said.

Kelly laughed, and picked up her bag, but before they could get too far, the reporter wanted to talk to them.

"How does it feel to be back doing gymnastics after so long?" the reporter asked.

"It feels great," Kelly said, "But I'm sure I'll be hurting tomorrow. I haven't used some of these muscles since before the tour. Doing backflips and walkovers onstage is nothing compared to doing a layout."

"How about you?" the reporter asked Jayna.

"It's been even longer for me," Jayna said. "Kelly at least had been working out at the college. I haven't done anything in that time except a few backflips."

"Will this pull you back into competitive gymnastics again?" the reporter asked Kelly.

"No," Kelly said. "I like gymnastics, but I love the band and I love to sing. I'll continue to do flips onstage, but that'll be the extent of it, except for things like this exhibition. I can get into shape quickly for this."

"Thank you for your time," the reporter said as she put her recorder away.

"You're welcome! Have a good afternoon!" Kelly hefted her bag onto her shoulder and she and Jayna walked out to Kelly's car. David had parked his truck next to her car in the lot.

"Who was that girl you were talking with earlier?" David asked.

"That's Jessica," Kelly said. "She used to be Ian's girlfriend but they broke up because she's the jealous type."

"She's a really good gymnast," he said.

"And she knows it," Jayna said.

"She made sure to tell me about her viral videos on You Tube," Kelly said. "I told her I have viral videos, too. She didn't like that."

"She'd pose for the camera every time it landed on her. I hope that isn't going to be a thing with her."

"It will be," Kelly and Jayna said in unison.

"Greaaat," David said. "Well, bye, sis."

"See you next Saturday."

Kelly woke up the next day very sore. She'd forgotten how much work it was to train, and had used muscles she hadn't used in a long time, even with her acrobatics onstage. Every muscle ached.

David emailed some photos of Kelly and Jayna the next day, to post on their social media pages. He got good pictures of Kelly working on her floor skills and Jayna working on the bars. He also sent Kelly a photo of her fall. She put that on her Instagram page, with the caption, "I need work!" She wasn't infallible, and wanted to show that. By the end of the day, every photo had more than a hundred reactions.

Kelly's phone *dinged*, and she picked it up off her nightstand.

"OOOOWWWW!!!!" Jayna had written.

"Yep. We're officially old," Kelly replied.

"At 22 years old."

At the Wednesday practice, Kelly noticed that Jessica wasn't there.

"She probably thinks she doesn't need any extra practice," Jayna said.

"Unfortunately, she's right," Kelly said. "She does this every day at UCLA."

Only half the girls came for the extra practice, mostly those who'd been out of school for a few years. It was a friendlier group, and they had fun and cheered each other on, helping each other with their skills.

For their floor routine, each girl selected a one and a half minute piece of music to do their routine to. Kelly picked "Classical Gas" and had it edited down to ninety seconds. Jayna picked "Fire Engine," an instrumental by Sweet.

The next six weeks were taken up with training and band practice for Kelly. Saturday day and Wednesday night with training, and Saturday nights with rehearsal.

"At least the 5-hour energy shots are working for me again," she said at band practice. "And I don't have to worry about breaking any rules with gymnastics since it's just an exhibition."

"Just take care of yourself," Dean said. "Jim's getting the Asian tour booked as we speak."

The exhibition was held at the Cal State University Long Beach gym. The equipment was brought in from several area schools and set up and checked for safety.

Kelly and Jayna had to be there at nine that morning to warm up and practice before the exhibition started two hours later. Kelly's parents would be there. David would also be there, recording the event for the record company, and it was being televised on CSULB's cable channel.

Kelly had pretty much kept to her high school weight, and still fit into one of her high school leotards in purple and silver. She pulled her long hair into a top knot, securing it with lots of bobby-pins, and then tied a purple ribbon around it. She put on minimal make-up, then pulled on her sweatpants and jacket and slipped her feet into her flip-flops.

Dean and the guys came to watch, dressed in jeans and t-shirts, trying to blend in with the rest of the college students arriving. Kelly caught sight of them, but didn't wave since they were trying to stay incognito, but they quickly waved to her and sat in the stands. Kelly waved to her parents, who gave her a thumbs up. Jayna's husband Marty and her parents sat near Kelly's and Kelly saw them talking together. The stands were filled, and there were several cameras and reporters set up around the floor, David being one of them.

Being in the gym again brought back so many fond memories for Kelly. It was like being back in high school again, being there with the old team, getting ready for a meet, even though this wasn't a competition. She hadn't realized how much she missed being a part of a gymnastics team, but she'd made the right decision for herself by being in the band, and performing the few skills she did at the end of the band's shows would satisfy her need for gymnastics.

All the girls lined up on the floor mats to be introduced and Miss Suzy went to the front of the audience to the microphone. Kelly and Jayna stood side by side. Jayna had also worn one of her high school leotards in red and gold. Jessica stood next to Kelly in her blue and gold leotard, her blond hair pulled into a sleek top knot with glitter, looking every bit the viral star as she looked down her nose at everyone.

"Thank you all so much for coming," Miss Suzy said. "And thank you for supporting the high school gymnastics program. All proceeds go directly to getting or replacing equipment as well as helping the girls with other costs. We've got a great line-up of talent this afternoon, so we hope you'll stick around to see all the girls perform."

Kelly smiled upon hearing that last statement. She and Jessica were going to perform in different events at different times, and she knew that a lot of people were only there to see them both. Kelly would go second on bars, Jessica was performing sixth on bars out of the fifteen girls there. Miss Suzy hadn't told the girls in what order they'd be performing on floor.

Miss Suzy finished her speech, then introduced all the girls. As she introduced them, she mentioned what they majored in if they were in college, what they wanted to be if they were still in high school, or their occupation if they weren't in school. There was applause for each girl and shouts out from their families.

"Our next gymnast was part of our high school team," Miss Suzy started, "and now she is the personal assistant and merchandise manager for the band Fate Struck—Jayna Campbell."

Jayna stepped forward and waved. Marty's shouts could be heard above the applause. Jayna smiled as she stepped back in line. Kelly squeezed her hand.

"Our last two gymnasts really need no introduction," Miss Suzy said. "Here, fresh off her band Fate Struck's European tour, is singer Kelly Brennen."

As Kelly smiled and stepped forward to wave, the applause and cheers were deafening. It took a few moments for the applause to die down so Miss Suzy could continue.

"And lastly, we have UCLA's newest viral darling…"

Oh, God, Kelly thought, rolling her eyes.

"Majoring in Finance—Jessica Jansen."

Jessica stepped forward and waved as the crowd's applause and cheers might have been slightly louder than for Kelly. Kelly didn't care; she wasn't there for the fame. She just wanted to participate and bring attention to the gymnastics program at her old high school.

Balance beam was first, and seven girls lined up for that, Kelly and Jayna watching on the sidelines to cheer them on. They watched as each girl performed her routine, shouting encouragement to each of them. Jessica went fourth on beam. She performed her routine perfectly and her dismount was impressive.

Kelly applauded along with the other girls and spectators. As Jessica ran off the mats, she gave Kelly a sly smile, then ran over to her former high school teammates who were also waiting their turn on the beam.

Uneven bars would be next, so while the rest of the girls took their turn on beam, Kelly and Jayna went over to wrap their wrists and put their grips on, many of the photographers and camera people following them. Kelly had gotten used to photographers following her, and didn't look at them while she prepared for the bars.

At the uneven bars, the girls chalked up their hands and did some warm-ups. Kelly did a couple of skills, then jumped down. After warm-ups, one of the high school girls went first. Her handstands were beautiful and her routine was perfect. It would be a hard act to follow.

Kelly stepped up to chalk up her hands again, then saluted the crowd and got into position to mount the bars. The crowd cheered, then quickly quieted down. Kelly stood for a moment, looking at the low bar, going through the mount in her head, then jumped and grabbed the bar to start her routine. She had worked hard on her routine, especially the one point that she always had trouble with—the transition from low to high bar. She had gotten it down in practice, and did it smoothly now. She did an open double tuck dismount. Kelly had a small step on her landing, and raised her hands in the air as the crowd applauded. The other girls came over and hugged her.

"A little rusty there, Brennen," Jessica said as she passed by.

"For not being on the bars at all for a year, I think she did pretty well," Jayna said.

"Let her say what she needs to so she can feel better about herself," Kelly said, staring at Jessica. "I'm not in competition with you, Jessica. Chill out."

When it came time for Jessica to do her routine, she walked up to the bars, saluted the crowd then blew a kiss at one of the cameras before she started her routine. Kelly could see why her routines went viral on You Tube; it was crisp and she hit every handstand, then for her dismount she did a double layout and stuck the landing. She turned and waved as the crowd cheered loudly for her.

"Nice job, Jansen," Kelly said.

Jessica curled her lip and rolled her eyes at Kelly, then went over to her friends.

"What a bitch," Kelly said under her breath.

The vault was next. Jayna would be going first. She put on her wrist guards and chalked up her hands, then saluted. She started running, did a round-off onto the springboard, a half-turn onto the vault then did a double twist and stuck her landing.

"Yes!" Kelly punched her fist in the air. The audience cheered, and Kelly could hear Marty's shouts above the others. She ran up to Jayna and hugged her. "That was beautiful!"

"Thanks!" Jayna said. "I was scared to death I was going to mess it up, though."

"It was perfect."

The last part of the exhibition was the floor routine. All fifteen girls would participate in that one. The girls all warmed up, running across the floor and doing their tumbling runs, then Miss Suzy called them over to give them the order they'd go in.

"Jayna will go first," Miss Suzy said. She called out a few more names, then looked at Kelly. "You'll go sixth."

"Awesome," Kelly said, relieved she wasn't last.

Miss Suzy continued to call out names.

"Although this isn't a competition, Jessica will be in the anchor spot," she finished.

"Yes!" Jessica said, pumping her arm in the air.

Miss Suzy came over to Kelly after the girls went to warm up.

"I wanted to put you in the anchor spot," she said, "but with Jessica's viral videos, I thought it was better to put her there."

"No, I agree," Kelly said. "I may not like her, but she's really good. It's a good choice."

"Thanks for being a good sport about this." Miss Suzy put her arm around Kelly's shoulders and hugged her.

Jayna's routine was fairly simple, since she'd been out of gymnastics for some time, but it was still a beautiful routine, and she nailed every landing. Kelly beamed as Jayna finished her routine and ran off amid applause and cheers from the audience.

"I'm so proud of you!" Kelly said, hugging her friend as cameras went off around them.

"Thanks," Jayna said, wiping tears from her eyes. "I didn't think I'd do so well."

"You were awesome," Kelly said, hugging her again.

Four other gymnasts did their routines to applause and cheers from the crowd. Kelly's turn came, and she chalked up her hands and feet and got into position on the floor as the crowd cheered, then became quiet. The music started and she began her routine. Everyone clapped in time with the music as she performed, doing her skills and sticking her landings. Kelly had worked hard on her routine, one that she had used in her last year of high school with just a few changes, until her muscles remembered doing the skills. While she did her routine, she momentarily forgot that she was a singer in a popular band and not back in high school at a competition. She was reminded of who she was, however, when she finished, as the audience applauded so loudly that it shook the gym. Kelly stood up and waved to everyone, then ran off the floor to the girls and hugged them.

When it came time for Jessica to perform, she strutted onto the floor and took her position and waited for the music to begin. Her music started softly, then picked up volume as the routine picked up pace. She did her viral UCLA floor routine and the audience got into the music, too, clapping along with the beat. When she finished, the applause sounded even louder than for Kelly. It was a good routine and she deserved the applause, even if she wasn't a very nice person. Jessica ran down the front of the audience, giving high-fives along the front row.

With that, the exhibition ended. Miss Suzy went up to the mic again.

"I want to thank all of you for coming," she said. "This has been a truly inspiring night. If you're able, I hope you will consider donating to the organization to help the current team and the incoming girls next year. The girls have agreed to take photos and sign autographs for anyone interested. Please keep it orderly. Thank you again for coming tonight."

The audience applauded again, and people got up and milled around. Some of the attendees, mostly young girls, wanted photos with the gymnasts and as expected, Jessica and Kelly were the more popular gymnasts.

Several reporters also came up to the gymnasts, asking questions. Kelly answered them between photos with the girls, who she thought were more important than the reporters. Jessica, on the other hand, stopped signing altogether while talking with the reporters.

"I want to grow up and be just like you," a girl of about ten years old said to Kelly. "I'm going to see if my mom will let me have purple hair."

"Oh, that'd be cool," Kelly said, signing a photo which Miss Suzy had for a small donation. "But if she says no, it's okay. You have lovely hair as it is."

"Thank you," the girl said shyly as Kelly handed the signed photo back to her.

When Kelly finished signing and taking pictures, the reporters came to her to interview her.

"Was it hard getting back into the routine of things?"

"A little," Kelly said, "but once my body remembered doing this, it got easier."

"How was it seeing some of your old team mates?" another asked.

"It was great! With some of them it was like being back in high school, talking about our routines, but also talking about how life is treating us all."

"Life seems to be treating you really well."

"With anything, it comes from working hard, and we've worked really hard to get to where we are now."

Half an hour later, the crowd had gone and the girls and young women picked up their belongings. Dean, Marty, and the guys had stayed in the background while Kelly and Jayna took photos with the girls, and came up now to congratulate them.

"You two were fantastic!" Dean said. "I never really knew how good you both were until now."

"So now maybe you won't freak out when I do my flips onstage?" Kelly asked.

"Not as much, anyway," he said.

"You should've heard him every time you twisted in the air," Isaac said. "'Oh my God, she's gonna break her neck.'"

They all gave Kelly and Jayna a kiss on the cheek. Kelly saw Jessica's expression when Ian kissed her and gave her a long hug. Jessica turned in a huff and went over to her boyfriend and gave him a long sensual kiss.

"I don't think Jessica is happy with us," Kelly said softly to Ian so only he could hear.

"She'd really flip if she knew what else we do," he said.

Kelly watched Jessica leave with her boyfriend.

"Toodles, Jess," Kelly shouted after her, waving her fingers at her.

Jessica didn't look back, but walked a little faster out the door.

"I'll see you tomorrow," Jayna said, as she linked her arm through Marty's as she got ready to leave.

"See ya, Jayna," Kelly said. "Great job today."

"You, too," Jayna said, and she and Marty left.

Kelly picked up her purse and dug into it, looking for her checkbook. She found it and pulled it out along with a pen, and wrote out a check to give to Miss Suzy.

"I'll be right back," Kelly said, and ran over to Miss Suzy.

"I hope you had fun today," Miss Suzy said.

"I did, thank you so much for asking me to come." She handed Miss Suzy the check, who looked at the amount and her eyes grew wide in surprise.

"Two thousand dollars?" Miss Suzy asked, and held the check out to Kelly. "I can't take this!"

"Why not?" Kelly asked, smiling.

"This is too much! I don't want you to go broke."

"I won't, believe me," Kelly said. "I couldn't do this three years ago. I can now."

"Thank you so much for this!" Miss Suzy said, and she hugged Kelly tight.

"You're welcome," Kelly said, and she turned and picked up her things and followed her friends out.

Chapter Twenty-One

The story about the gymnastic exhibition came out in the paper the next day. The paper had printed lots of photos of all the girls, with Kelly's and Jessica's photos more prominent. Kelly frowned at that, but it was done. She read the story and the quotes from the girls. The reporter mentioned the perceived animosity between Kelly and Jessica, and one of the other girls from their high school team told the reporter about the rivalry from high school.

"Kelly was always a class act," the girl had said. *"She didn't let the rivalry bother her."*

Kelly smiled, and was happy the girl hadn't said anything derogatory about Jessica.

Later that day, David called Kelly to let her know what the record company thought about the footage.

"They really like it," David said. "They want me to edit it down to about an hour. They'll have someone write out a narrative for it and I'll go back once that's done and sit down with Jim and see which shots would go with that."

"Cool!" Kelly said. "And you're still working on the tour video?"

"Yes." David laughed. "I have a lot of irons in the fire at the moment."

"Don't work too hard," Kelly said.

"You don't have to worry about that. I don't work nearly as hard as you do."

Tyrian Records released the dates of the Asian and South American tour later that week. The tour would start in the middle of October, which gave them two months to prepare for it, and it would last five weeks. Dean called a meeting with everyone to go over some things.

"A few updates," Dean said. "Your single has gone gold in England and Denmark."

"Woo hoo!" they shouted.

"That's fantastic!" Isaac said.

"We'll drive up to LA in a couple days to receive those. Now, the tour to Asia. They have *strict* laws on drugs, so that means you don't bring anything with you on the plane unless you want to end up in prison."

"So, how do we get it there?" Isaac asked.

"I'll check into it. If all else fails, I'm sure they have energy drinks there, or you can bring No Doz with you."

"Lame," Isaac said.

"That, of course, also means no pot."

"Super lame," Jake said.

"You'll live, I promise," Dean said.

Kelly didn't have anything to worry about, since the energy drinks worked for her again, after not taking or drinking anything for several weeks.

"We're not going to any countries where alcohol is banned, so you're good there," Dean said with a laugh.

"What countries are we hitting?" Paul asked.

"Japan, China, Thailand, Indonesia, and then a skip over to Australia and New Zealand. We'll hit South America on the way home."

"Awesome," Jake said.

"Once we're back home, ideally they'd like you to record another album."

"Already?" Kelly asked.

"Your first one will already be almost a year old by then," Dean said, "but we're not on any kind of timeline, so maybe take a break in there before recording."

"At least I'm not involved in that part," Jayna said. "I think Marty would like me to be home for a while."

"On your end, Jayna," Dean said, "just make sure you have enough stock of everything and make purchases if we're low on anything."

"Will do!" she said, making a note on her phone.

With the business part concluded, Dean invited them to stay and play games for a while. Jayna didn't want to play and left. Kelly stayed to watch and maybe try playing again. She played one round of Mario Kart with Paul and failed miserably.

"I'm just not good at games," Kelly said, handing the controller to Ian.

Kelly went home after that. As she drove up, she noticed a car parked a few houses down from hers. She didn't recognize it as one of the neighbor's cars. As soon as she got out of her car, two twenty-something guys got out of the vehicle and walked toward Kelly.

Oh crap, she thought, and didn't know if she should bolt for the house or just wait and see. Her mom was just a shout away if she needed help.

"You're Kelly Brennen from Fate Struck?" the taller one asked.

Well, at least they're fans.

"I am," Kelly said pleasantly.

"We saw your gymnastic show last week," said the blond guy. "You were fantastic!"

"Thank you so much," Kelly said.

"We knocked on your door to see if you were home. Your mom said you were in a meeting."

Okay, I wish they wouldn't bother my parents.

"Yeah, we were going over the Asian tour stuff."

"Can we get your autograph?" asked the taller guy, holding out Fate Struck's CD.

"Of course!" Kelly said, and she pulled out a silver Sharpie she carried with her just for these occasions, and signed her name on the CD booklet. She signed the other guy's booklet as well.

"Just one thing," she said. "If you can spread the word— please don't bother my parents. Just look for my car and if it's here, I'm here and I'll be happy to come talk to anyone."

"Okay," said the shorter guy. "We're sorry."

"It's okay, you didn't know. This is the first time that I'm aware of that anyone has come up to the house, so it's no biggie. You two have a good day!"

"Thank you, Kelly, you too," they said in unison, and they went back to their car and drove away.

Kelly blew out her breath. Hopefully this doesn't happen too often.

Inside her house, her mom asked her if those guys had talked to her.

"They did," Kelly said. "I also asked them to spread the word to not bother you guys when I'm not home."

"Oh, it was no bother," Mom said. "They were polite."

242

"Still, I don't like the idea of you guys being bugged because of me. If it gets too much I'll have a fence built with a security gate."

"Oh, Kelly, that won't be necessary! You worry too much."

"I signed up for this; you and Dad didn't. Just let me know and I'll do it for you."

"Thank you, sweetheart," Mom said, pulling Kelly into a hug.

Weekly rehearsals started that weekend for the tour. They now practiced at Dean's house, since the basement at Isaac's father's building wasn't appropriate anymore, considering they wanted to drink during practice, and the rental space was too far out of the way.

With only one week left before their tour of Asia, Kelly and Jayna surveyed what they'd need for the trip. Kelly stocked up on make-up, and bought a couple of blouses and some socks, and Jayna bought two pairs of pants.

Fate Struck had one more rehearsal before Bailey and Scott came to pack away the equipment for the trip. They would rent amplifiers and a PA system for each concert instead of shipping their amps, but they'd take their own instruments and foot pedals. Isaac's snare and bass drum would come on the flight with them in the cargo hold. Kelly took a couple of mics and her effects unit.

The day after, Dean picked them all up to drive to Los Angeles to pick up their new gold singles. Photos were taken, and Jake and Ian took those home for their walls.

Kelly, Jayna, Dean, and the guys deplaned in Tokyo after their nearly thirteen hour flight from LAX. As they walked out from the jetway, Kelly saw a man with a sign with the band's name on it. Dean saw it, too, and went over to talk with the man, then came back to the band.

"This is our driver, Genji, and he'll take us to our hotel," Dean told them. "He has a couple of guys with carts waiting by the carousel, so we'll go get that and we'll be on our way."

They got their luggage and headed to the waiting cars. Kelly was surprised how many of the signs were in English, but she supposed they got a lot of tourists there.

Once in the limo, with the luggage in the van behind them, Genji drove them to their hotel, which was only a short drive from the airport. Genji and his men helped take the luggage into the hotel and put it on another cart, and the hotel porter took over from there.

"Thank you so much," Dean said to Genji.

"My pleasure," he said, and with a tip of his hat, he and his men left. It was nearly four in the afternoon, although to Kelly it felt like it was the middle of the night.

The porters led them upstairs to their rooms—four rooms for the band and Dean, with the usual roommates together, and three more rooms for the roadies, techs, and sound guy. Kelly and Jayna went into their room and flopped onto their beds.

"I have never been on such a long flight," Jayna said.

"Same," Kelly said.

Both of their phones *dinged*, indicating a message, most likely from Dean. They pulled their phones out at the same time and read the message.

"Yay, we can rest for a while," Kelly said. "I should probably call my mom to let her know we got here okay."

"I need to call Marty, too," Jayna said.

Both girls made their calls, then they took a nap.

Kelly woke up three hours later. She looked at her phone and saw another text from Dean, telling them dinner would be at eight in the hotel restaurant if they wanted to eat. Kelly nudged Jayna awake.

"We're all meeting for dinner in an hour," she told her. "I figured you'd want to be awakened for that."

"Yeah," Jayna said, wiping her eyes as she sat up on her bed. "Do you want to shower first?"

"No, you can go ahead."

Jayna went in to shower while Kelly opened her suitcase to pull out something to wear. She and Jayna were both ready at the indicated time and went out to meet everyone at the elevator. Bailey, Scott, and the rest of the crew would join them.

The restaurant had partitioned off a section for them where they wouldn't be bothered. They ate their dinner, and Dean ordered Shochu, a Japanese hard liquor for all of them to try. Mixed with fruit juice, Kelly thought it tasted similar to a fruity martini. She stopped at one, as did Jayna, since that one drink made her very tipsy. She took a photo of the drink and posted to social media.

"First time trying Shochu. This drink really packs a punch!" she wrote to caption the photo.

Everyone squeezed together at the table for a picture of their first night in Tokyo. After dinner, they met in Dean's room to go over the itinerary for the next day.

"You've got a radio show to do in the morning," Dean told them. "Then you have a couple hours to yourselves to explore the area. Sound check at four with the show at eight. I will send a reminder to everyone in the morning. We're here for two nights, then we'll get a bus to travel to the other places in Japan, then we fly to Beijing and have one show there. Any questions?"

No one said anything.

"All right, group, that's all I have. Have a good night!"

***

Isaac and Jake waited at the elevator for Dean and the rest of the band to meet them for breakfast. They'd gotten up early even though they both had a hangover from the Shochu.

"Hey, guys," Dean said as he walked up to the elevator.

"Morning," Isaac said. "Though it feels like the afternoon."

"Yeah, we've lost a day," Dean said. "And to that end..." He held out two bags to Isaac. One had small pills in it, the other had gummy bears.

Isaac took them and quickly put them in his pocket.

"Fantastic," Isaac said. "Tell whoever got these 'thank you'."

"I will. Make sure you get rid of them before we board the flight to China."

"Definitely," Isaac said. "I'll dole these out later."

The rest of the group met them at the elevators and they went to breakfast.

After the radio show, they came back to the hotel to grab their stage clothes before being driven to the venue. When they walked into the dressing room, Isaac saw the usual Jack Daniels and Fireball, but also a couple bottles of Shochu.

"Fabulous," Isaac said. He turned to Dean. "Did you add this on?"

"I did," Dean said. "You all looked like you enjoyed it, so I added that onto the rider."

"Don't let Kelly see it, the lush," Jake said.

"Oh, you're funny," Kelly said, throwing a dinner roll from the table at him. He caught it and took a bite.

They grazed along the table before they did their sound check. The roadies and techs had everything set up perfectly for them. Fate Struck did their individual checks, then played a song to get the final mix set.

Isaac was glad he'd brought his own snare and bass drum. He liked the sound of his, and of course, the bass drum had Fate Struck's logo on it. The rest of the drums were rented.

"How's the setup for you?" Carlos, the drum tech, asked.

"It's great," Isaac said. "The bass drum might need tuning just a tad, though."

"I thought so, too, while listening to you play," Carlos said. "I'll get on that right away."

"Thanks, man," Isaac said.

Back in the dressing room, Isaac took a shower, then dried and dressed in his jeans and black t-shirt with multiple zippers on the front. He then sat at the counter and applied his dark eye liner, combed his short blond hair then ran his hands through it to muss it up a bit.

When he had finished getting ready for the show, he went to the food table and piled on some food. He expended a lot of energy when he drummed, and burned off what he ate. He could just sit behind his kit and hit the drums, but he wanted to give the fans a show, so he exaggerated his moves a lot when he drummed.

The rest of the band was ready and Dean invited the opener to the dressing room for the usual shot of Fireball. When the opener went onstage, Isaac poured himself a cup of Shochu, then took his Ritalin. The others did the same, though Kelly stuck with her energy shot and hard lemonade before the show instead of the Shochu.

Forty-five minutes later, it was time for Fate Struck's set. Isaac took a water bottle and a cup of Shochu with him onstage, and the audience cheered when they saw him. He set his drinks down on the small table behind his seat, and hit the bass drum a few times. It sounded better, and Isaac gave a thumb's up to Carlos. He got his computer ready, then picked up his drumsticks and pounded out the beat to their first song. Jake, Ian, and Paul came out next, playing their guitars, then Kelly ran out and took hold of the mic and stand and they started their first song.

By the end of the set, Isaac had worked up a sweat and had taken off his shirt. They finished their encore and the fans cheered louder than ever. Isaac came from behind his drum kit to take a bow with his bandmates, then Dean took the band photo with the fans. Isaac grabbed his shirt and drinks and they went back to the dressing room.

Isaac picked up a towel and dried off his face and chest, then put on a clean shirt. He fell onto the couch and laid his head back.

"Is there anything we need to discuss about the set?" Dean asked. "How was the lighting, set-up, sound, et cetera?"

"The sound was great for me," Ian said.

"Maybe tweak the lighting a bit," Kelly said. "I felt like I was in the dark when I went stage left."

Dean wrote that down on his phone notes.

"The drums were great," Isaac said. "Just had to have Carlos tune the bass drum."

They each brought up a couple more things, then Dean let in the fans that had backstage passes. Isaac noted there weren't as many as in the States, and they were all very polite. There was a mixture of Japanese and American fans, and the Japanese girls were bashful about talking to the guys, but loosened up after a while. The male fans wanted to talk about their instruments, and they all wanted photos with the band. Dean took the photos since Jayna was still at the merch table.

The party backstage started to wind down as the fans left without any prodding from Dean. The fans were very different from the fans in America.

"I couldn't get one girl to make out with me," Isaac said as Dean shut the door after the last fan left.

"Neither could I," Ian said.

"That could change in the other countries," Dean said.

They gathered up their belongings as best they could in their inebriated state, and went out to the waiting limo that would take them back to the hotel.

Isaac and the rest of the band gathered in Dean's room for video games and food. They would not be ready for sleeping for another few hours. Isaac saw Ian and Kelly slip out of the room, probably going to his room for their FWB playtime. He missed Hayley all the more.

He figured that if he couldn't have sex, he'd call Hayley. He did some quick calculating and figured it was ten in the morning the day before. He tapped out her number and waited for her to answer.

"Isaac!" Hayley said when she answered.

"Hey, beautiful," Isaac said.

"How are you?"

"I'm good! We just got back to the hotel from our show here."

"How did that go?"

"It was great! It seems we're very popular here."

"That's fantastic."

Paul and Jake shouted as they played their game.

"What's going on?" Hayley asked.

"We're in Dean's room, playing video games. We're too wired to go to sleep right now." Isaac told her. "It takes a while for the adrenaline to subside."

They talked for half an hour. Even though he'd only been gone for two days, it felt like a week. He could hardly wait to get back to her.

"Hey, switch to video so I can see you," Isaac said.

"No! I don't have any make-up on," Hayley protested.

"That's okay, I have enough on for both of us," he joked.

A moment later Hayley's beautiful face came up on his phone.

"God, you're gorgeous," he said. He turned on his camera for her.

"You weren't kidding about the make-up," she said.

"Yeah, I haven't taken it off yet. Too busy drinking and talking to fans."

"Not too much of either, I hope."

"The fans here are different. They wanted to talk shop and then they kind of left on their own before Dean asked them to."

Hayley looked at her clock and sighed.

"I hate to end this, but I have to get ready for work," Hayley said.

"Okay," Isaac said, drawing the word out. "I'll call you again soon. I love you so much, Hayley."

"I love you, too," she said.

They blew kisses to each other, then ended the call.

"How's Hayley?" Paul asked as he played his game.

"Beautiful, as usual," Isaac said.

"I gotta call Alexa later," Paul said. "She's already at work."

After taking a turn at the video game, Isaac finally felt like he could go to sleep, especially if he ate some of the edibles Dean had acquired. He went to his room and washed his face, then took off his clothes to his shorts, and got into bed. He ate two of the gummies and waited for sleep.

Chapter Twenty-Two

At brunch the next day, having slept through the usual breakfast time, several of the band and crew nursed their hangovers. Luckily, Kelly wasn't one of them, having only drunk her usual hard lemonade and shot of Fireball, and lots of water in between. The boys and a couple of the crew could only manage to eat some toast and eggs, with water and orange juice. Dean, of course, was bright eyed and bushy tailed, having resisted the urge to drink after the show.

"Someone's gotta keep you all in line," he said after Jake asked how he was so well off that morning. "The itinerary is the same today as yesterday—be ready to leave here at three-thirty for sound check at four."

Everyone said they'd be ready then. No one said anything about exploring the city more, which gave Kelly more time to read or watch movies. She didn't want to go out on her own, or with only Jayna. They'd gone out yesterday with the guys and saw what they wanted to see before the show, anyway, and took lots of photos, some of which ended up on the band's social media platforms.

The show that night went the same as the previous night's show. The crew had fixed the lighting issue that Kelly had brought up, and everything else went well. Kelly wore her purple Chucks that night, and did her usual routine for the audience, who went wild and screamed louder than before. Kelly waved to the fans, and after the band photo, Fate Struck left the stage.

The bus for the band arrived the next afternoon and upon first look, Kelly didn't know how they and all their stuff would fit inside; the bus wasn't much bigger than a motorhome. Kelly stepped inside and it had more room than the outside indicated, and with no bunks to sleep in, they'd be staying at hotels at night. Dean bought snacks and other groceries for them. The crew had a small truck that had all the band's gear. Genji hopped into the driver's seat, told everyone to take their seats, and quickly got onto the highway to take them to Nagoya, which would take about four hours.

They rolled up to the hotel at seven that night. Bailey led the crew inside to their rooms and Dean followed with the band. They all had rooms on the same floor.

Kelly woke up early the next morning. Jayna was still asleep, so Kelly scrolled through her personal Facebook page, then switched to the band's page where she had posted a lot of photos from Tokyo. The photos had a lot of likes and comments, and several people had uploaded videos of a few of their songs from the shows. Kelly still couldn't get used to seeing herself perform, so she skipped those for now. A lot of fans posted about that night's upcoming show, saying how excited they were to see the band live for the first time.

Her phone *dinged*. She closed Facebook and opened the text from Dean. Everyone was meeting for brunch in an hour. That gave her time to dress and put on her make-up.

Jayna stirred and then opened her eyes.

"Good morning!" Kelly greeted.

"Good morning," Jayna said through a yawn. "Was that a text I heard?"

"Yeah," Kelly said. "We're meeting for brunch in an hour with everyone."

"Nice! I like getting together for one meal each day. We get to talk to everyone that we don't normally see throughout the day."

"It's like one big happy family," Kelly said.

The girls got their clothes out, then took turns in the bathroom to change and put on their make-up. They were ready a few minutes before the indicated time, but went out to wait by the elevators. Isaac and Jake arrived at the elevators a few minutes later, and by the time Dean came to the elevator, everyone had turned up. They went down to the hotel restaurant. Dean had made reservations for the group, and the hotel staff had partitioned off an area for them.

It was hot and rainy outside, so only the crew left the hotel to go set up after eating, and the band and Jayna congregated in Dean's room to play video games and drink beer. Kelly and Jayna watched and cheered the boys on. Dean left for half an hour and came back bearing food.

"Yes!" Jake said, grabbing a burger from the bag. "I'm starving."

"This was fast and cheap," Dean said. "It should get you through sound check."

"I'll take it," Paul said.

By the time they finished eating, it was nearly time to leave for sound check. They all went back to their rooms to gather up what they needed for the night, then they went down to their bus for the drive to the venue.

The show that night went well, the enthusiastic crowd singing along to the songs. Kelly indulged more than she usually did in the hard lemonade and Shochu, and though it didn't affect her performance, she decided against doing any flips onstage, instead just doing an Illusion turn for the fans.

The shows over the next week went well for Fate Struck. They did one more show in Nagoya, then hit Kobe for one show, then flew over to China and then Manila for shows. Isaac heeded Dean's warning about carrying drugs with him, and, though he hated to do it, dumped the ten or so tablets left over into the toilet before they flew. No one wanted to risk getting caught buying or carrying anything, so the band had to settle for energy drinks and caffeine tablets before those shows. The bad thing with those was they crashed hard afterwards, sleeping for ten or more hours after the shows.

As the group got off the plane in Jakarta, airport security came and talked with Dean, whose face grew red and he ran his hands through his hair. Dean came over to the band, security following.

"We need to go with these nice gentlemen," Dean said sarcastically. "Apparently someone called in and said we were smuggling drugs in our luggage."

"What the fuck?" Isaac exclaimed. "None of us are stupid enough to do that."

"Well, whatever happened, we need to go with them so they can search us and our luggage."

Kelly's heart skipped a beat and she became light-headed and swayed on the spot and Jayna had to grab her arm to keep her from falling over. Dean noticed it, too.

"Kelly, it'll be okay," Dean told her. "They'll look and find nothing and send us on our way."

Dean and the band followed the men to an office across the airport and down a long hall. Kelly noticed that people got out of their way quickly and stared as they were led across the airport, with some photographers taking photos as they walked. One officer opened the door and they filed into the room where their luggage had been placed on tables. They sat down on the chairs along the wall facing the table. One male and one female officer stayed in the room while the others left.

They sat in the room for half an hour. Kelly wondered if there was something else going on. None of them would bring drugs through the airport, because none of them relished staying in prison. Tears spilled from her eyes, and she wiped them away with the back of her shaking hand. Jayna put her arm around her, their heads touching. *My mom is going to freak out when she hears about this,* Kelly thought, wiping her eyes again. She looked at the rest of the band. Isaac sat with his arms folded, looking pissed off. Ian and Jake were white as a sheet, and Paul had his face in his hands, elbows on his knees. None of them moved, waiting for something to happen. Kelly drew in a deep breath to try to settle her anxiety, a heaviness in her stomach making it hard to breathe.

Finally, two agents came back in and started to go through their luggage. They took out everything, leaving it strewn over the table, checking each container they found, opening it to check the contents. It took them an hour to go through all their luggage. They didn't find anything questionable.

The head agent stepped over to talk with Dean. Dean stood quickly.

"We're very sorry about this," the agent said in heavily accented English. "It looks like our information was wrong. Please accept our apologies."

"Thank you," Dean said, not too pleasantly.

Kelly sighed, the tears flowing again, this time from relief. The others looked just as relieved as they sat back in their chair or ran their hands over their face. The agents left the room and Kelly and the others stood up and organized their belongings back into the suitcases. Kelly's hand were still shaking.

"Who the hell would report us?" Ian asked, jamming his things back into his suitcase haphazardly.

"I couldn't come up with anyone who would do that," Isaac said. "My dad wouldn't do it. Having a son in prison wouldn't look good on him."

"Jessica?" Paul asked.

"No way," Ian said. "She'd be too scared to do something like that. It'd ruin her gymnastics career."

"Well, whoever it was," Dean said, zipping his suitcase up, "they're gonna pay for this. I'll get Tyrian Records legal team on this, because this is fucking bullshit."

They got their luggage back together and as they left the room, one of the agents led them to their driver, who sat waiting next to the desk. He jumped up when he saw Dean approach.

"Sorry for the wait," Dean said, shaking the gentleman's hand. "We had a bit of a delay but we're ready now."

"Some delay," Jake mumbled.

They followed the gentleman through the airport and to the waiting limo at the curb. As they walked through the airport, several reporters followed them, asking questions about the search.

"Obvious they found nothing," Dean said tersely "Otherwise we wouldn't be talking to you here."

They tried to ask Isaac a question, but Isaac just shoved the reporter away. They tried to talk to Kelly, but Ian and Dean both stepped in between her and the reporter and the reporter backed off.

They got to their hotel rooms without mishap. Kelly dropped her suitcase in front of a bed and threw her keycard on the dresser. No sooner had she sat on the bed she got a text from Dean, asking everyone to meet in his room.

She and Jayna grabbed their keycards and walked down the hall to Dean's room. Jake opened the door.

"Dean went out for a few minutes," he said as the girls walked in.

They sat on the couch next to Ian.

"Are you two okay?" he asked.

"Just peachy," Jayna said sarcastically.

"Brilliant," Kelly said.

Dean came back in a few minutes later with several bags with bottles of alcohol.

"I thought you could all use a belt," Dean said.

"You're not wrong," Jake said, taking the Jack Daniels out of the bag, opening it and pouring a good amount into one of the cups Dean had also brought.

Dean handed out the cups and they all poured what they wanted.

"I couldn't find any hard lemonade or seltzer," Dean said to Kelly.

"At this point, I don't care," Kelly said, pouring JD into her cup with a splash of cola.

No one said anything as they drank. Kelly was just glad they weren't detained for longer, but she knew that this was going to get out and her parents would no doubt call her. At that moment her phone *dinged*.

"Already?" she asked, looking at her phone to see who had texted her. If it was her mom, she wasn't going to answer it. She was already too drunk to be nice. It wasn't her mom, but Greg.

"I hope prison treats you well," was the message.

"The fucking vindictive son of a bitch!" she exclaimed.

"Whoa!" Jake said. "Never heard that before."

"What?" Dean asked.

She held out her phone, showing him the text.

"Sweet Jesus," Dean said. "It was Greg."

"Are you fucking kidding me?" Isaac asked. "What is his damn problem?"

Kelly was so angry she nearly threw her phone across the room. She thought better of it and tossed it onto the table.

"I thought he'd gotten over the breakup," Kelly said. "I guess not."

"I'll say he hasn't! And I thought this guy was nice when he started dating you," Paul said.

"I never thought he would stoop this low, to try to get us arrested," Kelly said. "But we did find out he had a temper. Remember in San Diego?"

"He nearly broke the window of the van," Isaac remembered.

Kelly picked up her phone and tapped out her reply.

"What did you say?" Dean asked.

"'In order to get arrested they would have to actually find drugs, which they didn't. Fuck you, asshole,'" Kelly read.

"Sounds good to me," Ian said.

"Well, at least we know who to prosecute," Dean said.

Kelly turned her phone to silent so she wouldn't hear when her mom texted or called.

They had to somehow get through the show that night. With the time difference, Kelly wouldn't hear from her parents for about twelve hours, but that only marginally comforted her. It was one-thirty in the afternoon and sound check was at the usual time. How was she and the rest of them going to get through it in the state they were in, or more specific, the state *she* was in? The guys can and have played drunk before. She hadn't.

"I'm going to bed," Kelly announced as she stood up.

"Want company?" Ian asked.

"No, I really need to sleep. Wake me up half an hour before we need to leave if I'm not awake. I'll set my alarm but the way I feel right now, I'll probably sleep through it."

"Will do," Dean said.

Kelly slowly walked back to her room two doors down, holding onto the wall for support. It took her three tries to get the keycard in correctly. The door finally opened, and she went straight to her bed. She set an alarm, hoping it was the correct time, and lay on the bed.

In her slightly inebriated state, she thought she was experiencing an earthquake. She rolled over quickly and almost jumped out of bed when she saw Jayna standing over her.

"Hey," Jayna said. "It's time to get ready to go."

Kelly rubbed her eyes as she sat up on the edge of the bed. She'd slept through her alarm.

"How are you feeling?" Jayna asked.

"Like crap," Kelly said. "I could sleep another four hours."

"Unfortunately that can't happen right now."

"I know."

Kelly stood and went to her luggage and pulled out a 5-hour energy shot.

"I guess I better start drinking these now if I want to be able to get onstage."

She drank the shot and then went to the bathroom to wash her face. She dried her face and came back out.

"I look like crap, too," Kelly said.

"I think we all do," Jayna said. "I didn't sleep and I'm not sure if anyone else did. But hey, that's what make-up is for, right?"

Kelly managed a weak smile.

"I know it's not a laughing matter, but it's over and we can only put it behind us now," Jayna said.

"Yeah, I know," Kelly said. "I've just never been in trouble like that before. It scared the hell out of me."

Kelly gathered up what she needed for the show that night, putting her clothes into a garment bag and her makeup in a shoulder bag. Jayna had her things together and they walked down to Dean's room and knocked.

"Dean's talking to Jim from Tyrian," Paul said when he answered the door. Kelly and Jayna stepped inside and shut the door.

"I don't care how you do it, just find him," Dean said. "I'll text you his address. I gotta go, we have sound check in half an hour…okay, thanks." Dean ended the call and turned to the girls.

"Jim will get right on getting Greg arrested," Dean told the group, handing his phone to Kelly. "Can you text Greg's address to him?"

"Sure," Kelly said. She tapped in the address and hit *Send*.

"How are you?" Dean asked.

"I've been better," Kelly said.

"Alcohol might not have been the best idea, but I knew you were all stressed."

"It's okay. I'll be okay," Kelly said.

They got to the venue and took their belongings to the dressing room, and after drinking some water, they went out for their sound check. Kelly's head hurt and by the looks of things, the guys felt just as bad. They managed to get through sound check without any issues, and went back to the dressing room to just sit and relax.

Food had been dropped off for them, but no one wanted to eat at the moment. Ian and Isaac took a bottle of beer from the table, though, and drank that.

"A little hair of the dog that bit you will make you feel better," Isaac said to Kelly.

"Does that work?" Kelly asked.

"It does for me," Isaac said with a shrug.

Kelly wasn't sure about Isaac's remedy. She already felt bad as it was. She took a long drink from her water bottle, knowing that, too, would help, but it would take time. Kelly went to take her shower before she had to get dressed. The hot water helped a bit with her slight headache.

After she finished dressing Kelly came out to put on her make-up. The color had finally returned to her face, so she put her make-up on as usual. Jayna helped her with her hair, and then ran out to work the merch table she had set up during sound check.

Feeling a little better and more energetic, Kelly went to the table and put some fruit on a plate and sat down to nibble on it while they waited for show time.

"Are we sticking to our preshow routine?" Dean asked.

"Of course," Ian said. "Can't screw with tradition."

"Okay, I'll ask the opener if they want to join us." Dean left the room, returning a few minutes later with the opener, a local hard rock group called Making Waves.

Dean went around the room and poured Fireball into everyone's cup, even Kelly. Dean made the toast, and they drank, then Isaac filled the cups again.

"Here's to no more incidents on this tour!" he said.

"Hear, hear!" they said, and drank again.

The opener left and the friends finally felt well enough to eat something before the show, but the guys still washing it down with JD. Kelly drank a can of hard seltzer with her food.

As the opener went onstage, Fate Struck did their warm-up routines. Kelly sat down on the floor and stretched her legs and back. The anxiety from earlier had gone and a calmness had come over her from the alcohol she'd drunk. When she finished stretching, she did her vocal warm-ups. Her high notes sounded a little shaky, so she practiced those a little more and they sounded better.

The opener's set ended, and Kelly put on her platform shoes before she and the guys went onstage. Isaac started the drum beat and the others followed, with Kelly coming out to the mic last. She greeted the fans and then began their first song.

Despite all of them not being at 100%, the show went well, even though Kelly missed coming in on one song, but the others just added another measure and Kelly came in. Isaac didn't miss any beats and the guitarists sounded great, although Ian stopped playing for just a moment when his fingers cramped up. He quickly stretched out his hand and came back in.

After the show, back in the dressing room, they sat around and rehydrated with water first, then opened up bottles of beer.

Kelly looked at her phone and saw she had two missed phone calls and ten text messages, all from her mom.

"I think it's about to hit the fan," Kelly said.

The others checked their phones and saw that they, too, had missed calls and texts.

"I'm not talking to my dad about this," Isaac said, tossing his phone onto the table.

"I'll talk to him," Dean said, "and that goes for the rest of you, if you want me to explain what happened to your parents or significant others."

"I'll talk to Hayley," Isaac said. "You can deal with my dad."

"It's what I'm here for," Dean said. "Backstage pass holders—yea or nay?"

"Yes!" Ian said. "Hopefully there's some girls who want to have some fun."

"Right?" Isaac said. "Not so many flirty girls in Asia."

Dean left the room and a few minutes later about twenty men and women came into the dressing room, mostly fans, but a few were photographers.

"What's with the cameras?" Ian asked.

"They're just rock photographers that asked for permission to come and take photos during and after the show," Dean said. "I vetted them thoroughly and they're legit. They just post photos on celebrity websites, only saying where and when the photo was taken."

"Okay," Ian said.

Kelly figured as long as Dean was comfortable with them and had cleared them to come in, she was okay with it. She trusted Dean to keep everything in their best interest.

Several guys made their way over to Kelly, who sat on the couch next to Jake, who had his own fans talking with him. Kelly felt much more comfortable with the male fans, confidently talking with them, but also making sure they knew nothing was going to happen between her and them.

"So what happened today at the airport?" one American fan asked.

"It was someone trying to get us in trouble," Kelly said. "Nothing was found because we don't use illegal drugs. And that someone is going to be prosecuted."

"I thought that was the case," the guy said. "You guys are too cool to use drugs."

Little does he know, she thought. But what she said was true. They weren't using illegal drugs. Even the edibles weren't going to get them put in jail in the States.

"Well, thanks, I appreciate that," Kelly said.

"You didn't do flips at the end of the show," one of the female Indonesian fans asked.

"Yeah, I'm sorry about that. Since we had kind of a rough start to our day here, I wasn't in the right frame of mind to do that." *Because I was drunk*, she added in her head. "But I'll definitely do it next time we're here."

"It's okay. I did gymnastics, too, for a while. It's fun!"

"I enjoy it a lot. In a month or so, there is going to be a video on You Tube of a gymnastics show I did for my old school, so watch for that. My brother is editing it."

"Your brother does videos?" another fan asked.

"He does! He's done all our music videos and he recorded the show in England, which will also be out soon."

"You have a talented family."

"Thanks!"

Kelly and the fans talked a little more, then they wanted the obligatory photo with her. Jayna had come back from the merch table and took the pictures for the fans.

"Thank you, Kelly, for talking with us," one of the male fans said.

260

"You're very welcome! I enjoy talking with our fans. You're the reason we're here, so thank you!"

After the fans had gone, Kelly decided it was time to deal with her mom and the detainment.

"Wish me luck, guys," Kelly said. "I'm calling my mom."

"Good luck!" they called out to her.

Kelly sat on the couch and punched in her mom's number. Her mom answered on the second ring.

"Finally!" Mom said. "Are you okay, honey? You had us worried."

"Yeah, I'm okay," Kelly said. "We're all okay, though it was really stressful."

"I'll bet," Mom said. "I have you on speaker so Dad can hear, too.

"Hi, Dad," Kelly said.

"Hi, Pumpkin," Dad said.

"Now, I want you to be honest with me," Mom said, "are you using drugs?"

"No! Absolutely not. No one is using illegal drugs on this tour, except for a few edibles, but no one has even had that for the past two weeks. We don't want to end up in prison over here."

"Thank God! I'm not worried about the edibles, that's a non-issue." Kelly slumped against the back of the couch in relief. "But I was worried that you were being exposed to other things that would get all of you in trouble."

"No, we're good. We've got energy drinks and caffeine tablets to keep us going right now."

"So do you know who called this in? It's got to be someone who really doesn't like the band."

"It was Greg."

"What? How do you know?"

"Because he sent me a text, saying good luck in prison."

"That son of a bitch," Dad said.

"Dean is getting Tyrian Records' legal department on it."

"Keep us updated," Mom said. "I'll be happy when you're back home."

"We've got another couple of weeks or so, then we'll be home."

"Stay safe!" Dad said.

261

"We will, and I'll let you know when I know more."

"Goodbye, Kelly, we love you!" Mom said.

"I love you both, too. Bye!"

She disconnected and dropped her hands to her lap.

"Well, that sounded like it went well," Dean said.

"My mom and dad were more concerned that I was okay than anything else, though she did ask if we were using drugs. You heard my answer."

"Very diplomatic," Isaac said. "'Not illegal drugs', ha ha."

"I just omitted the Ritalin, which is true—we haven't had that for a while."

***

While Kelly made her call to her parents, Ian called his parents. He sat in a chair in the corner, away from everyone else and tapped in his mom's number.

"It's about time," his mom said.

"We just finished our show," Ian said. "I couldn't call before because it would've been the middle of the night for you."

"Are you okay?" she asked.

"Yes, I'm fine, but I was pretty angry about the whole thing."

"So what were they looking for?"

"Drugs, of course," he said, "but they didn't find any because we're not stupid."

"Was it Jessica that set this up?"

"No, it was Kelly's ex Greg."

"Well, I hope he pays for this."

"He will, believe me. Dean's taking care of it, so it should be handled soon."

"Good, because I'd hate for this to ruin everything you've worked so hard for."

"I doubt it will do anything except make people want to know more about us."

"Find out what the bad press is about?"

"Yeah, something like that. Listen, I better let you go. We're heading back to our hotel in a few minutes."

"Okay. I love you, Ian, take care."

"I will, and I love you, too, Mom," Ian said, and he hung up.

***

Dean called his brother, Isaac's father. Steven had left several voice mails on Dean's phone and on Isaac's as well. Dean put the call on speaker so Isaac could hear what his father said.

"What the hell is going on over there?" Steven asked.

"Oh, the usual rock and roll stuff—sound checks, shows, drug searches, detainments," Dean said.

"Oh, you think this is funny?"

"No, I don't," Dean said. "But as usual you're jumping to the wrong conclusion."

"It doesn't sound like it. What drugs are you all into now?"

"None, Steve, unless you count energy drinks and caffeine as 'drugs.'"

"The news said that they were looking for cocaine and meth."

"Obviously none was found, otherwise I wouldn't be talking to you. It was the disgruntled ex of Kelly's that called it in, and now we're trying to get him arrested for that."

Steven was quiet for some time.

"Are you still there?" Dean asked.

"Yes, I'm still here. No drugs were found?"

"No."

"What a relief! I thought for sure that those kids were doing something."

Isaac shook his head. Of course his father would think the worst.

"I know you don't think too highly of the career choices that Isaac and I have made, but you don't need to worry about anything. Isaac and the rest of the kids are really smart. They're not going to jeopardize anything."

"Okay, well, thanks for calling. I'll let his mother know," Steven said.

"Thanks, tell Julia I said 'Hi'," Dean said.

"I will. Goodbye," Steven said and he hung up.

"That went about as I expected," Isaac said. "Once again he thinks the worst of me and this lifestyle."

"Remember what I told you?" Dean asked.

"Yeah," Isaac said. "It'll never be good enough for him."

"How'd it go with Hayley?" Jake asked, changing the subject.

"She was very understanding and didn't jump to conclusions," Isaac said. "She knew about the Ritalin, but I told her we haven't been using that much because we can't just go out and get it like at home."

"You better put a ring on it before I do," Jake said.

"That may happen sooner rather than later," Isaac said.

"Are you thinking about asking her to marry you?" Dean asked.

"Thinking about it," Isaac said, smiling. That was all he said about it.

Once everyone had spoken to their families, they got everything packed up and ready to go to the car. The band didn't stop to sign autographs this time, though it made Kelly sad not to, but they all just wanted to get back to the hotel and collapse.

Kelly got a text from Ian, asking if he should get Paul occupied so they could be together.

"Yes," she tapped out and hit *Send*.

When they got to the hotel, Ian didn't have to do anything, because they all wanted to play games in Dean's room to wind down. Ian and Kelly each grabbed a bottle of their preferred beverage and went to Ian and Paul's room. Once inside, they clinked their bottles and drank.

"What a fucking disaster," Ian said. "I don't know how you held it together."

"Alcohol," Kelly said. "That was the only way I could relax."

"This way is much more fun, though," he said and he kissed Kelly passionately. Kelly smiled as he kissed her, then returned the kiss. He deepened the kiss, and her tongue stroked his. He made a small sound that urged her to do more. She tugged at his t-shirt and they parted long enough to pull the shirt up over his head, and for him to pull her blouse off. He kissed her again as he reached behind her to unhook her bra, which fell to the floor.

264

He cupped her breasts in his hands and he backed her into the wall, her breaths coming faster. He tempered his kisses, and she closed her eyes as he ran his lips down her neck to her breasts. She became light-headed. Her hands were in his hair, and she opened her eyes as he came up again and looked at her face.

"You are so gorgeous," he breathed.

"So are you," Kelly said. She unbuttoned his pants and he stepped out of them. He did the same to her and stopped for a moment.

"Oh my God, that's hot!" he said. "When did you start wearing a thong?"

"About a week ago," Kelly said. "You like?"

"Oh, yes, I like," he whispered. "You wore that onstage?"

"Yeah."

"I'm glad I didn't know that then."

She smiled as he turned her around so she leaned against the wall. He took her breasts in his hands and kissed the back of her neck, then worked his way down to her ass, where he stopped. He placed light kisses over the small of her back and her derriere, sending tingles through her lower body. He kissed right above where the three strings of her thong came together. She half moaned, half sighed. *God, that feels good.* He reached between her legs and covered the lacy patch of fabric in front with his hand, and then slowly, sensually, pulled her thong off.

She turned around and then they both turned until Ian was against the wall. Kelly kissed her way down his chest and stomach, then hesitated.

"It's okay," Ian said. "You don't have to."

"I want to."

Kelly had never done what she was about to do before. He got the condom from his pants pocket and put it on. She only paused for a moment more, then took him into her mouth. His hands were immediately in her hair. When she finished, Ian picked her up and held her as he entered her. He again backed her to the wall, her arms around his head, his holding her around her waist, her legs circling his waist.

Ian then took Kelly to the bed where they continued to play. After they climaxed, he kissed her stomach then moved all the way down to her most sensual place, running his tongue over every inch. A warmth spread through her body.

"Ian," she whispered.

"Yes?"

"Fuck me again," she said.

"Your wish is my command," he said, and he was still hard enough to enter her again.

Fifteen minutes later, both satisfied, they lay in bed under the blankets, her back to his front, his arms around her.

"You are certainly full of surprises," Ian said.

"Why's that?" Kelly asked.

"I've always thought of you as kind of shy where sex is concerned, but man, you blow my mind."

"Is that a good thing?"

"Oh, yeah, it is."

Kelly looked at the clock and got out of bed to get dressed.

"I'd better go before Paul wants to sleep," she said.

"You're right," Ian said, throwing the blankets off of him. "We don't want him barging in again."

As Kelly pulled on her shoes, Ian got a text message.

"It's Paul, wondering if it's safe to come in." He tapped out a reply, saying aloud, "Yep."

Kelly picked up her bottle and went to her room, waving to Paul as he came down the hallway to his room. She opened the door and saw that Jayna wasn't there; still in Dean's room. Kelly went to the bathroom and removed her make-up then washed her face and brushed her teeth and changed into her pajamas. She sat on her bed and plugged her phone into the charger, and as she scrolled through Facebook Jayna came into their room.

"How are you feeling?" Jayna asked, sitting next to her friend.

"Better," Kelly said. "I don't know how I'll feel tomorrow, though, after drinking tonight."

"Drink some water before bed and I think you'll be fine."

Jayna went and took off her make-up and changed, then got into bed. Kelly put her phone down, drank half of her bottled water, and got into bed.

Chapter Twenty-Three

They met in Dean's room the next day for an update on everything. When Kelly and Jayna arrived, Dean was on the phone with someone, giving a recap of what happened the day before. He was still in his sweat pants and T-shirt he'd slept in.

"No, it was just someone trying to get back at us for something that happened," he said into the phone. "Right. Okay, thank you." Dean ended the call. "I've had about ten calls from various news agencies wanting to know what happened yesterday," he said. "They woke me up at six this morning. I'm going to start directing them to call Jim to find out what happened. I need coffee."

He went to his coffee maker and prepared a pot. He went into his bathroom to dress and when he came out the coffee was ready. He poured a cup and drank it black. "Anyone else want any?" he asked.

No one did. He sat down and gave them the run-down of the day.

"We have a short radio interview at one, then lunch and then sound check. Easy day."

"Good," Kelly said. "I'm beat."

They went to brunch. They finished just in time to head to the radio station for the interview. The radio station had an interpreter ready for them, and the interview went well. The subject of the search and detainment came up, and Isaac told them the same thing Kelly told her parents—no illegal drugs. At the end they asked Kelly to do a couple of skills for them, but she had to decline because she wasn't feeling 100% and didn't want to hurt herself. She promised the listeners she'd do one at the show that night.

The show that night went great. Kelly and the rest of the band were back to form, and Kelly stuck to her promise and did an illusion turn and a simple walkover for the fans at the end of the show.

The after-show didn't last too long, because they wanted to get back to the hotel to pack for their flight to Australia the next day. Kelly and Jayna took turns to shower and got all their belongings back into their luggage, leaving out what they were going to wear during travel.

"I think I'll be glad to leave here," Jake said as they crossed the lobby the next day.

"Same," Ian said. "Hopefully next time we come here we'll have a better start."

"And on that note," Dean said. "The police can't find Greg."

Kelly felt the color drain from her face and she stood stock-still.

"What?!" Kelly exclaimed.

"They checked his house and he's taken his clothes and left. They're checking flights but that will take some time."

"Fantastic," Kelly said as she started to walk again. "I hope he stays far away from me or I'll tear his fucking eyes out."

"Don't get on Kelly's bad side, folks," Isaac said. "I'm liking this feistiness, though."

"You guys are a bad influence on her," Dean said.

They landed in Perth, Australia seven hours later. They did three shows over the course of four days there—Perth, Melbourne, and Sydney, then flew to Peru.

At the hotel that afternoon, Isaac asked Dean about finding Ritalin there.

"The caffeine tablets just don't do the job," he said.

"The drug laws are a little more lax here," Dean said. "I'll see what I can do."

Back in the dressing room after sound check, Dean pulled out a bag and gave it to Isaac.

"Okay, I've got your Ritalin," Dean said. "He also got something for you to try, that's perfectly legal here."

"What's that?" Isaac asked, putting the bag in his pocket.

Dean held up a shopping bag with cans in it.

"Coca energy drinks," Dean said.

"Really?"

"They use the leaves of the coca plant for these, so not necessarily cocaine, but a derivative."

Isaac took the bag.

"I'll give it a whirl," he said.

Isaac set the bag down on the table and got a plate of food.

"What's in the bag?" Paul asked.

"Coca energy drinks," Isaac said. "I've also got Ritalin."

"Coca energy drinks? Like, cocaine?" Jake asked.

"Ha ha, no, not exactly. It's a derivative of the drug, but perfectly legal according to Dean."

"Awesome," Ian said.

"Should be interesting," Kelly said, who had started feeling tired again, even though she'd been taking the iron and vitamin supplements.

As the opening band went onstage, all of them drank one of the energy drinks, and half an hour later, Kelly had enough energy to run a marathon.

"I don't know what the crash will be like later," Dean said. "So just be prepared for it."

As Fate Struck went onstage, Kelly couldn't believe how much energy she had at that moment. Thankfully they all had a click track in their in-ear monitors for most of the songs, because Kelly felt like they were performing the songs too slow, but knew they weren't.

After the show, they were still wired, and they had a loud and spirited after party with the backstage pass holders. Isaac got a game of beer pong going, and everyone had a turn, even Kelly. Since she didn't drink beer, Isaac offered her a shot of Fireball instead.

Jayna came back after packing up the merchandise and played a round, happily drinking the beer. She hadn't drunk the energy drink, but she also wasn't running around onstage every other night, so didn't need the energy drink.

Later at the hotel, they all started to crash. Kelly and Jayna went to their room and Kelly barely had the energy to take off her make-up and change into her pajamas.

They flew to Brazil the next day for their next show. They spent the day being driven around by a tour guide to show them all the sights. He drove them to a parking lot and they walked up to see the Christ the Redeemer statue. Kelly had never seen anything to big and so beautiful. While not religious, she knew that this was an iconic statue and embraced the beauty of it and the surroundings.

Next the tour guide took them to Ipanema Beach and told them the story of how the song Girl From Ipanema came about.

"I always thought the song was older than that," Ian said.

"It's seems like it," the guide said. "But you're young, so it *has* been around for a long time."

The tour guide dropped them off back at the hotel in time for dinner. Dean had made reservations for the band and crew at the restaurant there in the hotel, then the guys left to check out the night life while Kelly and Jayna stayed in their room to watch a movie.

Their show the next night went without a hitch. They'd drunk the same energy drink but managed it better that night, and Kelly did her flips for the fans.

They had only two more shows to do on that part of the tour—Mexico City and Cancun. Mexico City was an opening spot for The Warning, then in Cancun, they played at a two-day festival, appearing both days on one of the smaller stages. They had a lot of fans there, however, and when they were in the pool to watch other bands, their fans stopped to say hello and buy them drinks. Kelly had to turn down drinks since she started to get a little tipsy.

Before they flew back home to California, Dean had some news regarding Greg.

"They picked up his trail in Mexico," Dean said.

"Are you kidding me?" Kelly said. "I'm glad I didn't know that until now, or I wouldn't have gone onstage."

"Obviously nothing happened, but I'd recommend that you stay inside until we all leave for the airport."

"You don't have to tell me twice," Kelly said. "Where in Mexico?"

"They don't know yet. Mexico police are cooperating, but it's hard to track him if he's on foot."

"The faster we get out of here, the better I'll feel," Kelly said.

"We'll be out of here early tomorrow and be back home by dinner time."

As promised, the band touched down at LAX at three the next day, and they stopped to eat dinner before dropping everyone off at their homes.

When Kelly walked into her house, Mom stood up from the couch and wrapped her arms around her daughter.

"Oh, my gosh, I was so worried about you," Mom said. She pulled away to look at Kelly. "You don't look the worse for wear, thank goodness."

"I'm really glad to be home," Kelly said as she fell into the nearest chair. "I found out yesterday that Greg was in Mexico somewhere. I'm glad I didn't know before the show or I'm not sure how I would've gotten through it."

"Well, hopefully he'll stay away forever."

"If they find him in Mexico they'll extradite him back for trial."

"I'd be happy with that, too," Mom said.

Kelly talked with her mom for a few minutes, then took her luggage to her room to sort through it. She'd also gathered a lot of souvenirs in her travels, and she displayed those around her room. By the time she'd finished unloading her luggage, her father had come home from playing golf. She brought out the gifts she'd bought her parents in Indonesia.

"I have something for you both, from Indonesia," Kelly said, handing them each a wrapped parcel.

"Oh, you didn't have to bring us anything, sweetheart," Mom said.

"Well, I wanted to," Kelly told her. "You've been so supportive of my career, I wanted to bring you something. It's not much, but I liked them."

They both unwrapped their gift and they each held a figure made out of bamboo and wood. It was a matched set—Mom got the girl and Dad got the boy.

"These are beautiful," Mom said.

"Outstanding, pumpkin," Dad said.

"Do you like them?"

"I love them!" Mom said. "Thank you so much."

"You're welcome! I would've got more but my suitcase was getting full."

"These are fabulous, Kelly," Dad said. "We can put them together on the shelf."

"I'd hoped you would. I have something for David, too."

271

Kelly called her brother the next day and asked if he was free for lunch, and they made plans to meet at Stonefire Grill at noon.

"I'm so happy you're back home," David said, hugging his sister as they met outside of the restaurant. They went inside and stood in line to place their order.

"Me, too," Kelly said. "It was fun but exhausting."

The line moved quickly and they placed their order, then found an open table and sat down.

"So, what happened at the airport?" David asked.

"We didn't know what happened at the time," Kelly said. "But Greg called in and said we had drugs in our luggage, so they detained us and searched through our suitcases and obviously didn't find anything. They made a mess of everything, though."

"I bet that was rough," David said as he took a forkful of the salad that had just arrived.

"I didn't tell Mom and Dad this, but I was really scared. I knew that no one had anything, but I didn't know if these agents were just doing their job, or if they were corrupt and would plant something on one of us. It was tense and I was in tears because I've never been in trouble before. Not like that, anyway."

"Greg obviously knew that someone used drugs in the band," David said.

"The guys have used Ritalin for energy onstage, and they smoke pot every now and then. Isaac gave me CBD gummy bears when I was having trouble sleeping, none of which we took with us."

"So have they found Greg yet?"

Kelly told him what Dean had told her about Greg possibly being in Mexico.

"Hopefully they find him soon," David said. "To give you peace of mind."

Their meals arrived and they started to eat.

"How's life on the road?" David asked.

"It was fun, but tiring. We did get to do a few things in a couple of the places we visited—I'm sure you've seen the photos—and it was nice to eat all together for breakfast in the hotel. Like a big happy family."

"No sleeping in a bus this time?"

"No. We had a small bus to drive us to the different cities in the country, but we got to stay in hotels this time."

"How's Ian?" David asked.

"He's good, and I know what you're going to ask—yes, we're still friends with benefits."

"Just curious if anything had changed."

"No, nothing has changed. He's a good friend no matter what."

When they finished eating, Kelly pulled David's gift out from her bag.

"This is for you," she said, handing him the package.

"Aw, you didn't have to get me anything," he said.

"I know, but I wanted to. Open it!"

Kelly rested her chin on her folded hands as David carefully unwrapped the gift—a wooden carving of Buddha.

"This is fantastic!" David exclaimed as he turned the carving over to look at all of it. It still had the bark from the tree on the back of it. "Wow! Thank you so much!"

"You're welcome. I wanted to bring back more, but like I told Mom and Dad, my suitcase was getting full."

They talked a little longer before David had to get back to work.

"I'm working on the gymnastics meet right now," he told her. "The concert from England is done and I'm just waiting to see if Tyrian Records wants me to change anything."

"Oh, awesome! I'm excited to see them both."

They hugged again at Kelly's car and promised to do lunch again soon.

Chapter Twenty-Four

The band had been home a month when Dean texted them to come meet at his house. They hadn't had an actual meeting since they'd been home, Dean keeping them updated on things via text. They'd had a couple of rehearsals, just to work on some new songs, but nothing major had been discussed.

Kelly arrived at the set time and when everyone had arrived and gotten their drinks, Dean told them the good news.

"The gymnastic video is done and approved," Dean said.

"Yes!" Kelly said. She'd been anxious to see how it came out.

"Tyrian Records wants to have a screening for all who participated, so that will happen within the next couple weeks."

"You mean I gotta see Jessica again?" Ian asked.

"We'll keep her separated from you and Kelly."

"Knowing her, she won't come, because it won't compare to her viral videos," Kelly said.

"Last but not least, the concert video is done!"

Everyone cheered and clapped.

"Tyrian Records wants to have a Hollywood premiere for it, even though it's going straight to streaming, then released on DVD. That's set for two weeks from tomorrow night. They are very happy with David's team's work and want him to do more for them, not just for Fate Struck."

"That's fantastic!" Kelly said.

After Kelly got home, she lay on her bed and thought about how much had happened to the band already, and more was to come, especially what would come after the premiere of their video. Dean hinted that Tyrian Records had plans for them and Kelly looked forward to it all.

Rock and Roll.

Fate Struck Lyrics

The Lies That You Tell
(Kelly Brennen and Ian Ketchner)

First Verse:
You think that I don't notice
The little things you do
That make me question
everything
If you only knew
I play dumb to keep the peace
Your honesty is due

Chorus:
The lies that you tell
Put me through hell
I wish we could go back
To how things used to be

Second Verse:
You lose your patience with
me
But try to play it cool
I saw the look you didn't
think I saw
But baby, I'm no fool
Late nights away from home
Your honesty is cruel

Chorus

Third Verse:
Misunderstandings hurt us
Am I always to blame?
I don't care what you say
It takes two to fan the flame
Questions to me at every turn
Your honesty's a game

Chorus and Fade

Bad Vibes
(Kelly Brennen and Ian Ketchner)

First Verse:
I feel it every time you're near
The urgency to get away
I look for you in a crowd
Happy when you're not found

Chorus:
The vibes you give
When you're around
Make me want to run away
I've got to run away

Second Verse:

Following me around all day
Trying to change my mind
The day your jealousy came into play
Was the day I told you to just walk away

Chorus

Bridge:
Unpredictable
Unexpected
Holding me hostage
Even when you're not around

Chorus

Jealousy Rules
(Ian Ketchner)

First Verse:
In the moments that we're together
And things are really good
It's hard to imagine the other times
The changes in your mood

Chorus:
You swear you'll change
That you'll behave
But jealousy rules your heart
And we have to be apart.

Second Verse:
Confronted with your jealousy
You fly into a rage
You think I've been unfaithful to you
Your mood is hard to gauge

Chorus

Third Verse:
I gave myself completely to you
I thought you were the one
Making promises you just can't keep
I don't give a damn, we're done.

Chorus

Psychobabble—Disciples of Man
(Erik Dawson, Stevie Royce, Will Talbot)

First Verse:
The voices inside my head
Get louder every day
Calling, calling to me
Please make them go away

Chorus:
I lie upon your couch
A clipboard in your hand
Don't give my your psychobabble
Just give me what I need

Second Verse:
I think I'm going crazy
I cannot tell for sure
Maybe I'm just lazy
Is there any cure?

Chorus

Bridge:
These thoughts inside my head
They make me go insane
When I'm high on my meds
I feel so free

Chorus

Thank you so much for reading *Routine,* Book Two in the Rock and Roll Gymnast Series. If you enjoyed it, please consider leaving a review on Amazon or Goodreads and tell your friends! If you found any typos, etc, please email me at jedi_anegram@hotmail.com.

I started this story, intending it to be just one book, but Kelly's story wasn't finished with one book. I wrote every day for a year to see if I could (developing that habit) and I wrote this book, the second in the series, in about four months. I wrote four books in this series in that year, and I'm still going! Book Five is nearly finished and I have ideas for Book Six, which should be the final book in the series.

I'd like to thank the writing communities I'm a part of, both online and here in Colorado. Ink Authors and Christine Whitmarsh, Sparkly Badgers of Facebook, Bryan Cohen, 500 Words a Day, 20 Books to 50K, and Pikes Peak Writers have all been a great help to me whenever I need it. You rock!

Other books by Margena Adams Holmes

The Rock and Roll Gymnast Series

Fate Struck (Book One)

The Elixir Series

The Elixir War
The Elixir Deception
Evalycer's War
Coming Soon! The Elixir Vengeance

Dear Moviegoer Series

Dear Moviegoer: Tales From Behind The Velvet
Curtain
Dear Moviegoer 2: Unmasked Mayhem

On The Line

Dark Harmony

Moments From A Lifetime
A Collection of Poems and Short Stories